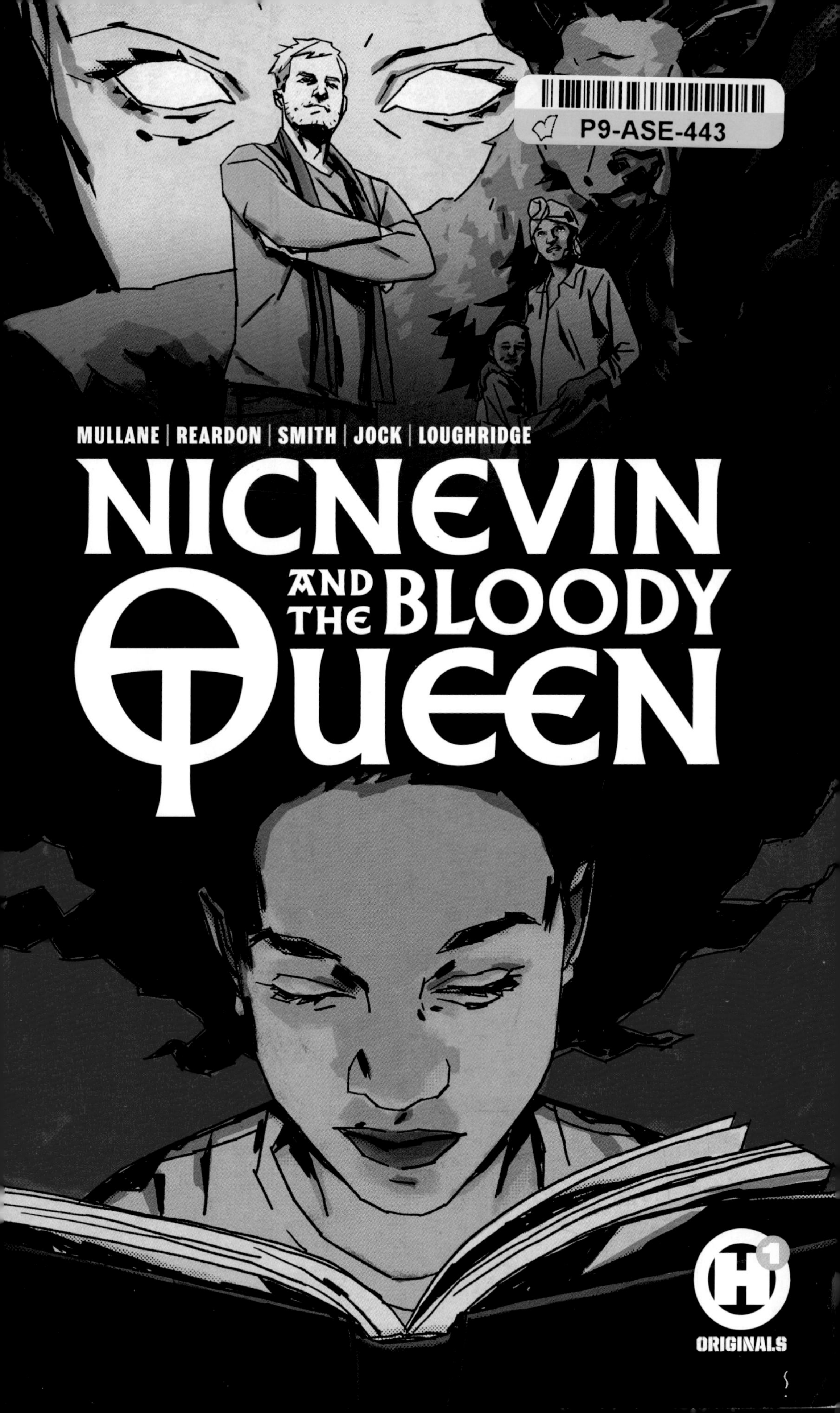
MULLANE | REARDON | SMITH | JOCK | LOUGHRIDGE
NICNEVIN AND THE BLOODY QUEEN
H1 ORIGINALS

WRITER | **HELEN MULLANE**
ARTIST | **DOM REARDON**
LAYOUTS ARTIST [PGS 69-123]
& TITLE PAGE ILLUSTRATION | **MATTHEW DOW SMITH**
COVER & PAGE 3 ILLUSTRATION | **JOCK**
COLOR ARTIST | **LEE LOUGHRIDGE**
LETTERS | **ROBIN JONES**

DIRECTOR OF CREATIVE DEVELOPMENT | **MARK WAID**
CHIEF CREATIVE OFFICER | **JOHN CASSADAY**
EDITORS | **ALEX DONOGHUE & FABRICE SAPOLSKY**
ASSISTANT EDITOR | **ALISA TRAGER**
LOGO DESIGN | **RIAN HUGHES**
SENIOR ART DIRECTOR | **JERRY FRISSEN**

CEO AND PUBLISHER | **FABRICE GIGER**
COO | **ALEX DONOGHUE**
CFO | **GUILLAUME NOUGARET**
SENIOR EDITORS | **FABRICE SAPOLSKY & ROB LEVIN**
ASSISTANT EDITOR | **AMANDA LUCIDO**
SALES AND MARKETING ASSISTANT | **ANDREA TORRES**
SALES REPRESENTATIVE | **HARLEY SALBACKA**
PRODUCTION COORDINATOR | **ALISA TRAGER**
DIRECTOR, LICENSING | **EDMOND LEE**
CTO | **BRUNO BARBERI**
RIGHTS AND LICENSING | **LICENSING@HUMANOIDS.COM**
PRESS AND SOCIAL MEDIA | **PR@HUMANOIDS.COM**

SPECIAL THANKS TO RYAN LEWIS

Library of Congress Control Number: 2019910051

H1 is an imprint of Humanoids, Inc.

SPECIAL THANKS FROM HELEN MULLANE:
This book is dedicated to Jen, whose passion, power and magic inspired every page.

HUMANOIDS

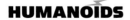

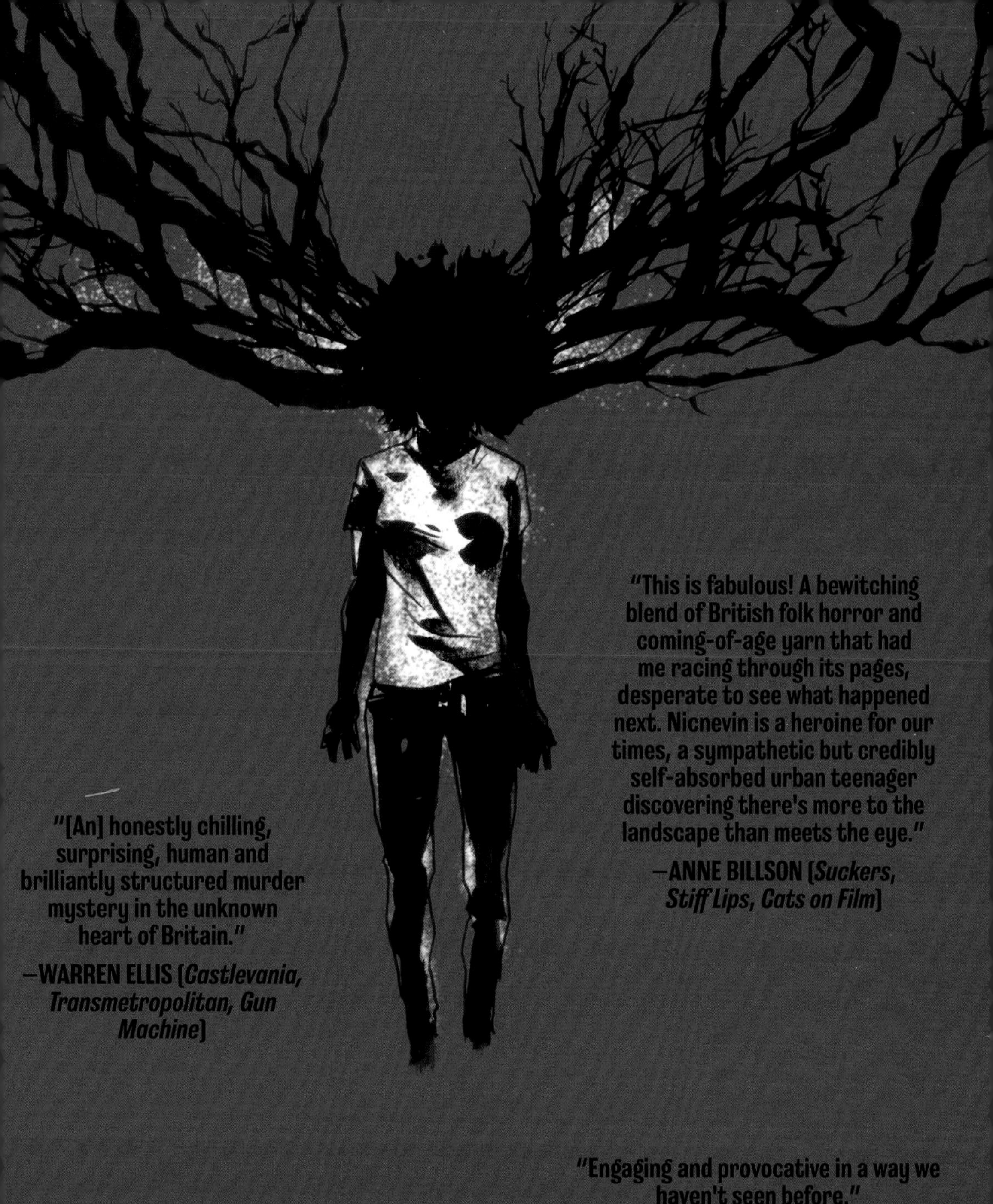

"This is fabulous! A bewitching blend of British folk horror and coming-of-age yarn that had me racing through its pages, desperate to see what happened next. Nicnevin is a heroine for our times, a sympathetic but credibly self-absorbed urban teenager discovering there's more to the landscape than meets the eye."

—ANNE BILLSON [*Suckers, Stiff Lips, Cats on Film*]

"[An] honestly chilling, surprising, human and brilliantly structured murder mystery in the unknown heart of Britain."

—WARREN ELLIS [*Castlevania, Transmetropolitan, Gun Machine*]

"Engaging and provocative in a way we haven't seen before."

—ALAN JONES [*Dario Argento: The Man, The Myths & The Magic, The Rough Guide to Horror Movies*]

"Darkly magical and strange, *Nicnevin and the Bloody Queen* explores British landscape and myth in the style of folk horror film and TV from the 1960s and '70s but with a contemporary edge ..."

—KIM NEWMAN [*Anno Dracula* series, *Nightmare Movies: A critical history of the horror film, 1968–88*]

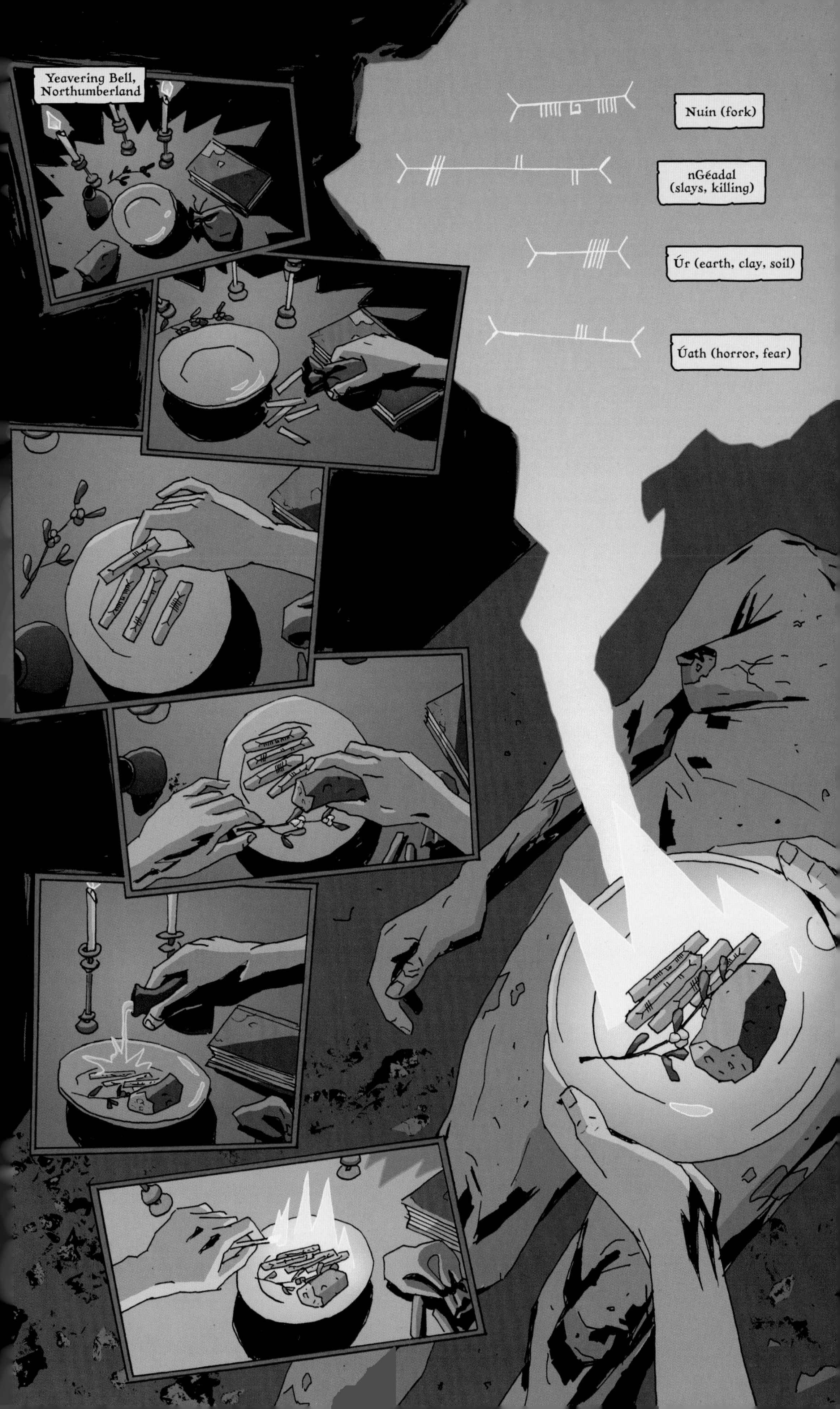
Yeavering Bell, Northumberland
Nuin (fork)
nGéadal (slays, killing)
Úr (earth, clay, soil)
Úath (horror, fear)

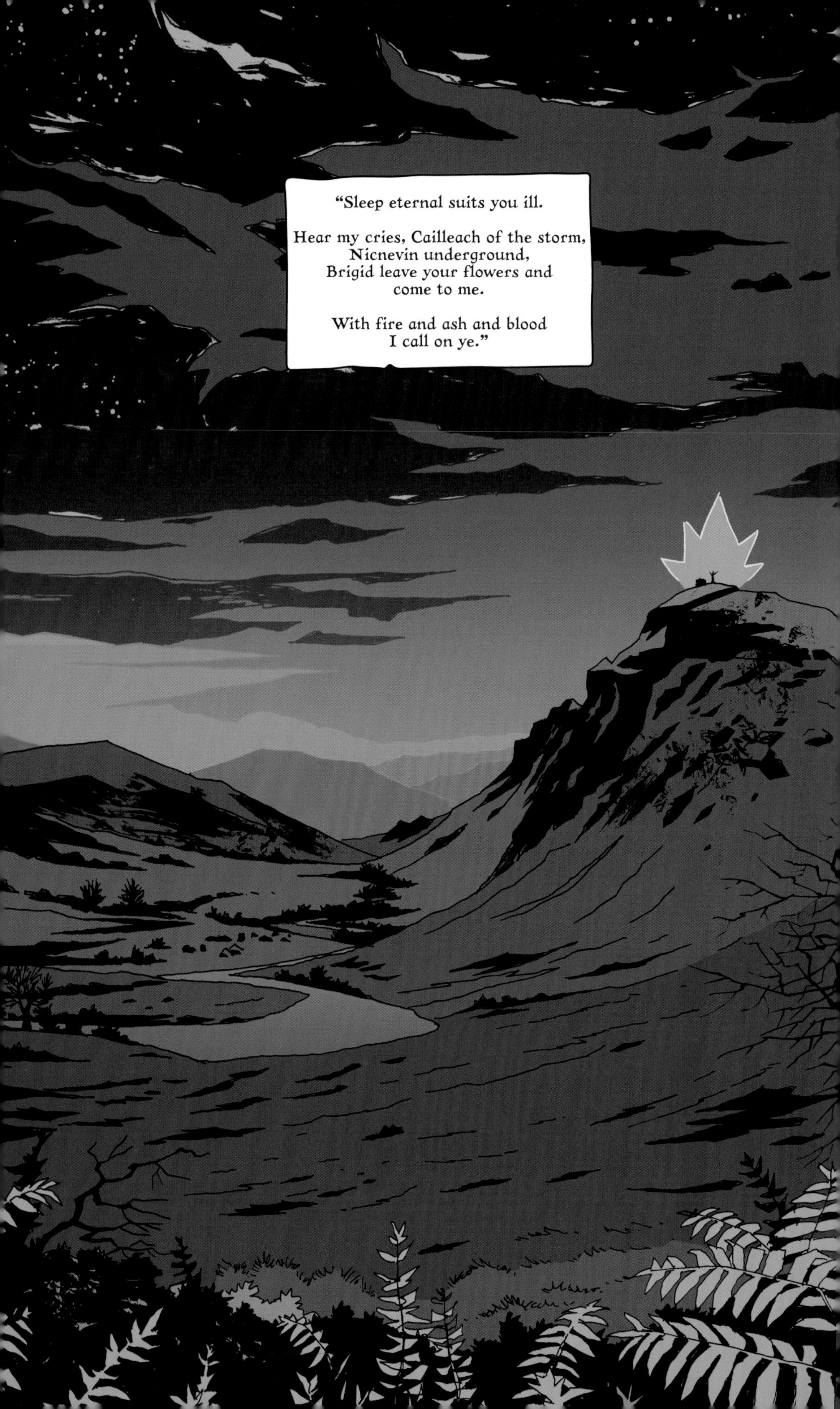
"Sleep eternal suits you ill.
Hear my cries, Cailleach of the storm, Nicnevin underground, Brigid leave your flowers and come to me.
With fire and ash and blood I call on ye."

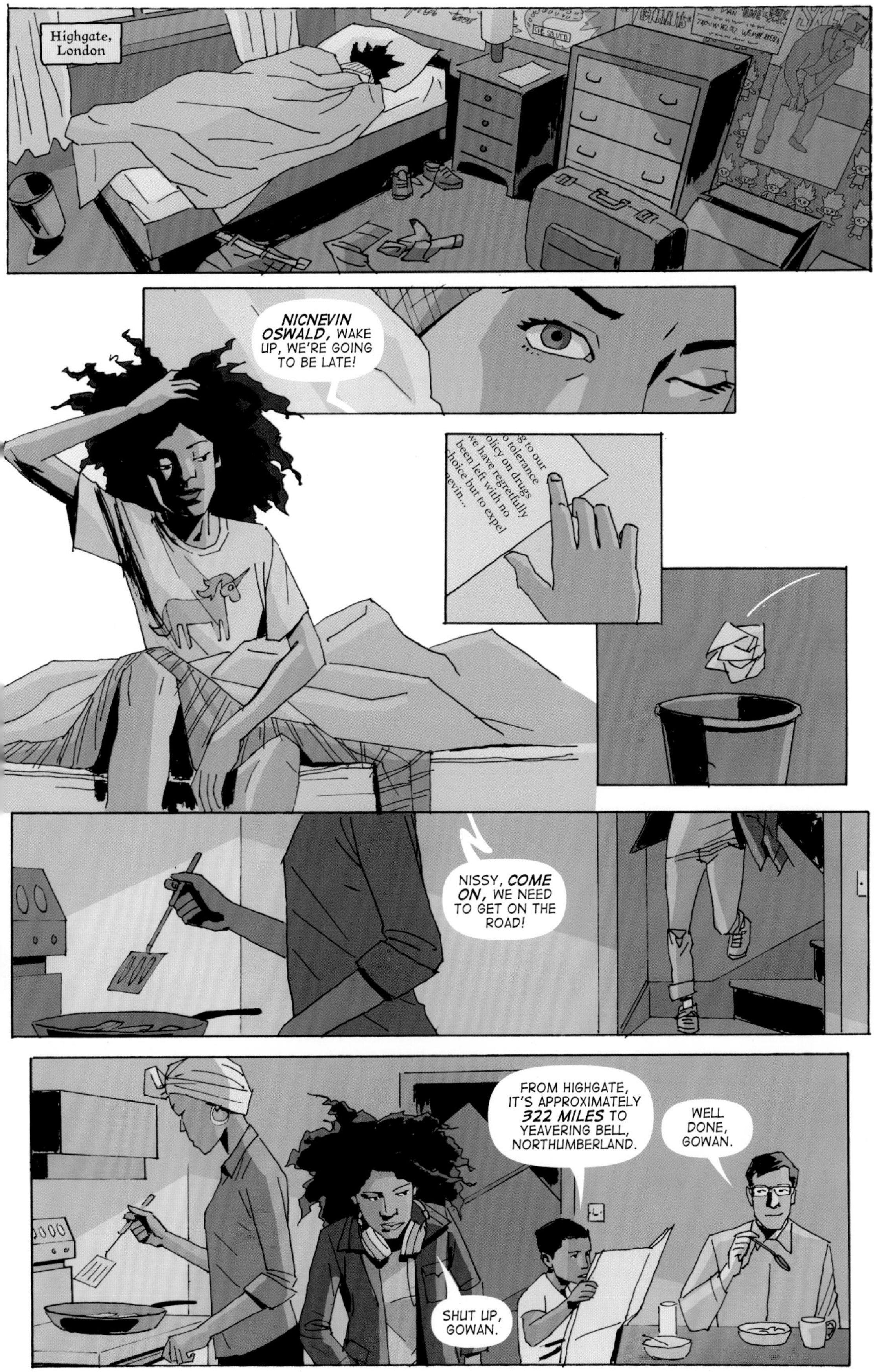
Highgate, London
NICNEVIN OSWALD, WAKE UP, WE'RE GOING TO BE LATE!
g to our
o tolerance
olicy on drugs
we have regretfully
been left with no
choice but to expel
nevin...
NISSY, COME ON, WE NEED TO GET ON THE ROAD!
FROM HIGHGATE, IT'S APPROXIMATELY 322 MILES TO YEAVERING BELL, NORTHUMBERLAND.
WELL DONE, GOWAN.
SHUT UP, GOWAN.

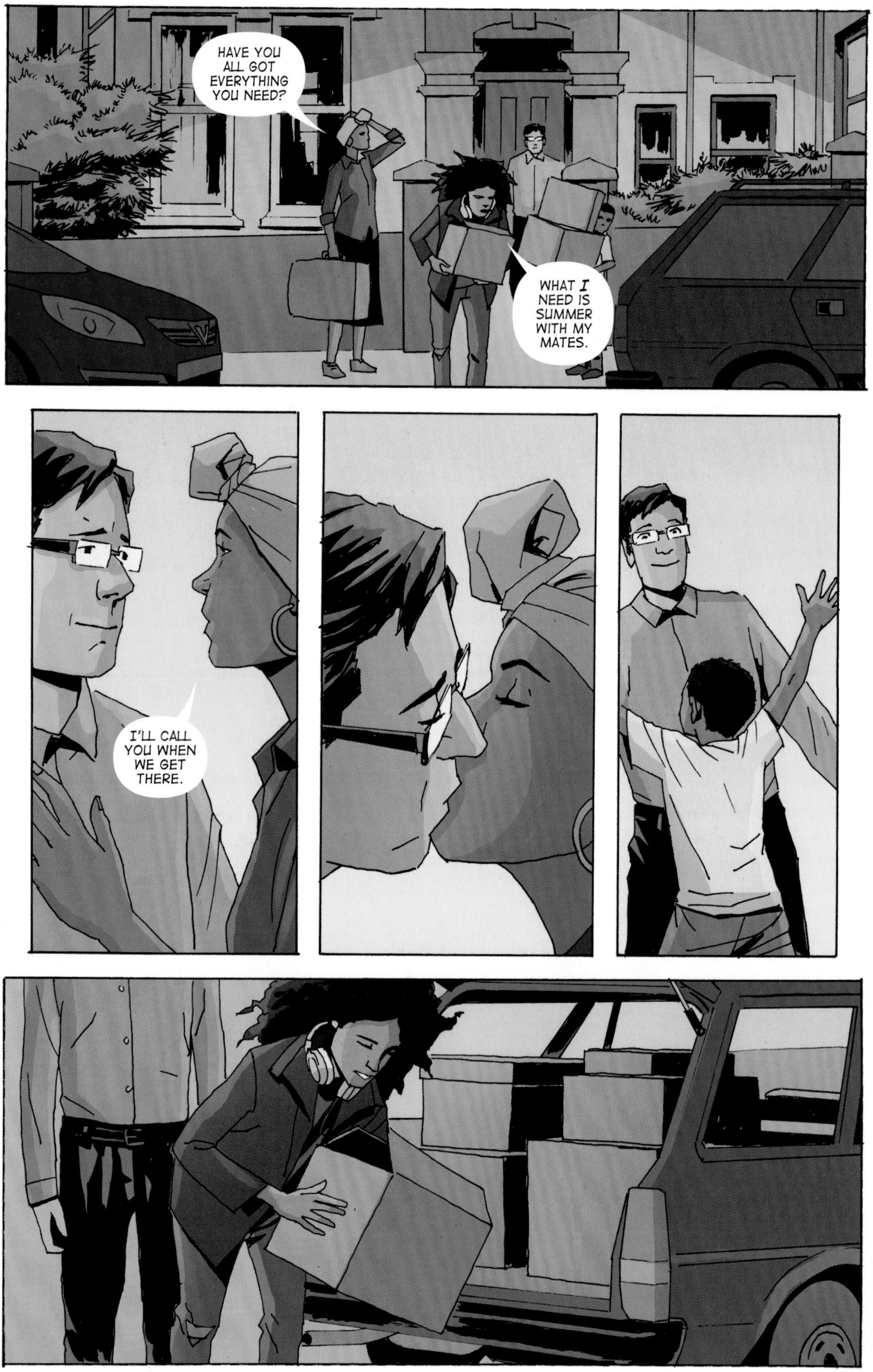
HAVE YOU ALL GOT EVERYTHING YOU NEED?
WHAT I NEED IS SUMMER WITH MY MATES.
I'LL CALL YOU WHEN WE GET THERE.

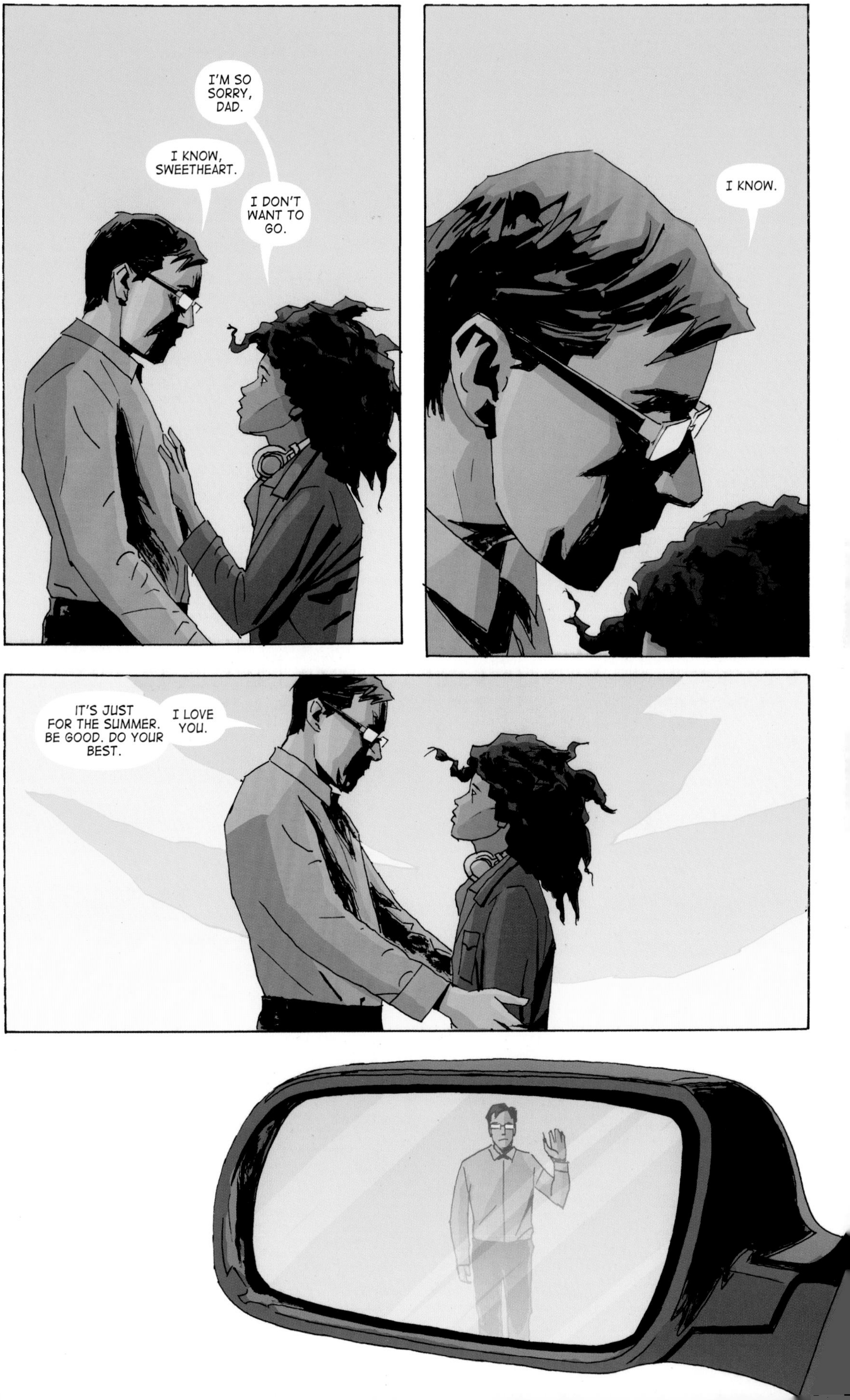
I'M SO SORRY, DAD.
I KNOW, SWEETHEART.
I DON'T WANT TO GO.
I KNOW.
IT'S JUST FOR THE SUMMER. BE GOOD. DO YOUR BEST.
I LOVE YOU.

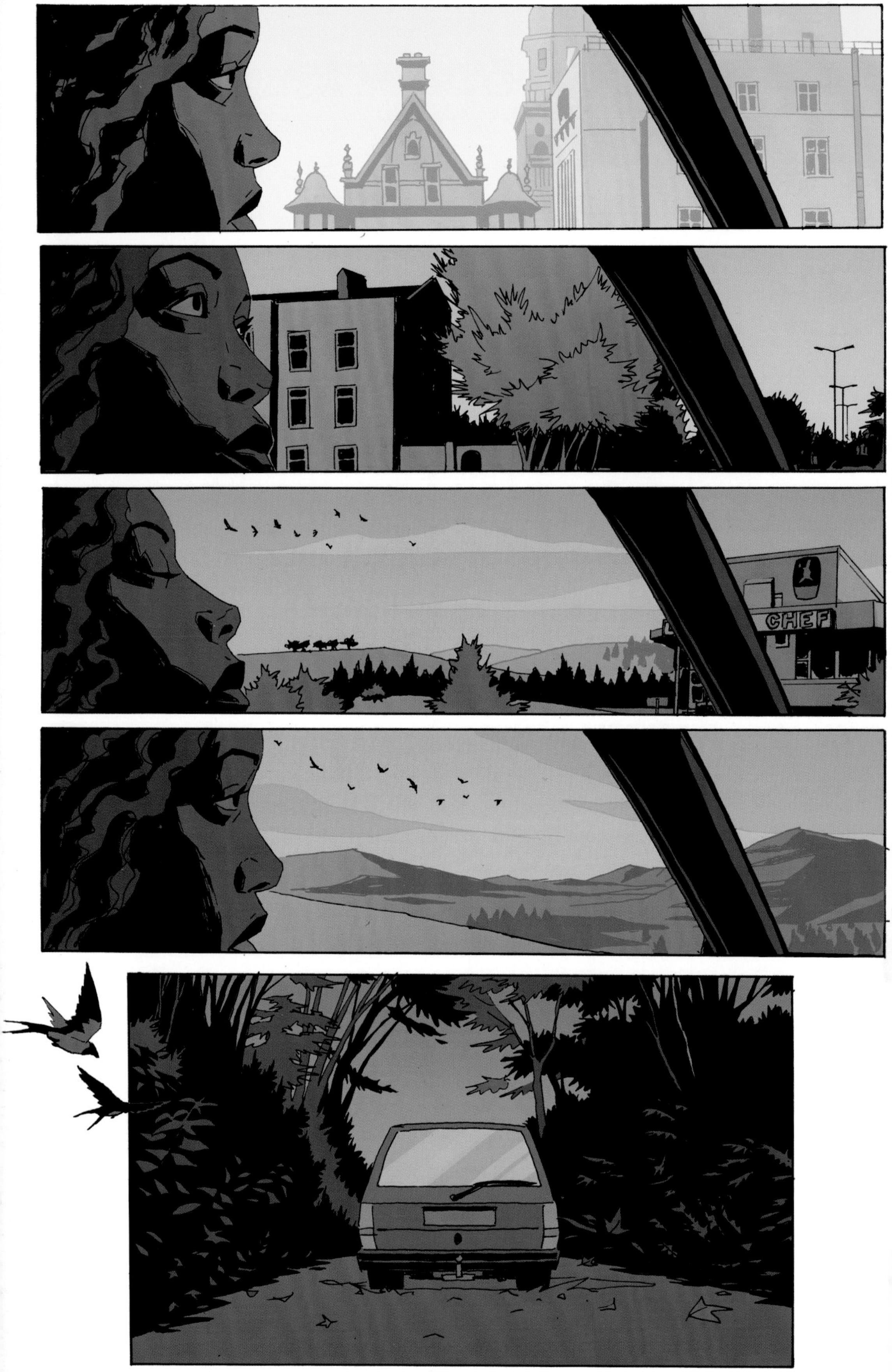
CHEF

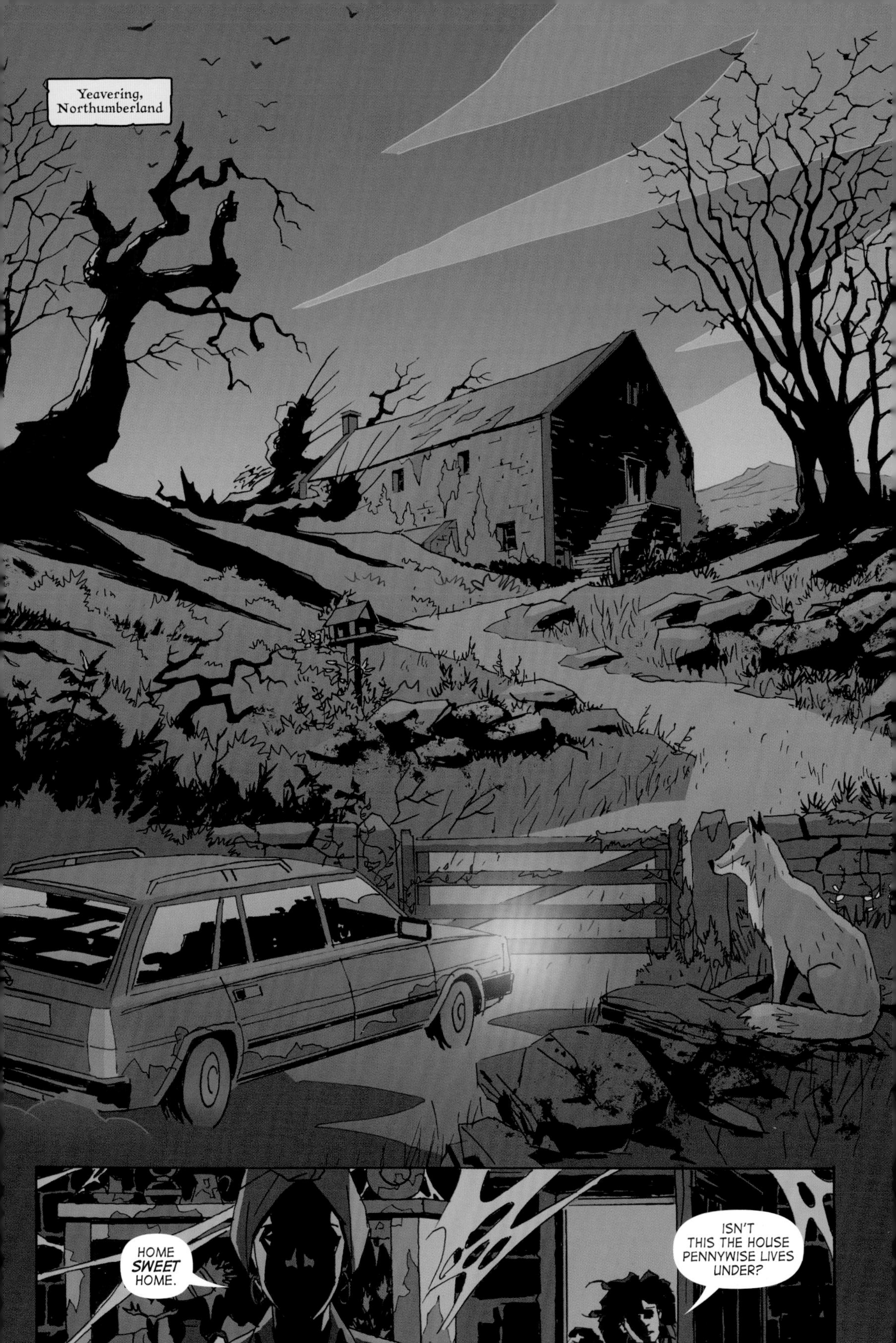
Yeavering,
Northumberland

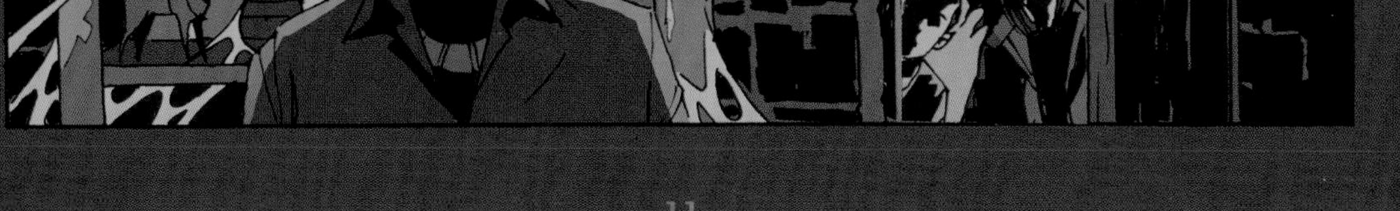
HOME SWEET HOME.
ISN'T THIS THE HOUSE PENNYWISE LIVES UNDER?

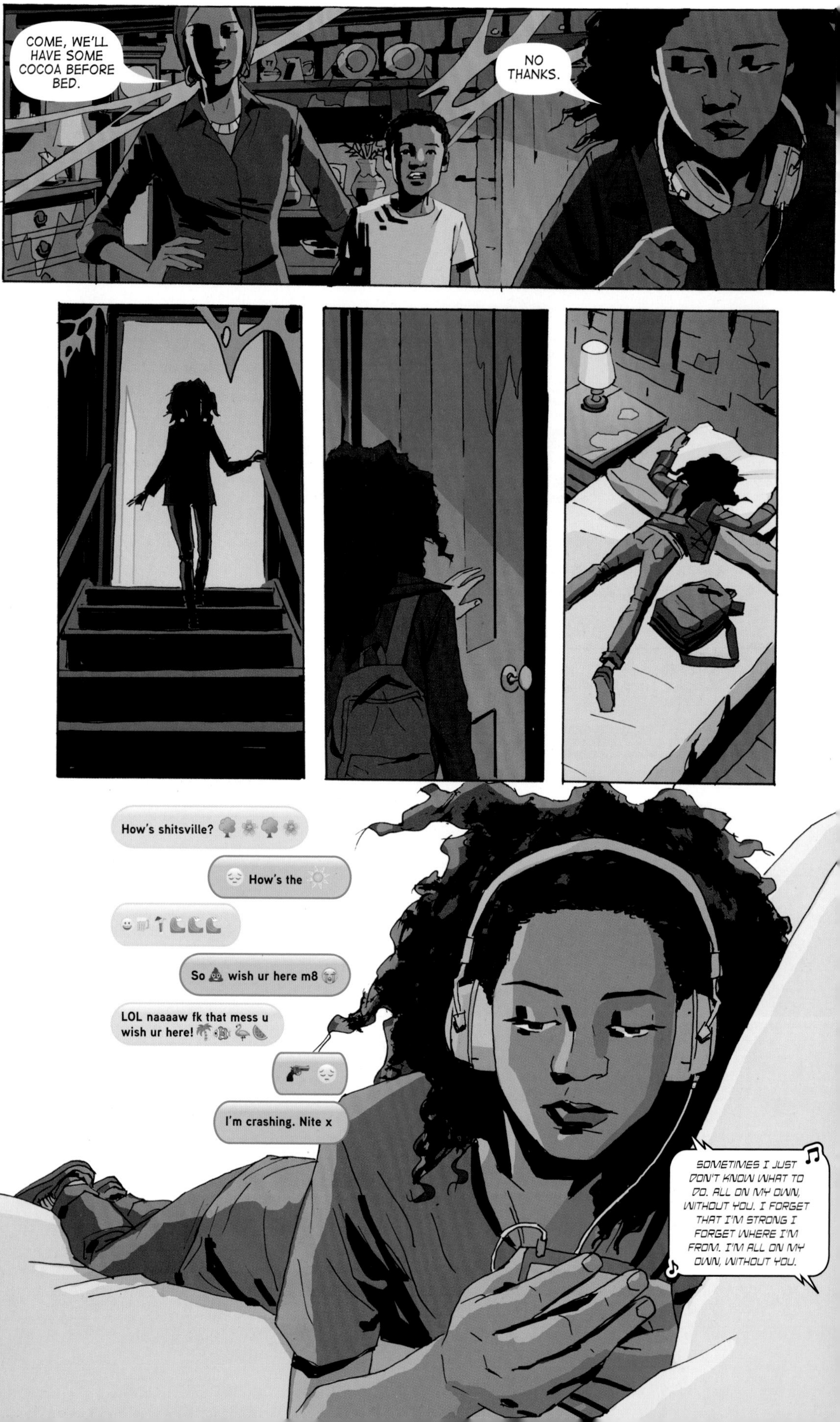
COME, WE'LL HAVE SOME COCOA BEFORE BED.
NO THANKS.
How's shitsville?
How's the
So wish ur here m8
LOL naaaaw fk that mess u wish ur here!
I'm crashing. Nite x
SOMETIMES I JUST DON'T KNOW WHAT TO DO. ALL ON MY OWN, WITHOUT YOU. I FORGET THAT I'M STRONG I FORGET WHERE I'M FROM. I'M ALL ON MY OWN, WITHOUT YOU.

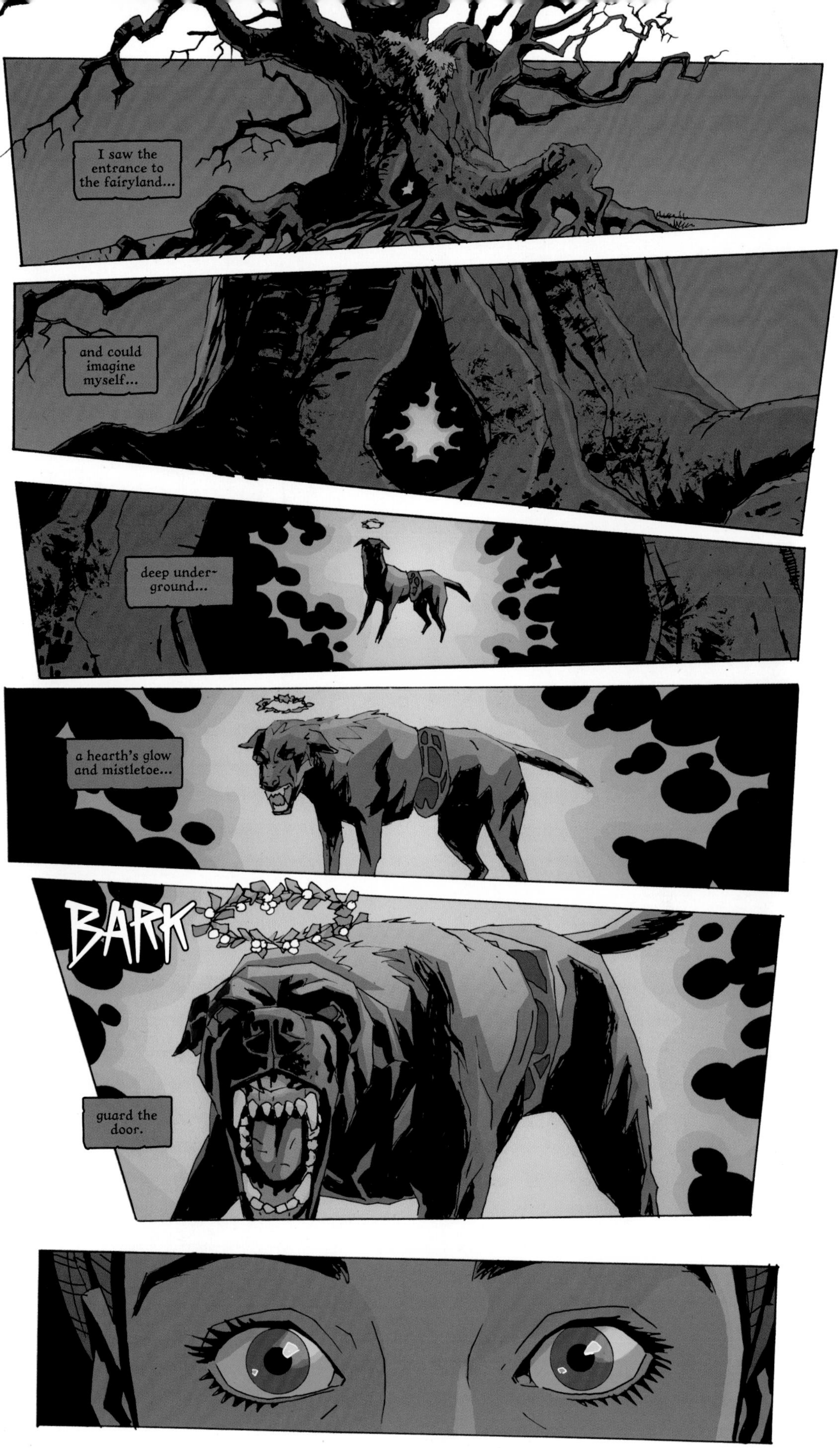
I saw the entrance to the fairyland...
and could imagine myself...
deep under-ground...
a hearth's glow and mistletoe...
BARK
guard the door.

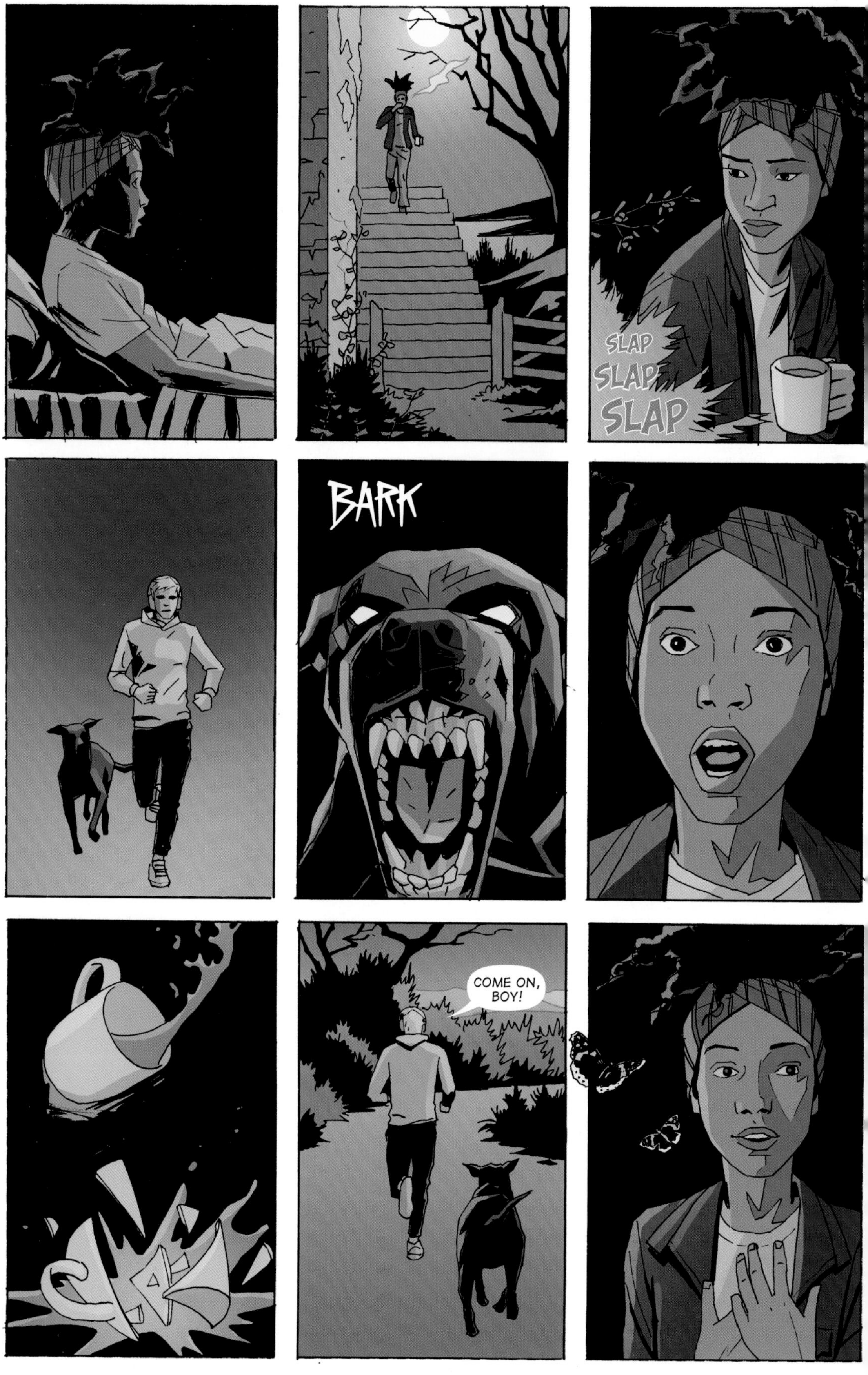
SLAP
SLAP
SLAP
BARK
COME ON, BOY!

MILK, BREAD, BUTTER, TEA, COFFEE, WASHING UP LIQUID...

AND GET SOME EGGS AND BACON. WE'LL HAVE A NICE BREKKIE WHEN YOU GET BACK. OOH AND SOME TREATS FOR LATER.

AND BRING YOUR BROTHER.

YOU'D BETTER BE CAREFUL, BRO

WHY?

BRAAGS.

WHAT?

YEAH, THEY'RE LIKE GOBLINS.

THE WOODS ARE FULL OF THEM.

NO WAY! YOU'RE LYING!

THEY SAY THEY SHAPESHIFT AND LURE THEIR VICTIMS DEEP INTO THE FOREST, NEVER TO BE SEEN AGAIN. WATCH OUT IS ALL I'M SAYING.

NO WAY!

EDITH MAYFEILD

MISSING
CE TUESD   JUNE
INFORMATION CONTACT
0 - 081811   81

SEE!

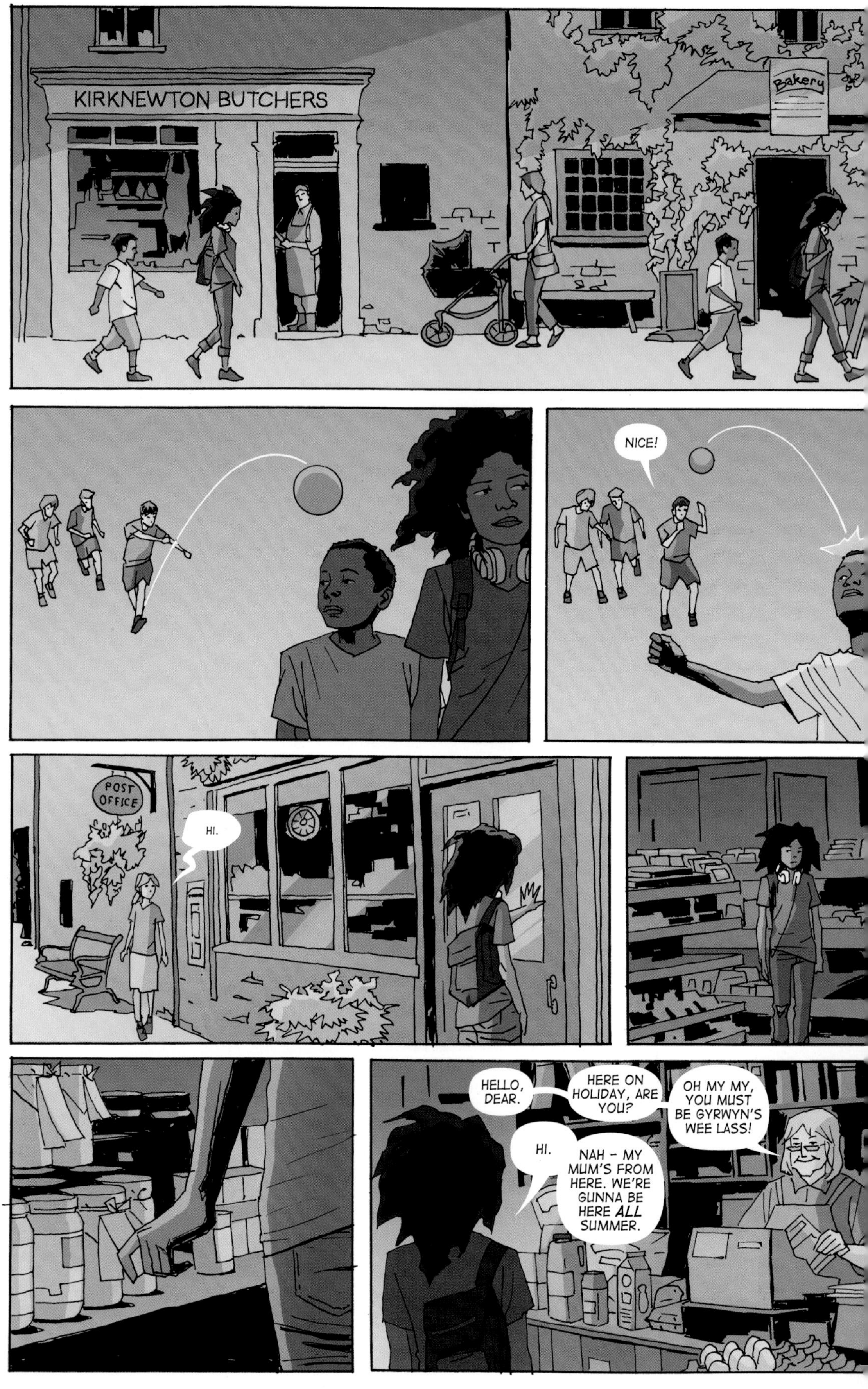
KIRKNEWTON BUTCHERS
Bakery
NICE!
POST OFFICE
HI.
HELLO, DEAR.
HERE ON HOLIDAY, ARE YOU?
OH MY MY, YOU MUST BE GYRWYN'S WEE LASS!
HI.
NAH - MY MUM'S FROM HERE. WE'RE GUNNA BE HERE ALL SUMMER.

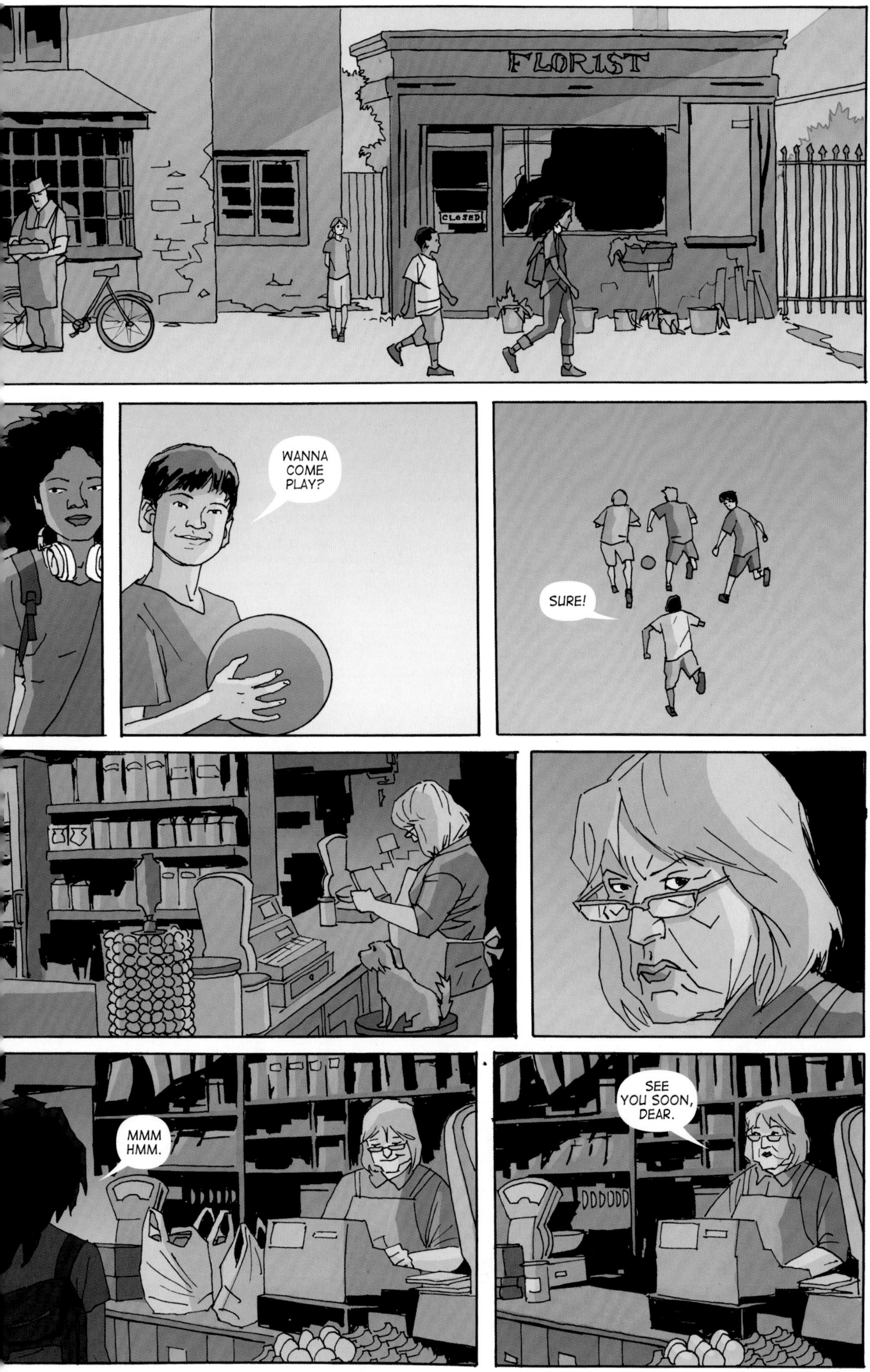
FLORIST
CLOSED
WANNA COME PLAY?
SURE!
MMM HMM.
SEE YOU SOON, DEAR.

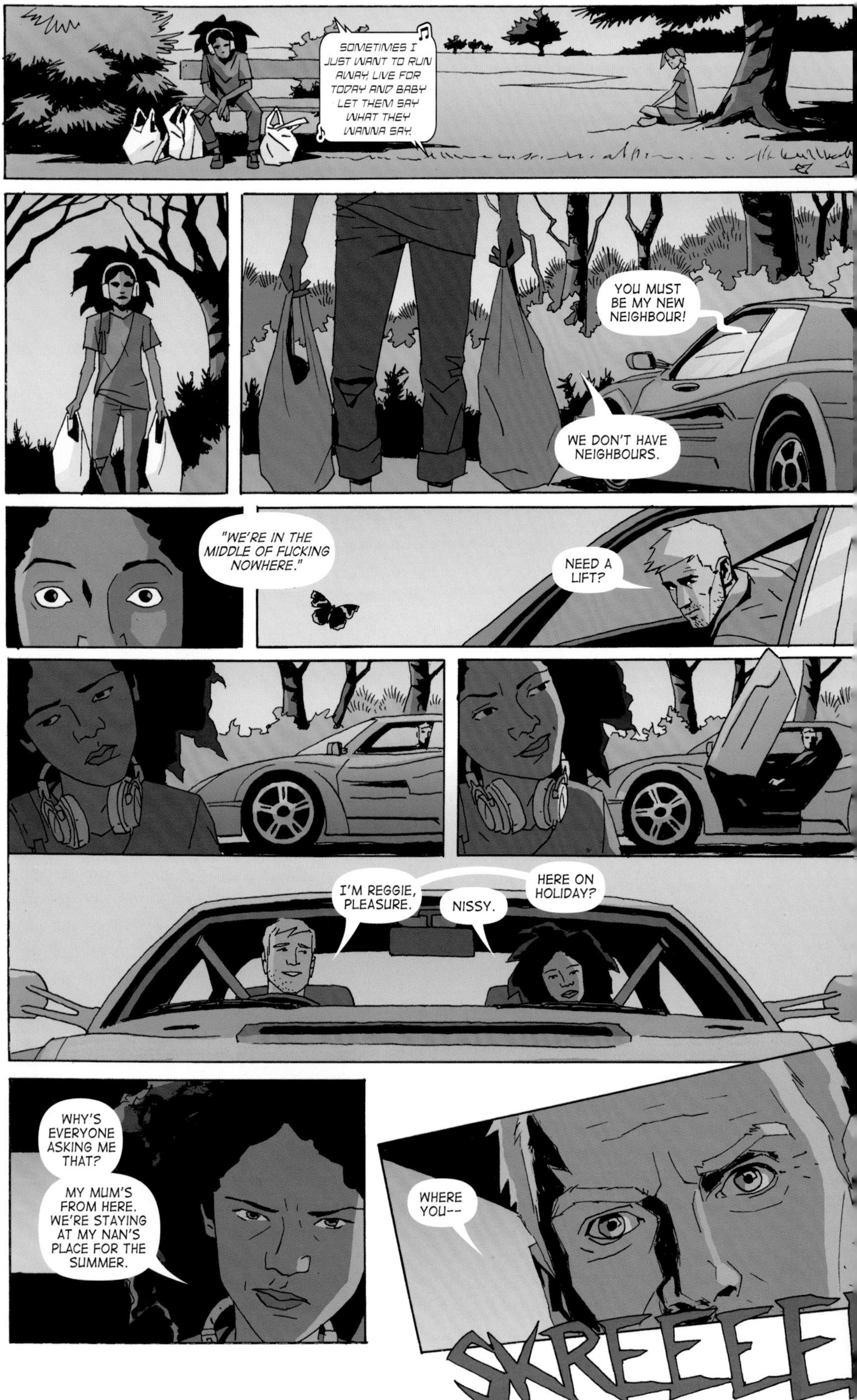
SOMETIMES I JUST WANT TO RUN AWAY, LIVE FOR TODAY AND BABY LET THEM SAY WHAT THEY WANNA SAY.
YOU MUST BE MY NEW NEIGHBOUR!
WE DON'T HAVE NEIGHBOURS.
"WE'RE IN THE MIDDLE OF FUCKING NOWHERE."
NEED A LIFT?
I'M REGGIE, PLEASURE.
NISSY.
HERE ON HOLIDAY?
WHY'S EVERYONE ASKING ME THAT?
MY MUM'S FROM HERE. WE'RE STAYING AT MY NAN'S PLACE FOR THE SUMMER.
WHERE YOU--
SKREEEE

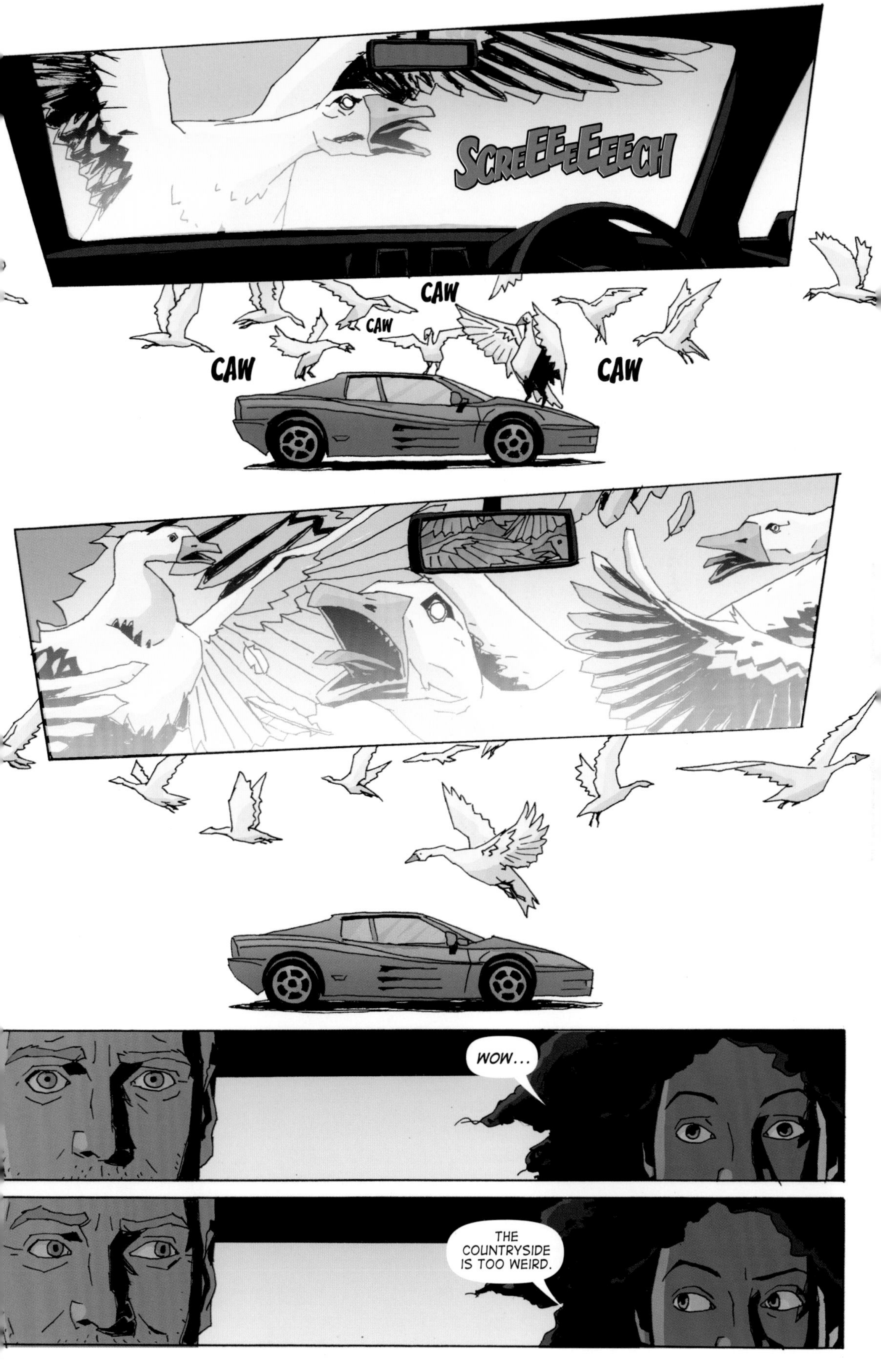
SCREEEEEEECH
CAW
CAW
CAW
CAW
WOW...
THE COUNTRYSIDE IS TOO WEIRD.

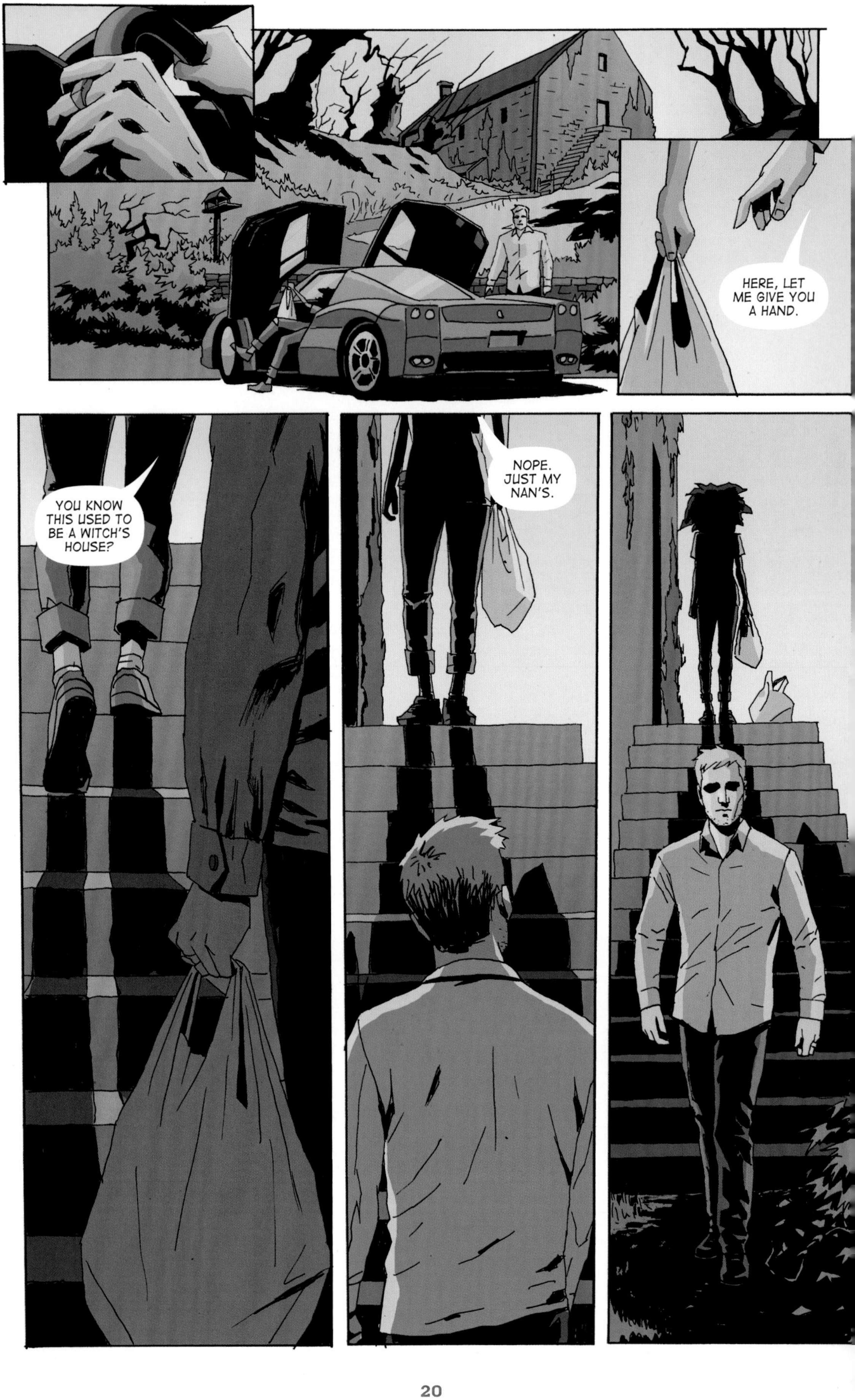
HERE, LET ME GIVE YOU A HAND.
YOU KNOW THIS USED TO BE A WITCH'S HOUSE?
NOPE. JUST MY NAN'S.

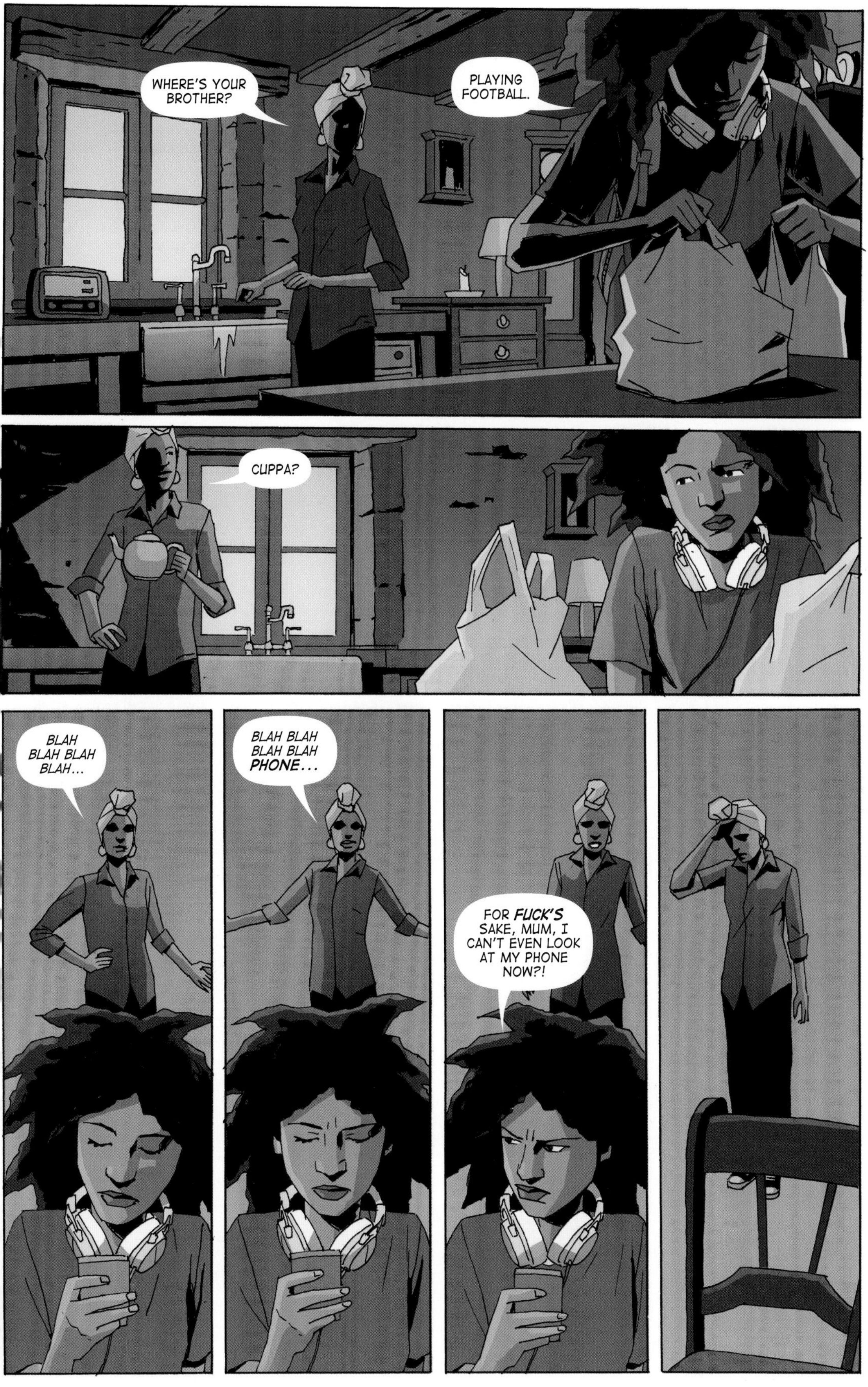
WHERE'S YOUR BROTHER?
PLAYING FOOTBALL.
CUPPA?
BLAH BLAH BLAH BLAH BLAH...
BLAH BLAH BLAH BLAH **PHONE...**
FOR **FUCK'S** SAKE, MUM, I CAN'T EVEN LOOK AT MY PHONE NOW?!

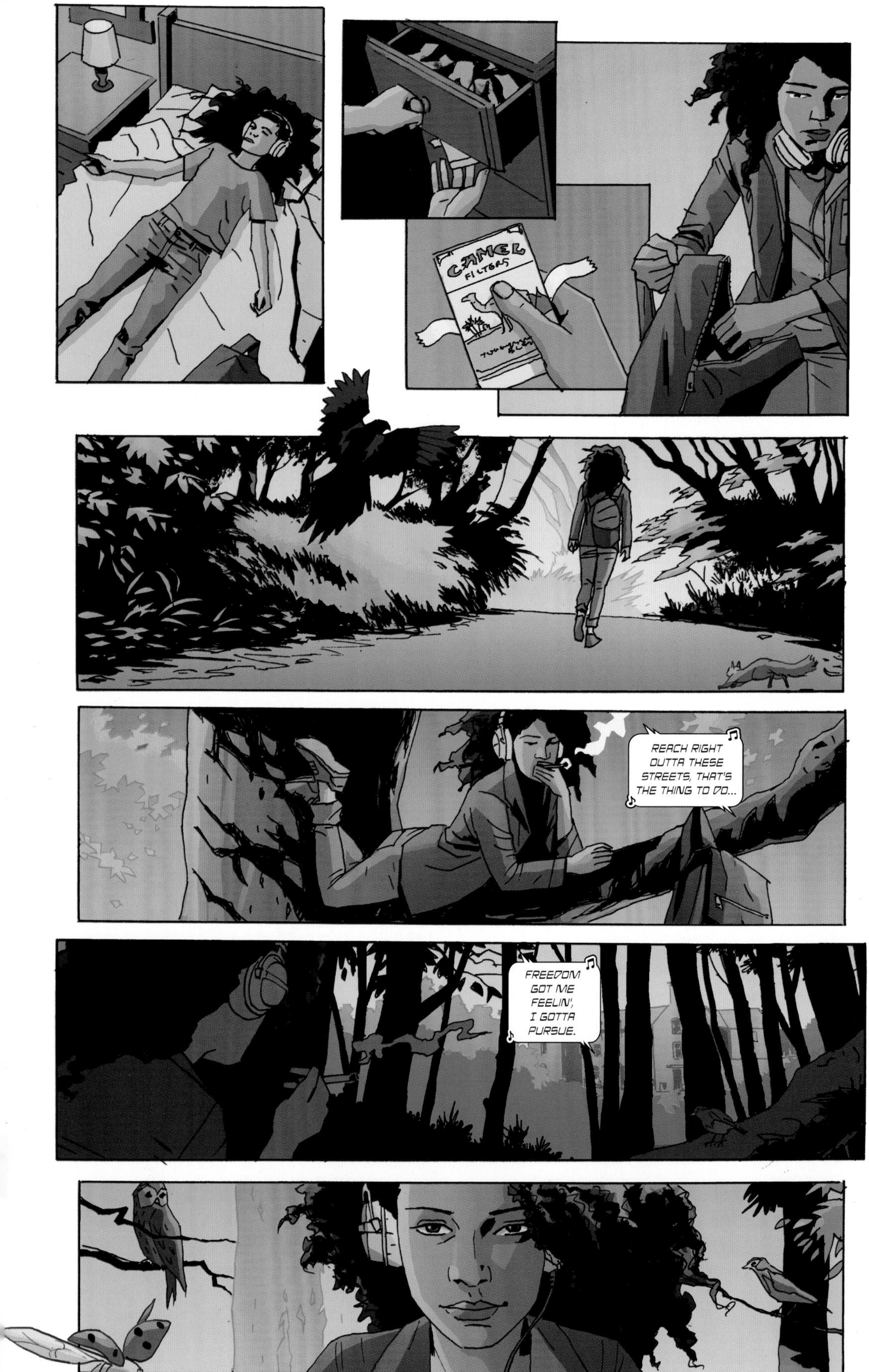
CAMEL
FILTERS
REACH RIGHT OUTTA THESE STREETS, THAT'S THE THING TO DO...
FREEDOM GOT ME FEELIN', I GOTTA PURSUE.

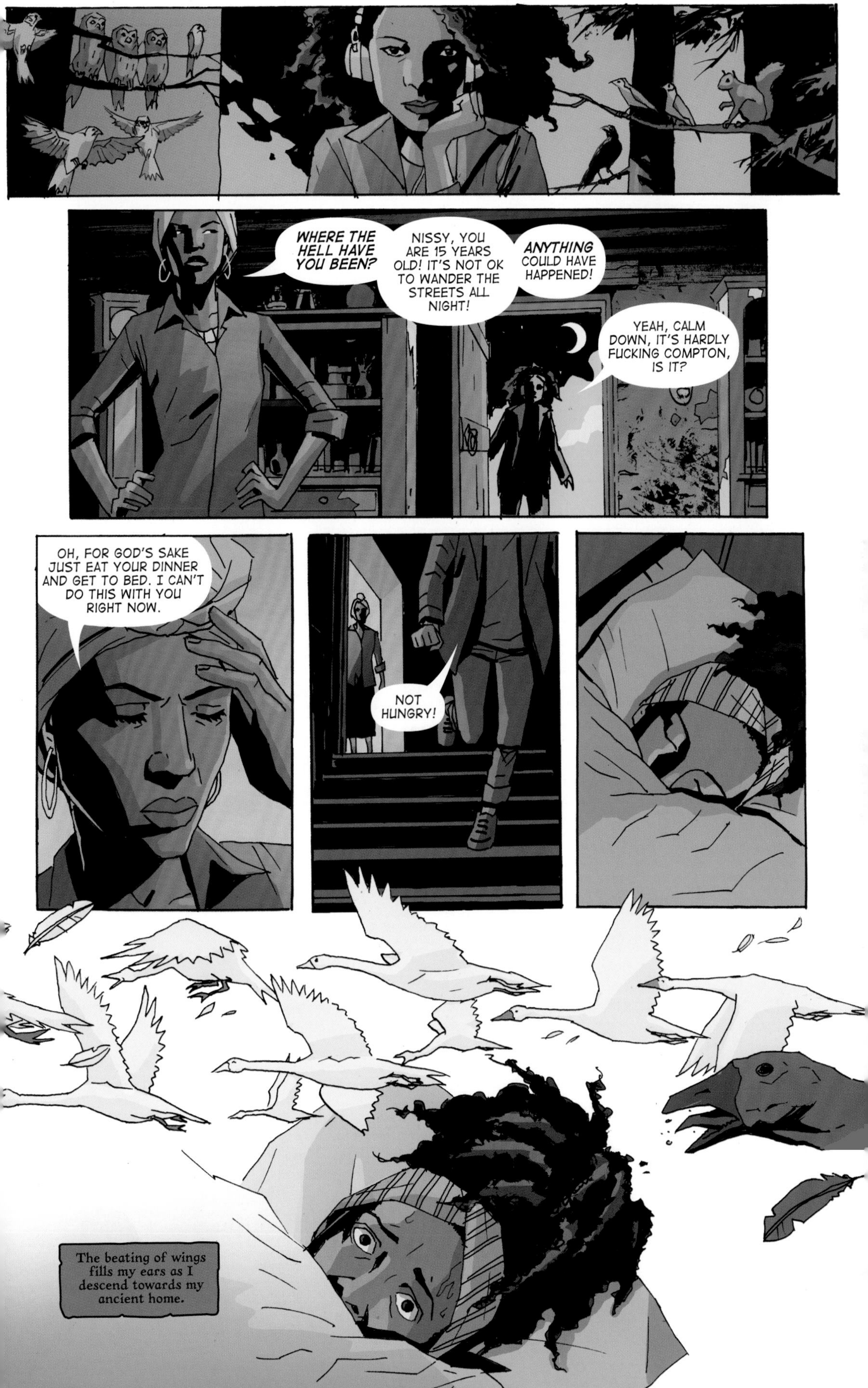
WHERE THE HELL HAVE YOU BEEN?
NISSY, YOU ARE 15 YEARS OLD! IT'S NOT OK TO WANDER THE STREETS ALL NIGHT!
ANYTHING COULD HAVE HAPPENED!
YEAH, CALM DOWN, IT'S HARDLY FUCKING COMPTON, IS IT?
OH, FOR GOD'S SAKE JUST EAT YOUR DINNER AND GET TO BED. I CAN'T DO THIS WITH YOU RIGHT NOW.
NOT HUNGRY!
The beating of wings fills my ears as I descend towards my ancient home.

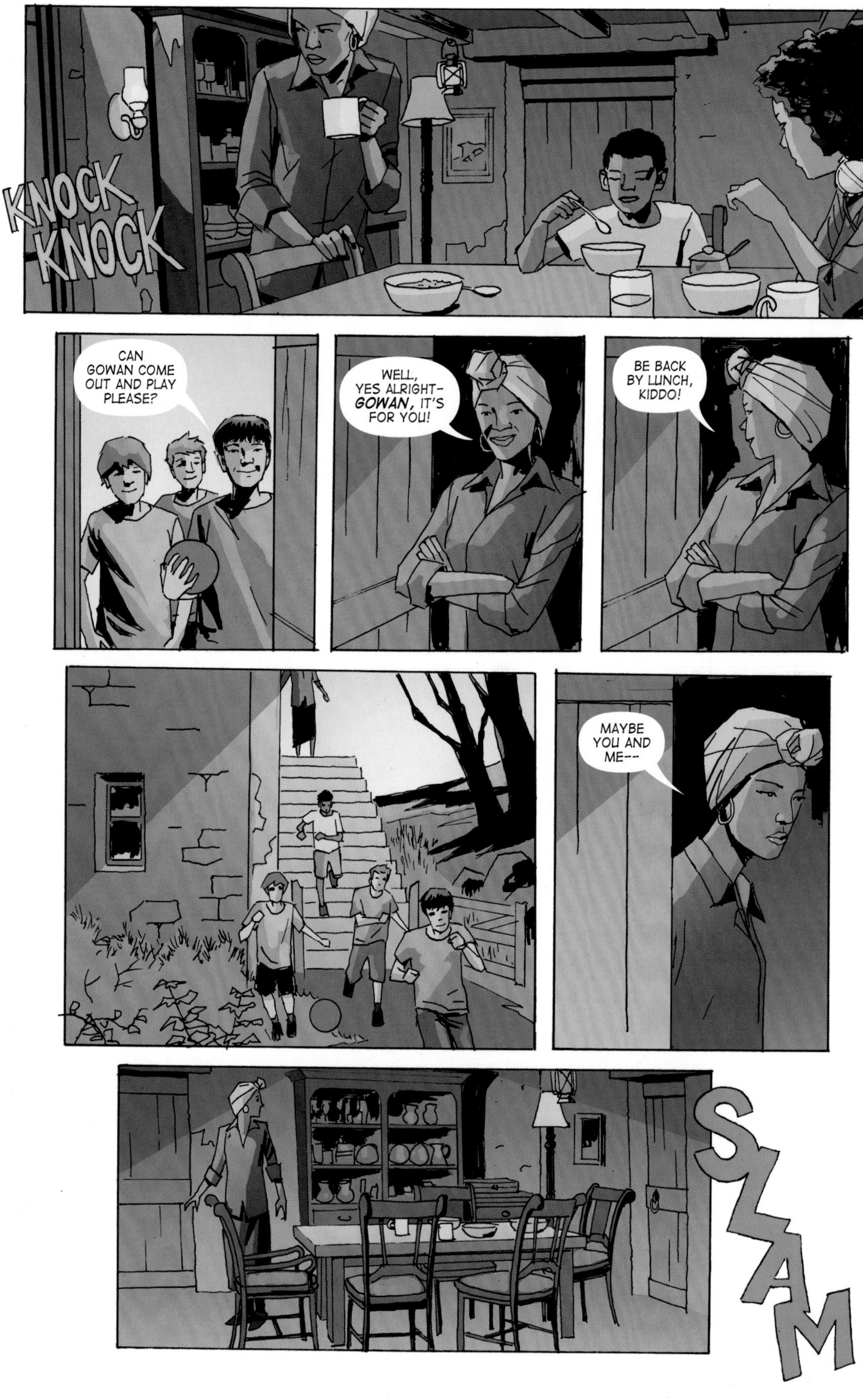
KNOCK KNOCK
CAN GOWAN COME OUT AND PLAY PLEASE?
WELL, YES ALRIGHT- GOWAN, IT'S FOR YOU!
BE BACK BY LUNCH, KIDDO!
MAYBE YOU AND ME--
SLAM

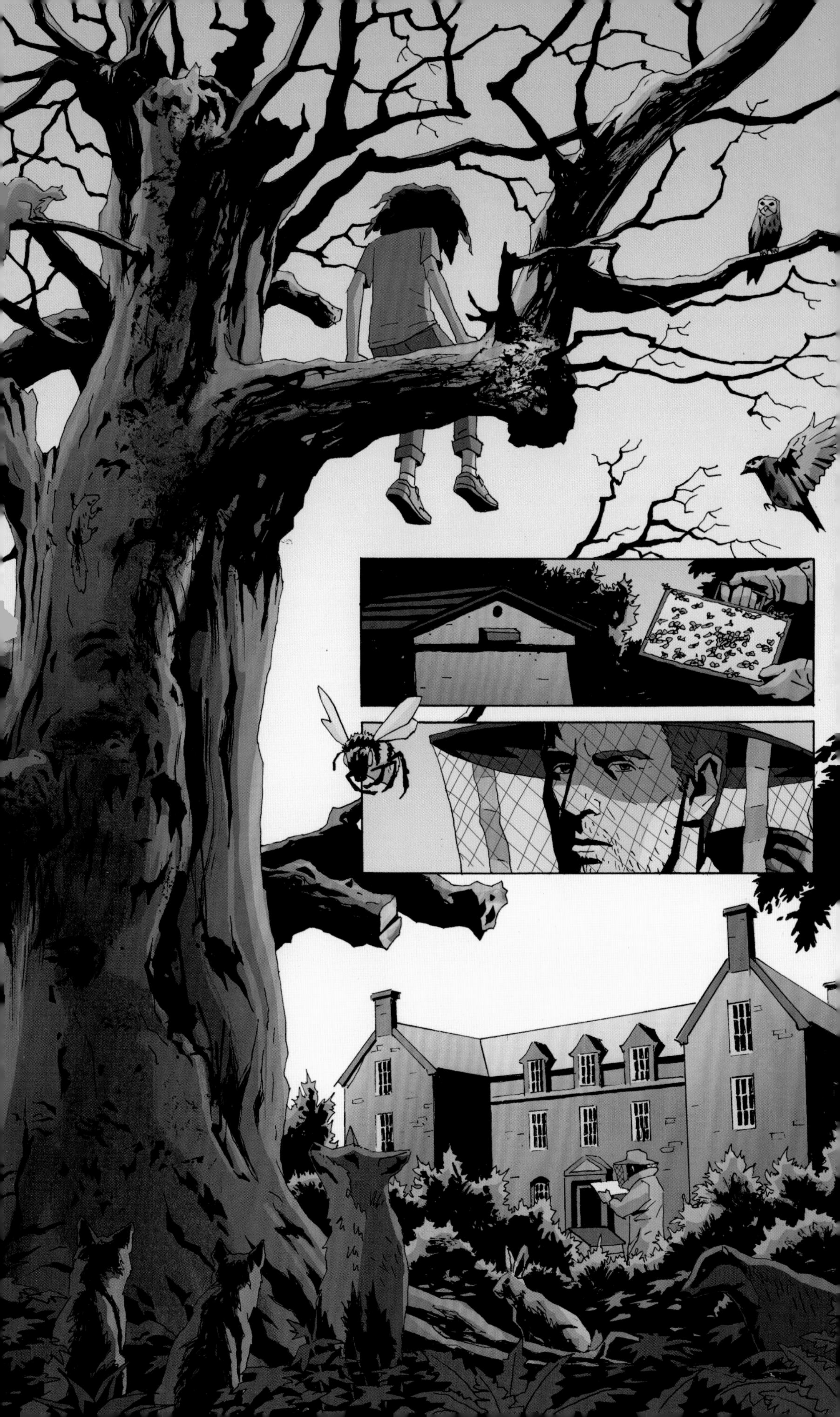

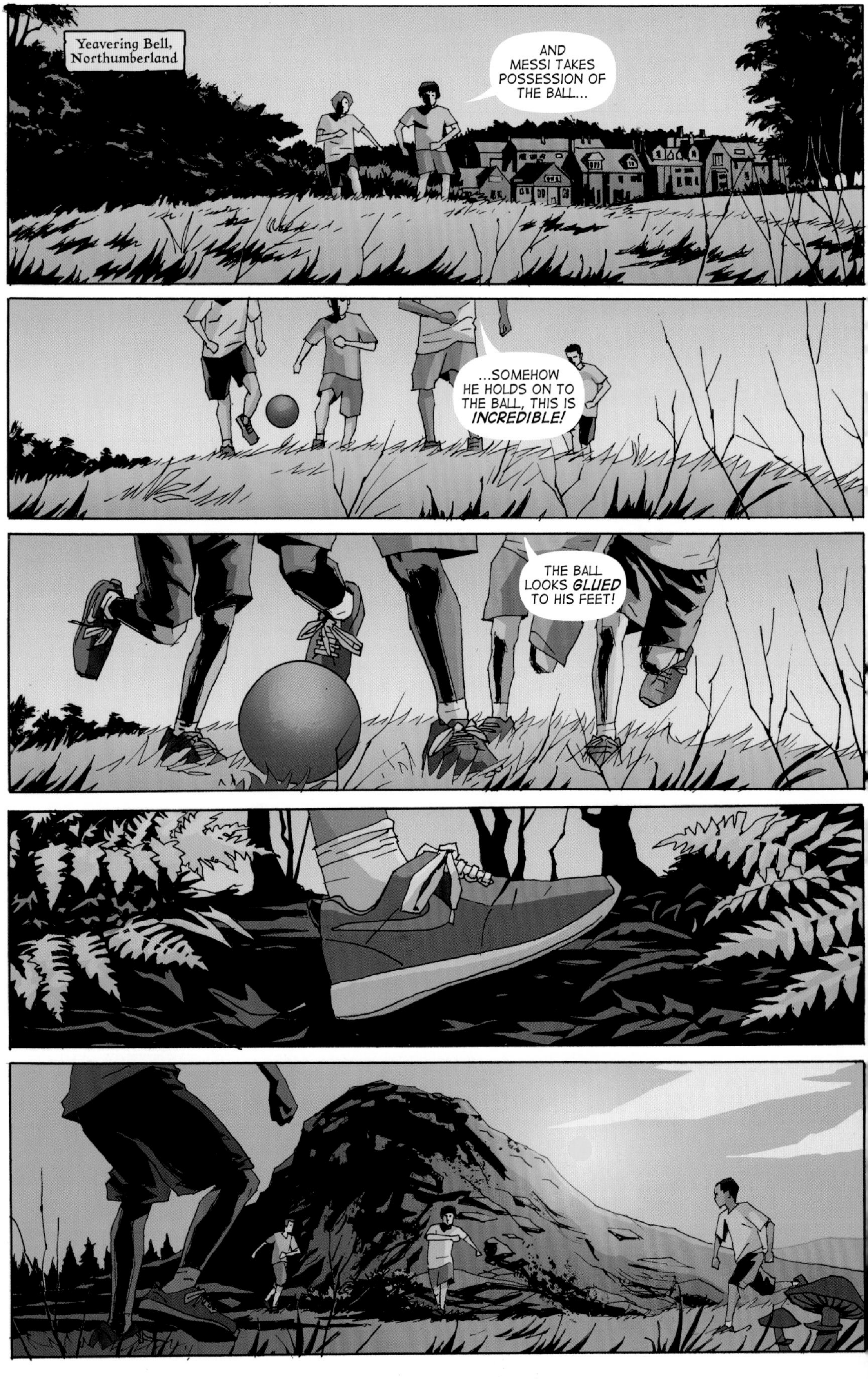
Yeavering Bell, Northumberland
AND MESSI TAKES POSSESSION OF THE BALL...
...SOMEHOW HE HOLDS ON TO THE BALL, THIS IS *INCREDIBLE!*
THE BALL LOOKS *GLUED* TO HIS FEET!

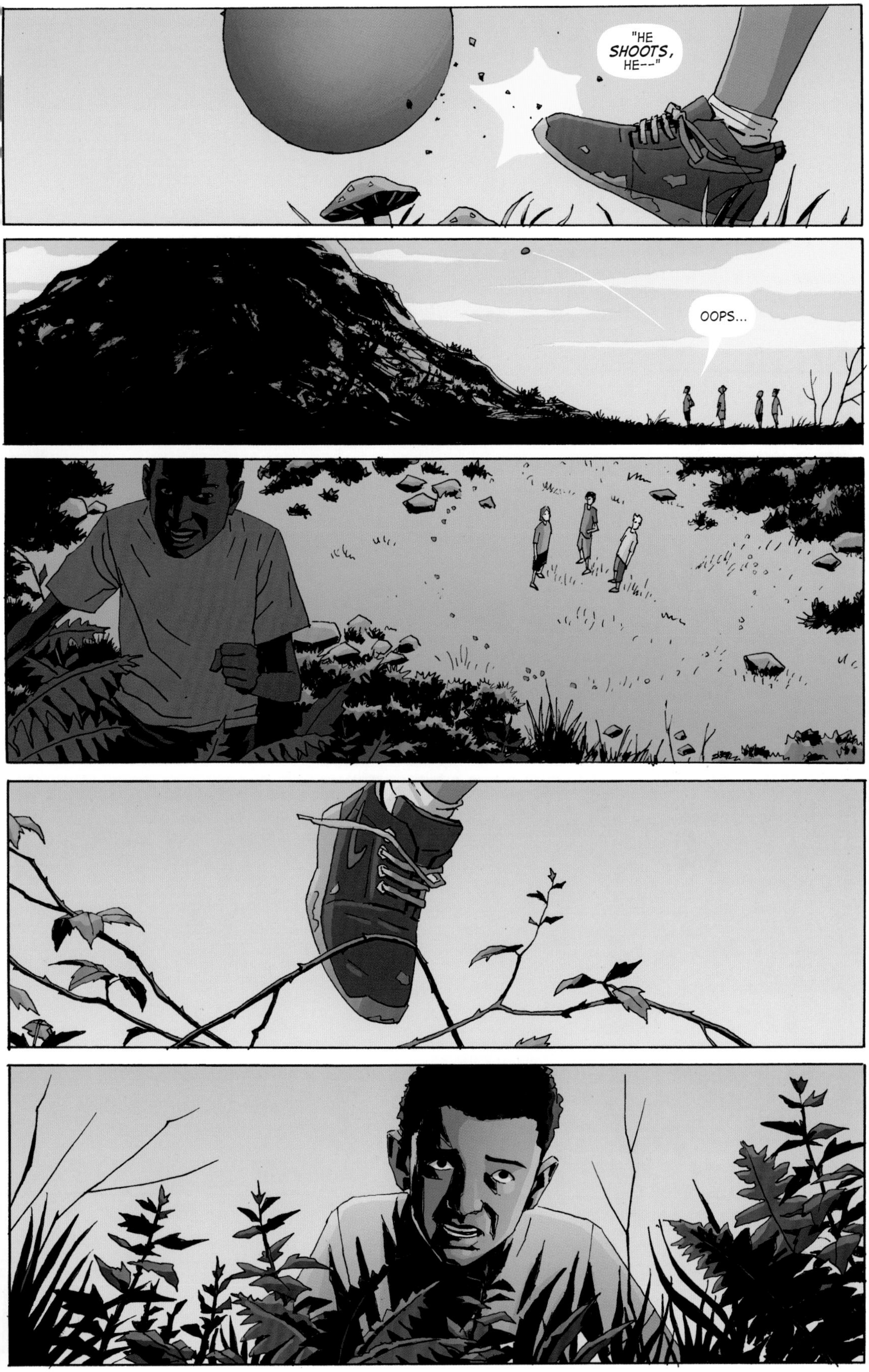
"HE SHOOTS, HE--"
OOPS...

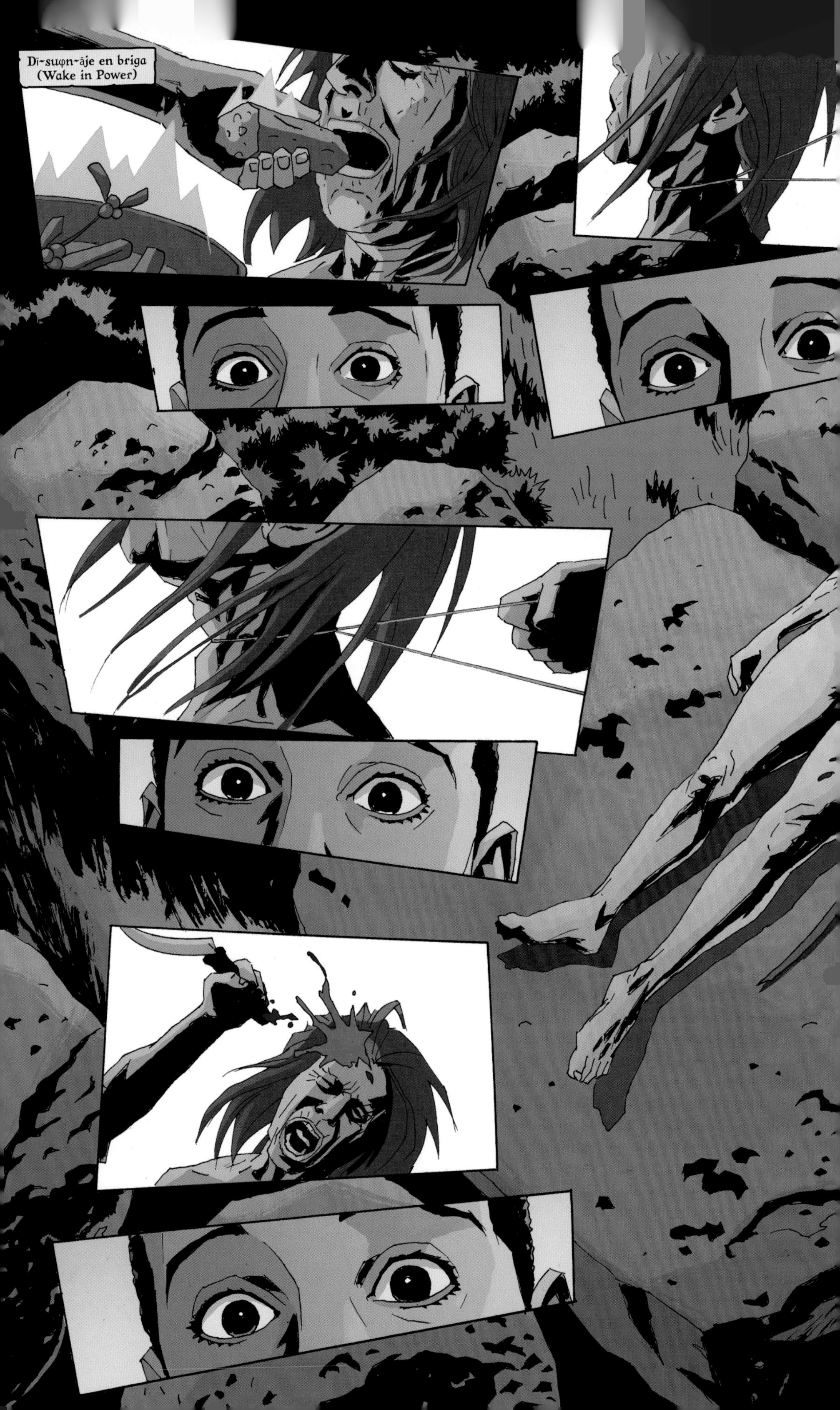
Dī~suφn~āje en briga
(Wake in Power)

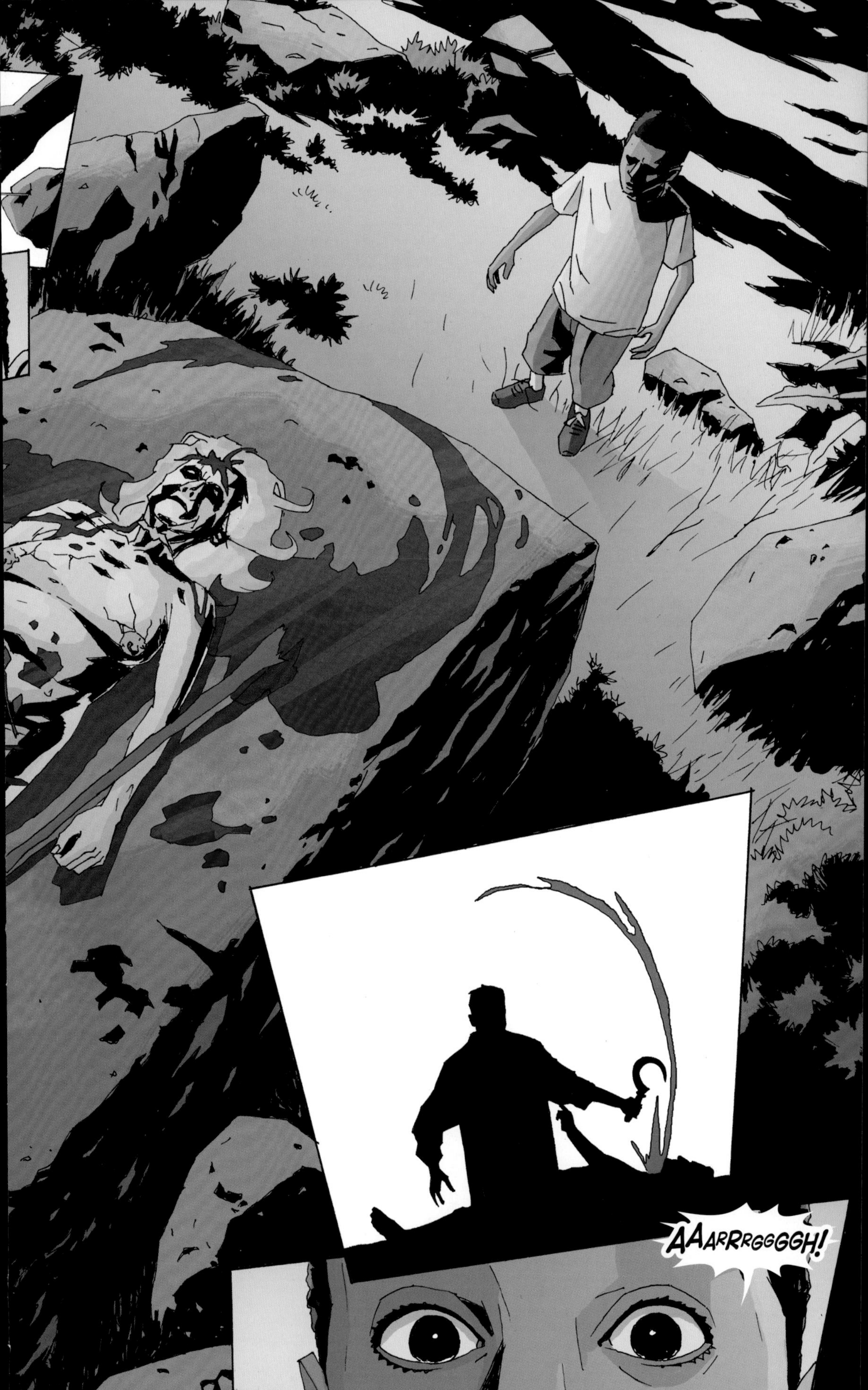
AAARRRGGGGH!

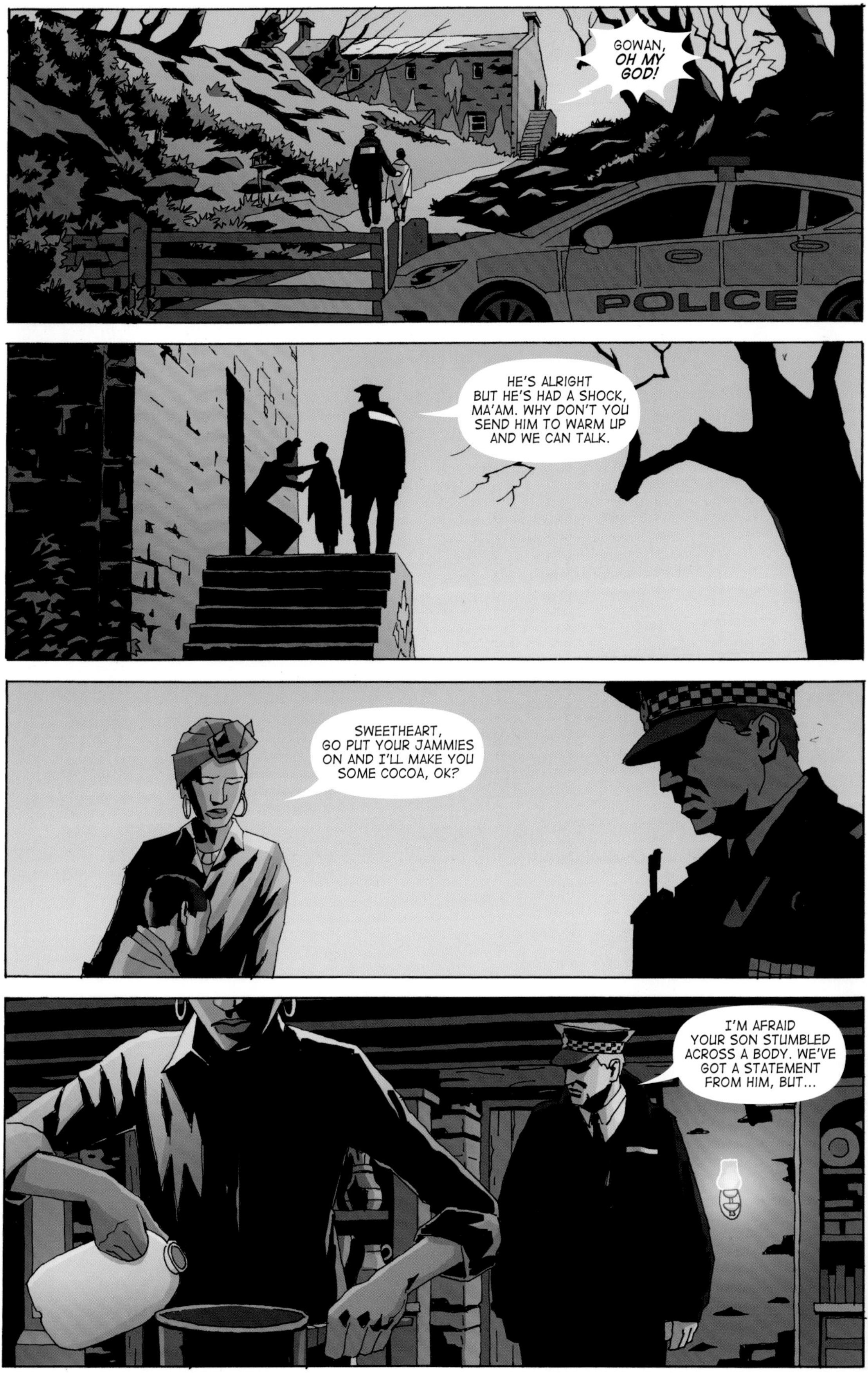
GOWAN, OH MY GOD!
POLICE
HE'S ALRIGHT BUT HE'S HAD A SHOCK, MA'AM. WHY DON'T YOU SEND HIM TO WARM UP AND WE CAN TALK.
SWEETHEART, GO PUT YOUR JAMMIES ON AND I'LL MAKE YOU SOME COCOA, OK?
I'M AFRAID YOUR SON STUMBLED ACROSS A BODY. WE'VE GOT A STATEMENT FROM HIM, BUT...

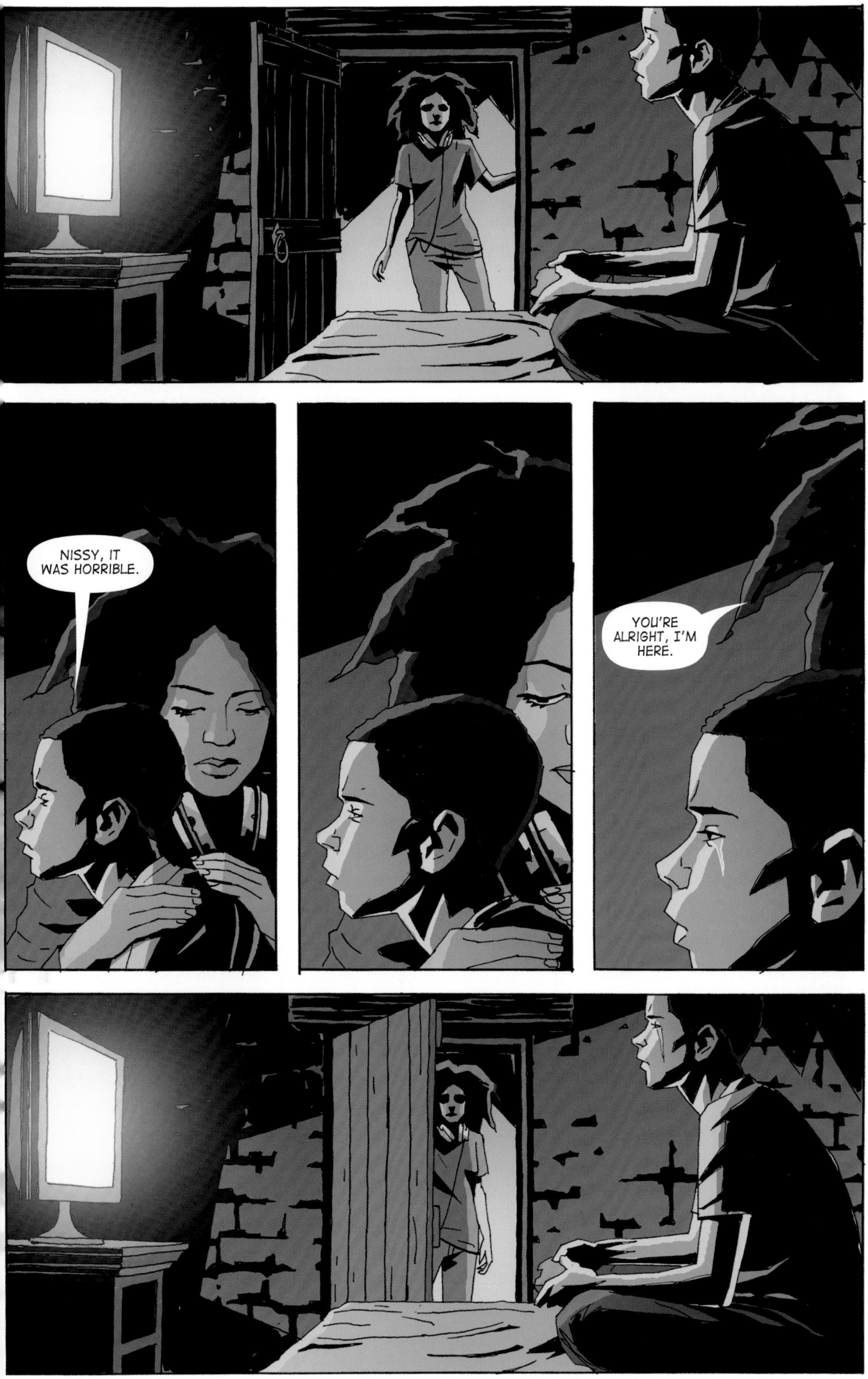
NISSY, IT WAS HORRIBLE.
YOU'RE ALRIGHT, I'M HERE.

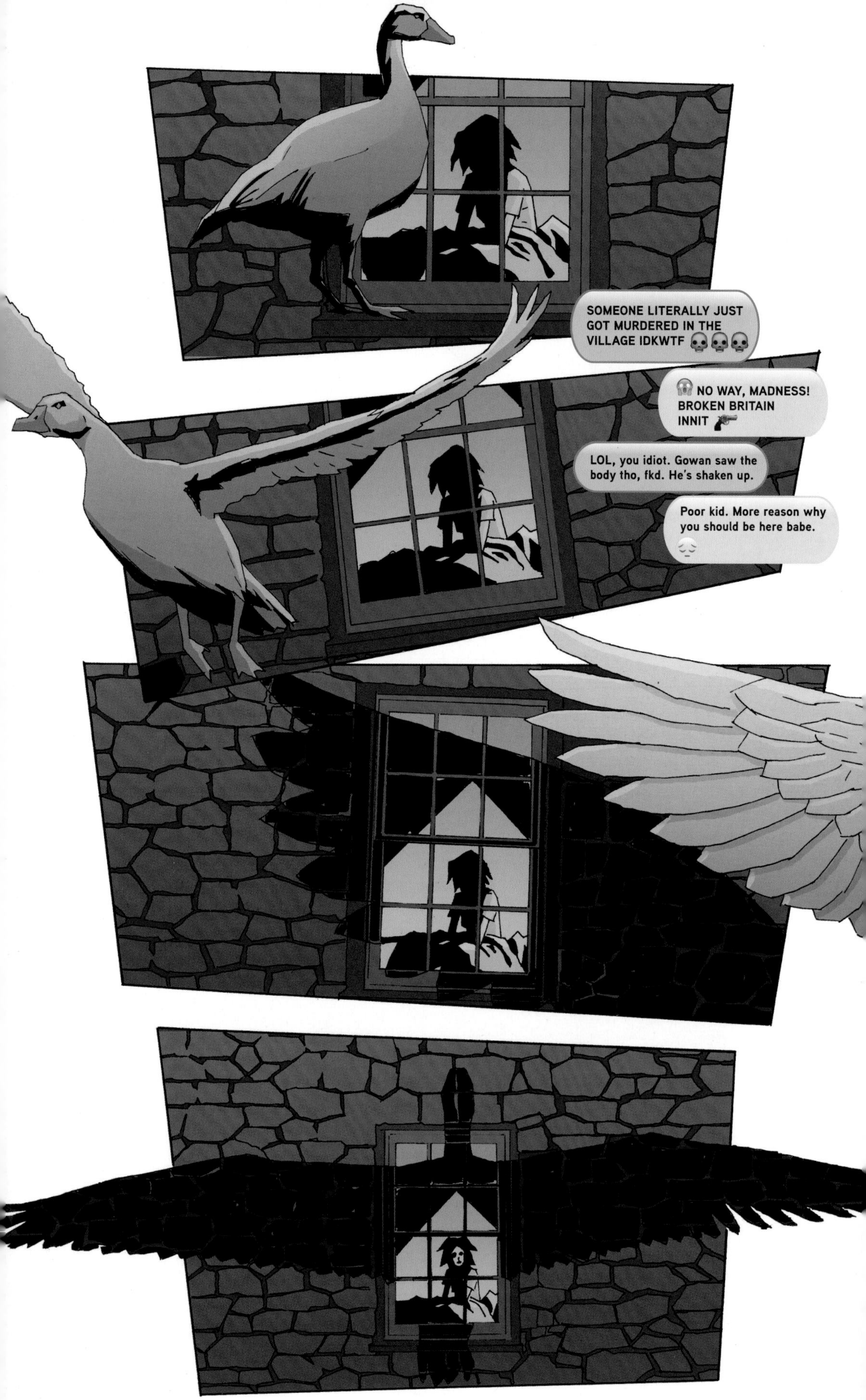

SOMEONE LITERALLY JUST GOT MURDERED IN THE VILLAGE IDKWTF 💀💀💀
😱 NO WAY, MADNESS! BROKEN BRITAIN INNIT 🔫
LOL, you idiot. Gowan saw the body tho, fkd. He's shaken up.
Poor kid. More reason why you should be here babe. 😔

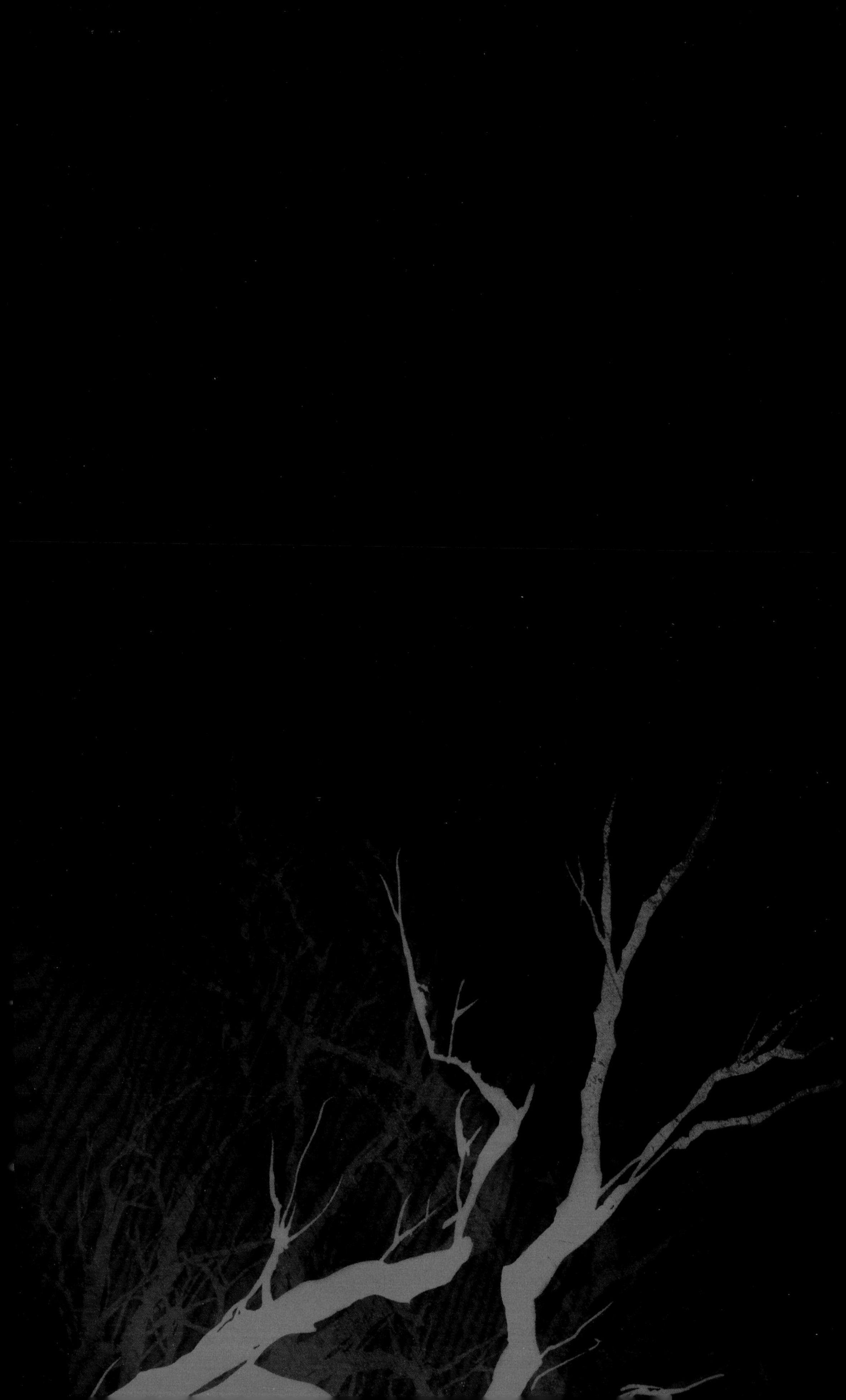

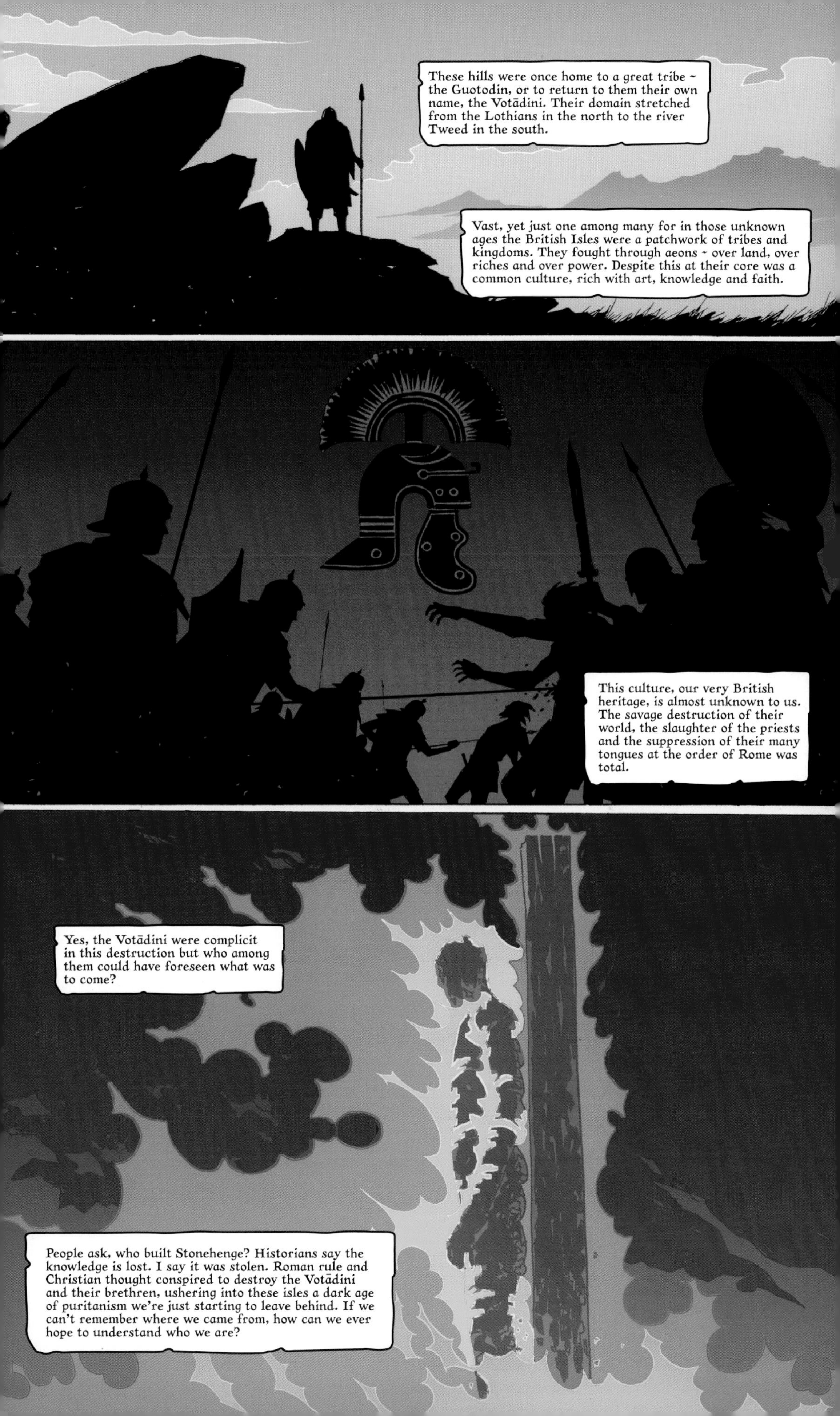
These hills were once home to a great tribe ~ the Guotodin, or to return to them their own name, the Votādini. Their domain stretched from the Lothians in the north to the river Tweed in the south.
Vast, yet just one among many for in those unknown ages the British Isles were a patchwork of tribes and kingdoms. They fought through aeons ~ over land, over riches and over power. Despite this at their core was a common culture, rich with art, knowledge and faith.
This culture, our very British heritage, is almost unknown to us. The savage destruction of their world, the slaughter of the priests and the suppression of their many tongues at the order of Rome was total.
Yes, the Votādini were complicit in this destruction but who among them could have foreseen what was to come?
People ask, who built Stonehenge? Historians say the knowledge is lost. I say it was stolen. Roman rule and Christian thought conspired to destroy the Votādini and their brethren, ushering into these isles a dark age of puritanism we're just starting to leave behind. If we can't remember where we came from, how can we ever hope to understand who we are?

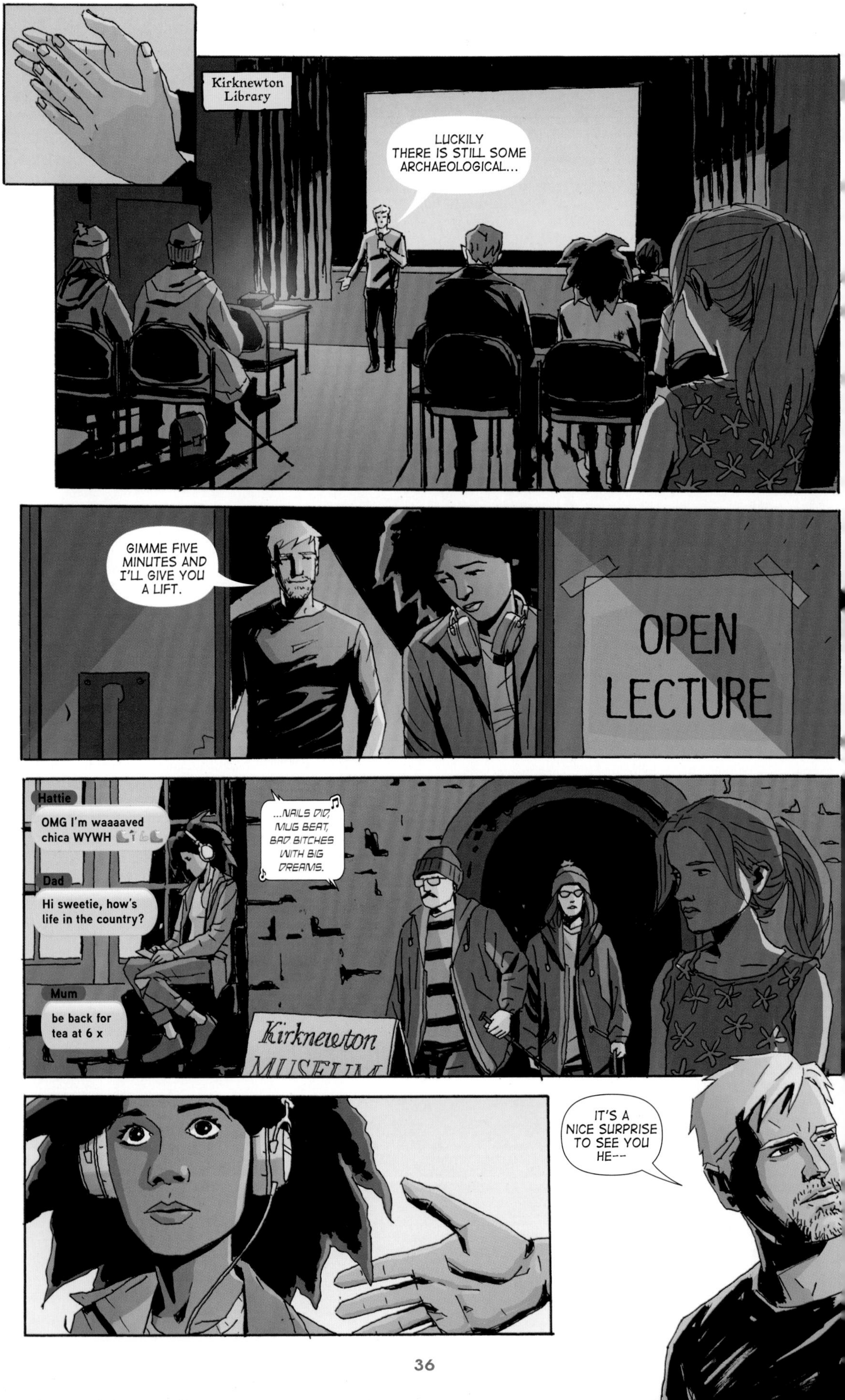
Kirknewton Library
LUCKILY THERE IS STILL SOME ARCHAEOLOGICAL...
GIMME FIVE MINUTES AND I'LL GIVE YOU A LIFT.
OPEN LECTURE
Hattie
OMG I'm waaaaved chica WYWH
Dad
Hi sweetie, how's life in the country?
Mum
be back for tea at 6 x
...NAILS DID, MUG BEAT, BAD BITCHES WITH BIG DREAMS.
IT'S A NICE SURPRISE TO SEE YOU HE--

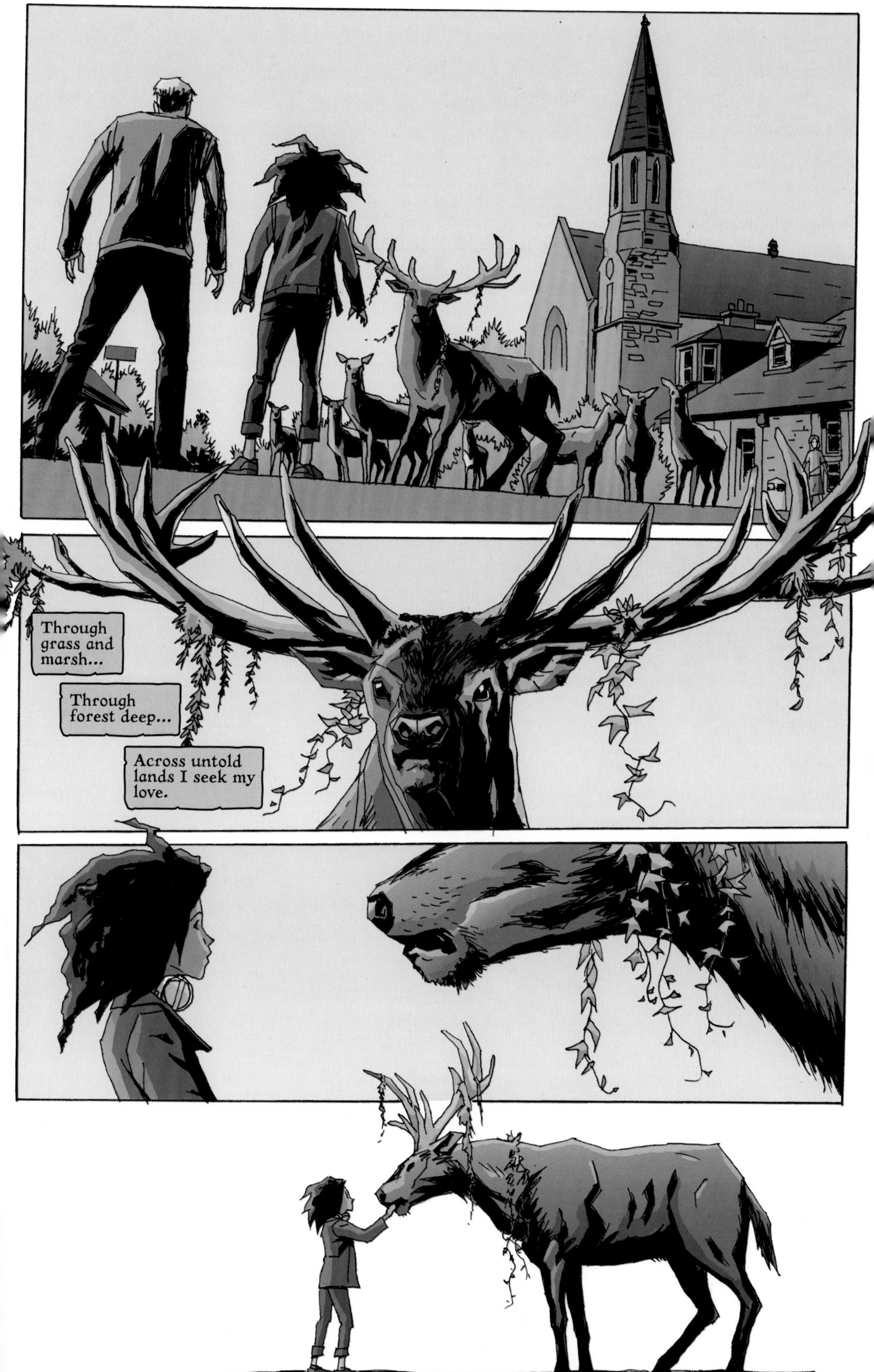
Through grass and marsh...
Through forest deep...
Across untold lands I seek my love.

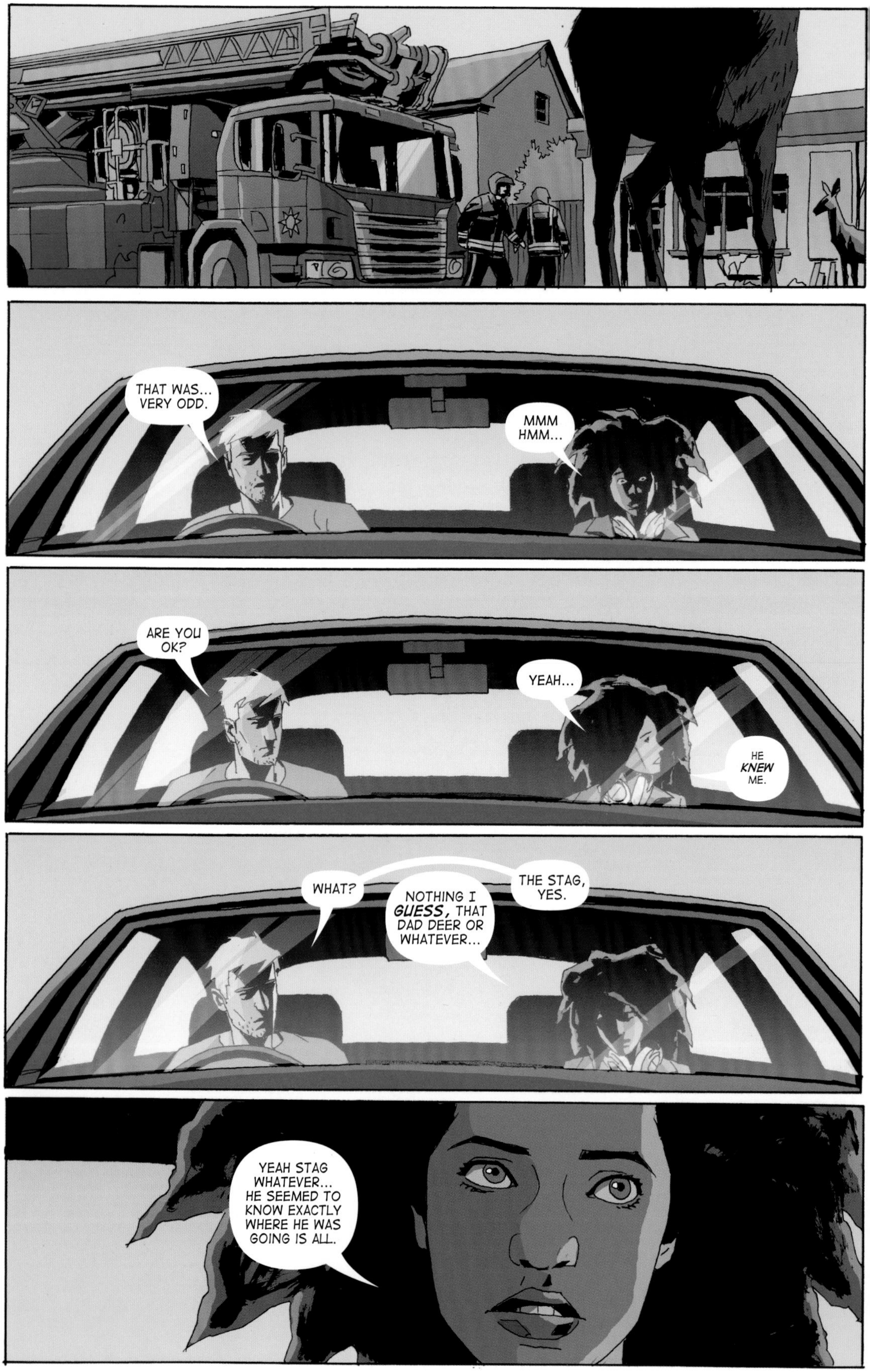
THAT WAS... VERY ODD.
MMM HMM...
ARE YOU OK?
YEAH...
HE KNEW ME.
WHAT?
THE STAG, YES.
NOTHING I GUESS, THAT DAD DEER OR WHATEVER...
YEAH STAG WHATEVER... HE SEEMED TO KNOW EXACTLY WHERE HE WAS GOING IS ALL.

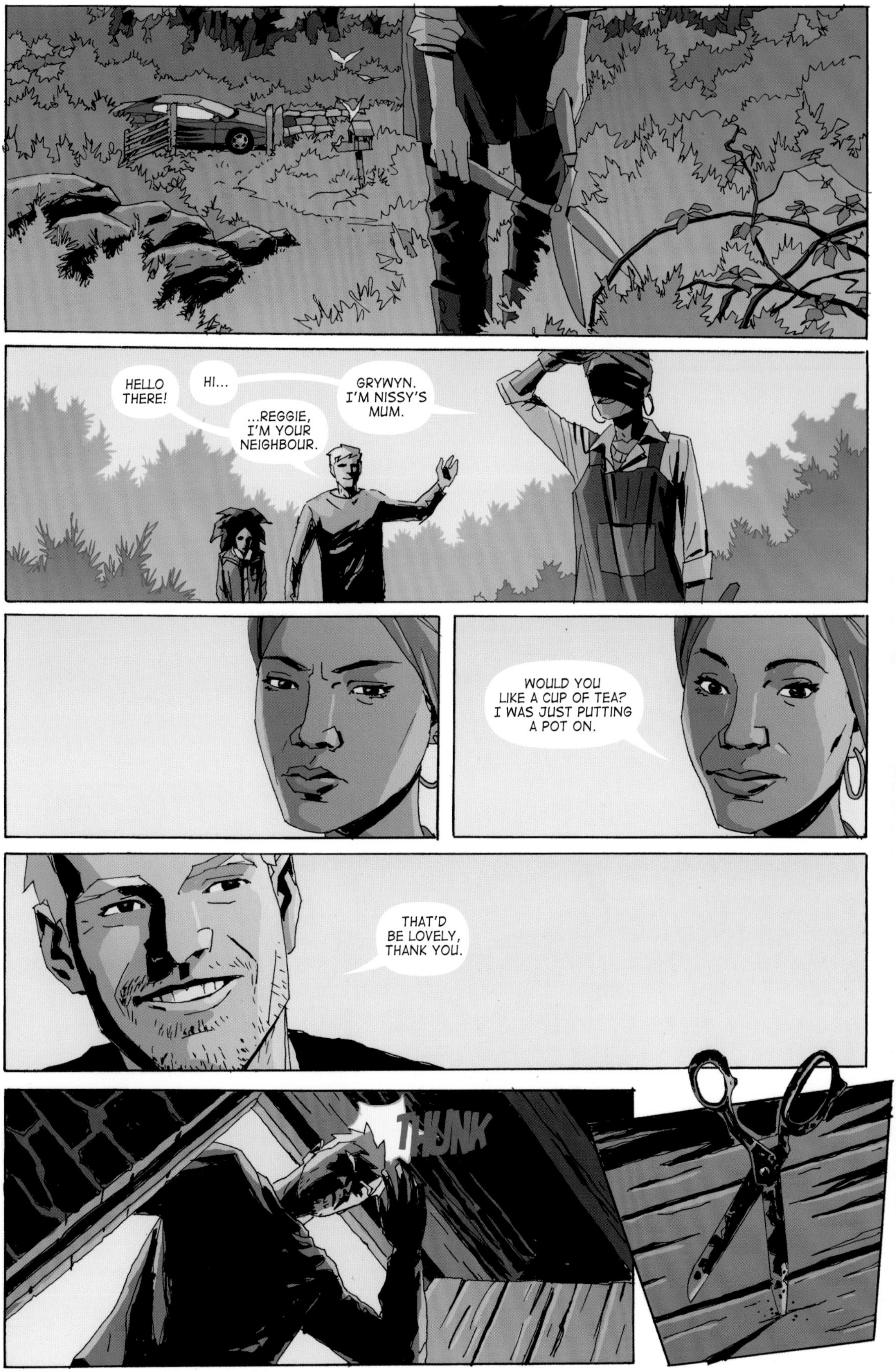
HELLO THERE!
HI...
...REGGIE, I'M YOUR NEIGHBOUR.
GRYWYN. I'M NISSY'S MUM.
WOULD YOU LIKE A CUP OF TEA? I WAS JUST PUTTING A POT ON.
THAT'D BE LOVELY, THANK YOU.
THUNK

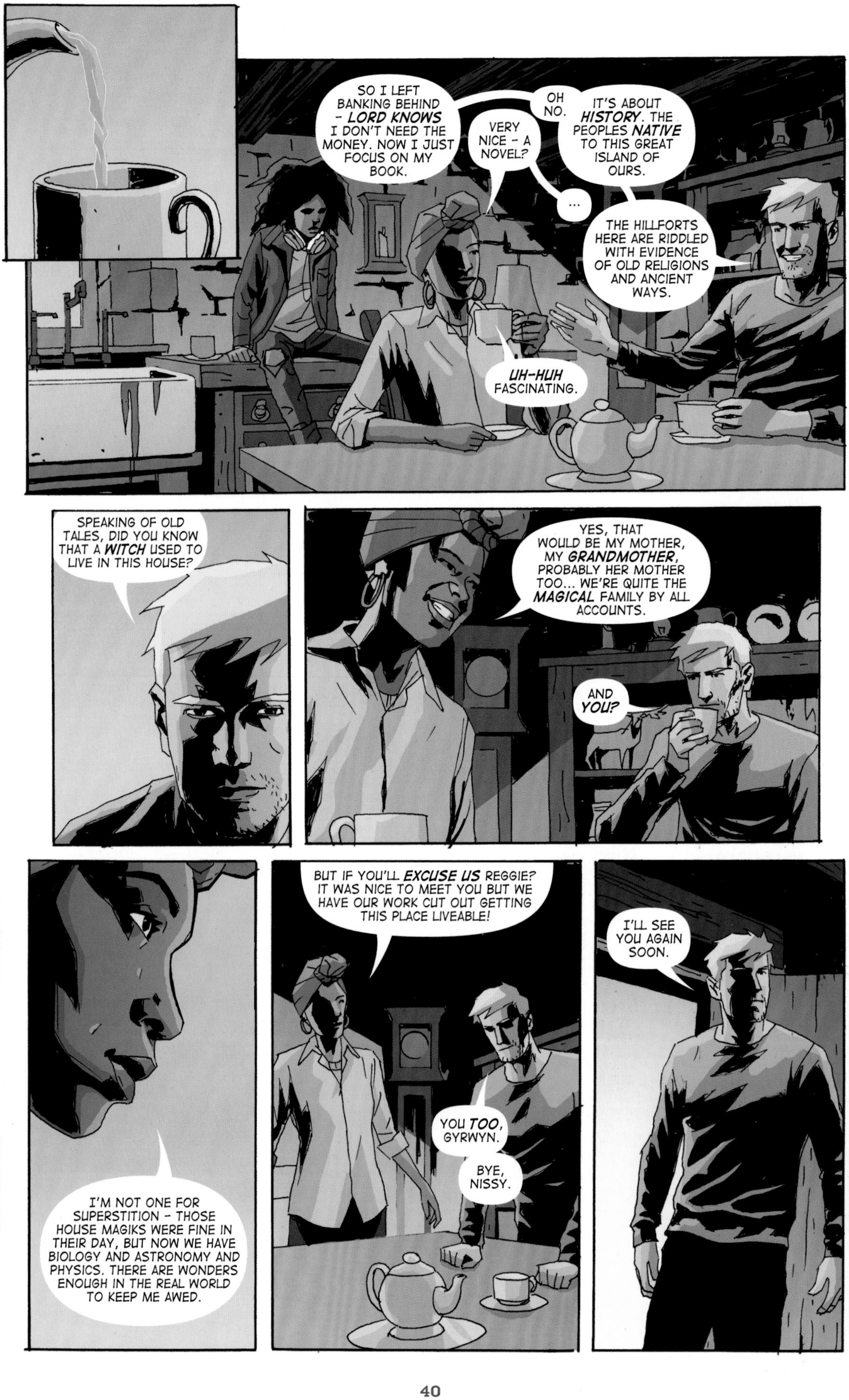
SO I LEFT BANKING BEHIND – LORD KNOWS I DON'T NEED THE MONEY. NOW I JUST FOCUS ON MY BOOK.
VERY NICE – A NOVEL?
OH NO.
IT'S ABOUT HISTORY. THE PEOPLES NATIVE TO THIS GREAT ISLAND OF OURS.
...
THE HILLFORTS HERE ARE RIDDLED WITH EVIDENCE OF OLD RELIGIONS AND ANCIENT WAYS.
UH-HUH FASCINATING.
SPEAKING OF OLD TALES, DID YOU KNOW THAT A WITCH USED TO LIVE IN THIS HOUSE?
YES, THAT WOULD BE MY MOTHER, MY GRANDMOTHER, PROBABLY HER MOTHER TOO... WE'RE QUITE THE MAGICAL FAMILY BY ALL ACCOUNTS.
AND YOU?
I'M NOT ONE FOR SUPERSTITION – THOSE HOUSE MAGIKS WERE FINE IN THEIR DAY, BUT NOW WE HAVE BIOLOGY AND ASTRONOMY AND PHYSICS. THERE ARE WONDERS ENOUGH IN THE REAL WORLD TO KEEP ME AWED.
BUT IF YOU'LL EXCUSE US REGGIE? IT WAS NICE TO MEET YOU BUT WE HAVE OUR WORK CUT OUT GETTING THIS PLACE LIVEABLE!
YOU TOO, GYRWYN.
BYE, NISSY.
I'LL SEE YOU AGAIN SOON.

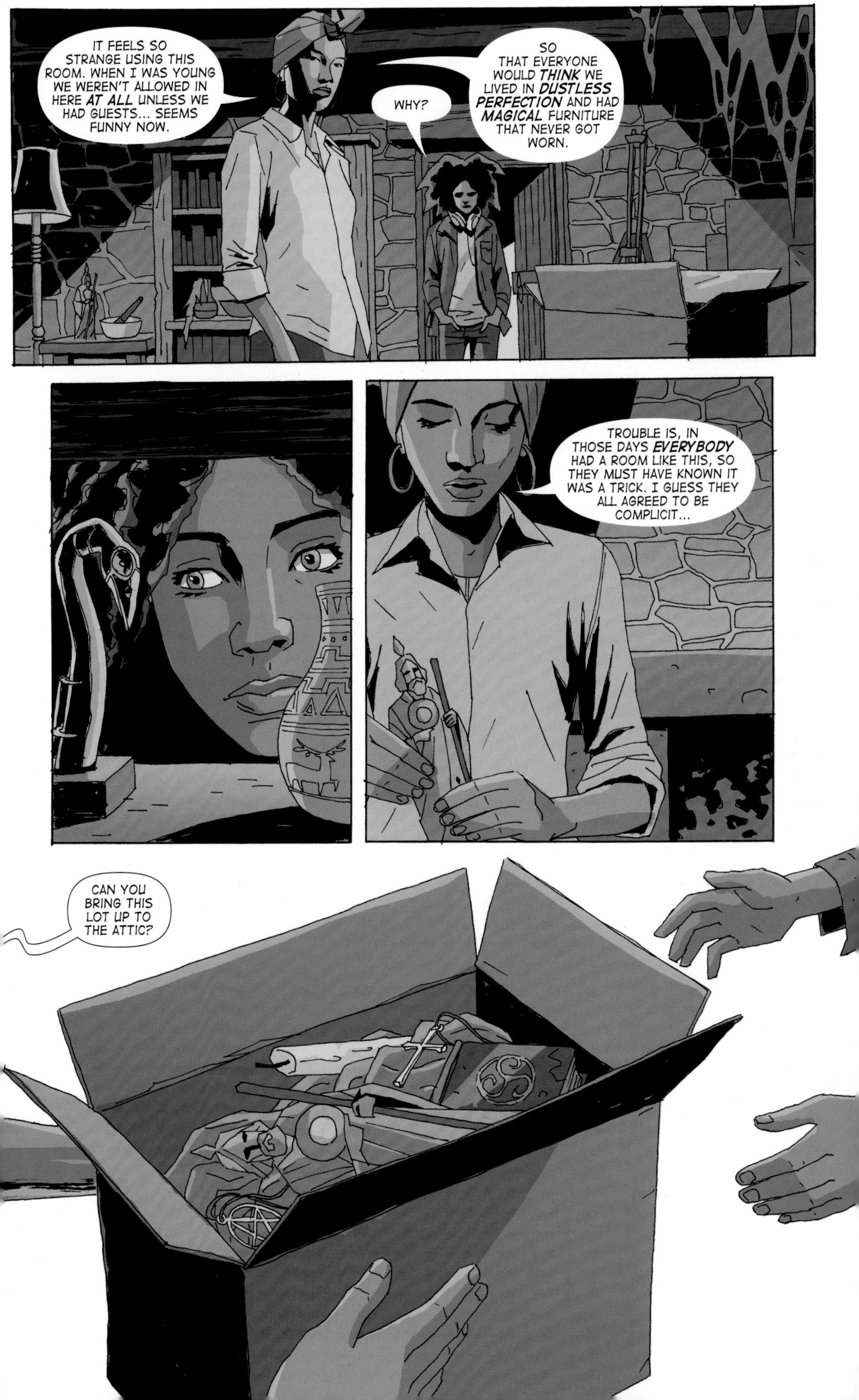
IT FEELS SO STRANGE USING THIS ROOM. WHEN I WAS YOUNG WE WEREN'T ALLOWED IN HERE AT ALL UNLESS WE HAD GUESTS... SEEMS FUNNY NOW.
WHY?
SO THAT EVERYONE WOULD THINK WE LIVED IN DUSTLESS PERFECTION AND HAD MAGICAL FURNITURE THAT NEVER GOT WORN.
TROUBLE IS, IN THOSE DAYS EVERYBODY HAD A ROOM LIKE THIS, SO THEY MUST HAVE KNOWN IT WAS A TRICK. I GUESS THEY ALL AGREED TO BE COMPLICIT...
CAN YOU BRING THIS LOT UP TO THE ATTIC?

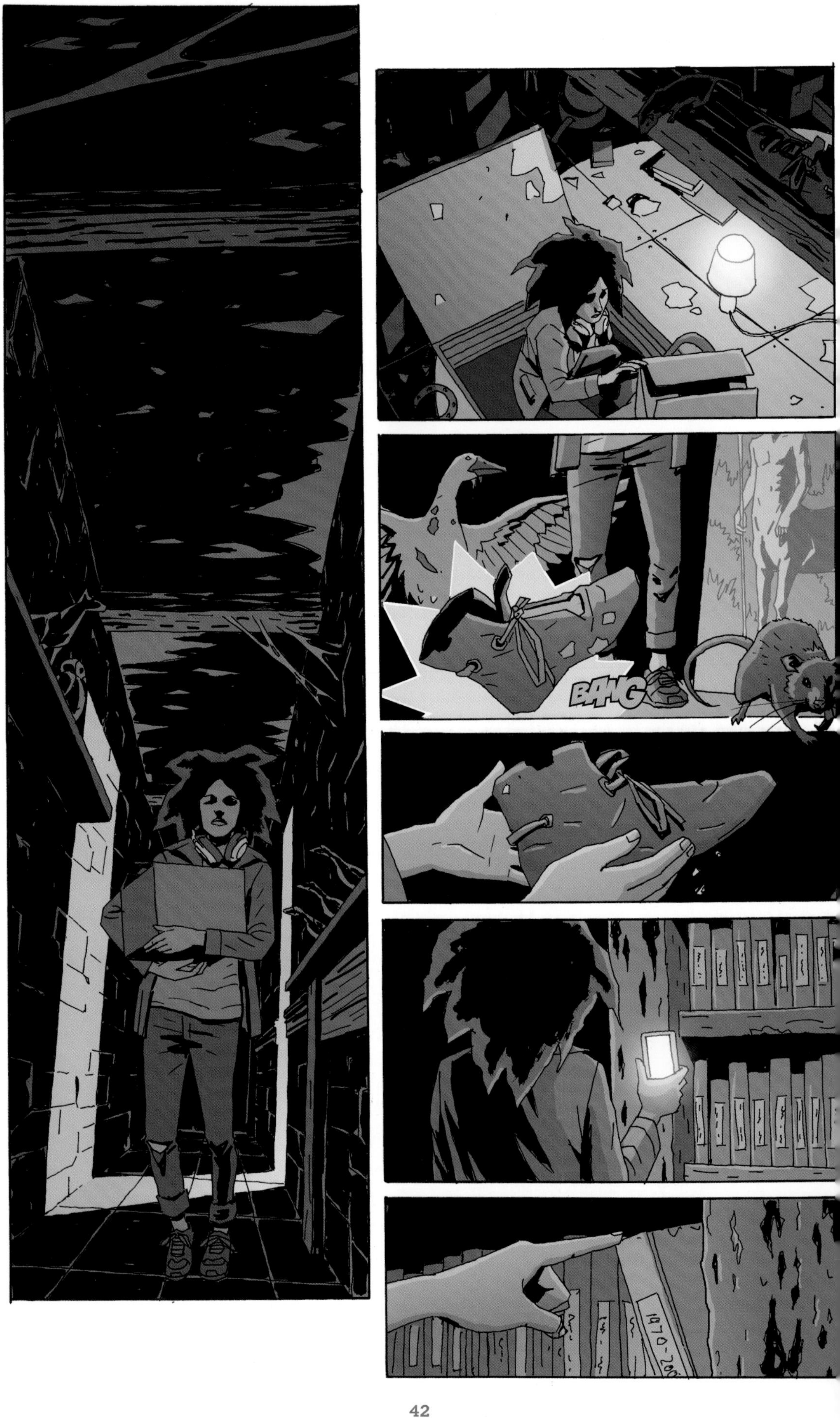
BANG

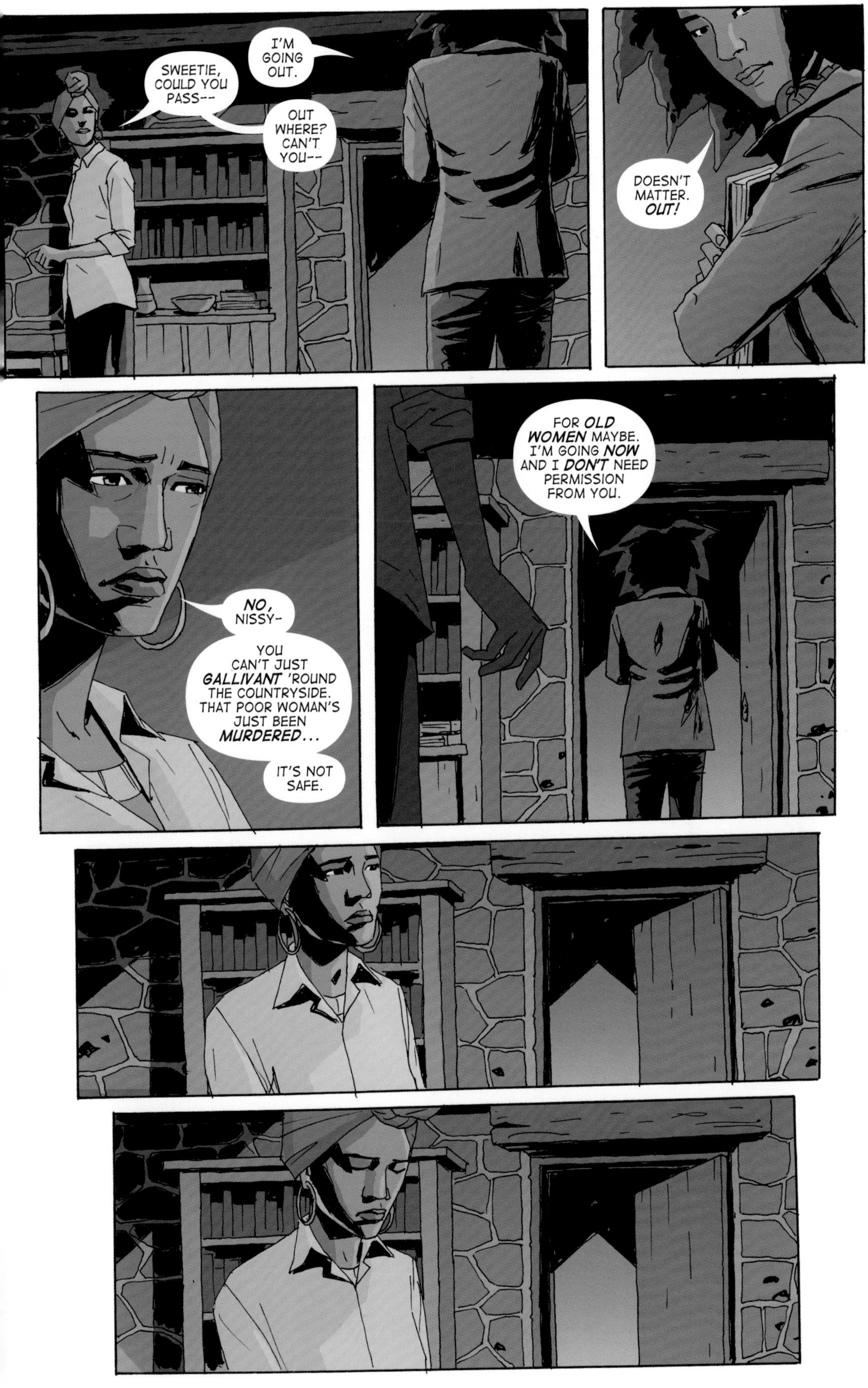
SWEETIE, COULD YOU PASS--
I'M GOING OUT.
OUT WHERE? CAN'T YOU--
DOESN'T MATTER. OUT!
NO, NISSY-
YOU CAN'T JUST GALLIVANT 'ROUND THE COUNTRYSIDE. THAT POOR WOMAN'S JUST BEEN MURDERED...
IT'S NOT SAFE.
FOR OLD WOMEN MAYBE. I'M GOING NOW AND I DON'T NEED PERMISSION FROM YOU.

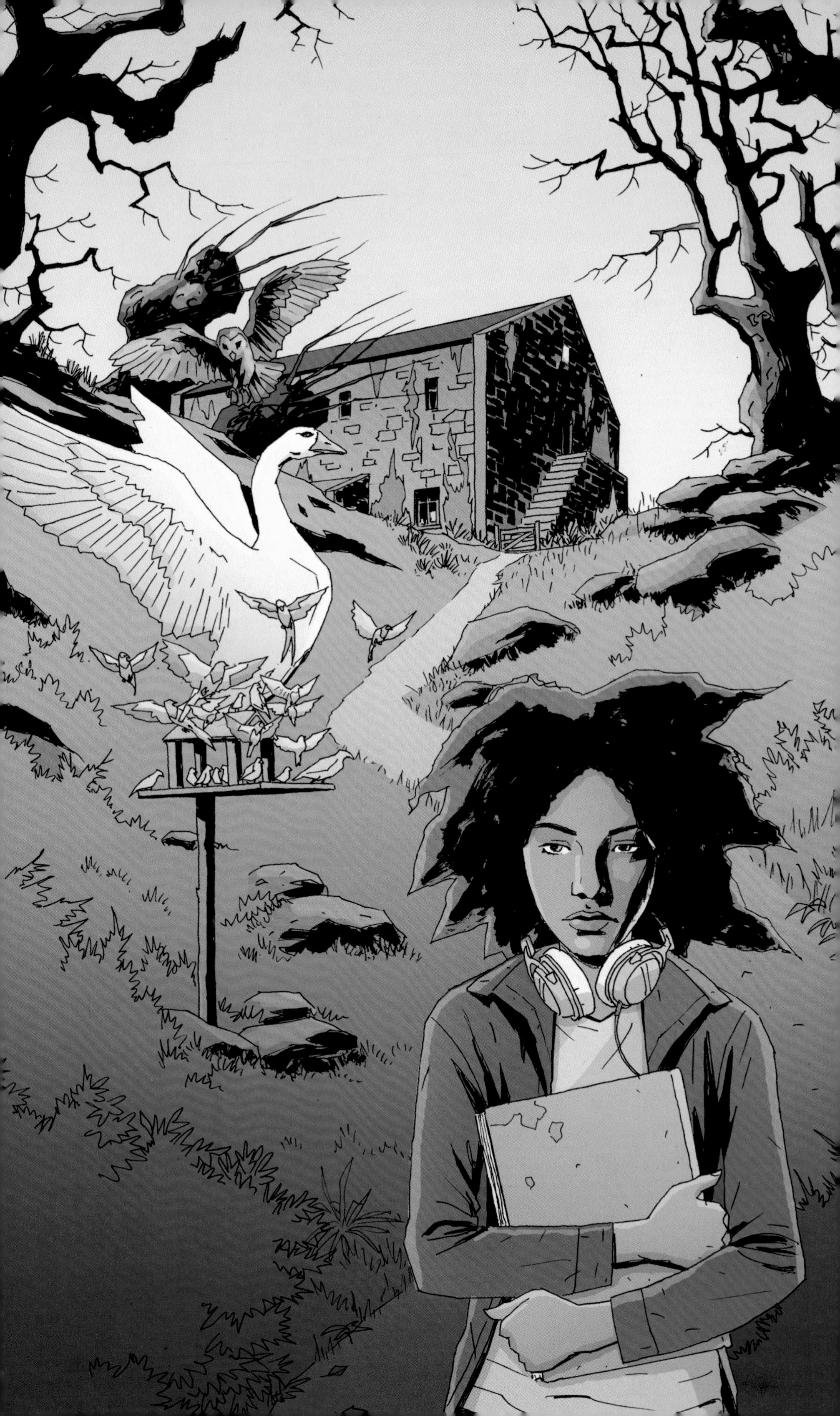

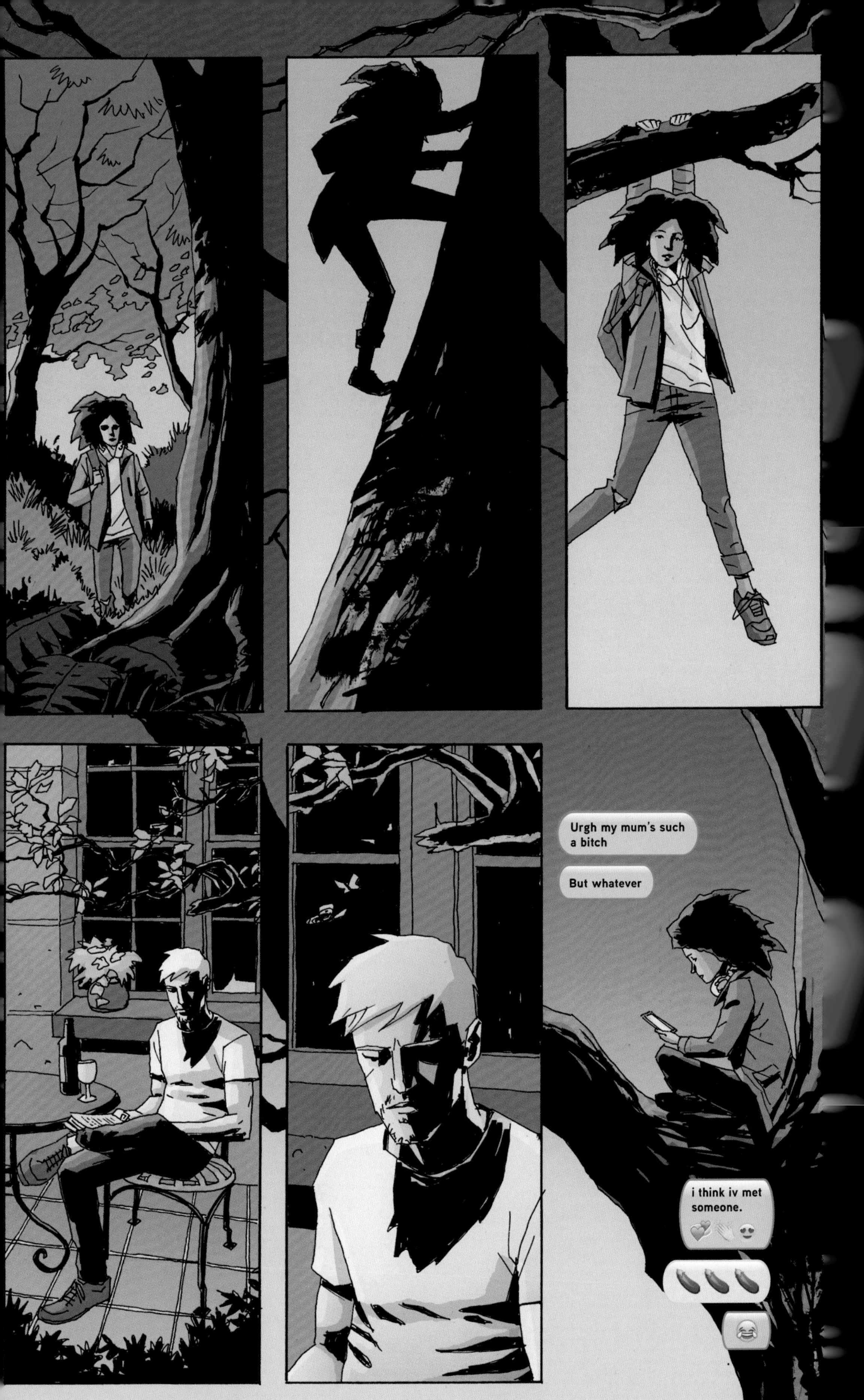
Urgh my mum's such a bitch
But whatever
i think iv met someone.

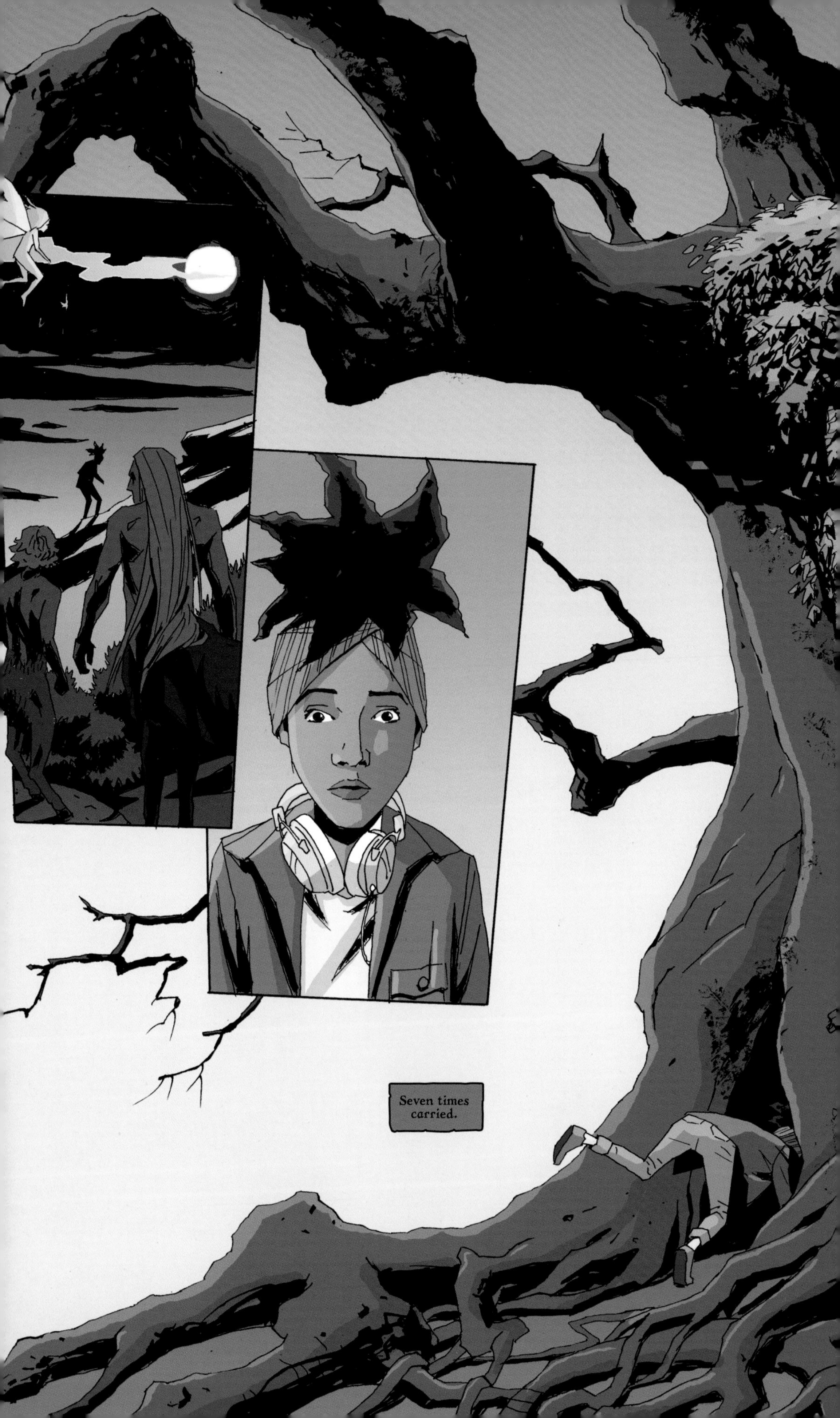
Seven times
carried.

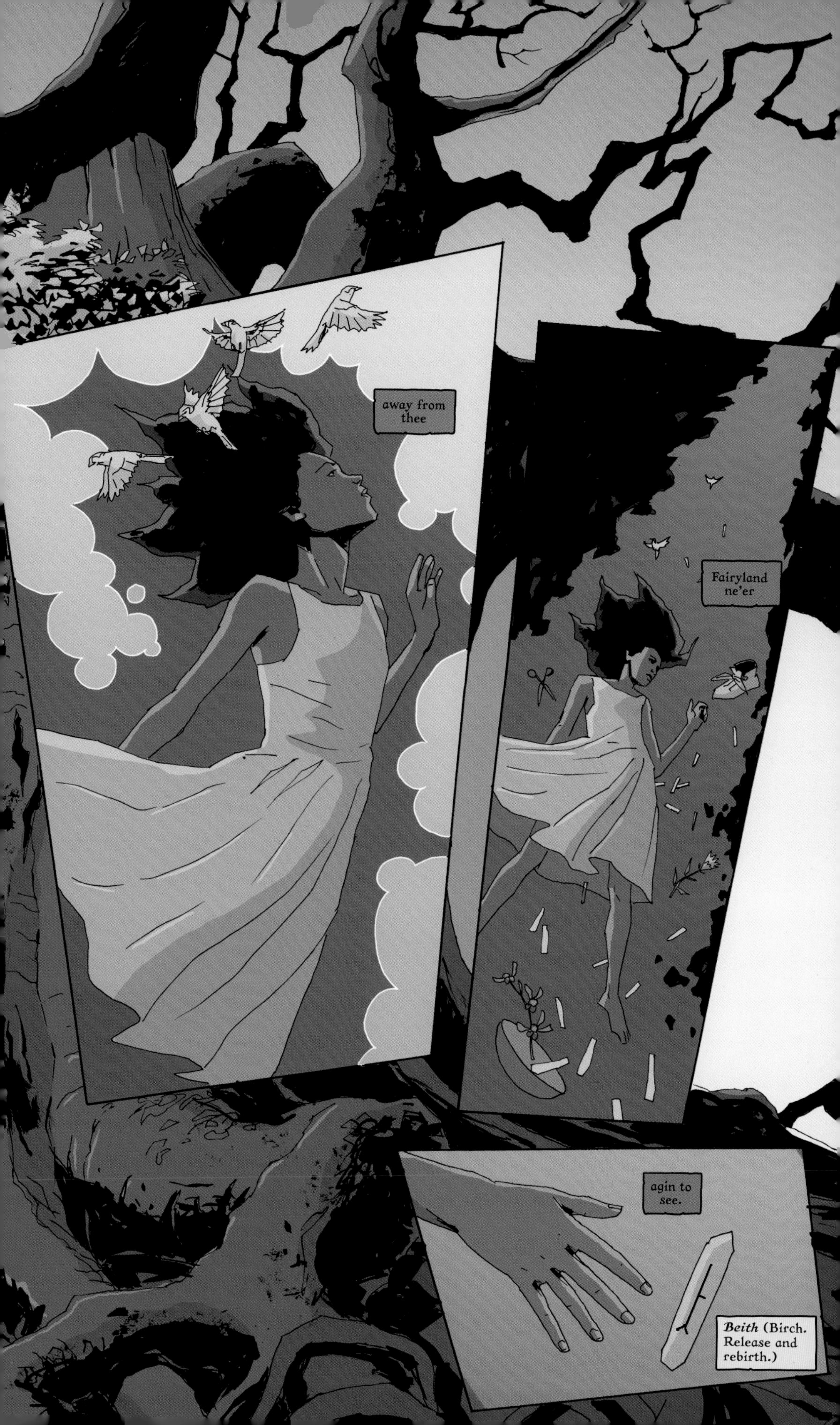
away from thee
Fairyland ne'er
agin to see.
Beith (Birch. Release and rebirth.)

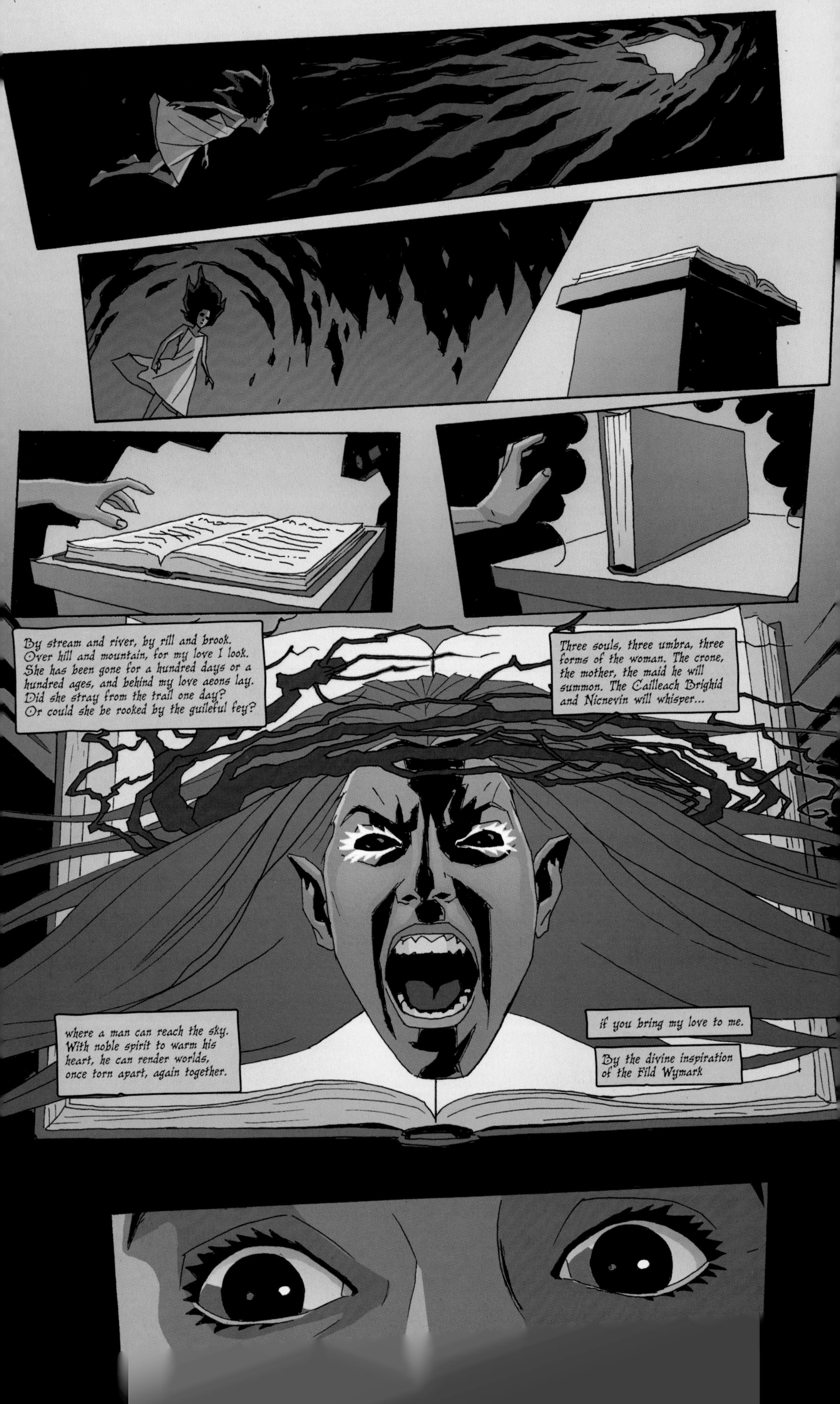
By stream and river, by rill and brook. Over hill and mountain, for my love I look. She has been gone for a hundred days or a hundred ages, and behind my love aeons lay. Did she stray from the trail one day? Or could she be rooked by the guileful fey?
Three souls, three umbra, three forms of the woman. The crone, the mother, the maid he will summon. The Cailleach Brighid and Nicnevin will whisper...
where a man can reach the sky. With noble spirit to warm his heart, he can render worlds, once torn apart, again together.
if you bring my love to me.
By the divine inspiration of the Fild Wymark

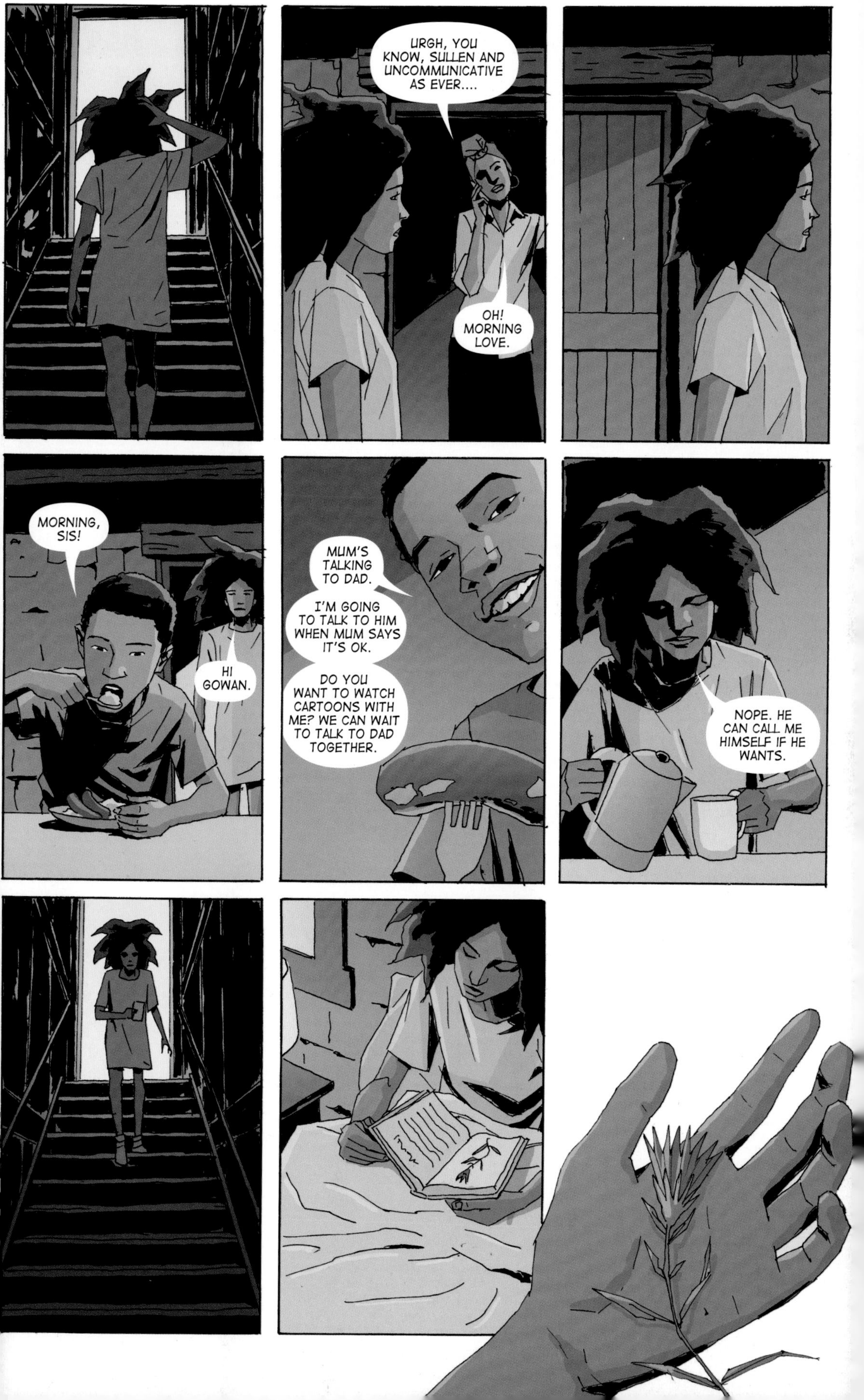
URGH, YOU KNOW, SULLEN AND UNCOMMUNICATIVE AS EVER....
OH! MORNING LOVE.
MORNING, SIS!
HI GOWAN.
MUM'S TALKING TO DAD.
I'M GOING TO TALK TO HIM WHEN MUM SAYS IT'S OK.
DO YOU WANT TO WATCH CARTOONS WITH ME? WE CAN WAIT TO TALK TO DAD TOGETHER.
NOPE. HE CAN CALL ME HIMSELF IF HE WANTS.

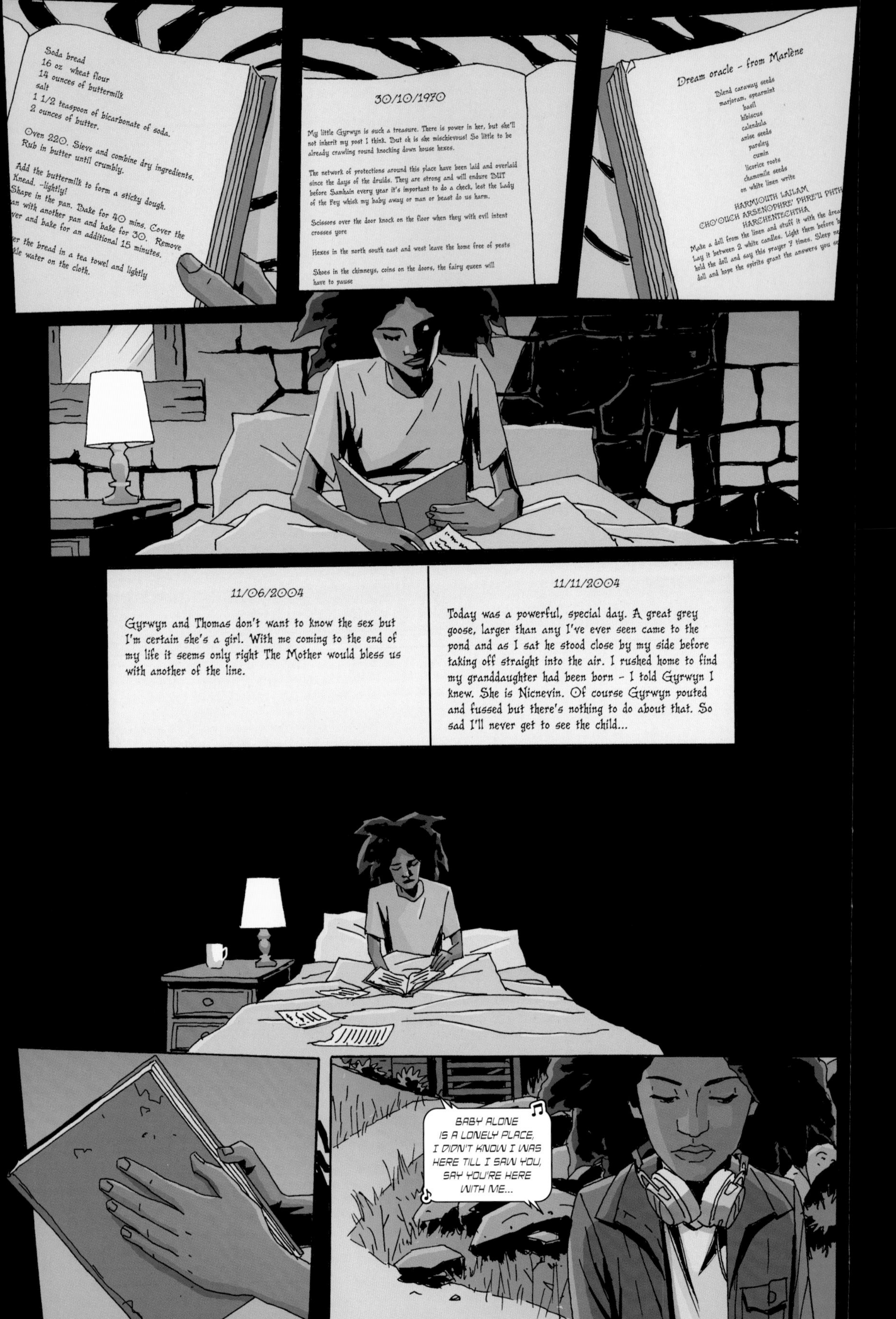

Soda bread
16 oz wheat flour
14 ounces of buttermilk
salt
1 1/2 teaspoon of bicarbonate of soda.
2 ounces of butter.
Oven 220. Sieve and combine dry ingredients.
Rub in butter until crumbly.
Add the buttermilk to form a sticky dough.
Knead. -lightly!
Shape in the pan. Bake for 40 mins. Cover the
an with another pan and bake for 30. Remove
ver and bake for an additional 15 minutes.
er the bread in a tea towel and lightly
kle water on the cloth.
30/10/1970
My little Gyrwyn is such a treasure. There is power in her, but she'll not inherit my post I think. But oh is she mischievous! So little to be already crawling round knocking down house hexes.
The network of protections around this place have been laid and overlaid since the days of the druids. They are strong and will endure BUT before Samhain every year it's important to do a check, lest the Lady of the Fey whisk my baby away or man or beast do us harm.
Scissors over the door knock on the floor when they with evil intent crosses yore
Hexes in the north south east and west leave the home free of pests
Shoes in the chimneys, coins on the doors, the fairy queen will have to pause
Dream oracle – from Marlène
Blend caraway seeds
marjoram, spearmint
basil
hibiscus
calendula
anise seeds
parsley
cumin
licorice roots
chamomile seeds
on white linen write
HARMIOUTH LAILAM
CHO'OUCH ARSENOPHRE' PHRE'U PHTH
HARCHENTECHTHA
Make a doll from the linen and stuff it with the drea
Lay it between 2 white candles. Light them before b
hold the doll and say this prayer 7 times. Sleep ne
doll and hope the spirits grant the answers you se
11/06/2004
Gyrwyn and Thomas don't want to know the sex but I'm certain she's a girl. With me coming to the end of my life it seems only right The Mother would bless us with another of the line.
11/11/2004
Today was a powerful, special day. A great grey goose, larger than any I've ever seen came to the pond and as I sat he stood close by my side before taking off straight into the air. I rushed home to find my granddaughter had been born – I told Gyrwyn I knew. She is Nicnevin. Of course Gyrwyn pouted and fussed but there's nothing to do about that. So sad I'll never get to see the child...
BABY ALONE IS A LONELY PLACE, I DIDN'T KNOW I WAS HERE TILL I SAW YOU, SAY YOU'RE HERE WITH ME...

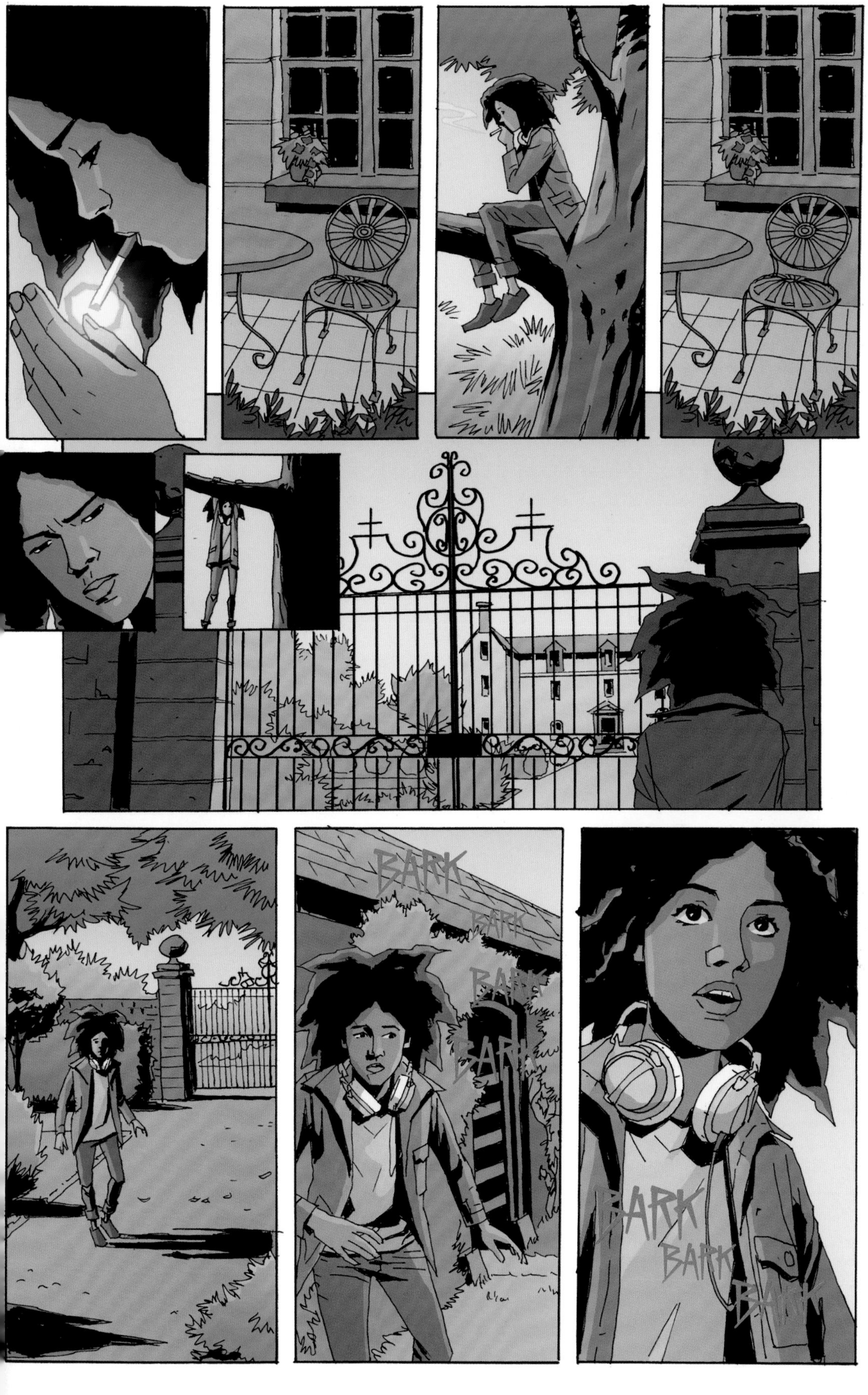
BARK
BARK
BARK
BARK
BARK
BARK
BARK

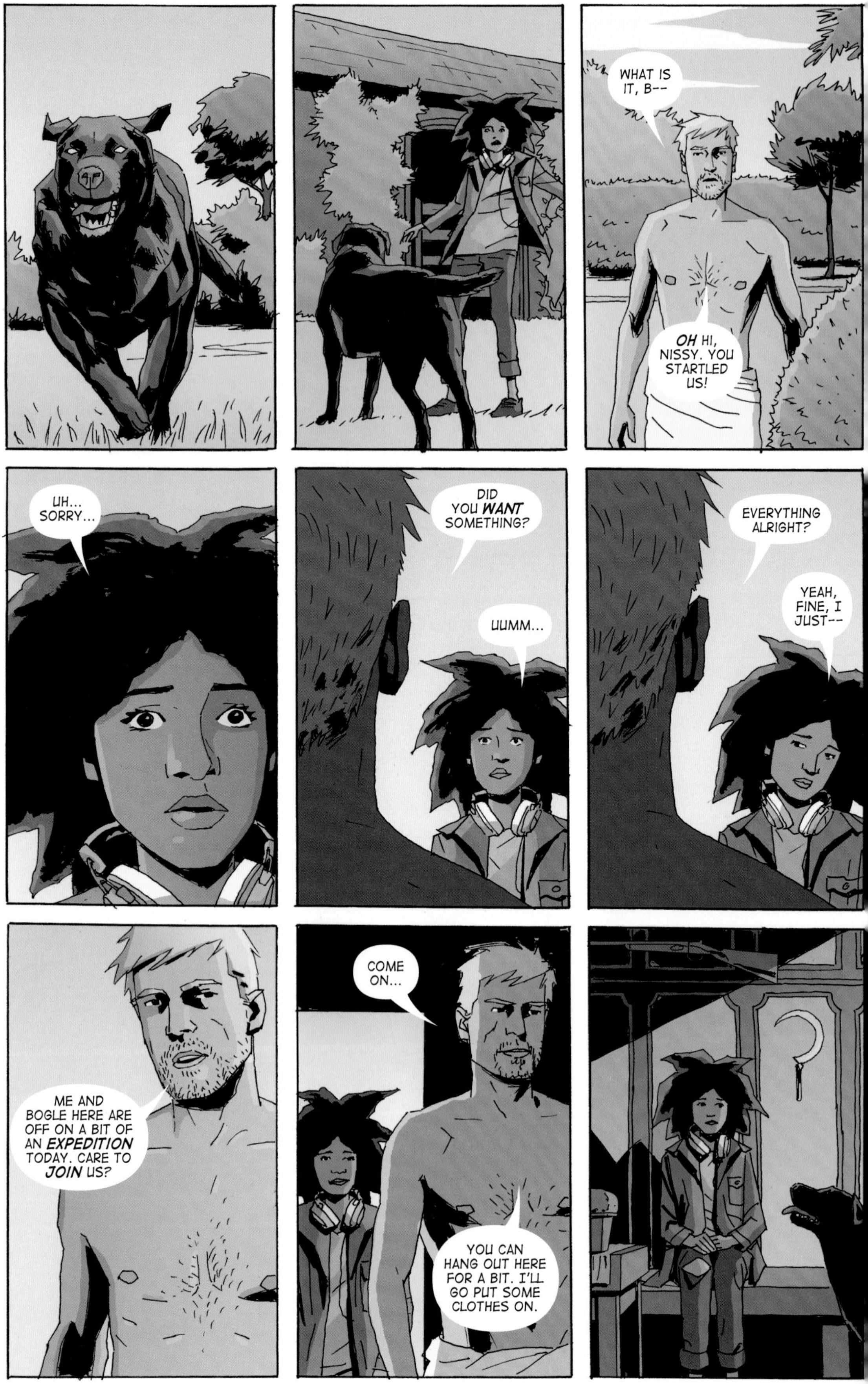
WHAT IS IT, B--
OH HI, NISSY. YOU STARTLED US!
UH... SORRY...
DID YOU WANT SOMETHING?
UUMM...
EVERYTHING ALRIGHT?
YEAH, FINE, I JUST--
ME AND BOGLE HERE ARE OFF ON A BIT OF AN EXPEDITION TODAY. CARE TO JOIN US?
COME ON...
YOU CAN HANG OUT HERE FOR A BIT. I'LL GO PUT SOME CLOTHES ON.

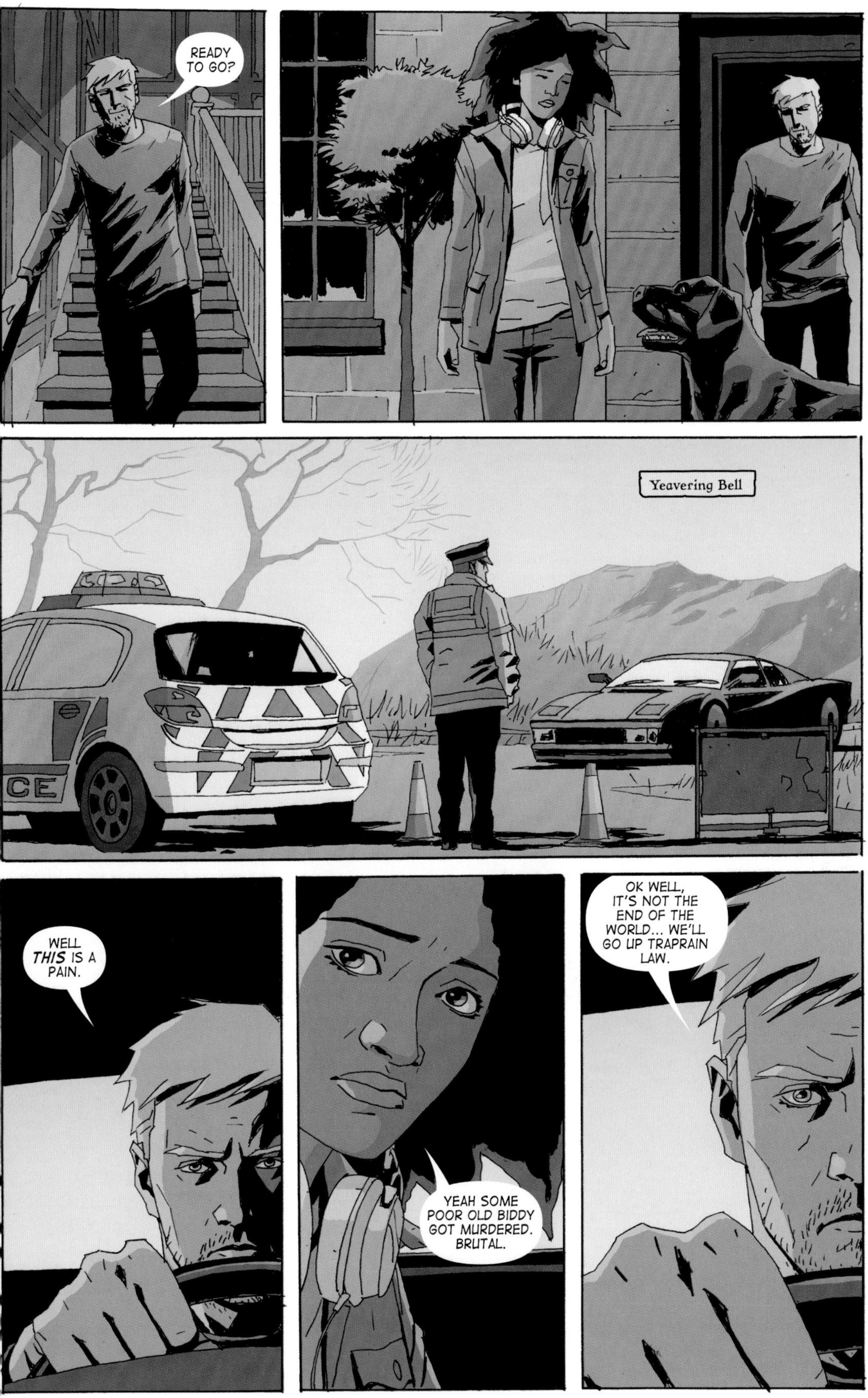
READY TO GO?
Yeavering Bell
WELL *THIS* IS A PAIN.
YEAH SOME POOR OLD BIDDY GOT MURDERED. BRUTAL.
OK WELL, IT'S NOT THE END OF THE WORLD... WE'LL GO UP TRAPRAIN LAW.

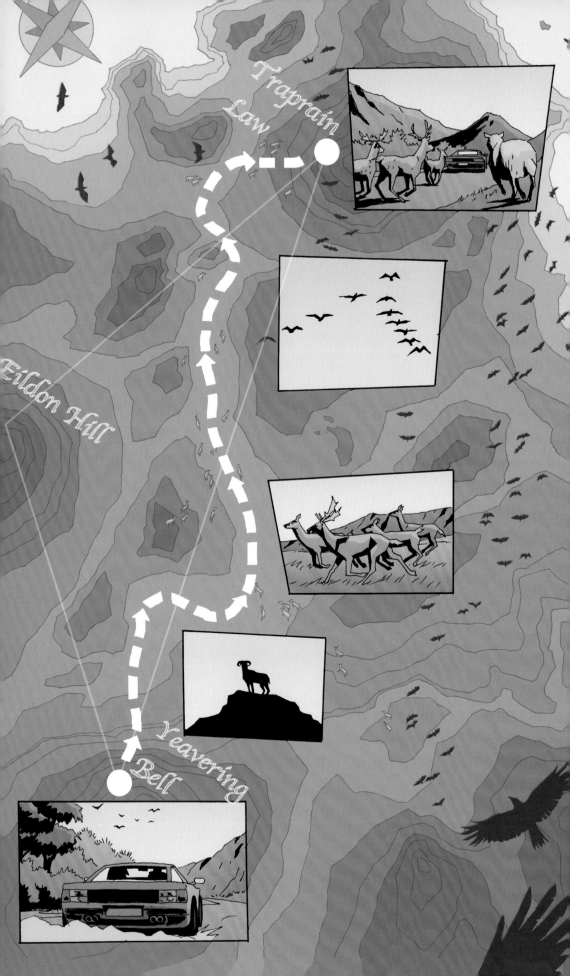

Traprain Law

Eildon Hill

Yeavering Bell

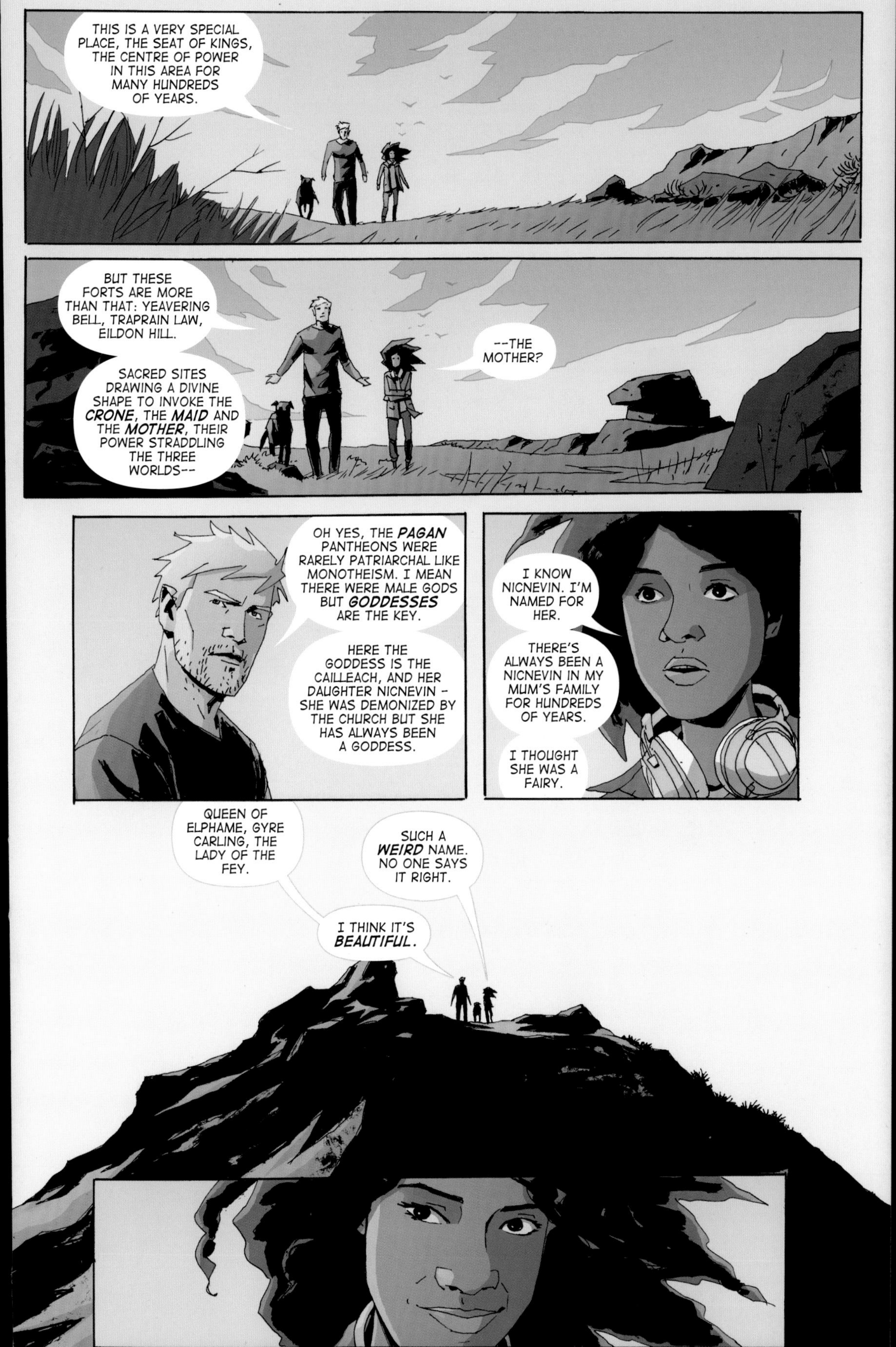

THIS IS A VERY SPECIAL PLACE, THE SEAT OF KINGS, THE CENTRE OF POWER IN THIS AREA FOR MANY HUNDREDS OF YEARS.
BUT THESE FORTS ARE MORE THAN THAT: YEAVERING BELL, TRAPRAIN LAW, EILDON HILL.
SACRED SITES DRAWING A DIVINE SHAPE TO INVOKE THE CRONE, THE MAID AND THE MOTHER, THEIR POWER STRADDLING THE THREE WORLDS--
--THE MOTHER?
OH YES, THE PAGAN PANTHEONS WERE RARELY PATRIARCHAL LIKE MONOTHEISM. I MEAN THERE WERE MALE GODS BUT GODDESSES ARE THE KEY.
HERE THE GODDESS IS THE CAILLEACH, AND HER DAUGHTER NICNEVIN - SHE WAS DEMONIZED BY THE CHURCH BUT SHE HAS ALWAYS BEEN A GODDESS.
I KNOW NICNEVIN. I'M NAMED FOR HER.
THERE'S ALWAYS BEEN A NICNEVIN IN MY MUM'S FAMILY FOR HUNDREDS OF YEARS.
I THOUGHT SHE WAS A FAIRY.
QUEEN OF ELPHAME, GYRE CARLING, THE LADY OF THE FEY.
SUCH A WEIRD NAME. NO ONE SAYS IT RIGHT.
I THINK IT'S BEAUTIFUL.

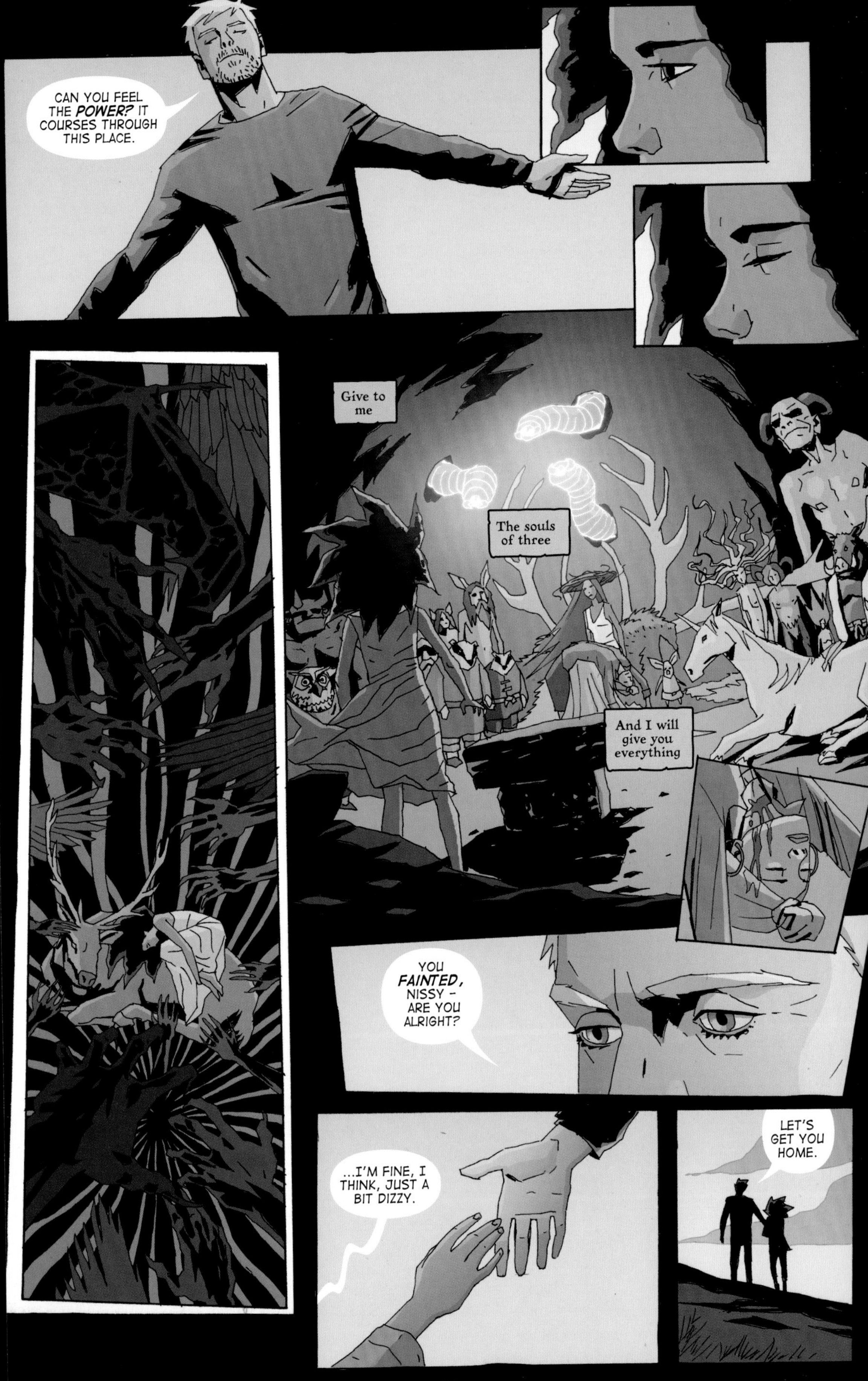
CAN YOU FEEL THE POWER? IT COURSES THROUGH THIS PLACE.
Give to me
The souls of three
And I will give you everything
YOU FAINTED, NISSY - ARE YOU ALRIGHT?
...I'M FINE, I THINK, JUST A BIT DIZZY.
LET'S GET YOU HOME.

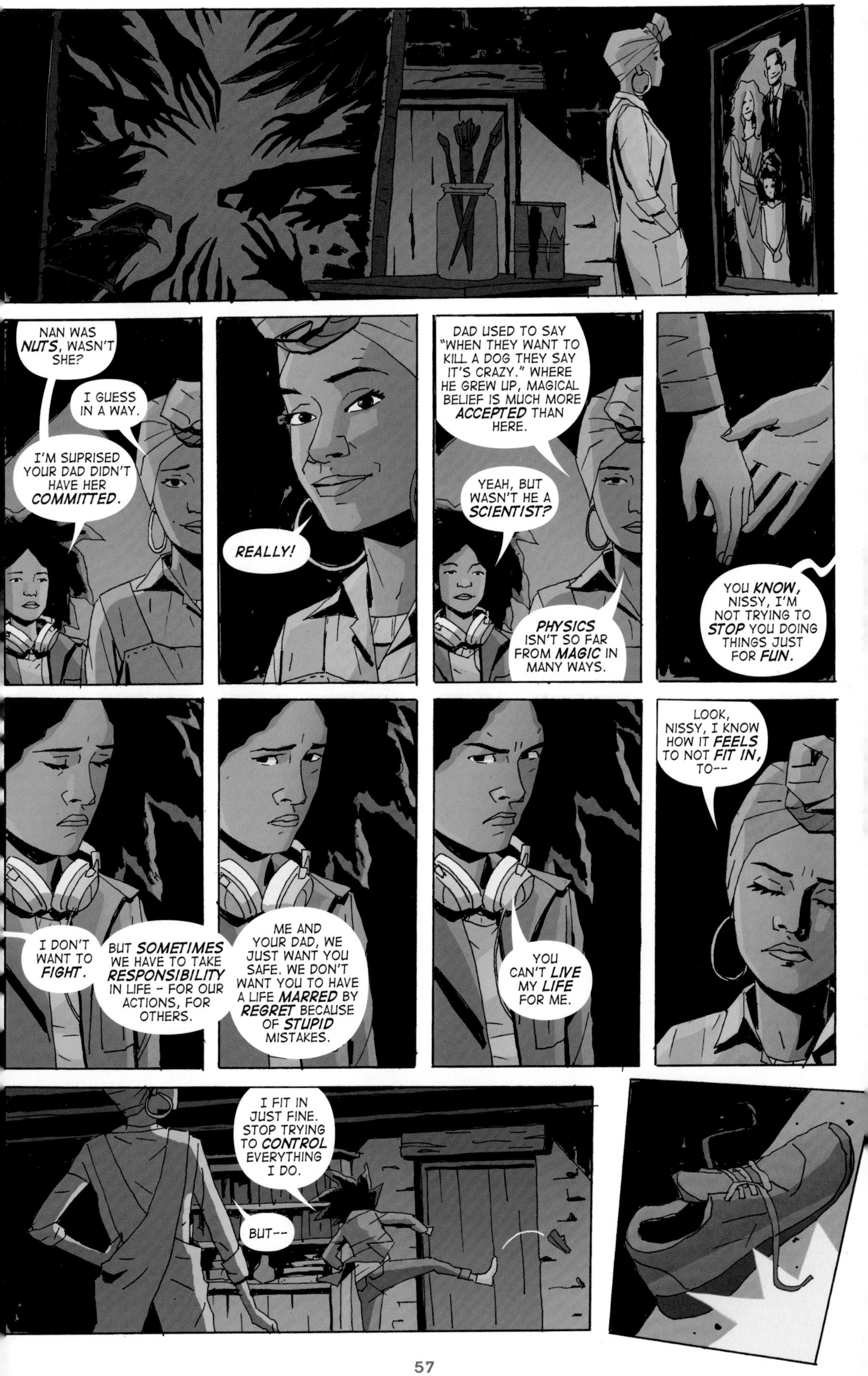

NAN WAS NUTS, WASN'T SHE?
I GUESS IN A WAY.
I'M SUPRISED YOUR DAD DIDN'T HAVE HER COMMITTED.
REALLY!
DAD USED TO SAY "WHEN THEY WANT TO KILL A DOG THEY SAY IT'S CRAZY." WHERE HE GREW UP, MAGICAL BELIEF IS MUCH MORE ACCEPTED THAN HERE.
YEAH, BUT WASN'T HE A SCIENTIST?
PHYSICS ISN'T SO FAR FROM MAGIC IN MANY WAYS.
YOU KNOW, NISSY, I'M NOT TRYING TO STOP YOU DOING THINGS JUST FOR FUN.
I DON'T WANT TO FIGHT.
BUT SOMETIMES WE HAVE TO TAKE RESPONSIBILITY IN LIFE - FOR OUR ACTIONS, FOR OTHERS.
ME AND YOUR DAD, WE JUST WANT YOU SAFE. WE DON'T WANT YOU TO HAVE A LIFE MARRED BY REGRET BECAUSE OF STUPID MISTAKES.
YOU CAN'T LIVE MY LIFE FOR ME.
LOOK, NISSY, I KNOW HOW IT FEELS TO NOT FIT IN, TO--
I FIT IN JUST FINE. STOP TRYING TO CONTROL EVERYTHING I DO.
BUT--

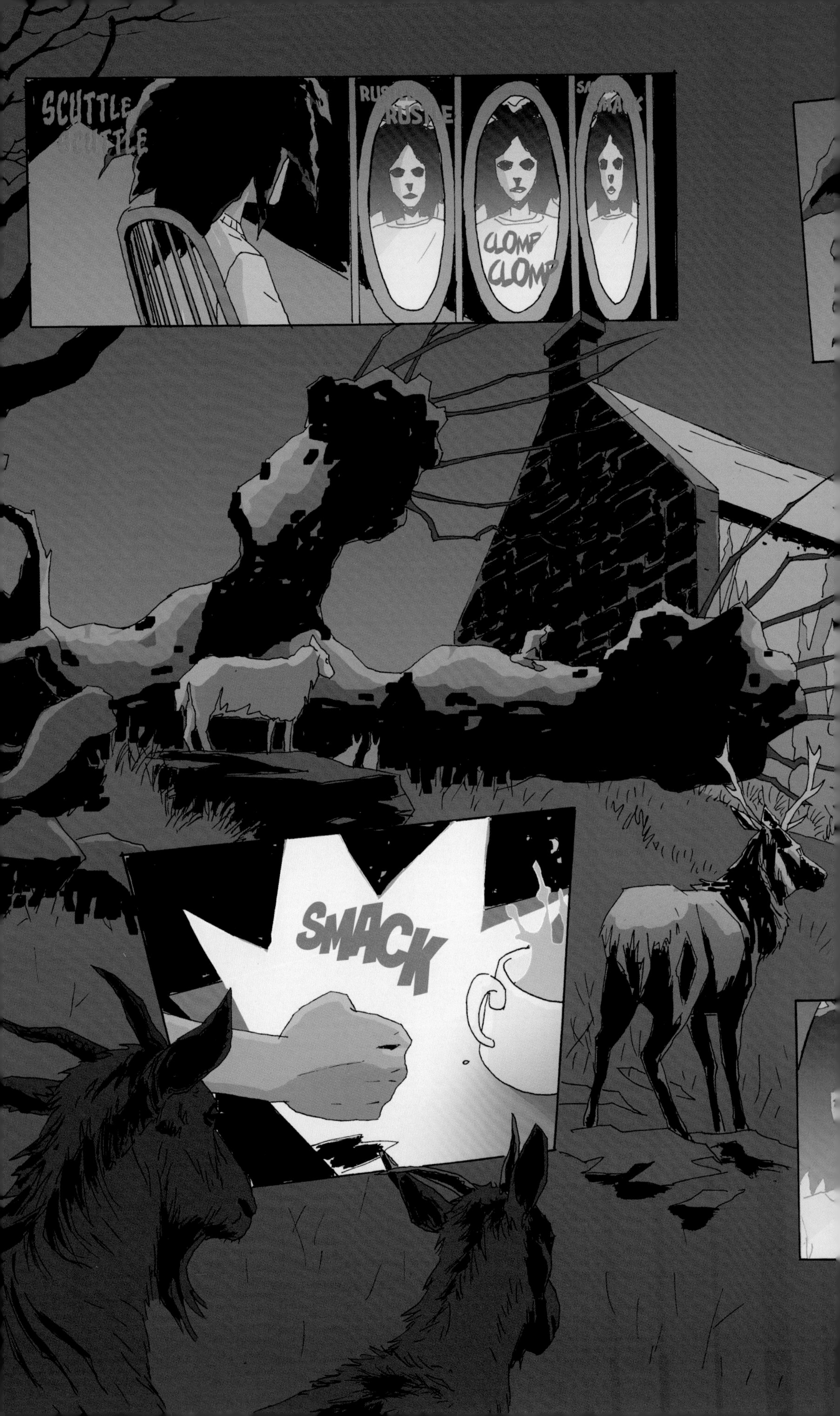
SCUTTLE
RUSTLE
CLOMP
CLOMP
SMACK

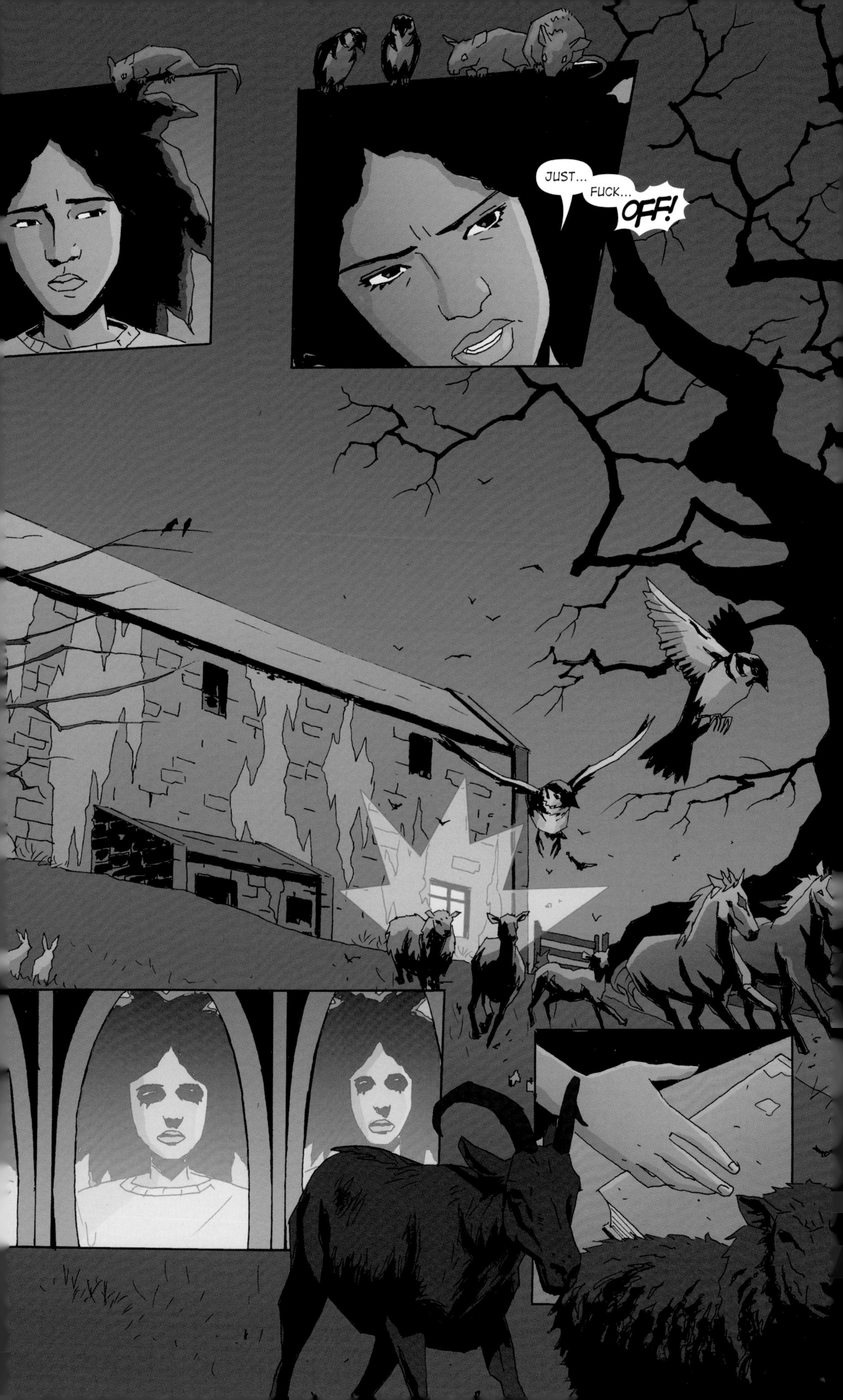
JUST... FUCK... OFF!

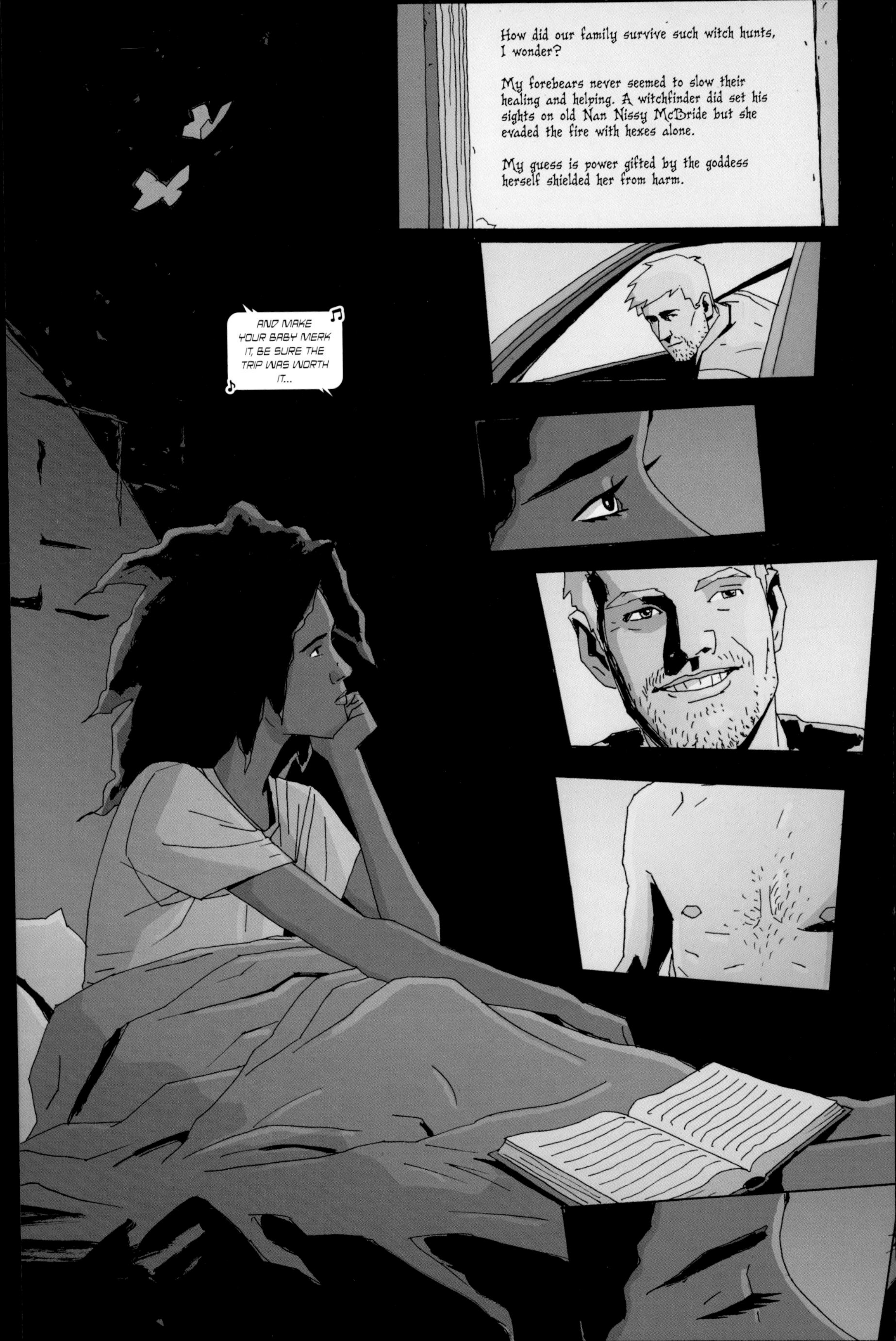
How did our family survive such witch hunts, I wonder?
My forebears never seemed to slow their healing and helping. A witchfinder did set his sights on old Nan Nissy McBride but she evaded the fire with hexes alone.
My guess is power gifted by the goddess herself shielded her from harm.
AND MAKE YOUR BABY MERK IT, BE SURE THE TRIP WAS WORTH IT...

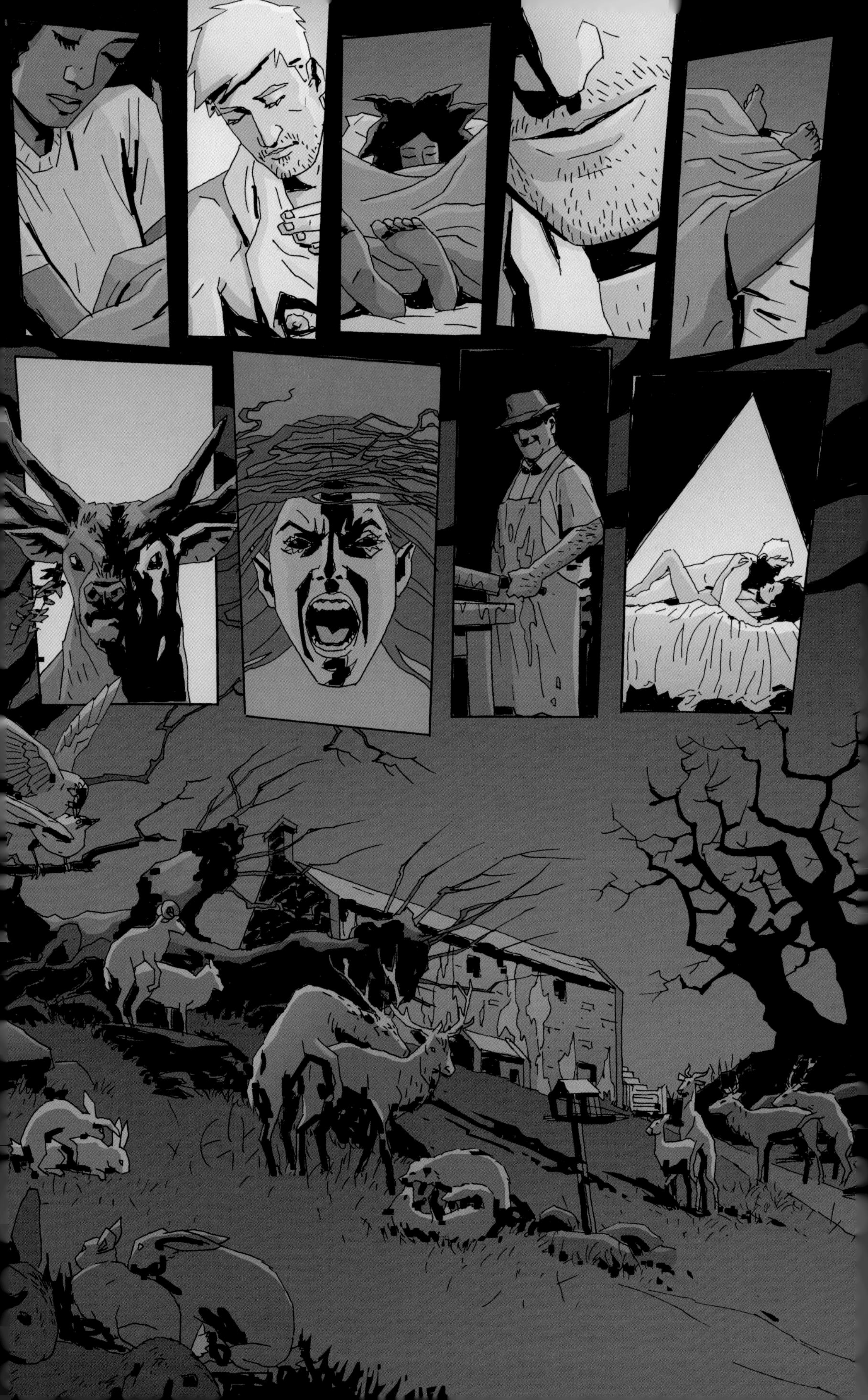

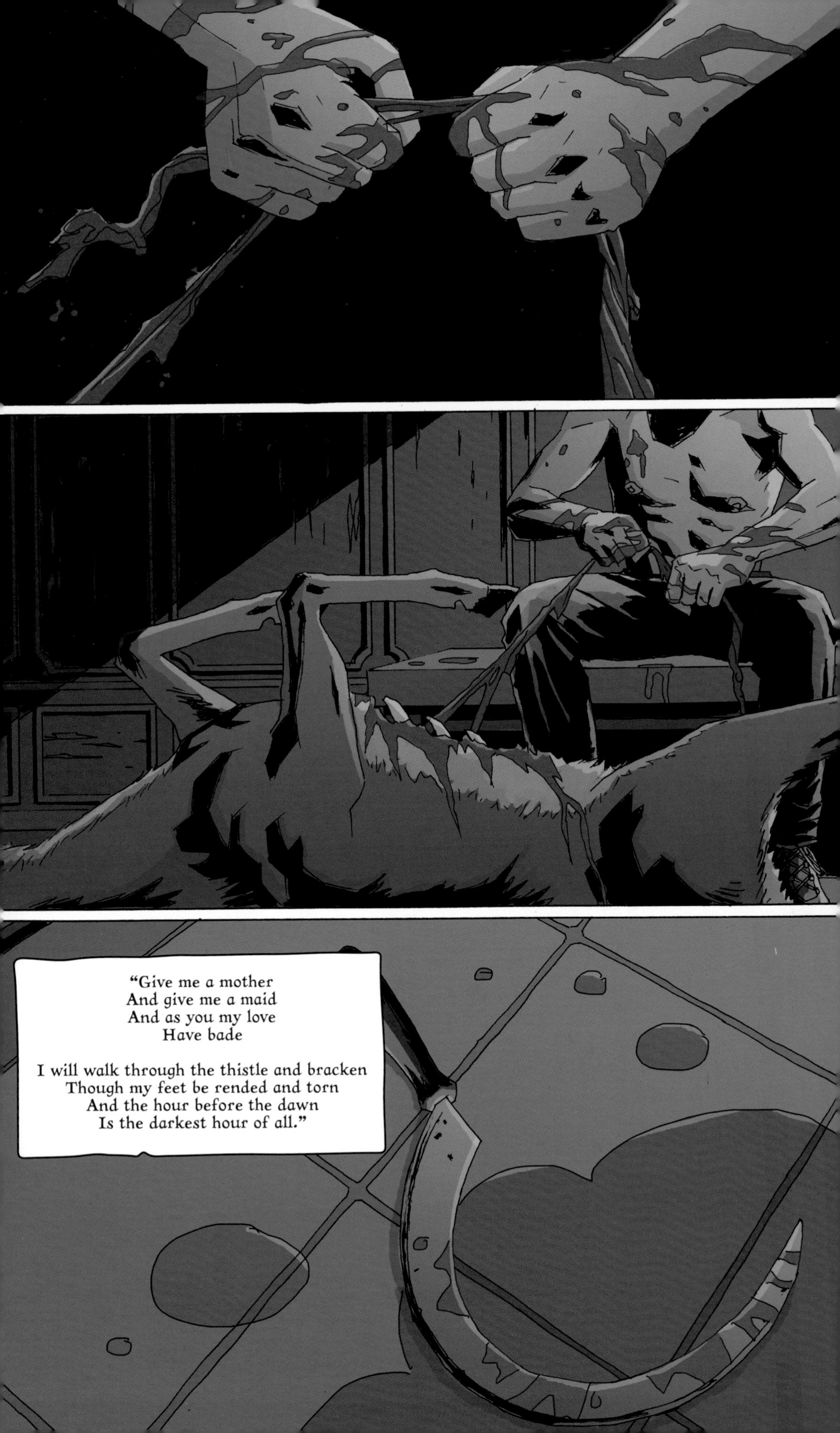
"Give me a mother
And give me a maid
And as you my love
Have bade

I will walk through the thistle and bracken
Though my feet be rended and torn
And the hour before the dawn
Is the darkest hour of all."

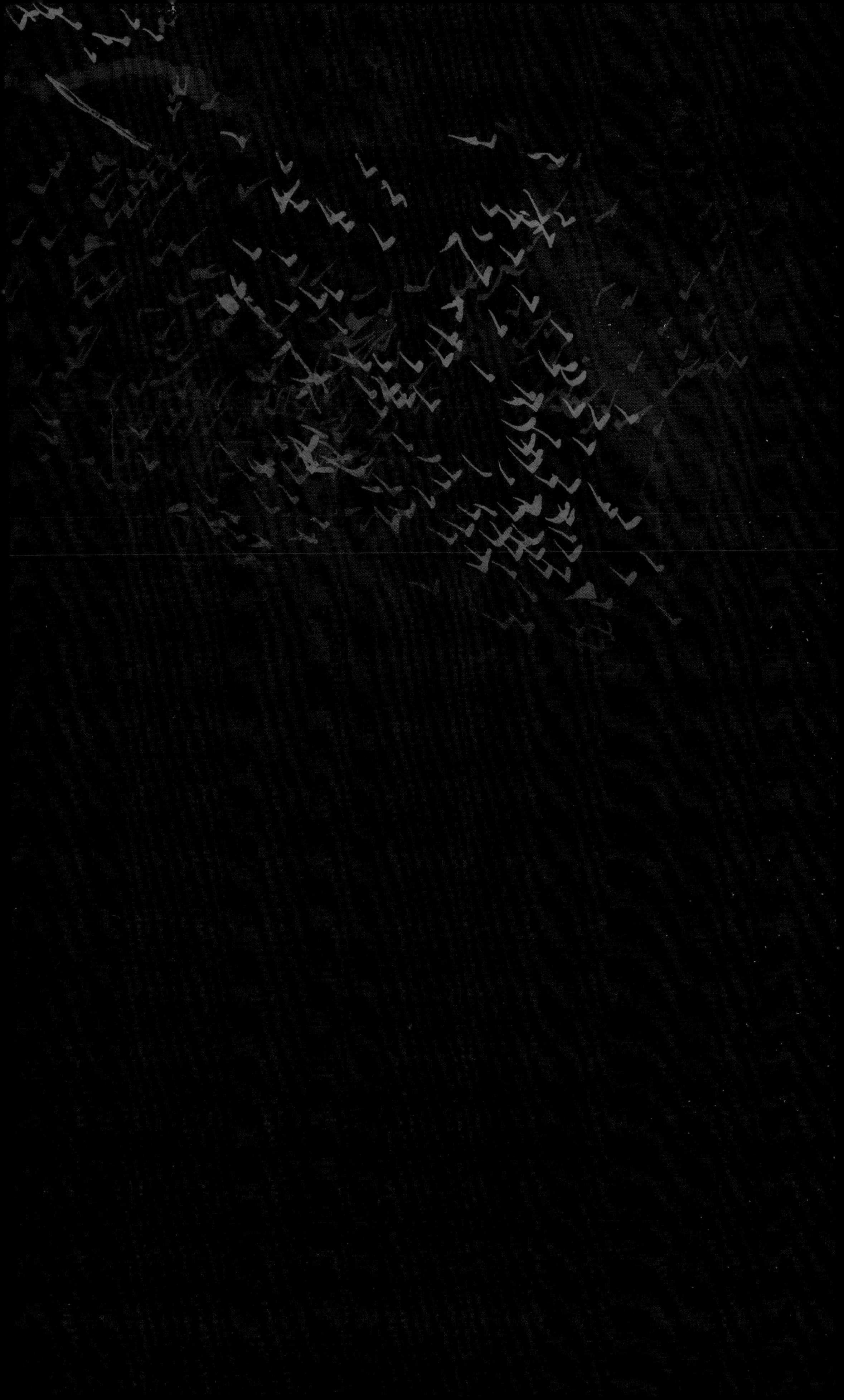

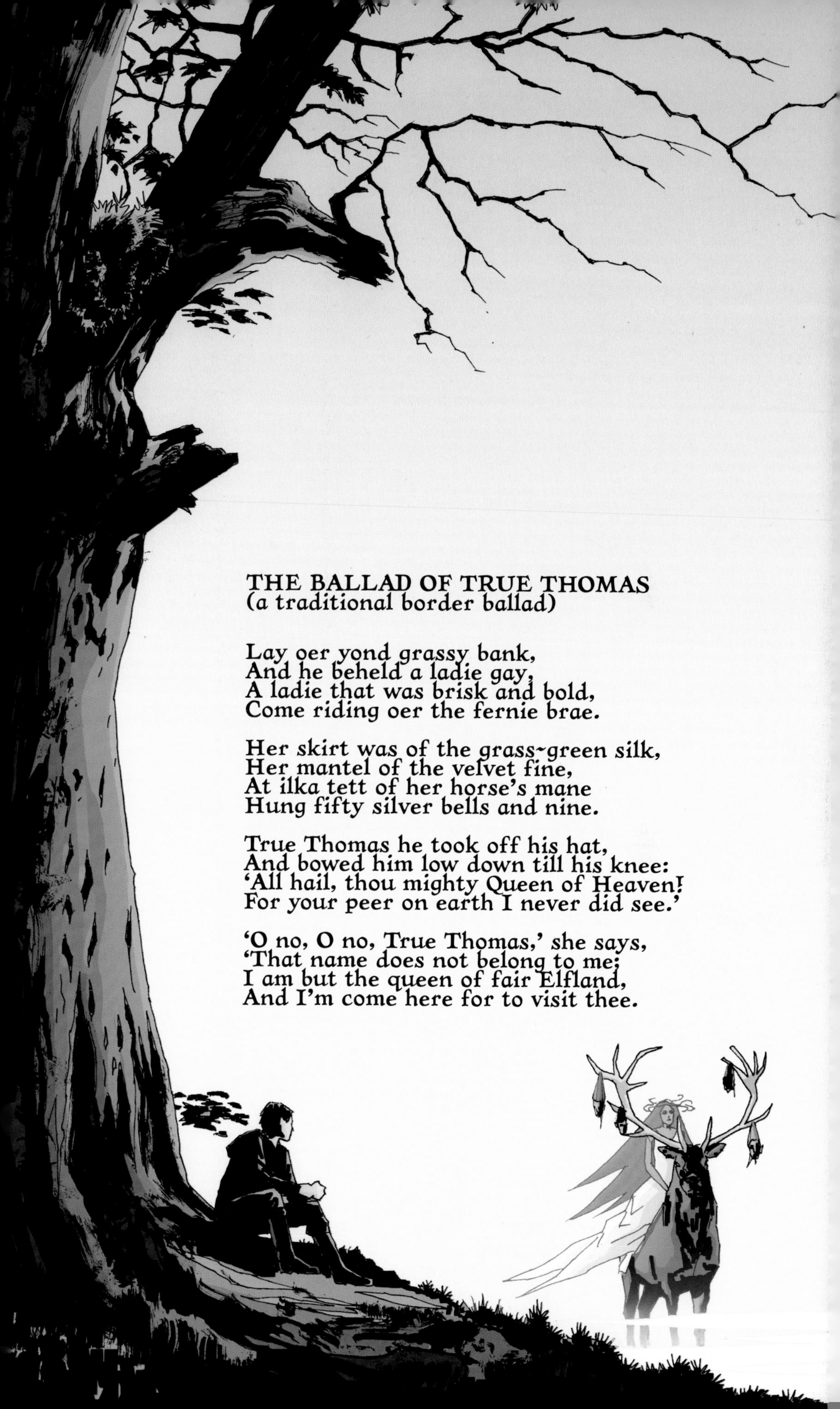

THE BALLAD OF TRUE THOMAS
(a traditional border ballad)

Lay oer yond grassy bank,
And he beheld a ladie gay,
A ladie that was brisk and bold,
Come riding oer the fernie brae.

Her skirt was of the grass-green silk,
Her mantel of the velvet fine,
At ilka tett of her horse's mane
Hung fifty silver bells and nine.

True Thomas he took off his hat,
And bowed him low down till his knee:
'All hail, thou mighty Queen of Heaven!
For your peer on earth I never did see.'

'O no, O no, True Thomas,' she says,
'That name does not belong to me;
I am but the queen of fair Elfland,
And I'm come here for to visit thee.

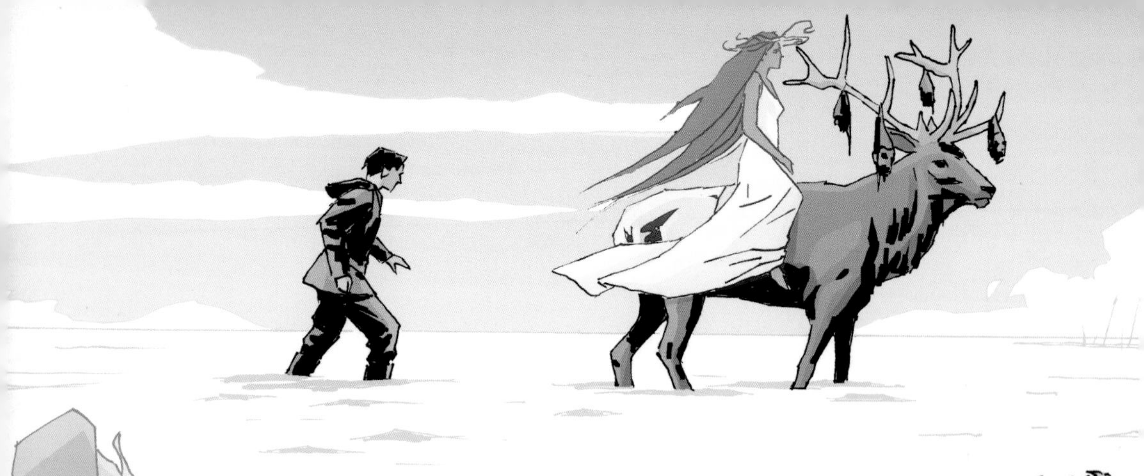

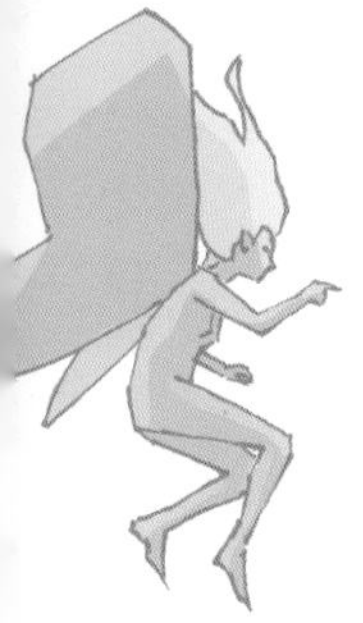

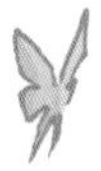

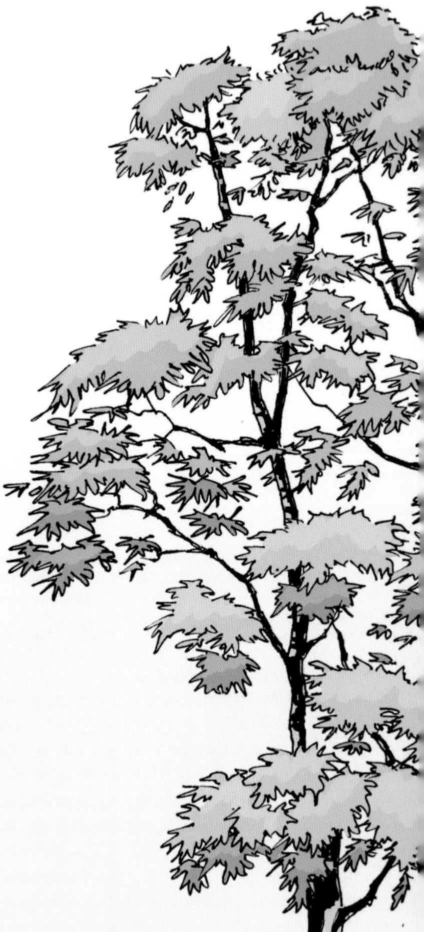

'But ye maun go wi me now, Thomas,
True Thomas, ye maun go wi me,
For ye maun serve me seven years,
Thro weel or wae as may chance to be.'

She turned about her milk-white steed,
And took True Thomas up behind,
And aye wheneer her bridle rang,
The steed flew swifter than the wind.

For forty days and forty nights
He wade thro red blude to the knee,
And he saw neither sun nor moon,
But heard the roaring of the sea.

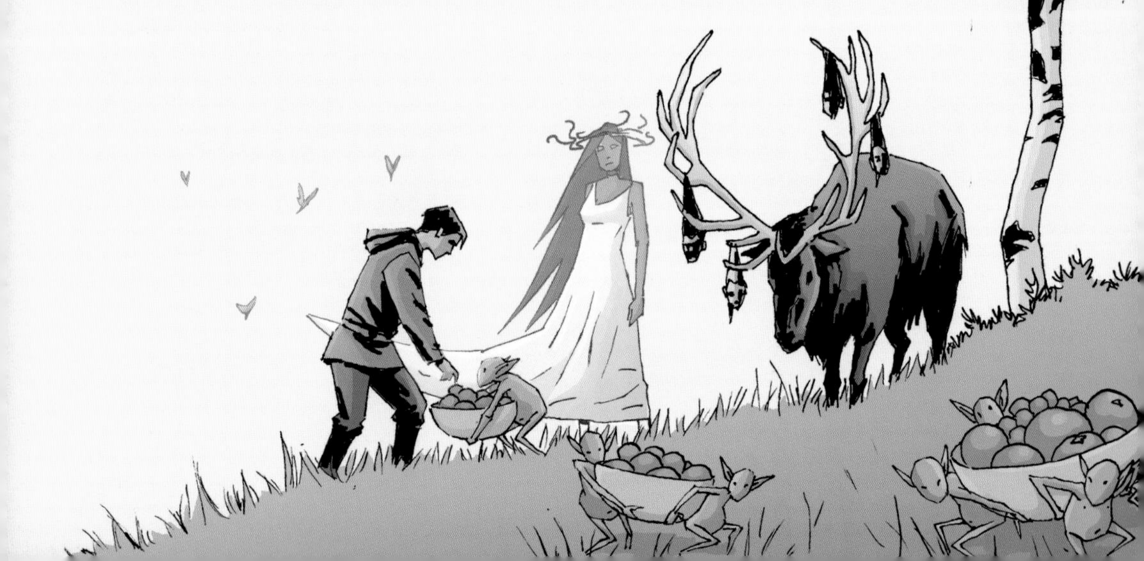

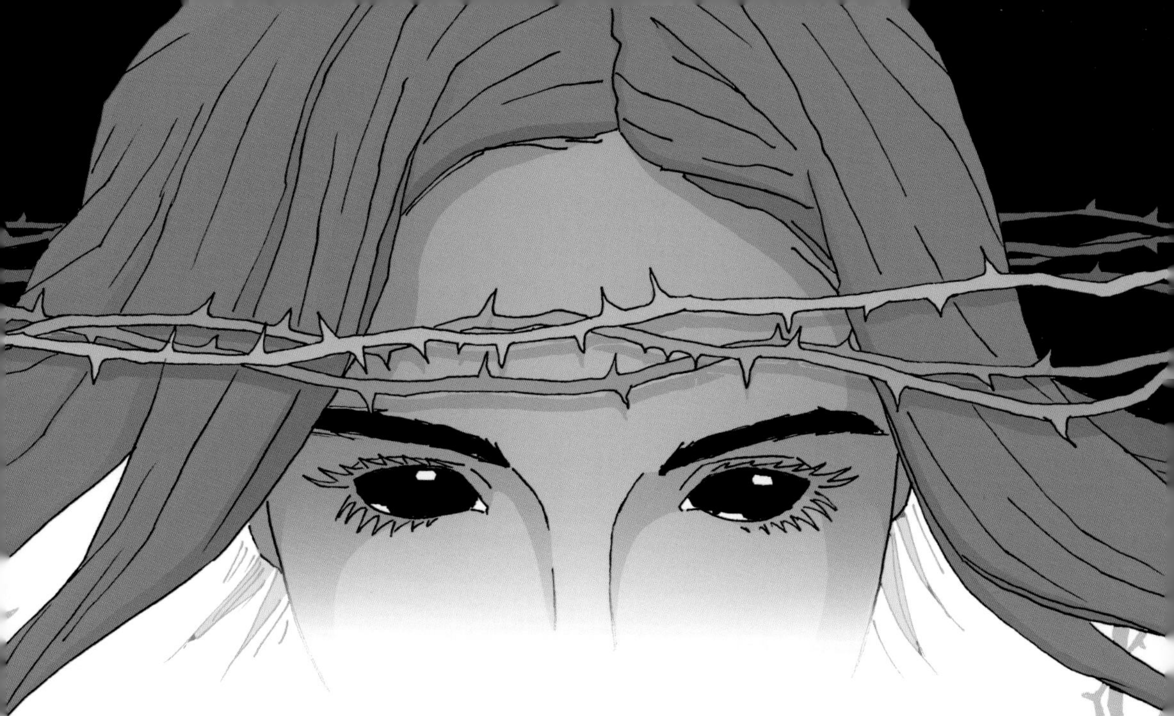

O they rade on, and further on,
Until they came to a garden green:
'Light down, light down, ye ladie free,
Some of that fruit let me pull to thee.'

'O no, O no, True Thomas,' she says,
'That fruit maun not be touched by thee,
For a' the plagues that are in hell
Light on the fruit of this countrie.

'But I have a loaf here in my lap,
Likewise a bottle of claret wine,
And now ere we go farther on,
We'll rest a while, and ye may dine.'

When he had eaten and drunk his fill,
'Lay down your head upon my knee,'
The lady sayd, ere we climb yon hill,
And I will show you fairlies three.

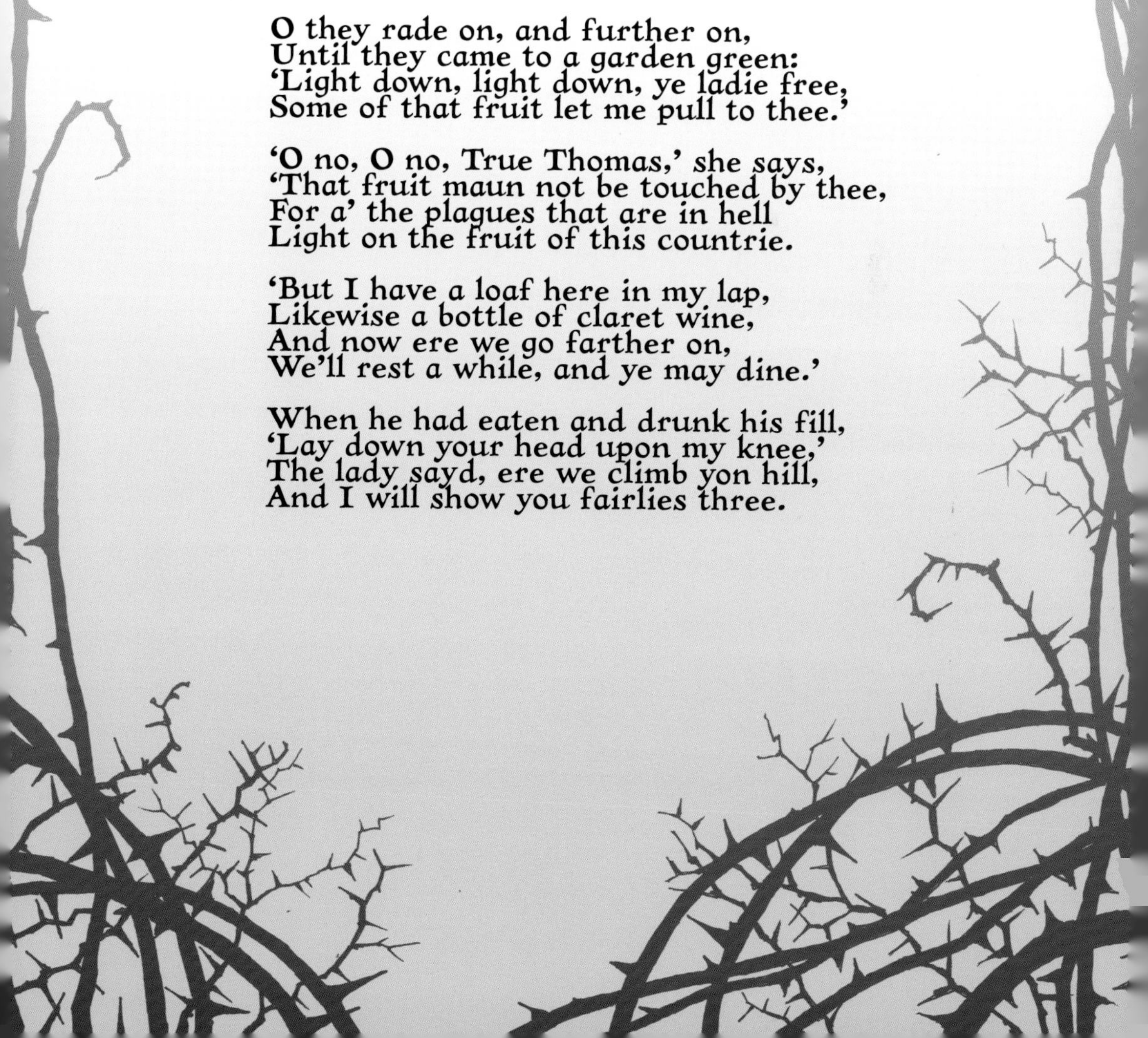

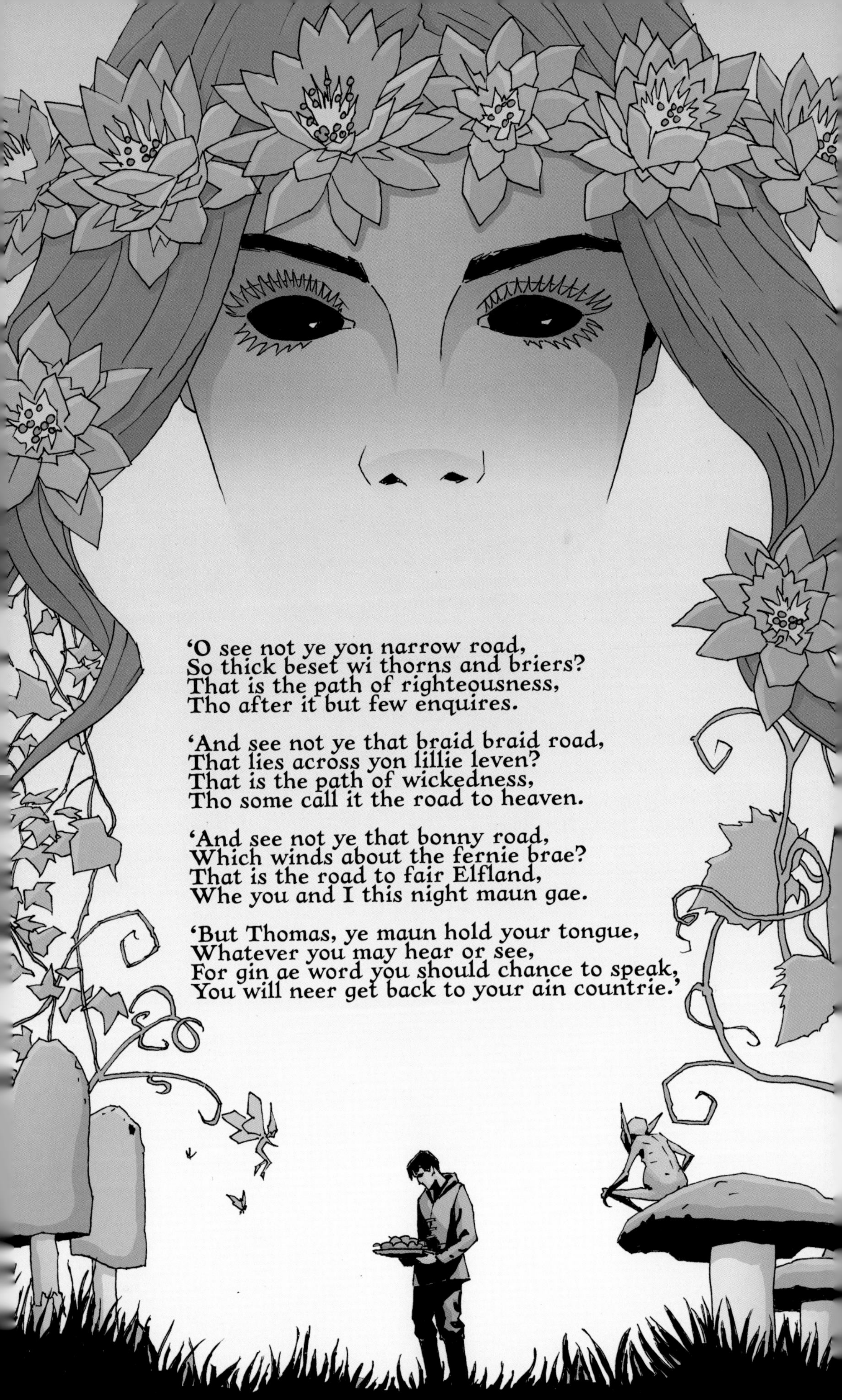

'O see not ye yon narrow road,
So thick beset wi thorns and briers?
That is the path of righteousness,
Tho after it but few enquires.

'And see not ye that braid braid road,
That lies across yon lillie leven?
That is the path of wickedness,
Tho some call it the road to heaven.

'And see not ye that bonny road,
Which winds about the fernie brae?
That is the road to fair Elfland,
Whe you and I this night maun gae.

'But Thomas, ye maun hold your tongue,
Whatever you may hear or see,
For gin ae word you should chance to speak,
You will neer get back to your ain countrie.'

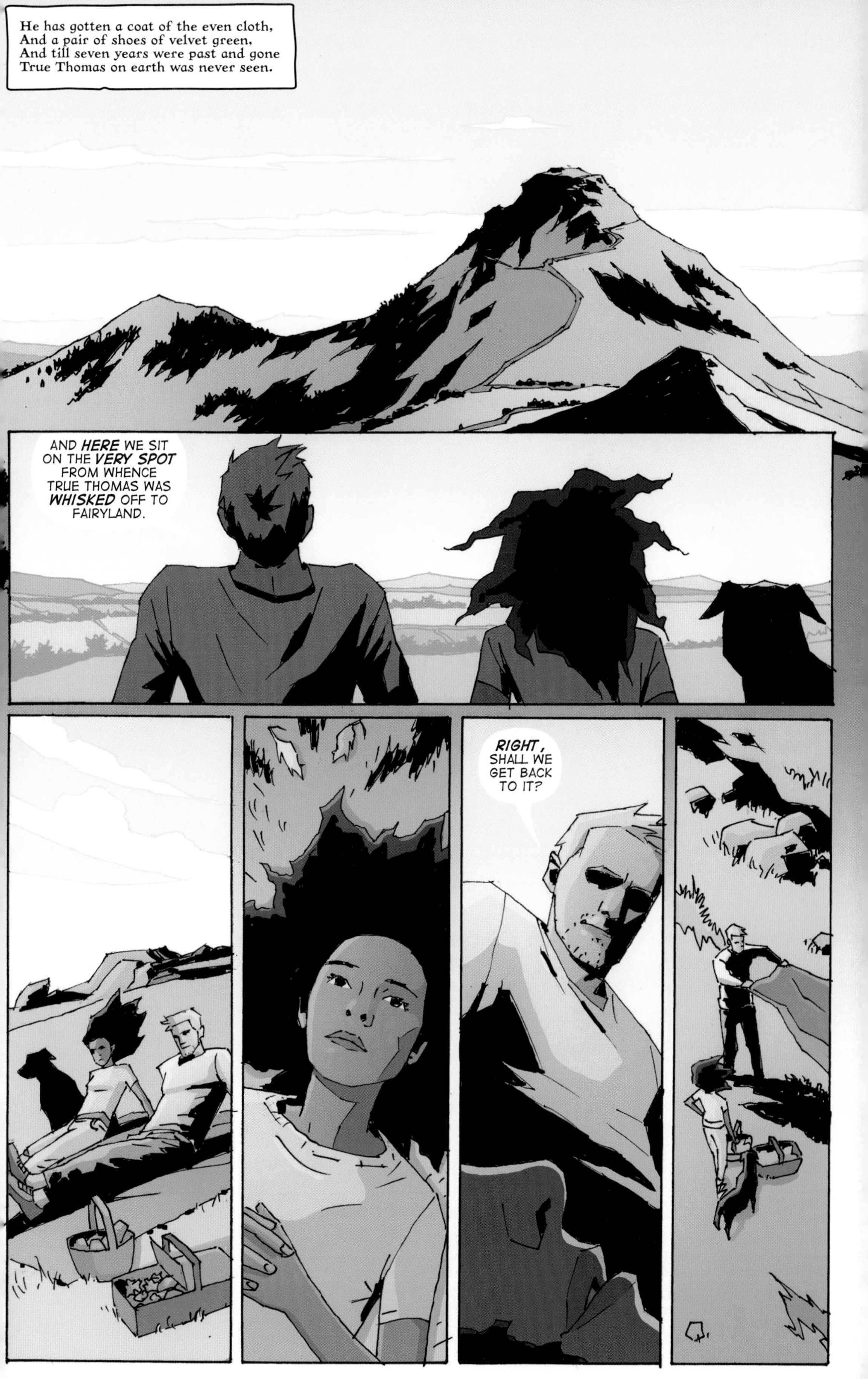
He has gotten a coat of the even cloth,
And a pair of shoes of velvet green,
And till seven years were past and gone
True Thomas on earth was never seen.
AND *HERE* WE SIT ON THE *VERY SPOT* FROM WHENCE TRUE THOMAS WAS *WHISKED* OFF TO FAIRYLAND.
RIGHT, SHALL WE GET BACK TO IT?

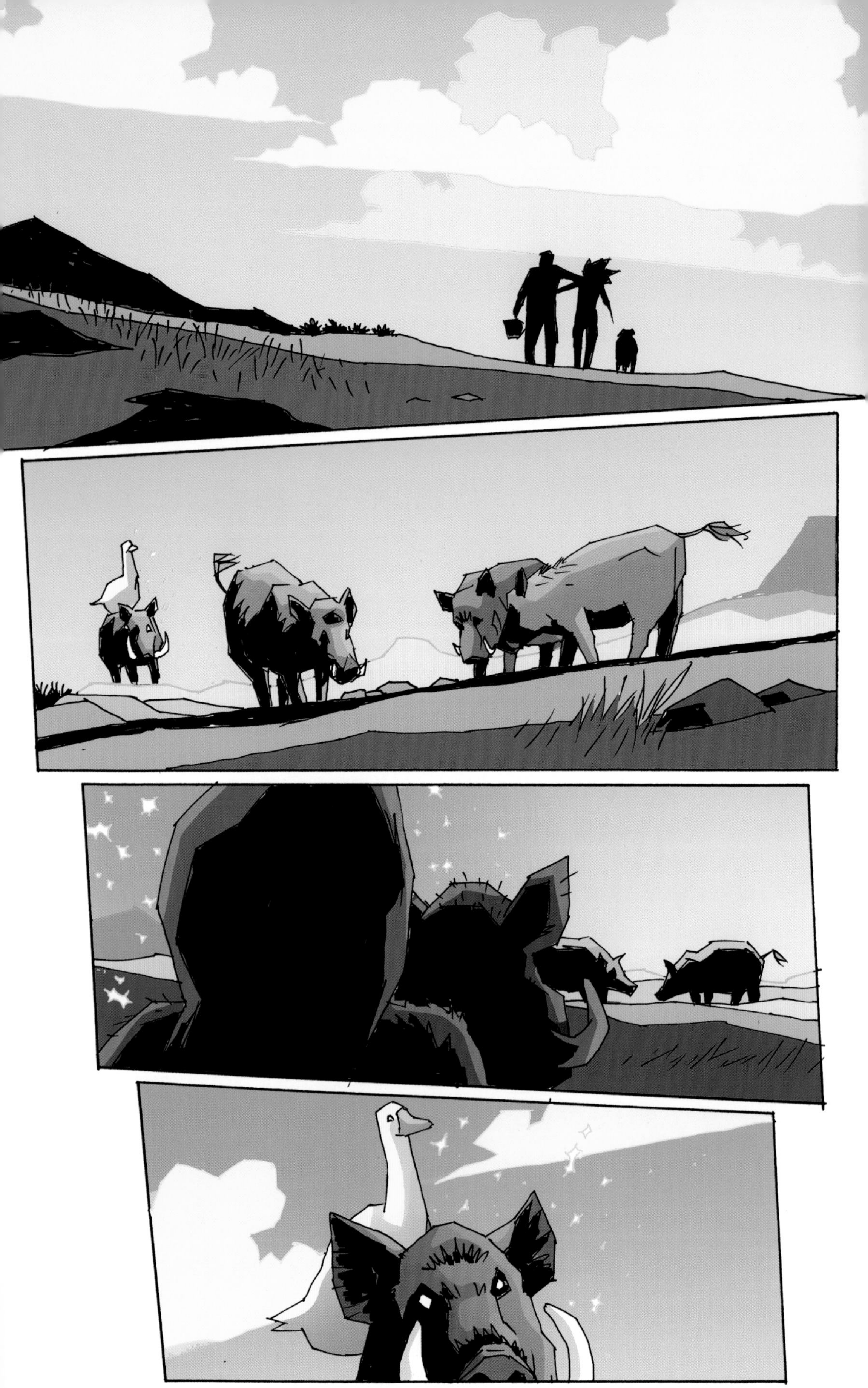

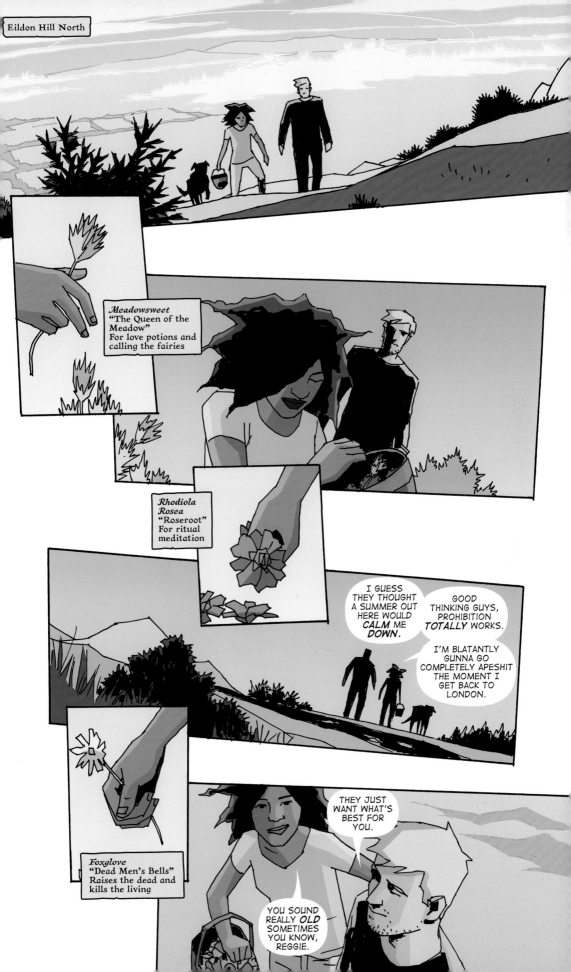

Meadowsweet
"The Queen of the Meadow"
For love potions and calling the fairies

Rhodiola Rosea
"Roseroot"
For ritual meditation

I GUESS THEY THOUGHT A SUMMER OUT HERE WOULD *CALM* ME *DOWN.*

GOOD THINKING GUYS, PROHIBITION *TOTALLY* WORKS.

I'M BLATANTLY GUNNA GO COMPLETELY APESHIT THE MOMENT I GET BACK TO LONDON.

Foxglove
"Dead Men's Bells"
Raises the dead and kills the living

THEY JUST WANT WHAT'S BEST FOR YOU.

YOU SOUND REALLY *OLD* SOMETIMES YOU KNOW, REGGIE.

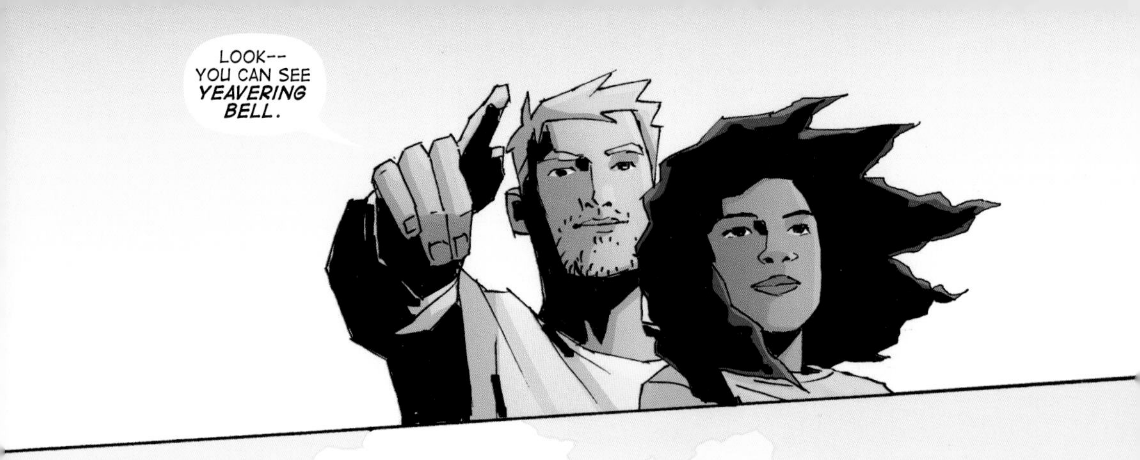
LOOK-- YOU CAN SEE YEAVERING BELL.

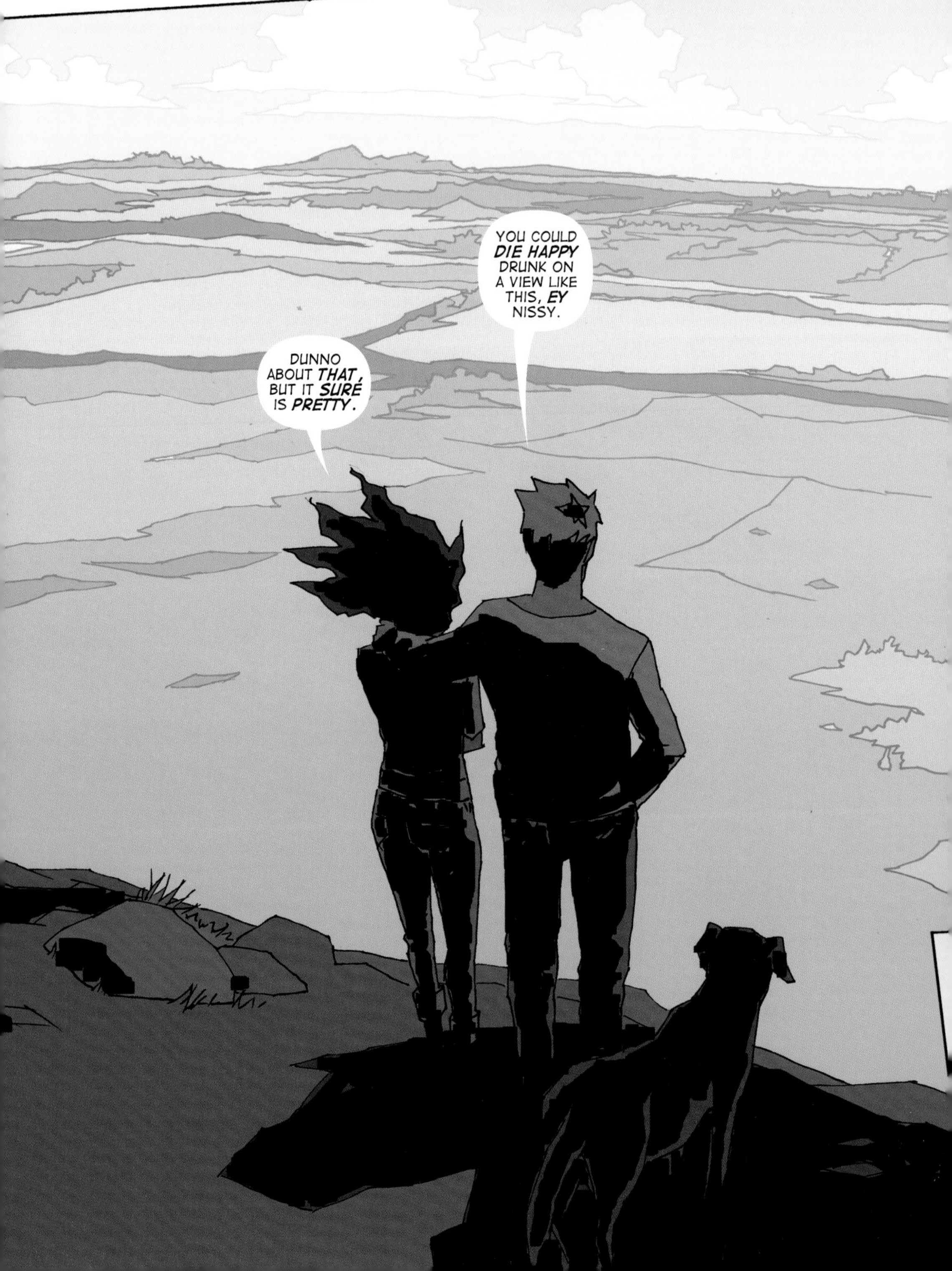
YOU COULD DIE HAPPY DRUNK ON A VIEW LIKE THIS, EY NISSY.
DUNNO ABOUT THAT, BUT IT SURE IS PRETTY.

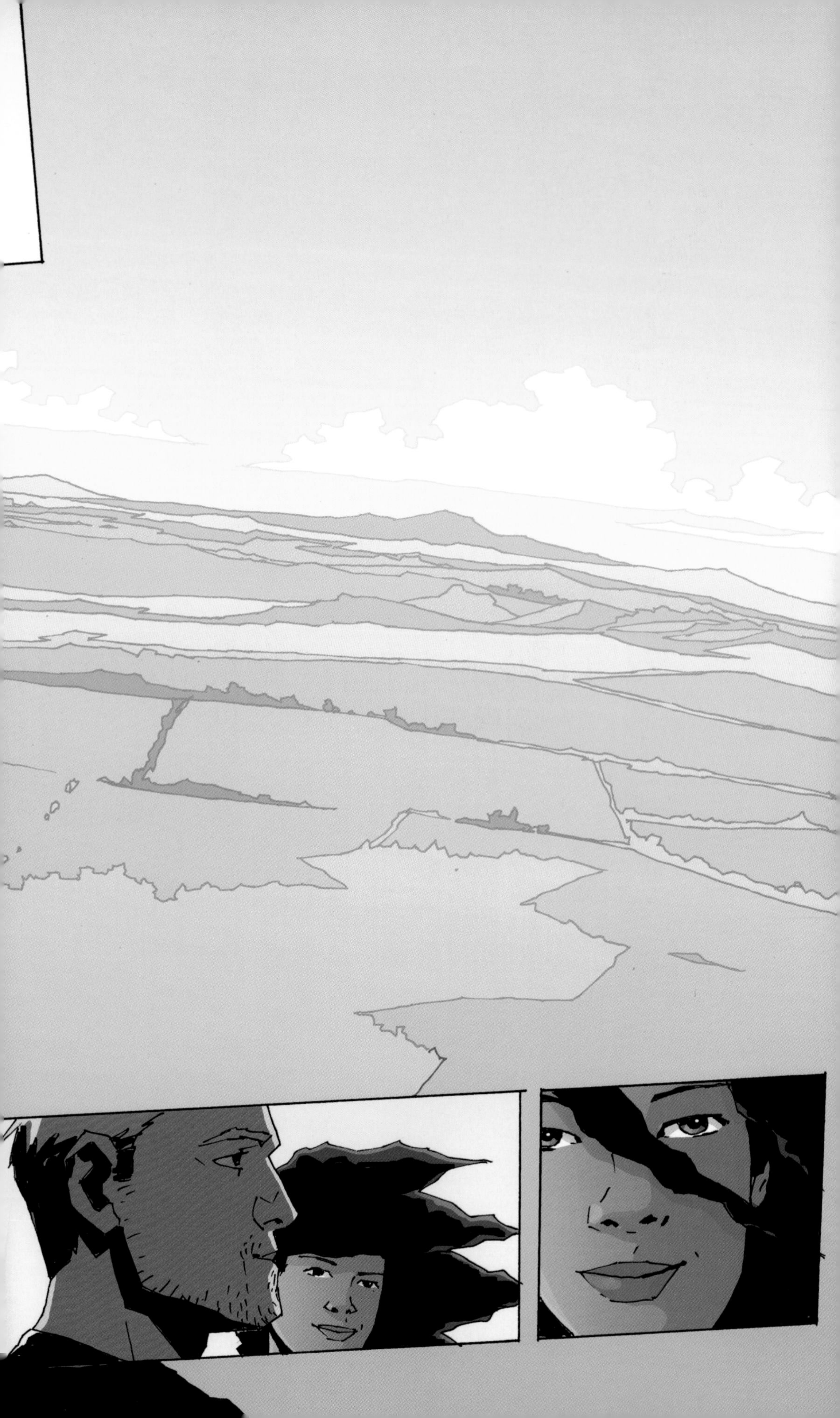

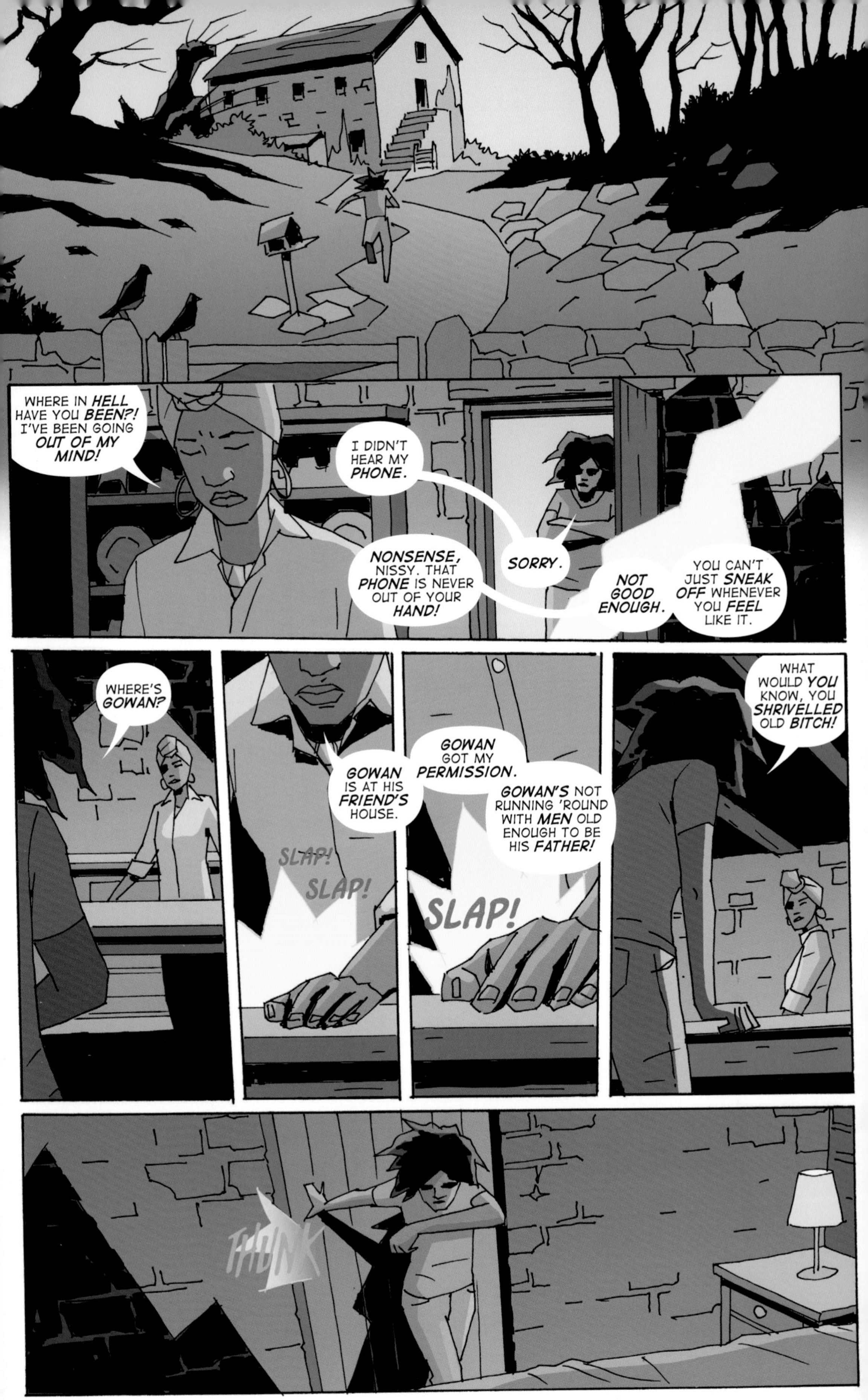
WHERE IN HELL HAVE YOU BEEN?! I'VE BEEN GOING OUT OF MY MIND!
I DIDN'T HEAR MY PHONE.
SORRY.
NONSENSE, NISSY. THAT PHONE IS NEVER OUT OF YOUR HAND!
NOT GOOD ENOUGH.
YOU CAN'T JUST SNEAK OFF WHENEVER YOU FEEL LIKE IT.
WHERE'S GOWAN?
GOWAN IS AT HIS FRIEND'S HOUSE.
SLAP!
SLAP!
GOWAN GOT MY PERMISSION.
GOWAN'S NOT RUNNING 'ROUND WITH MEN OLD ENOUGH TO BE HIS FATHER!
SLAP!
WHAT WOULD YOU KNOW, YOU SHRIVELLED OLD BITCH!
THUNK

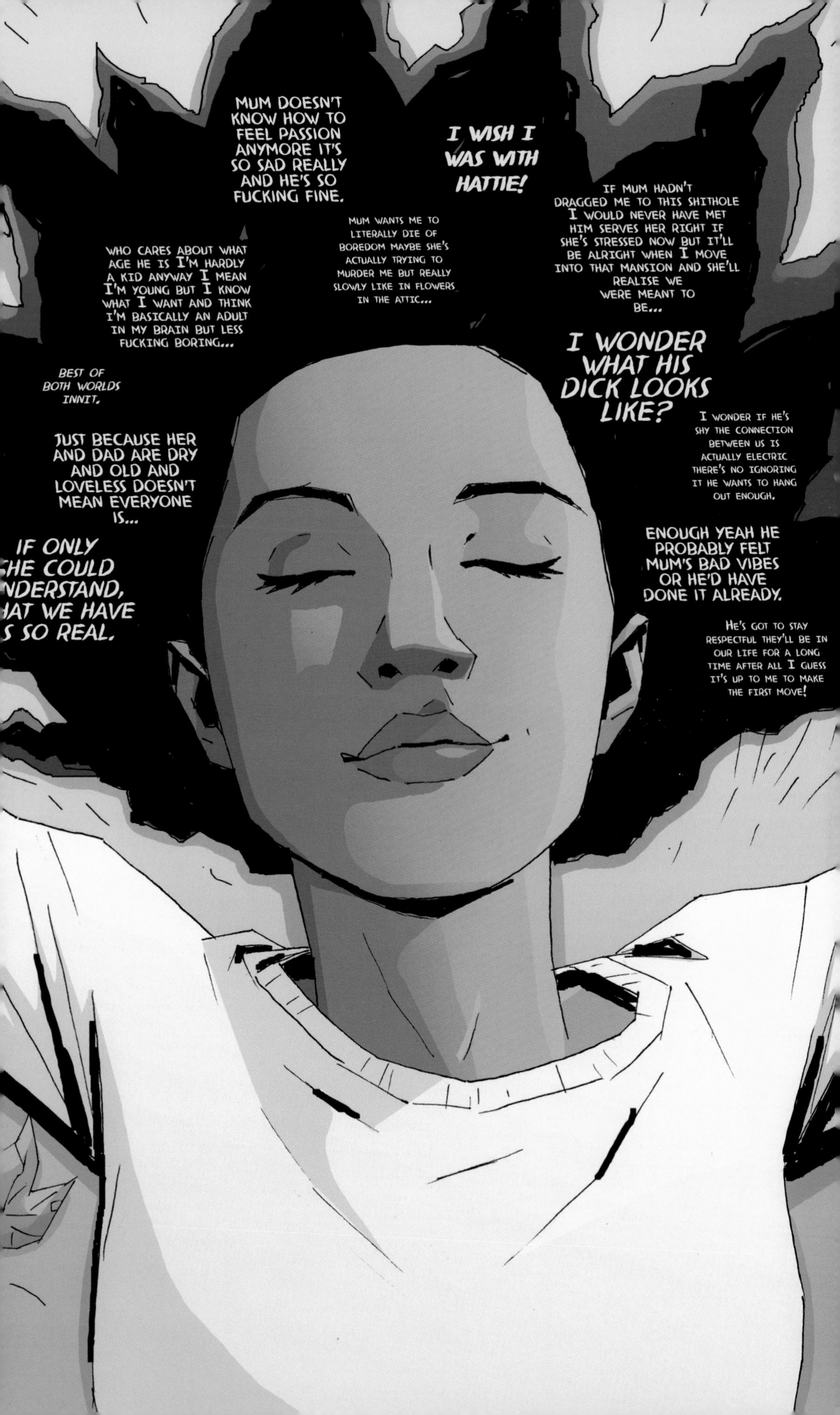
MUM DOESN'T KNOW HOW TO FEEL PASSION ANYMORE IT'S SO SAD REALLY AND HE'S SO FUCKING FINE.
I WISH I WAS WITH HATTIE!
IF MUM HADN'T DRAGGED ME TO THIS SHITHOLE I WOULD NEVER HAVE MET HIM SERVES HER RIGHT IF SHE'S STRESSED NOW BUT IT'LL BE ALRIGHT WHEN I MOVE INTO THAT MANSION AND SHE'LL REALISE WE WERE MEANT TO BE...
MUM WANTS ME TO LITERALLY DIE OF BOREDOM MAYBE SHE'S ACTUALLY TRYING TO MURDER ME BUT REALLY SLOWLY LIKE IN FLOWERS IN THE ATTIC...
WHO CARES ABOUT WHAT AGE HE IS I'M HARDLY A KID ANYWAY I MEAN I'M YOUNG BUT I KNOW WHAT I WANT AND THINK I'M BASICALLY AN ADULT IN MY BRAIN BUT LESS FUCKING BORING...
BEST OF BOTH WORLDS INNIT.
I WONDER WHAT HIS DICK LOOKS LIKE?
I WONDER IF HE'S SHY THE CONNECTION BETWEEN US IS ACTUALLY ELECTRIC THERE'S NO IGNORING IT HE WANTS TO HANG OUT ENOUGH.
JUST BECAUSE HER AND DAD ARE DRY AND OLD AND LOVELESS DOESN'T MEAN EVERYONE IS...
ENOUGH YEAH HE PROBABLY FELT MUM'S BAD VIBES OR HE'D HAVE DONE IT ALREADY.
HE'S GOT TO STAY RESPECTFUL THEY'LL BE IN OUR LIFE FOR A LONG TIME AFTER ALL I GUESS IT'S UP TO ME TO MAKE THE FIRST MOVE!

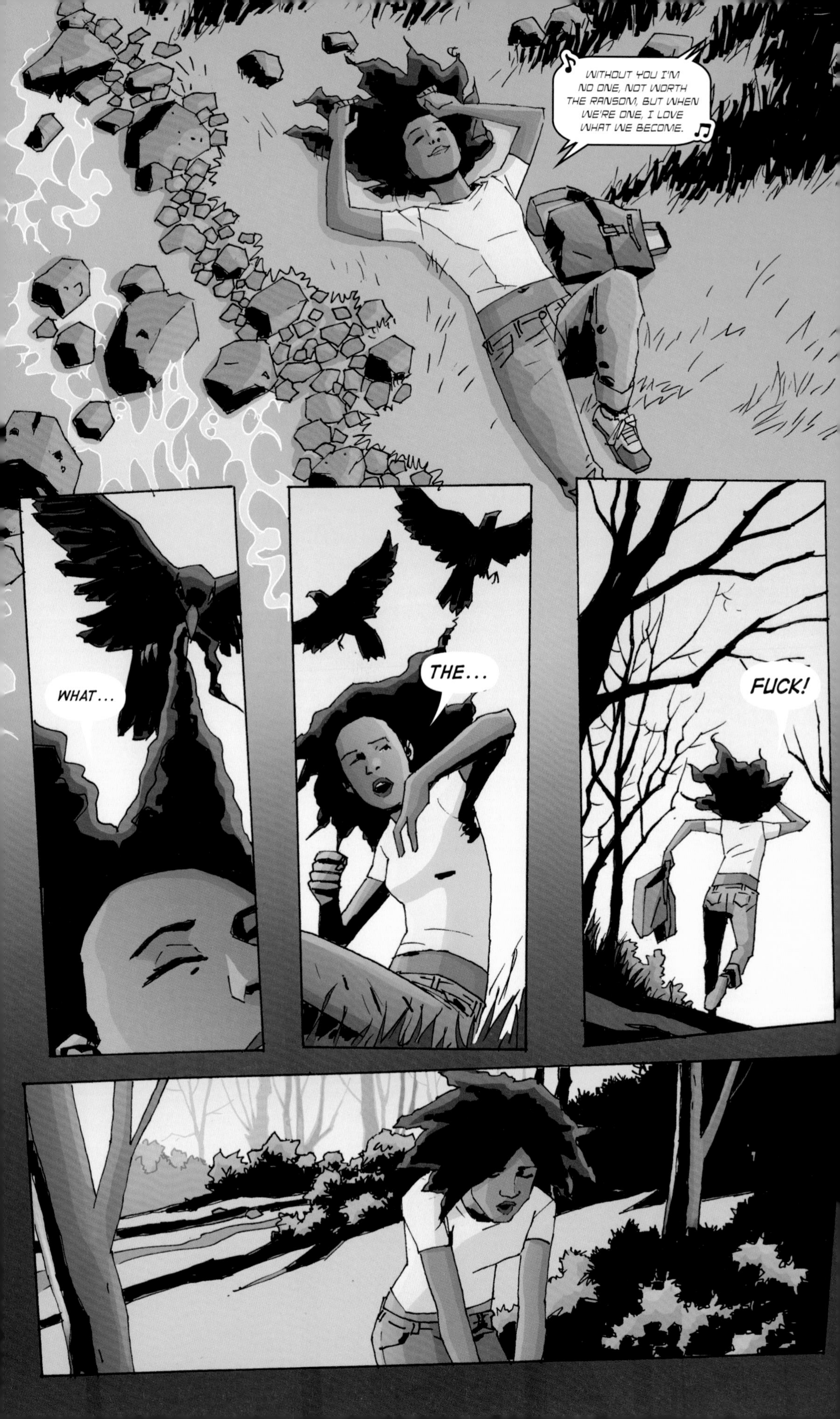
WITHOUT YOU I'M NO ONE, NOT WORTH THE RANSOM, BUT WHEN WE'RE ONE, I LOVE WHAT WE BECOME.
WHAT...
THE...
FUCK!

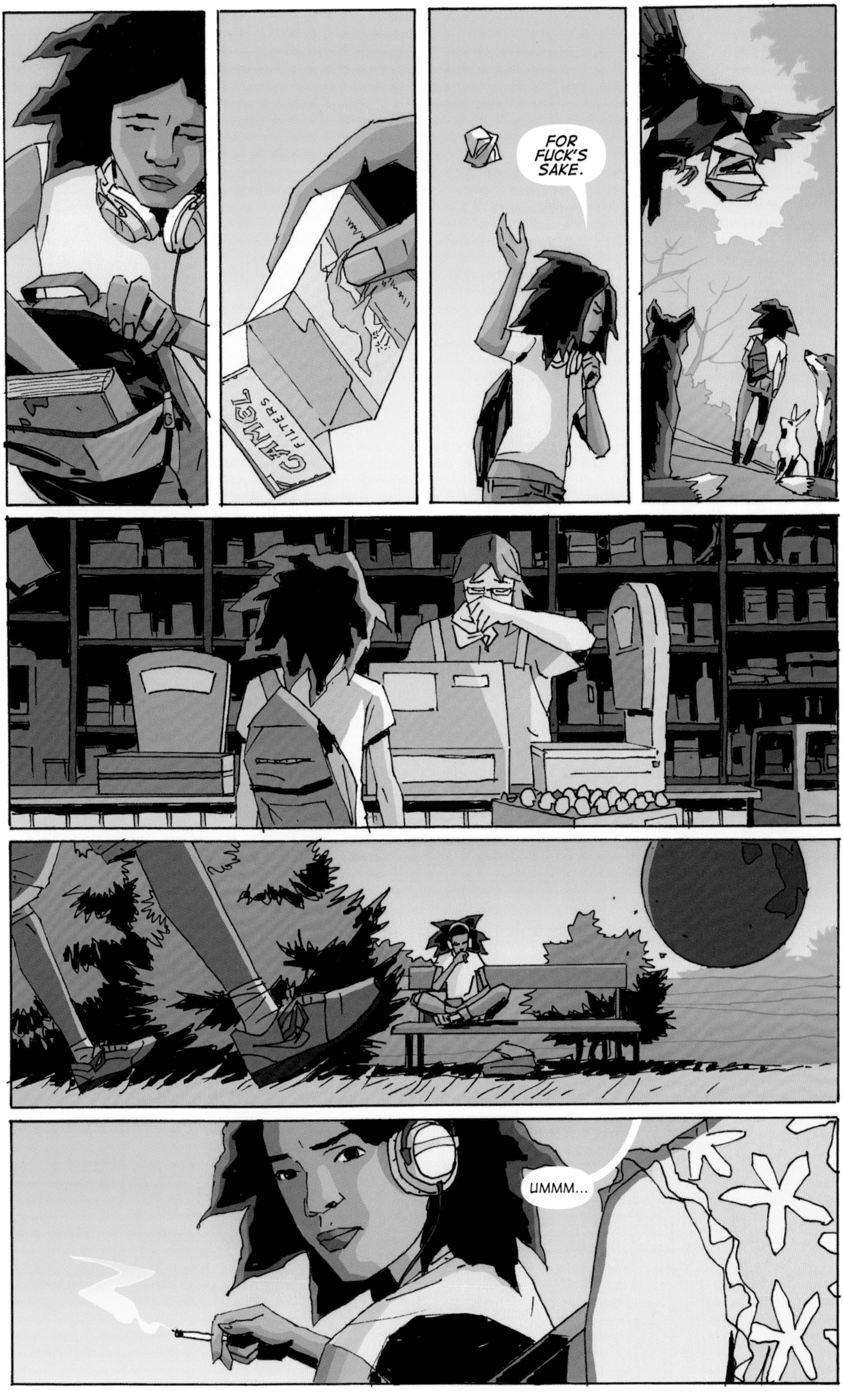
CAMEL
FILTERS
FOR FUCK'S SAKE.
UMMM...

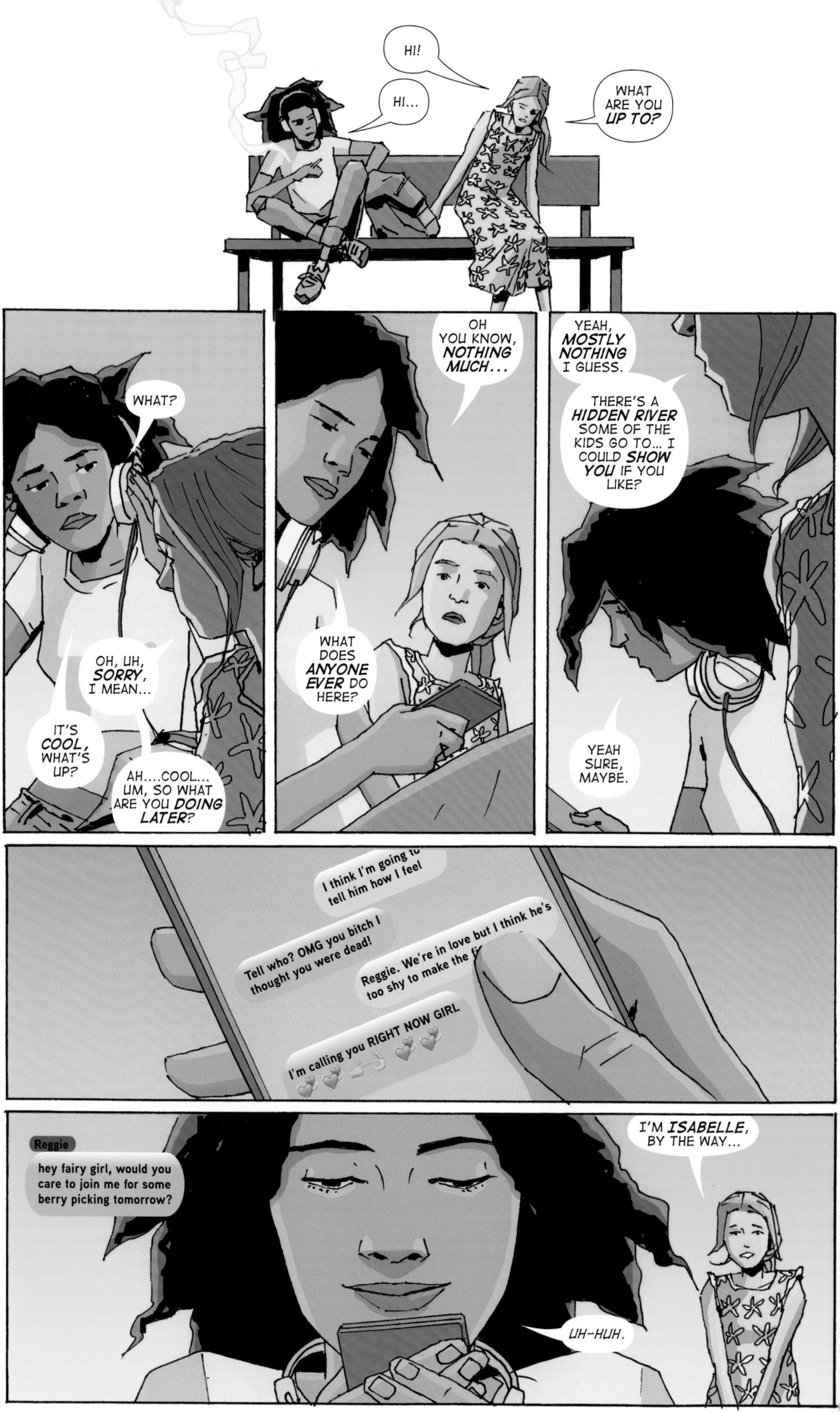
HI!
HI...
WHAT ARE YOU UP TO?
WHAT?
OH, UH, SORRY, I MEAN...
IT'S COOL, WHAT'S UP?
AH....COOL... UM, SO WHAT ARE YOU DOING LATER?
OH YOU KNOW, NOTHING MUCH...
WHAT DOES ANYONE EVER DO HERE?
YEAH, MOSTLY NOTHING I GUESS.
THERE'S A HIDDEN RIVER SOME OF THE KIDS GO TO... I COULD SHOW YOU IF YOU LIKE?
YEAH SURE, MAYBE.
tell him how I feel
Tell who? OMG you bitch I thought you were dead!
Reggie. We're in love but I think he's too shy to make the
I'm calling you RIGHT NOW GIRL
Reggie
hey fairy girl, would you care to join me for some berry picking tomorrow?
I'M ISABELLE, BY THE WAY...
UH-HUH.

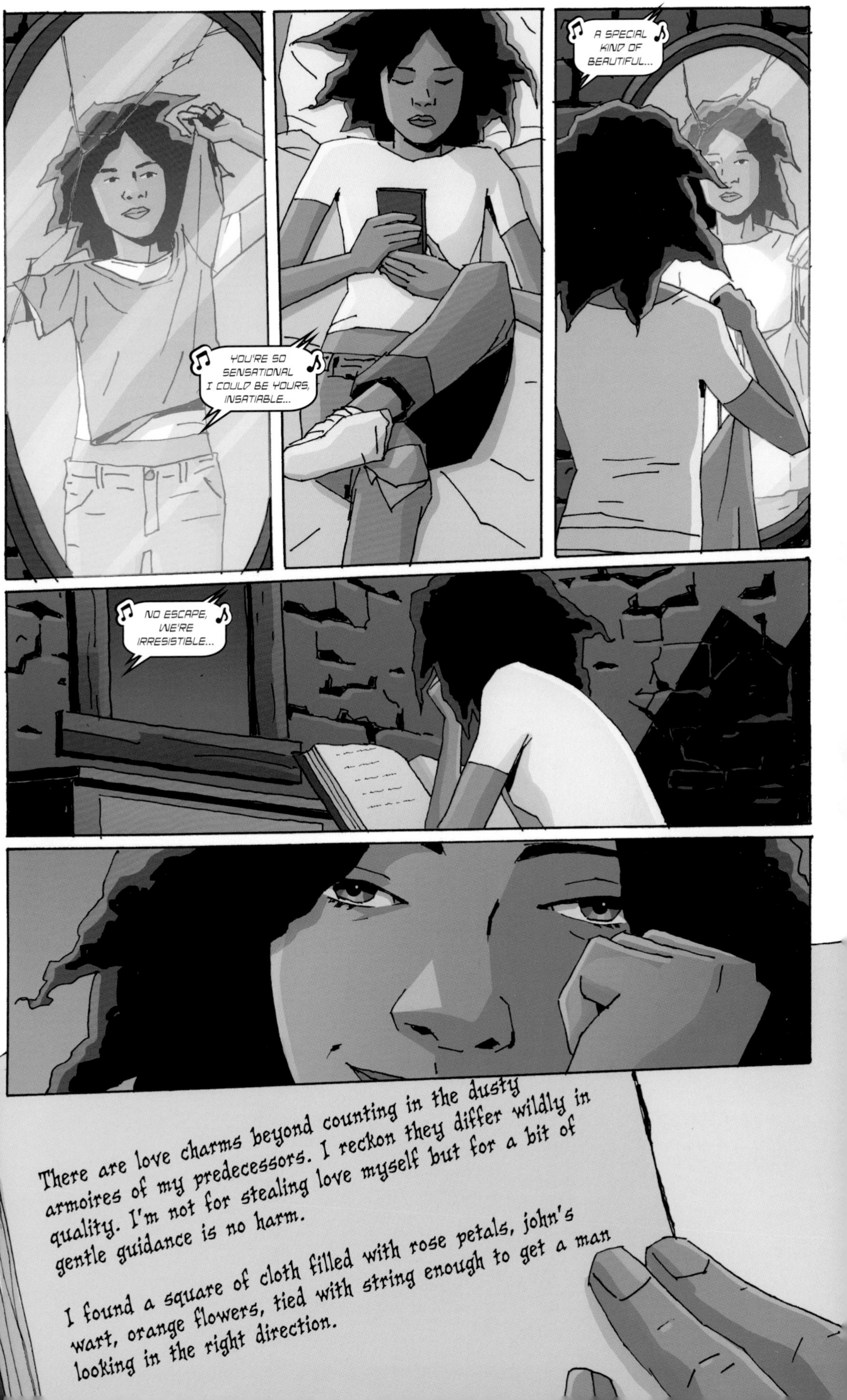
YOU'RE SO SENSATIONAL I COULD BE YOURS, INSATIABLE...
A SPECIAL KIND OF BEAUTIFUL...
NO ESCAPE, WE'RE IRRESISTIBLE...
There are love charms beyond counting in the dusty armoires of my predecessors. I reckon they differ wildly in quality. I'm not for stealing love myself but for a bit of gentle guidance is no harm.
I found a square of cloth filled with rose petals, john's wart, orange flowers, tied with string enough to get a man looking in the right direction.

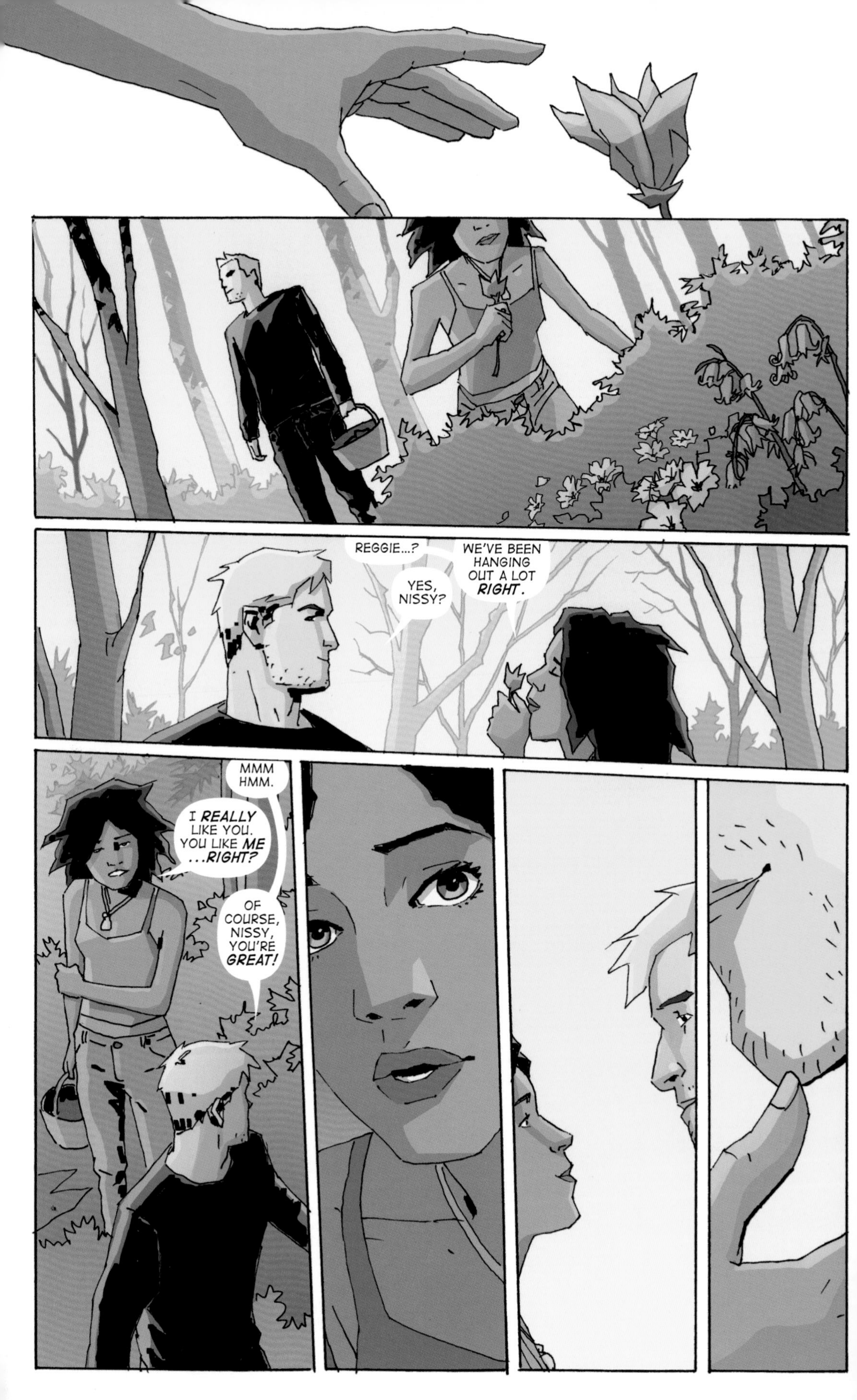
REGGIE...?
YES, NISSY?
WE'VE BEEN HANGING OUT A LOT RIGHT.
MMM HMM.
I REALLY LIKE YOU. YOU LIKE ME ...RIGHT?
OF COURSE, NISSY, YOU'RE GREAT!

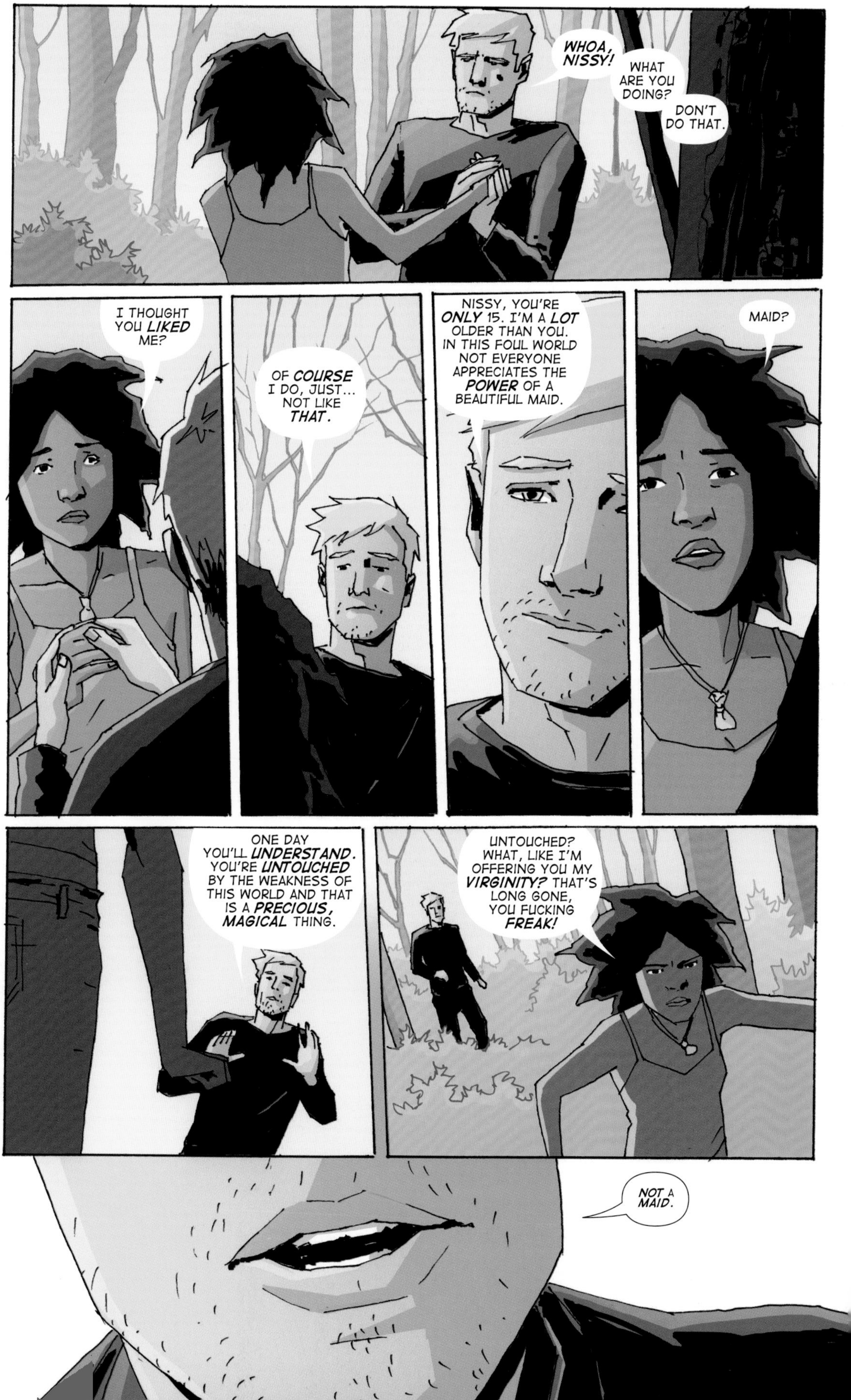
WHOA, NISSY!
WHAT ARE YOU DOING?
DON'T DO THAT.
I THOUGHT YOU LIKED ME?
OF COURSE I DO, JUST... NOT LIKE THAT.
NISSY, YOU'RE ONLY 15. I'M A LOT OLDER THAN YOU. IN THIS FOUL WORLD NOT EVERYONE APPRECIATES THE POWER OF A BEAUTIFUL MAID.
MAID?
ONE DAY YOU'LL UNDERSTAND. YOU'RE UNTOUCHED BY THE WEAKNESS OF THIS WORLD AND THAT IS A PRECIOUS, MAGICAL THING.
UNTOUCHED? WHAT, LIKE I'M OFFERING YOU MY VIRGINITY? THAT'S LONG GONE, YOU FUCKING FREAK!
NOT A MAID.

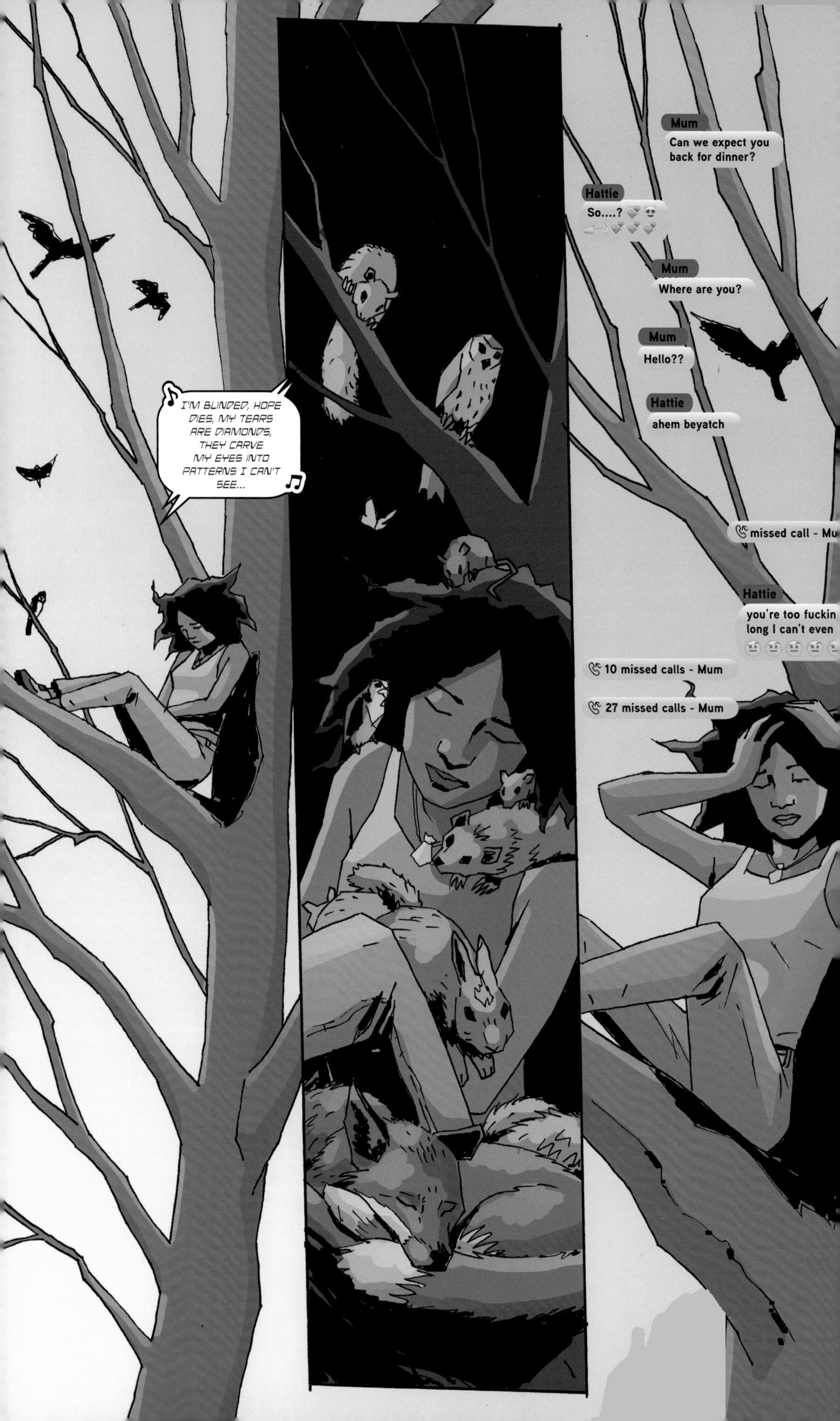

Mum
Can we expect you back for dinner?
Hattie
So....?
Mum
Where are you?
Mum
Hello??
Hattie
ahem beyatch
I'M BLINDED, HOPE DIES, MY TEARS ARE DIAMONDS, THEY CARVE MY EYES INTO PATTERNS I CAN'T SEE...
missed call - Mu
Hattie
you're too fuckin long I can't even
10 missed calls - Mum
27 missed calls - Mum

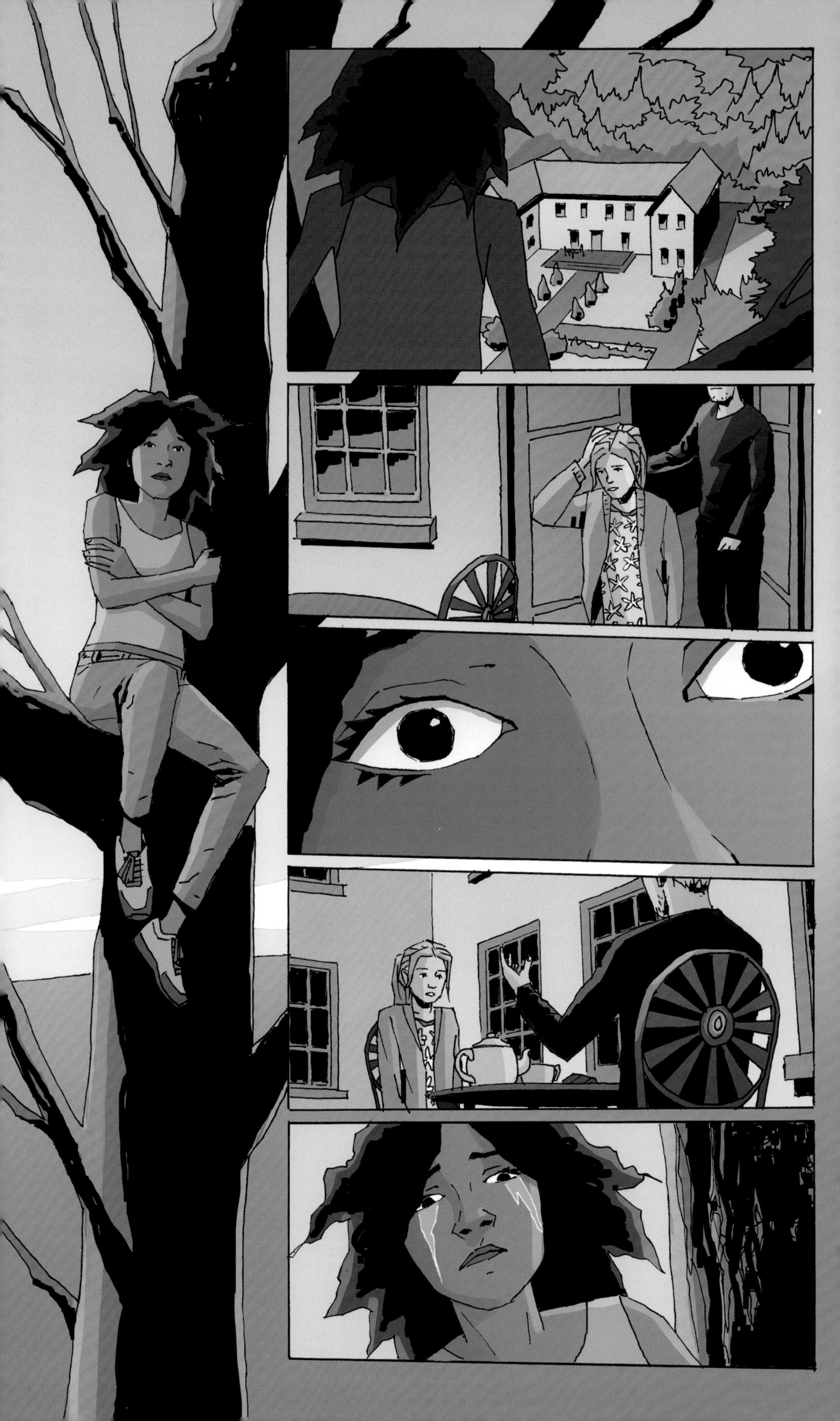

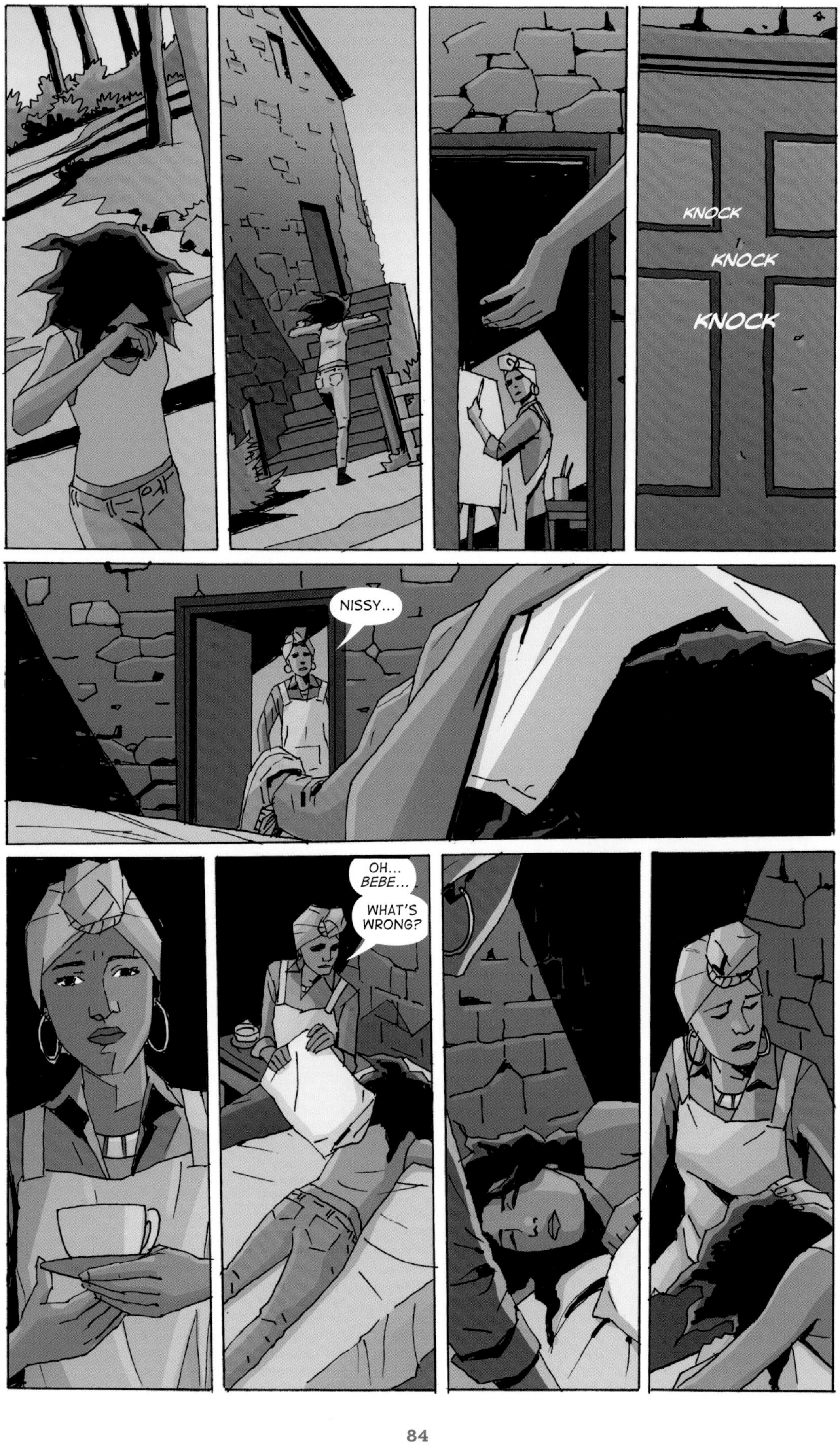
KNOCK
KNOCK
KNOCK
NISSY...
OH... BEBE...
WHAT'S WRONG?

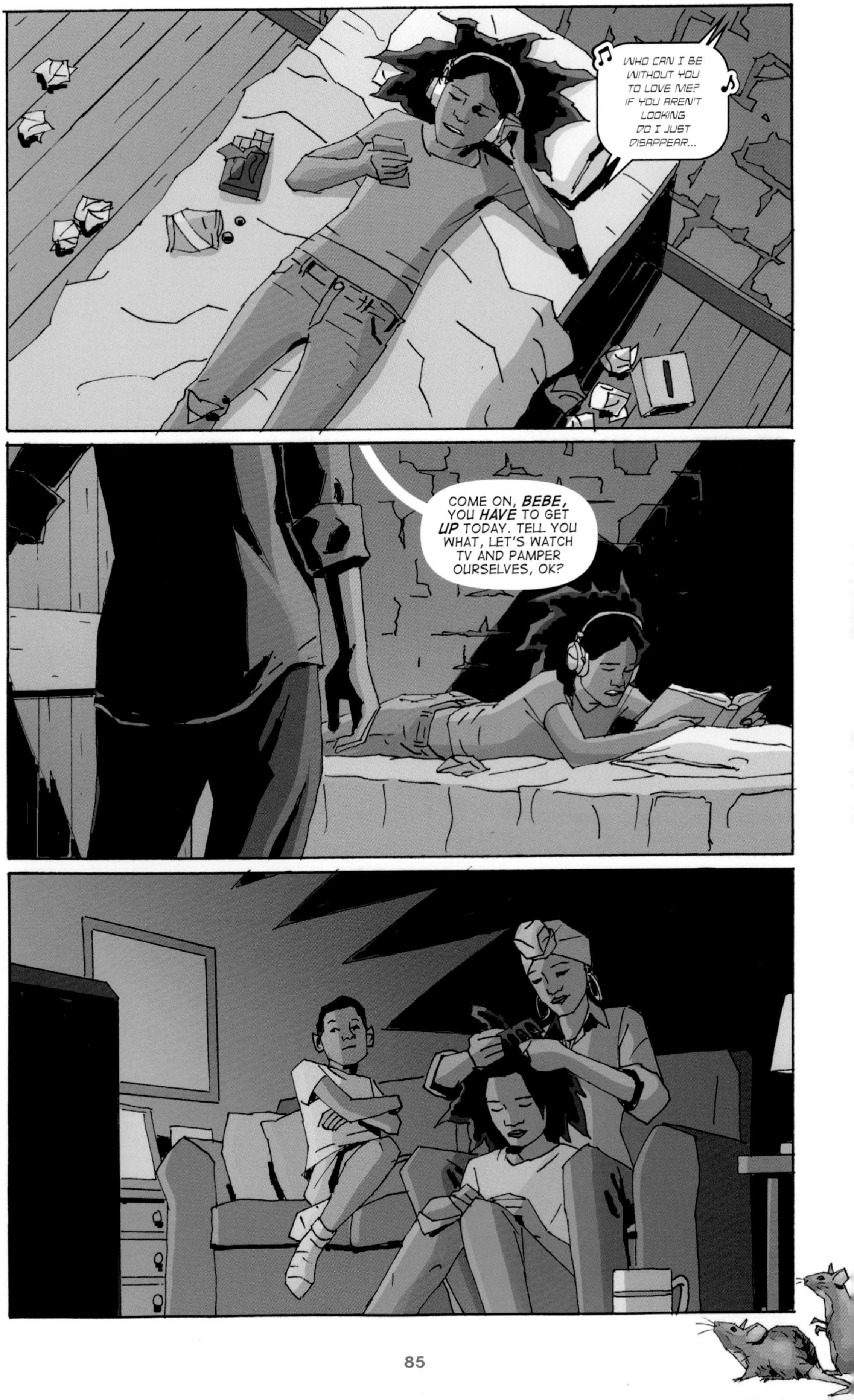
WHO CAN I BE WITHOUT YOU TO LOVE ME? IF YOU AREN'T LOOKING DO I JUST DISAPPEAR...
COME ON, **BEBE,** YOU **HAVE** TO GET **UP** TODAY. TELL YOU WHAT, LET'S WATCH TV AND PAMPER OURSELVES, OK?

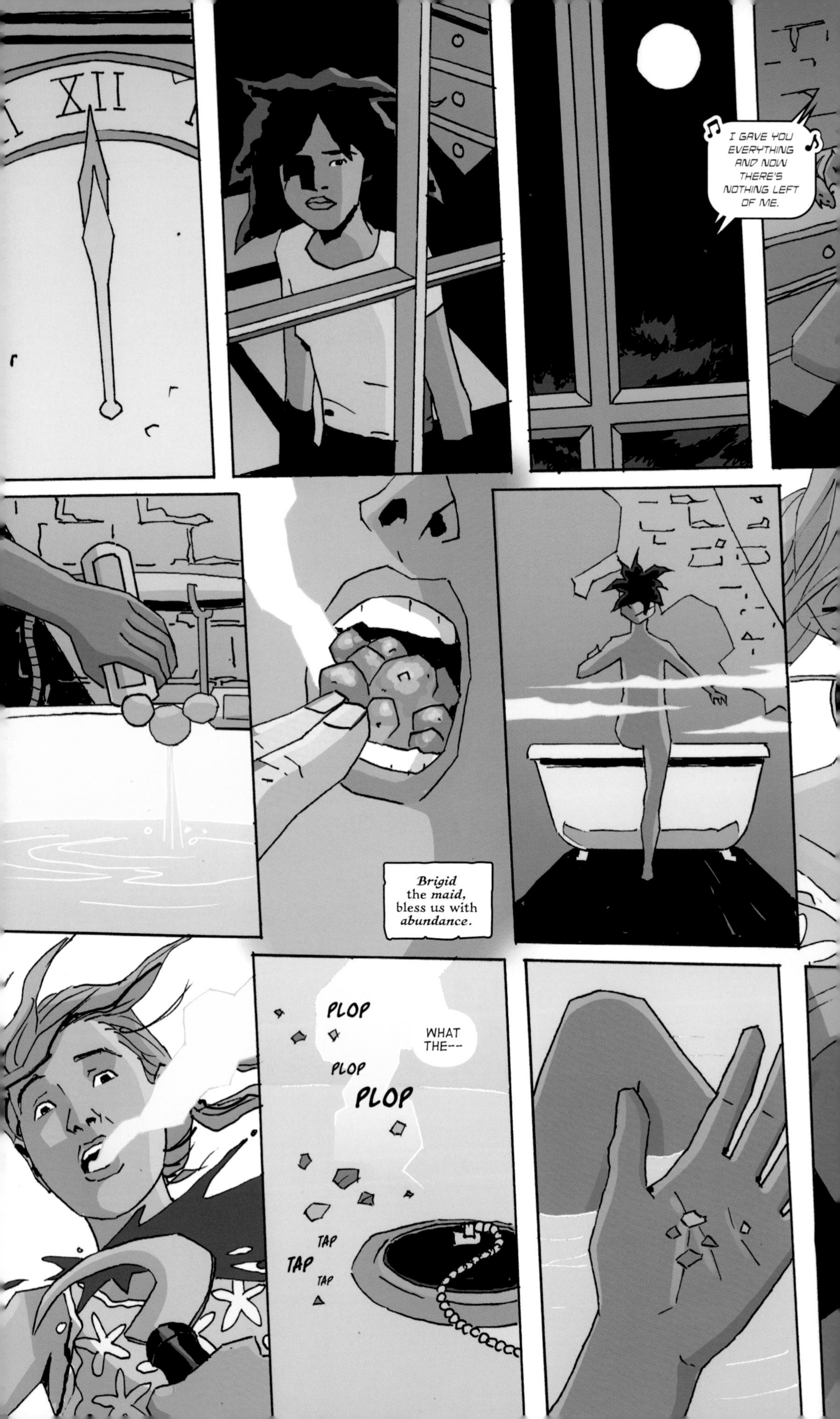

I GAVE YOU EVERYTHING AND NOW THERE'S NOTHING LEFT OF ME.
Brigid the *maid,* bless us with *abundance.*
PLOP
WHAT THE--
PLOP
PLOP
TAP
TAP
TAP

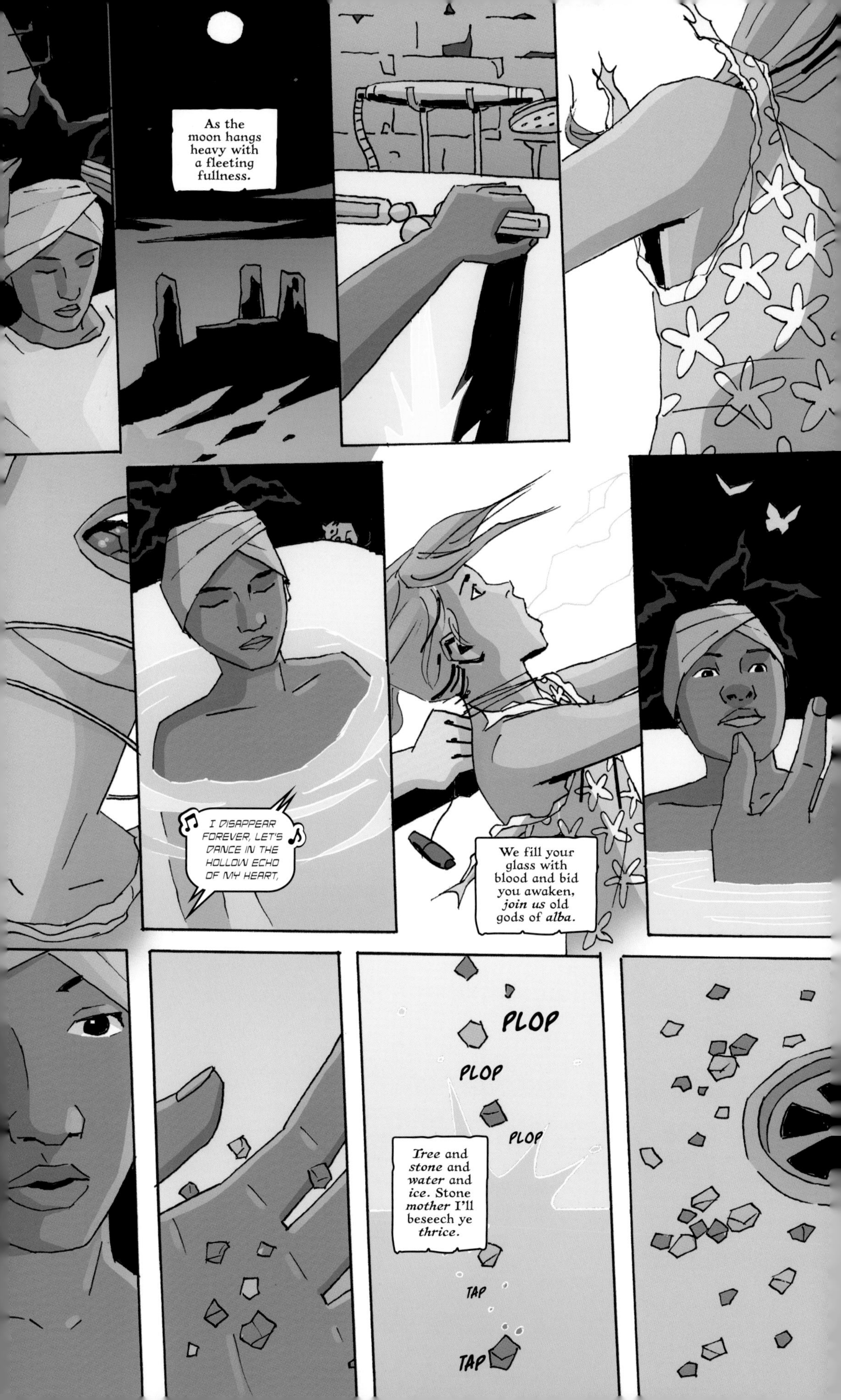

As the moon hangs heavy with a fleeting fullness.
I DISAPPEAR FOREVER, LET'S DANCE IN THE HOLLOW ECHO OF MY HEART,
We fill your glass with blood and bid you awaken, *join us* old gods of *alba*.
PLOP
PLOP
PLOP
Tree and *stone* and *water* and *ice*. Stone *mother* I'll beseech ye *thrice*.
TAP
TAP

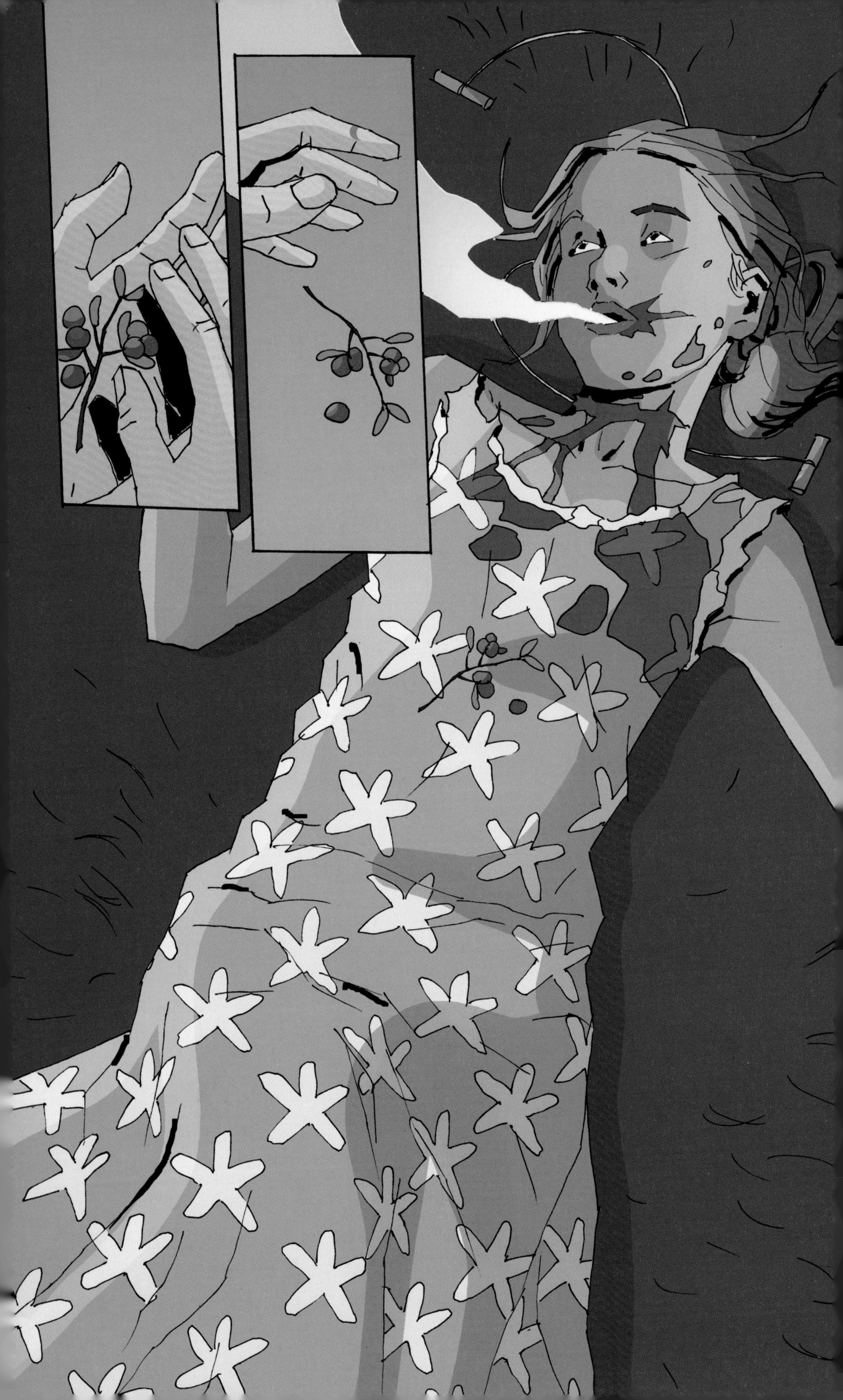

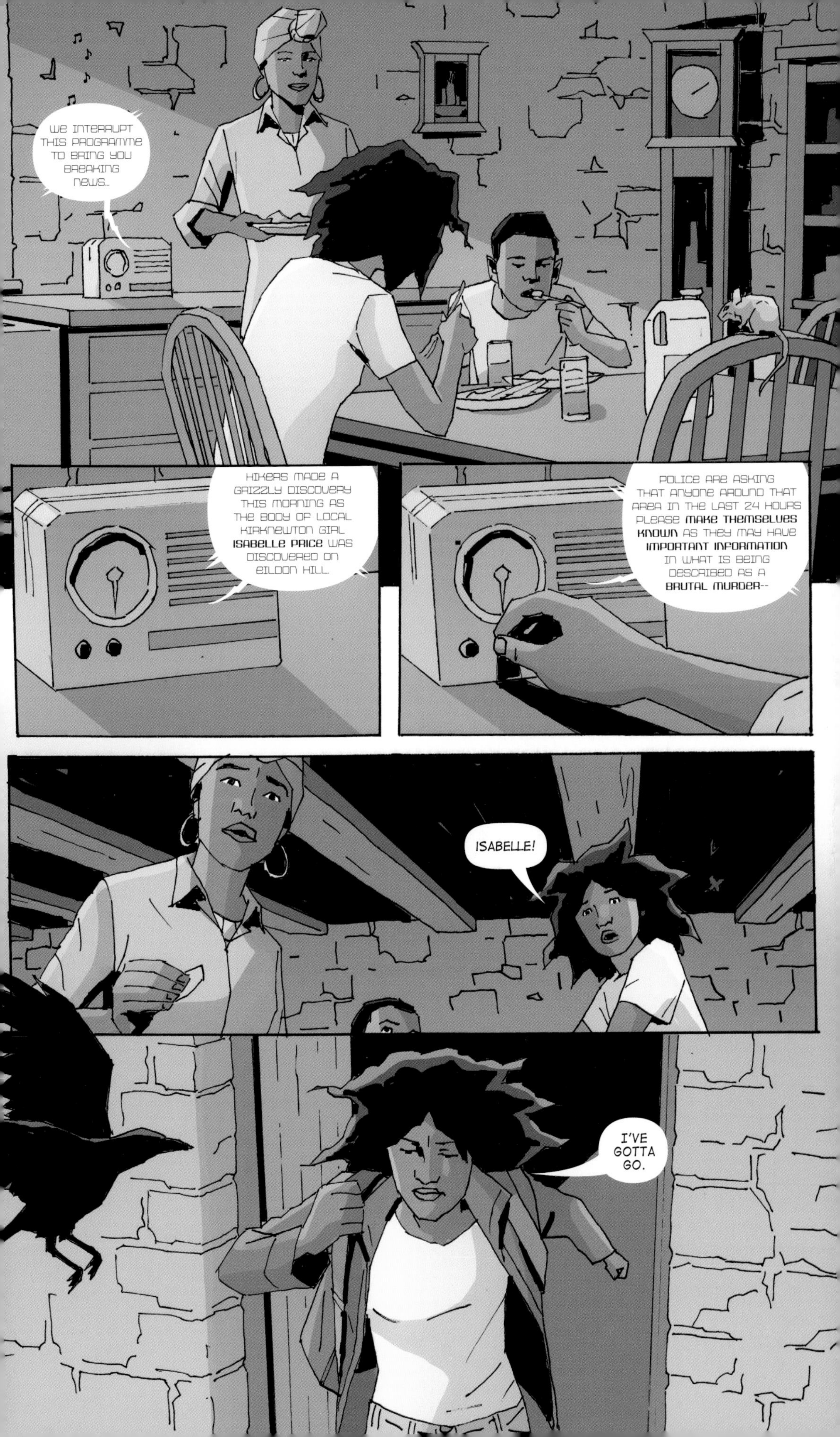

WE INTERRUPT THIS PROGRAMME TO BRING YOU BREAKING NEWS...
HIKERS MADE A GRIZZLY DISCOVERY THIS MORNING AS THE BODY OF LOCAL KIRKNEWTON GIRL ISABELLE PRICE WAS DISCOVERED ON EILDON HILL.
POLICE ARE ASKING THAT ANYONE AROUND THAT AREA IN THE LAST 24 HOURS PLEASE MAKE THEMSELVES KNOWN AS THEY MAY HAVE IMPORTANT INFORMATION IN WHAT IS BEING DESCRIBED AS A BRUTAL MURDER--
ISABELLE!
I'VE GOTTA GO.

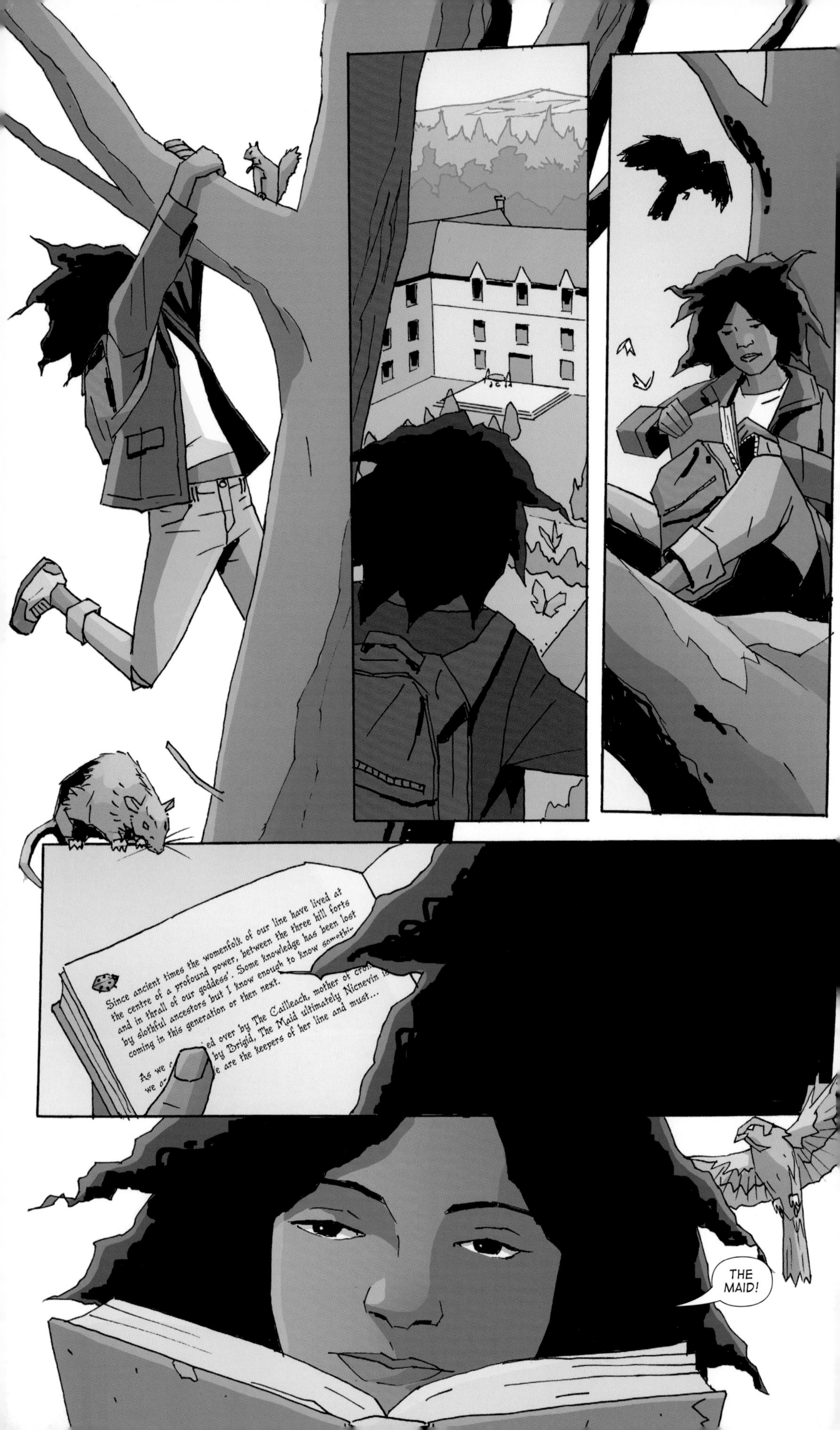
Since ancient times the womenfolk of our line have lived at the centre of a profound power, between the three hill forts and in thrall of our goddess'. Some knowledge has been lost by slothful ancestors but I know enough to know somethi… coming in this generation or then next.
…ed over by The Cailleach, mother of cro… …by Brigid, The Maid ultimately Nicnevin i… …e are the keepers of her line and must…
As we…
we a…
THE MAID!

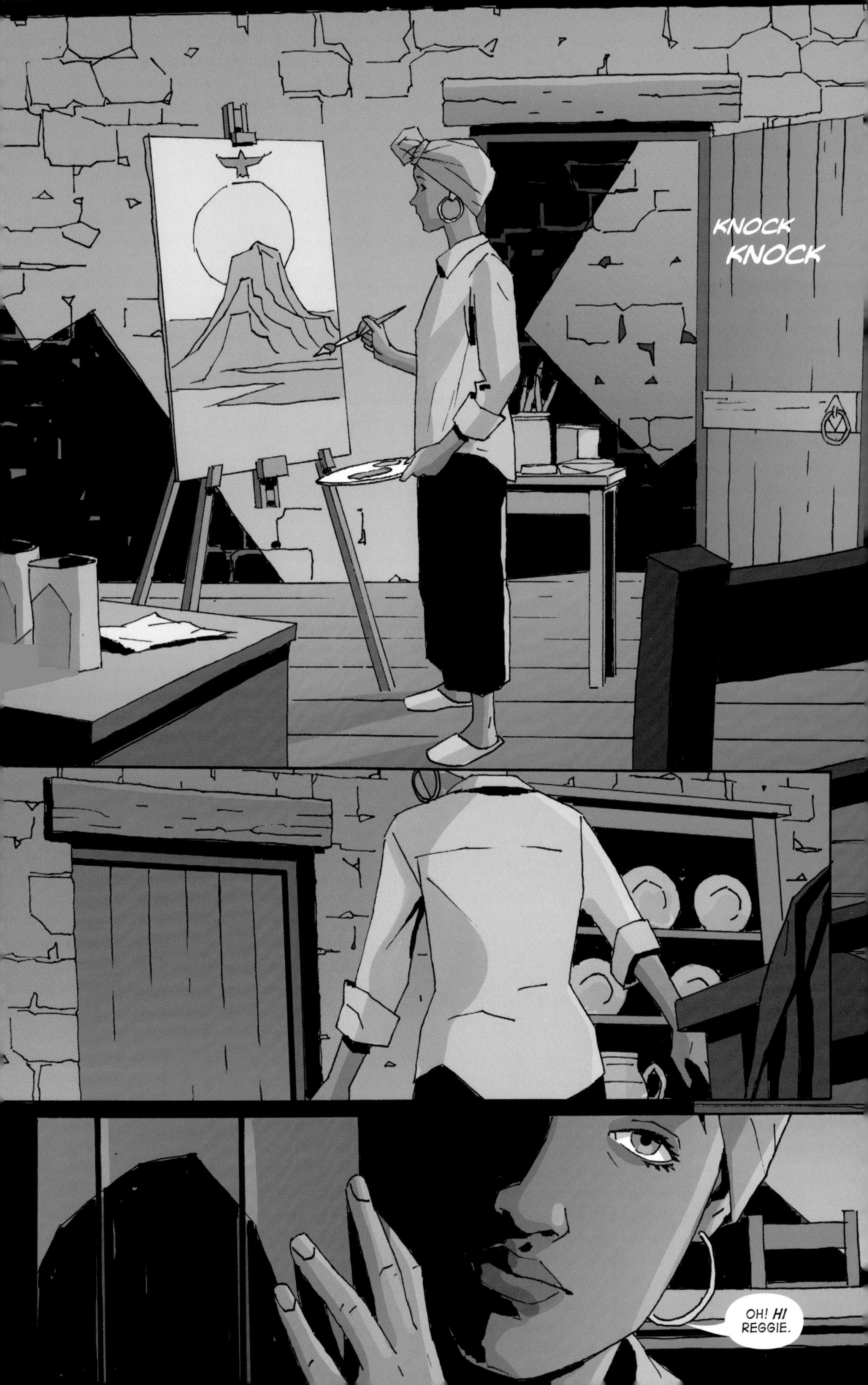
KNOCK
KNOCK
OH! HI REGGIE.

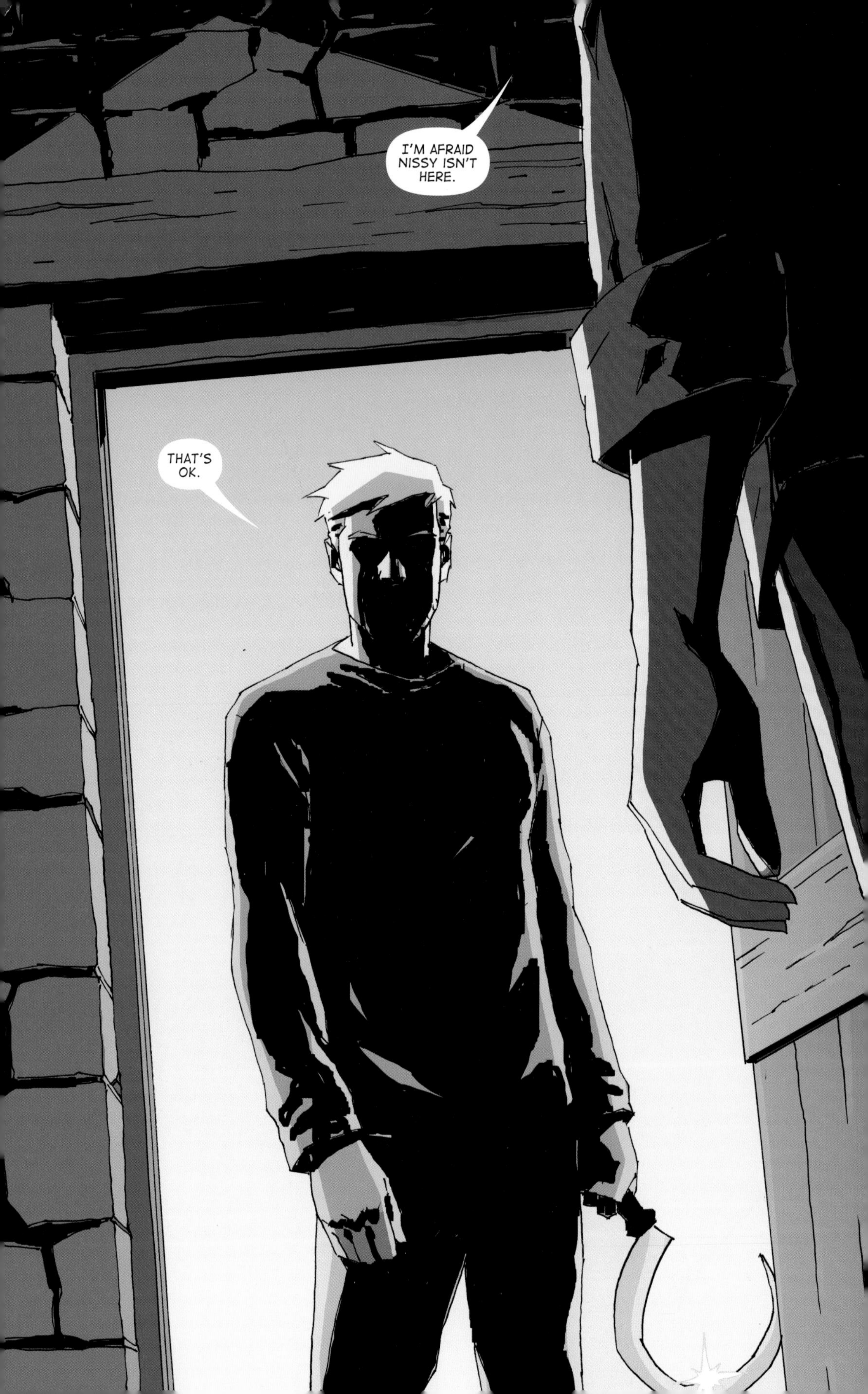
I'M AFRAID NISSY ISN'T HERE.
THAT'S OK.

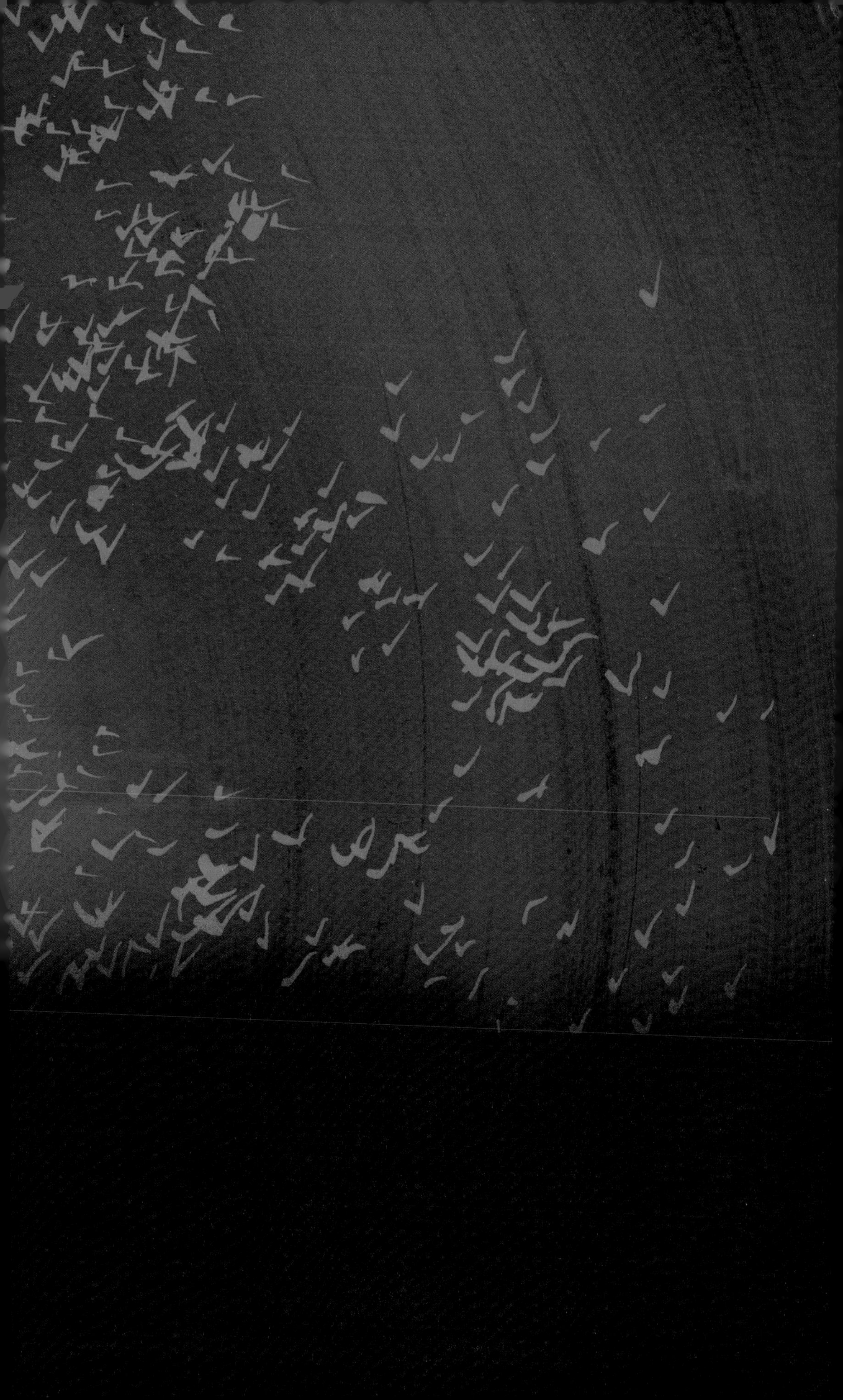

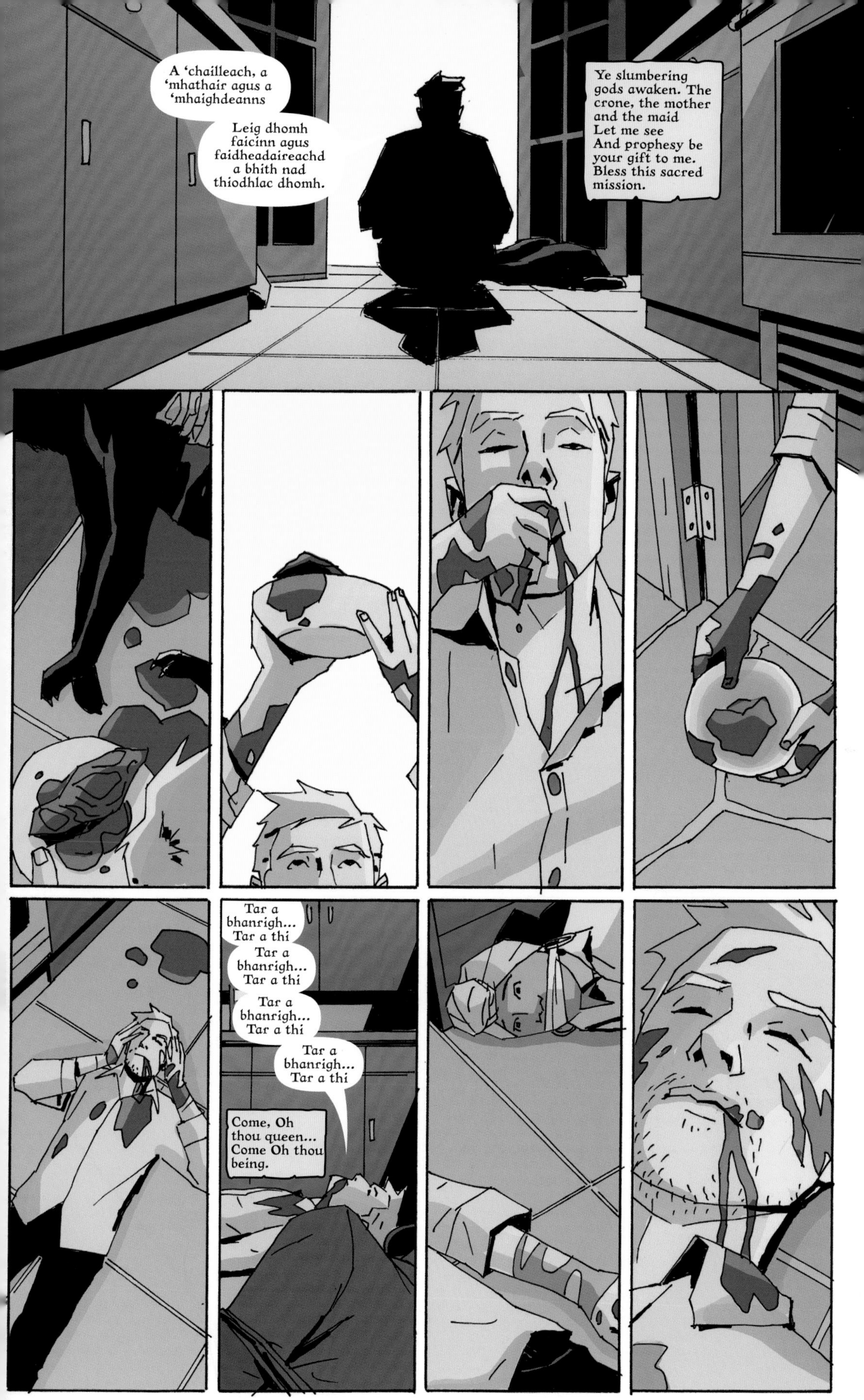
A 'chailleach, a 'mhathair agus a 'mhaighdeanns
Leig dhomh faicinn agus faidheadaireachd a bhith nad thiodhlac dhomh.
Ye slumbering gods awaken. The crone, the mother and the maid Let me see And prophesy be your gift to me. Bless this sacred mission.
Tar a bhanrigh... Tar a thi
Tar a bhanrigh... Tar a thi
Tar a bhanrigh... Tar a thi
Tar a bhanrigh... Tar a thi
Come, Oh thou queen... Come Oh thou being.

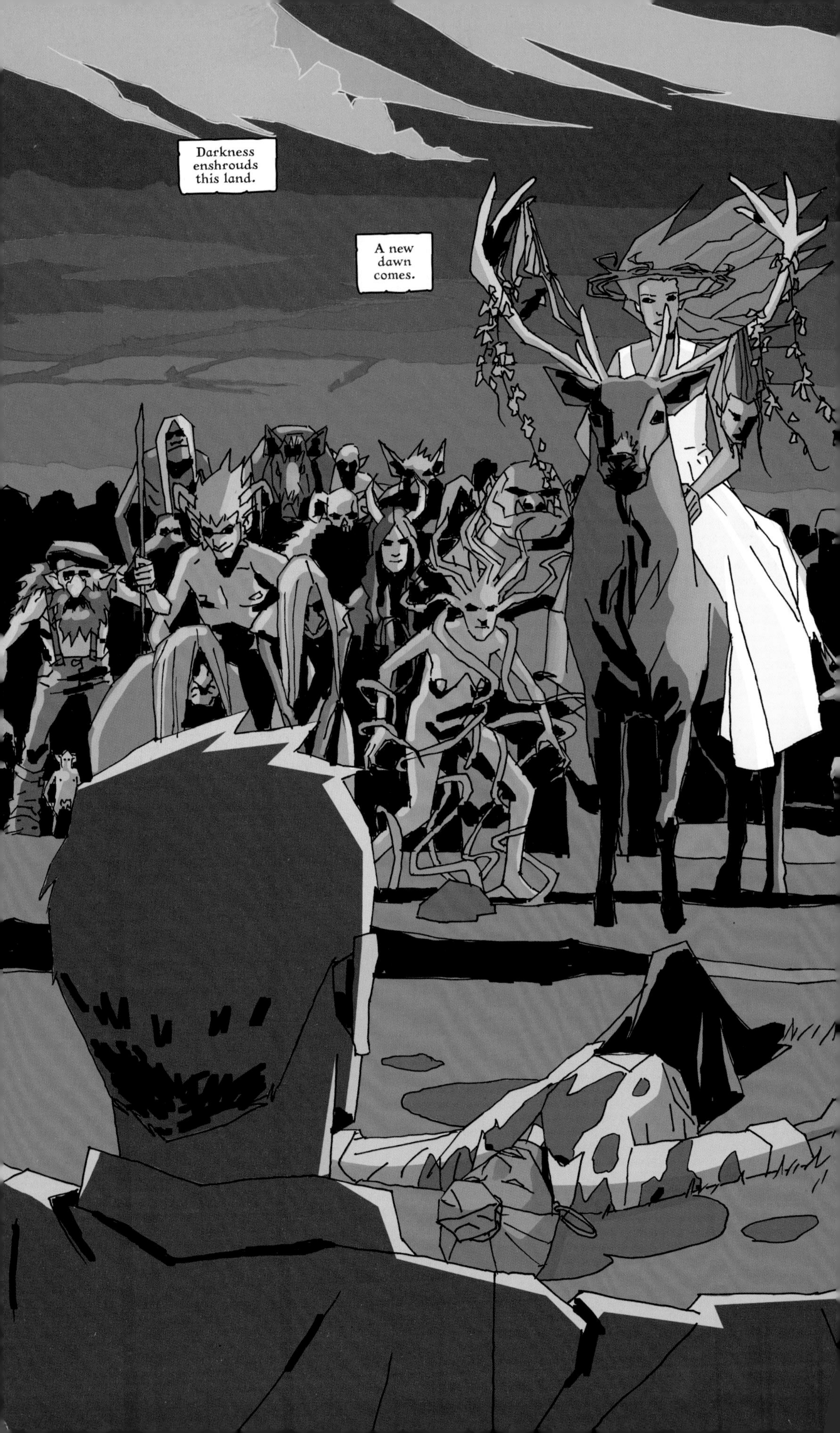
Darkness enshrouds this land.
A new dawn comes.

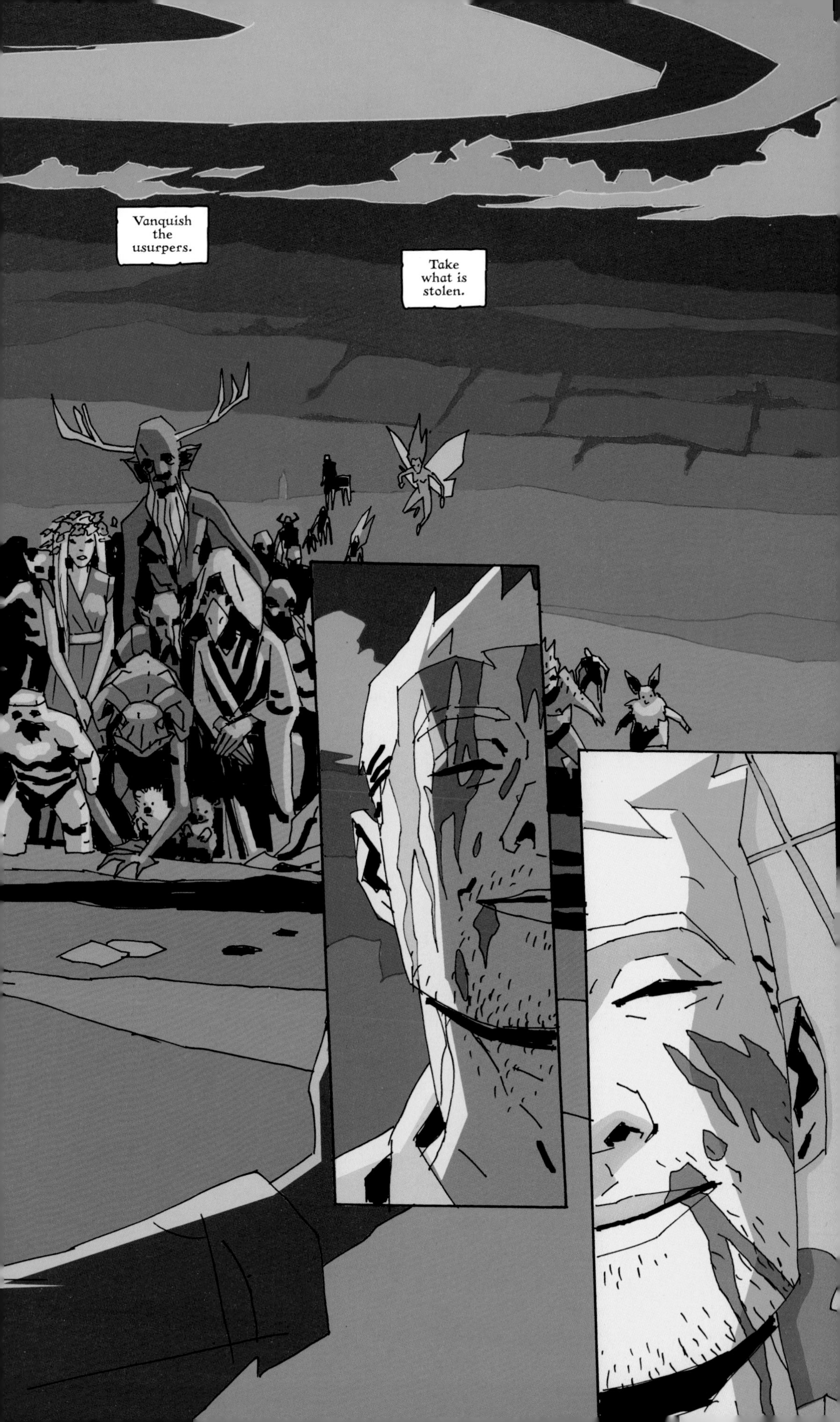
Vanquish the usurpers.
Take what is stolen.

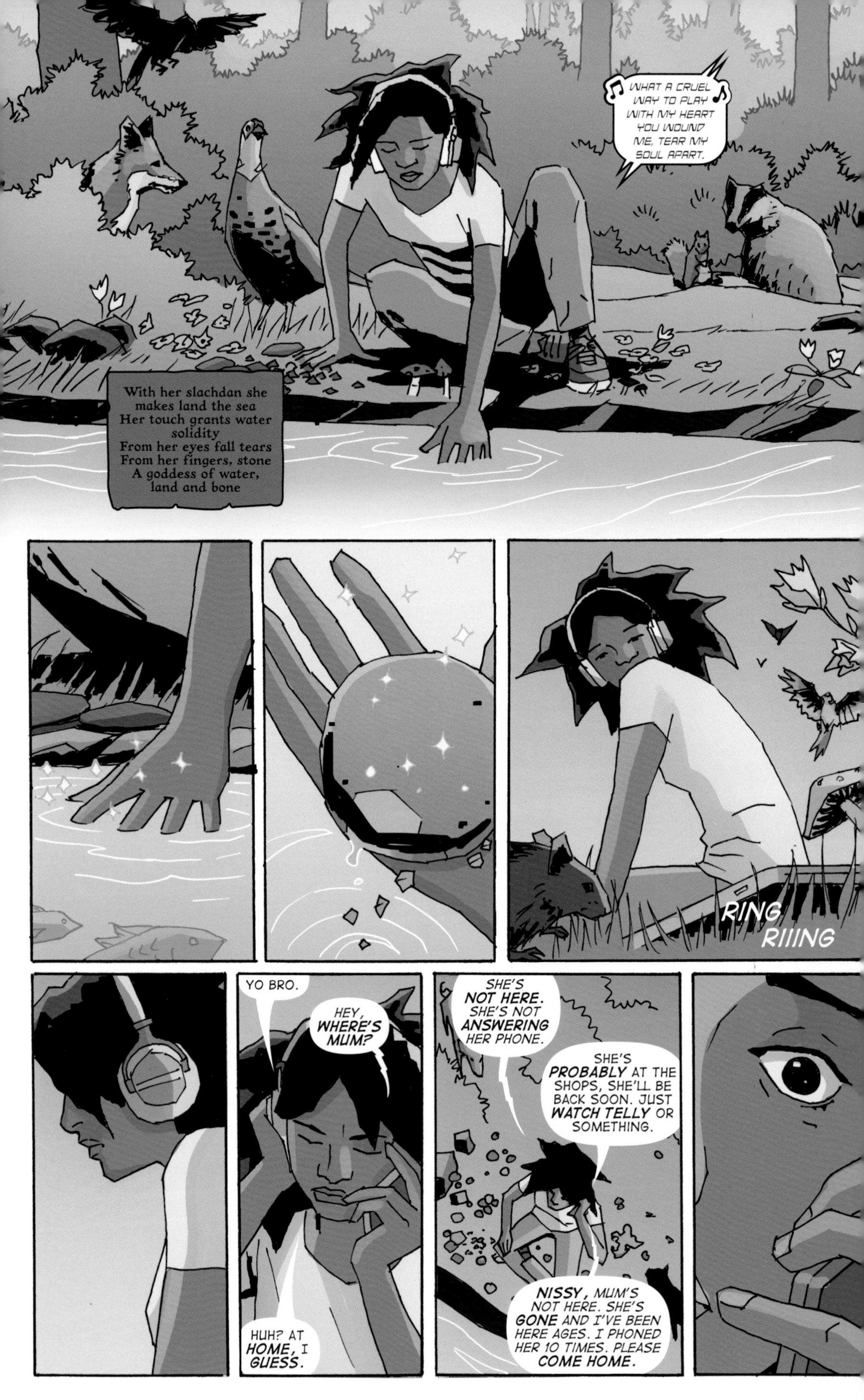
WHAT A CRUEL WAY TO PLAY WITH MY HEART YOU WOUND ME, TEAR MY SOUL APART.
With her slachdan she makes land the sea Her touch grants water solidity From her eyes fall tears From her fingers, stone A goddess of water, land and bone
RING RIIING
YO BRO.
HEY, WHERE'S MUM?
HUH? AT HOME, I GUESS.
SHE'S NOT HERE. SHE'S NOT ANSWERING HER PHONE.
SHE'S PROBABLY AT THE SHOPS, SHE'LL BE BACK SOON. JUST WATCH TELLY OR SOMETHING.
NISSY, MUM'S NOT HERE. SHE'S GONE AND I'VE BEEN HERE AGES. I PHONED HER 10 TIMES. PLEASE COME HOME.

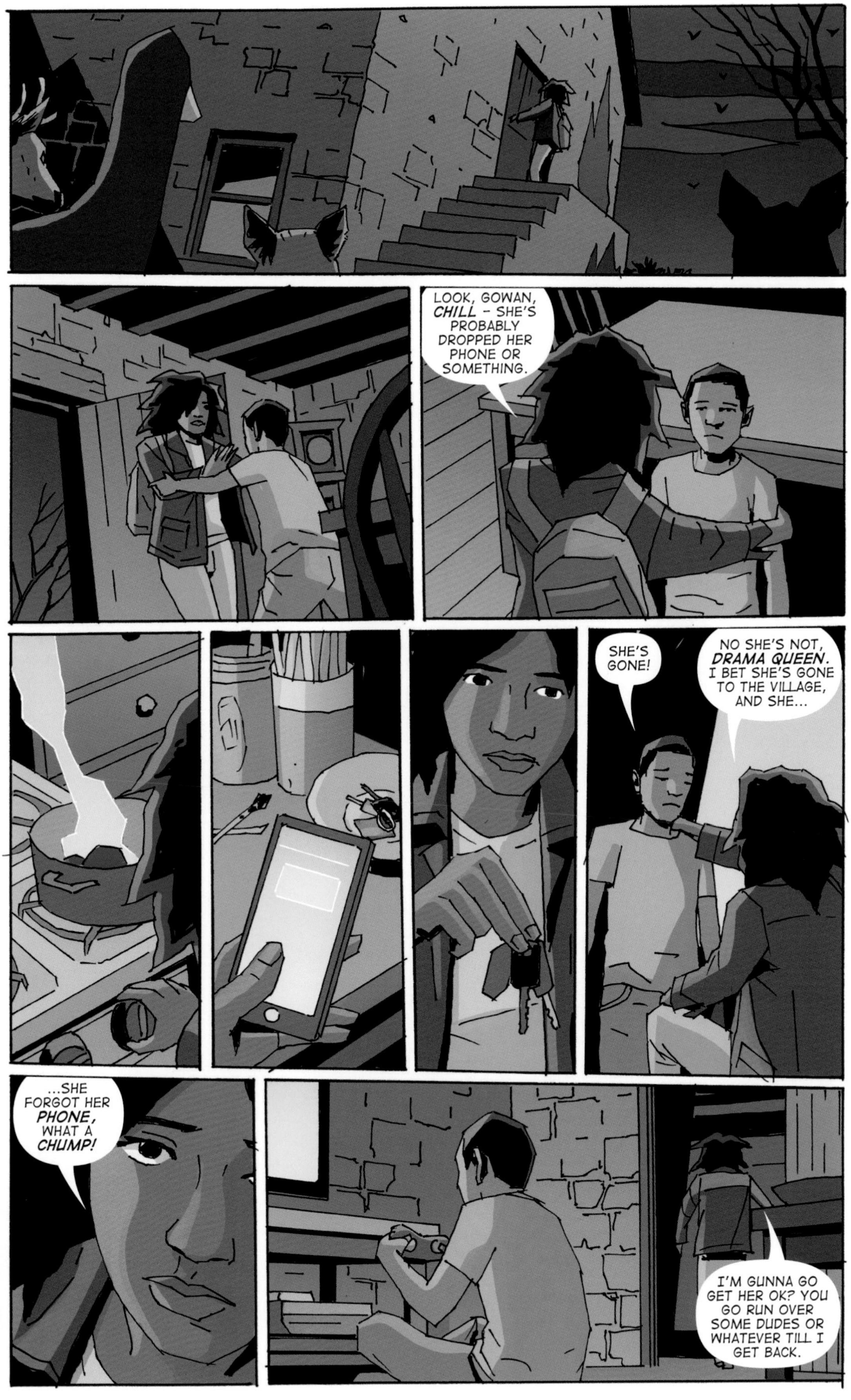
LOOK, GOWAN, CHILL - SHE'S PROBABLY DROPPED HER PHONE OR SOMETHING.
SHE'S GONE!
NO SHE'S NOT, DRAMA QUEEN. I BET SHE'S GONE TO THE VILLAGE, AND SHE...
...SHE FORGOT HER PHONE, WHAT A CHUMP!
I'M GUNNA GO GET HER OK? YOU GO RUN OVER SOME DUDES OR WHATEVER TILL I GET BACK.

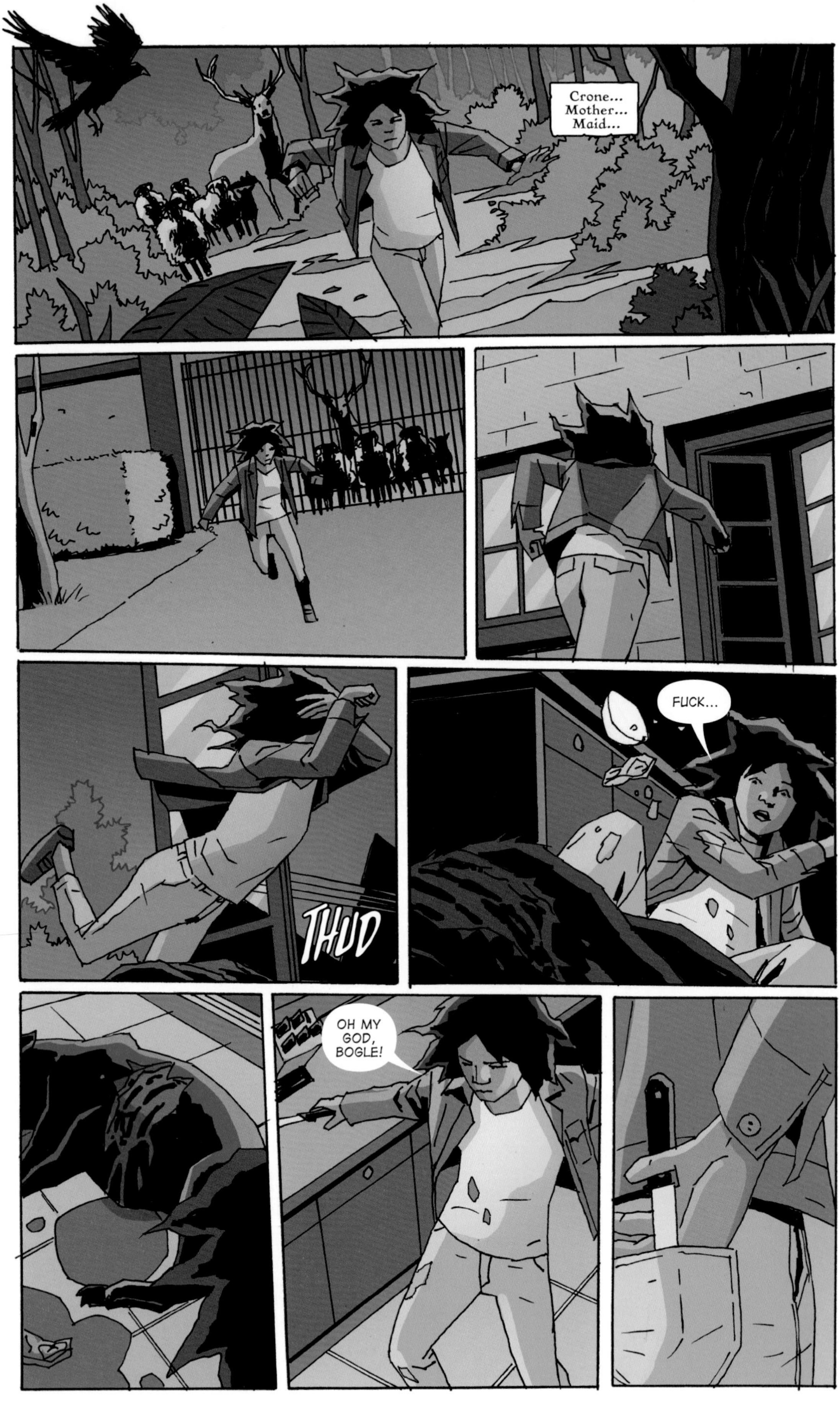
Crone... Mother... Maid...
THUD
FUCK...
OH MY GOD, BOGLE!

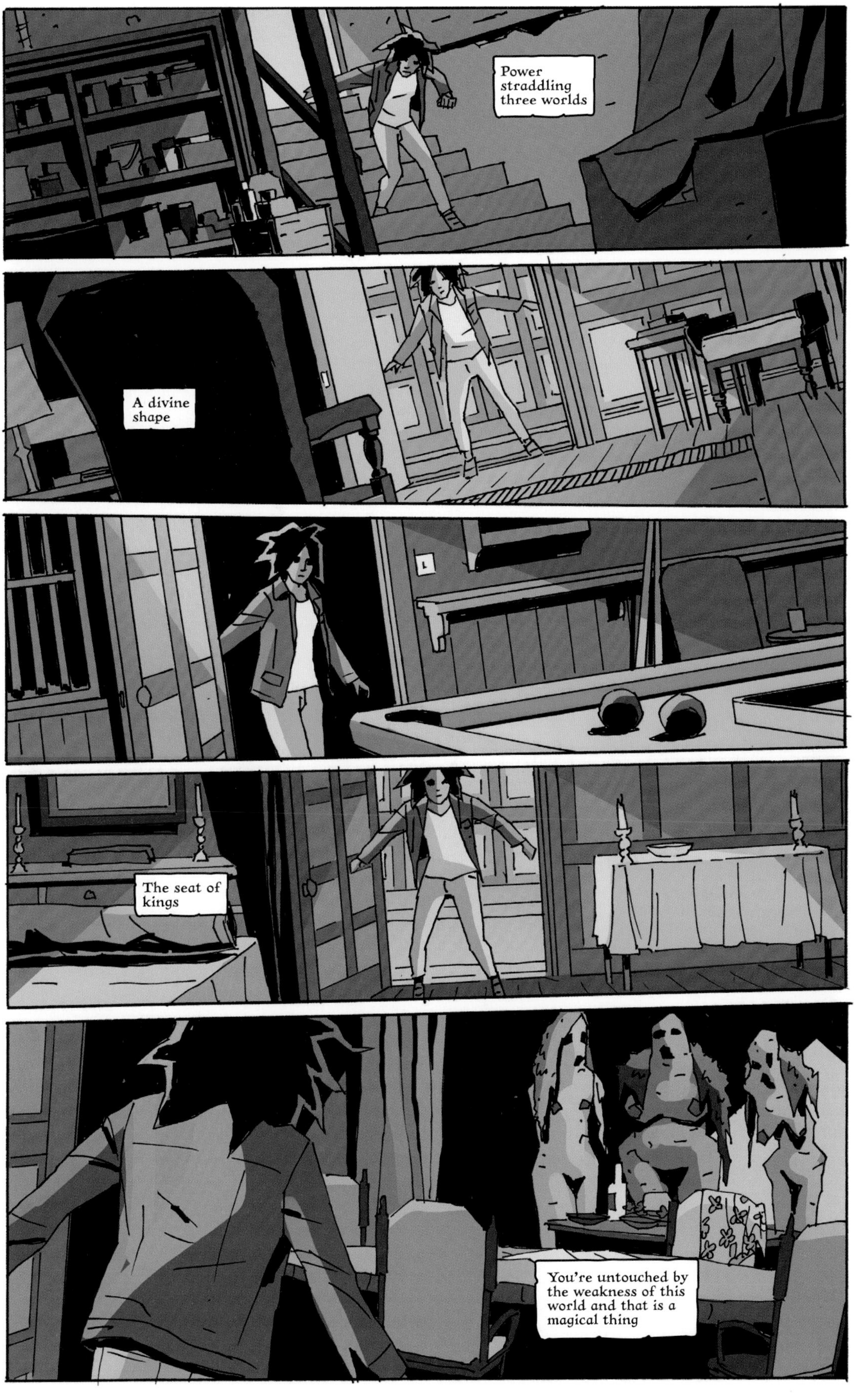
Power straddling three worlds
A divine shape
The seat of kings
You're untouched by the weakness of this world and that is a magical thing

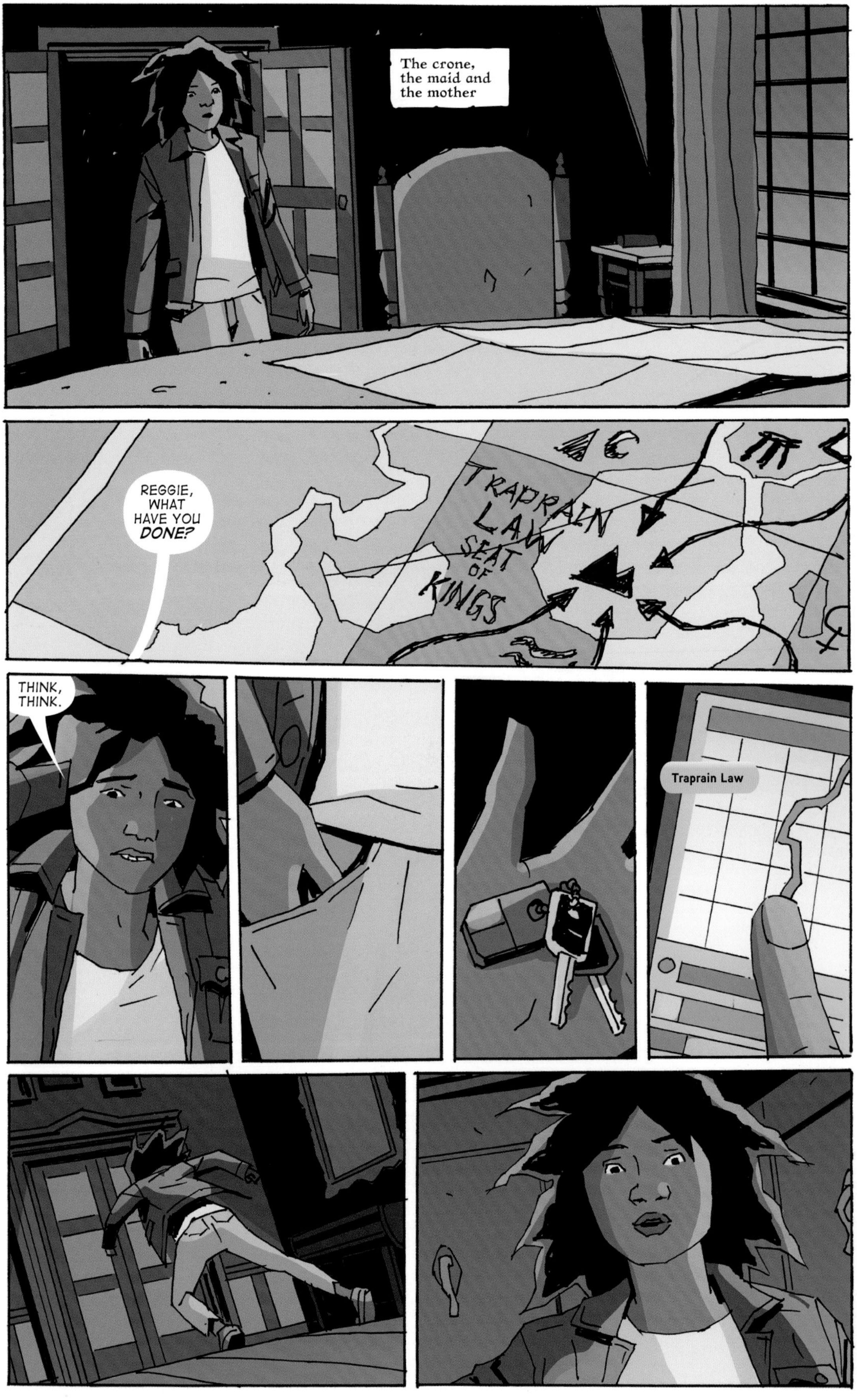
The crone, the maid and the mother
REGGIE, WHAT HAVE YOU DONE?
TRAPRAIN LAW SEAT OF KINGS
THINK, THINK.
Traprain Law

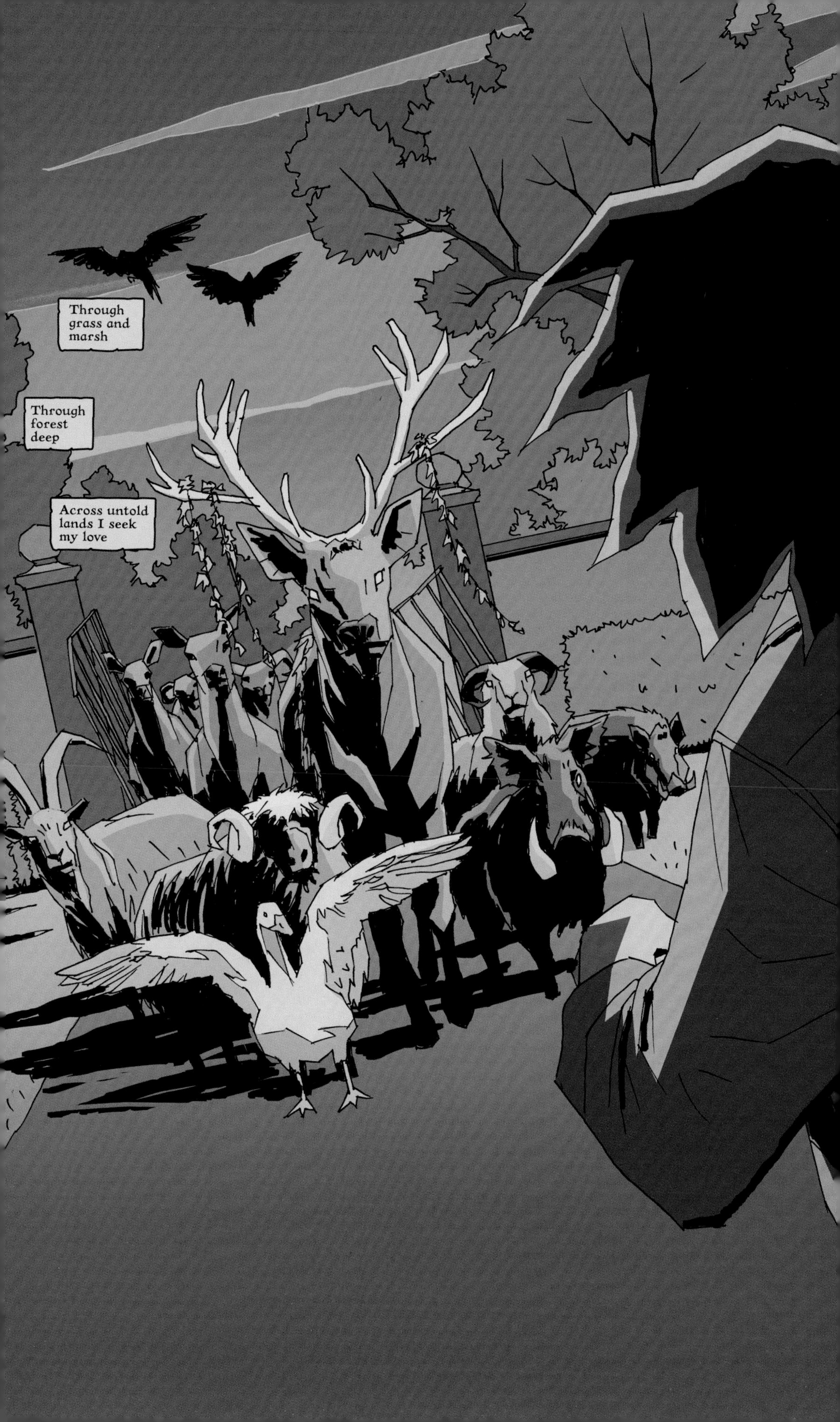
Through grass and marsh
Through forest deep
Across untold lands I seek my love

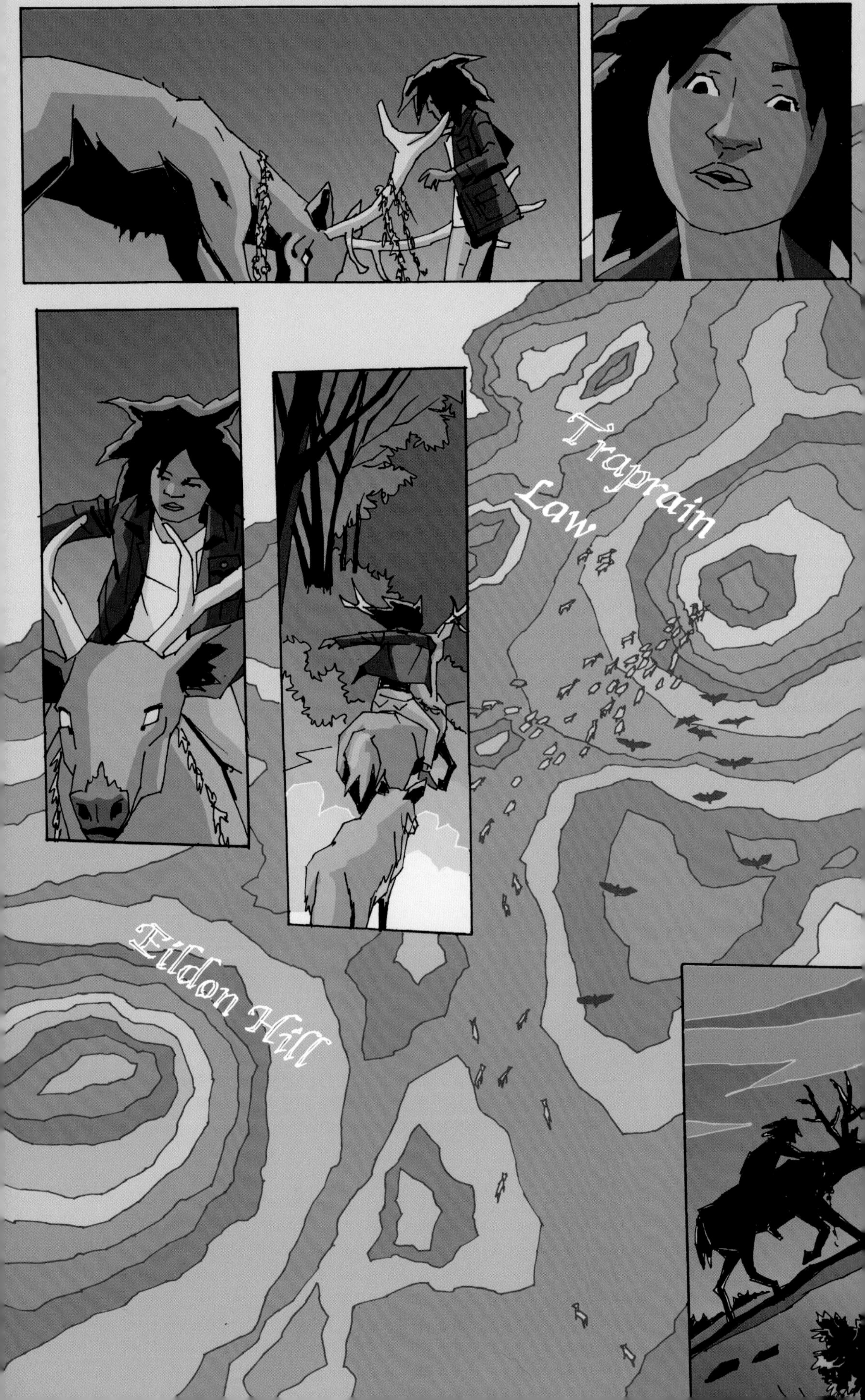
Traprain Law
Eildon Hill

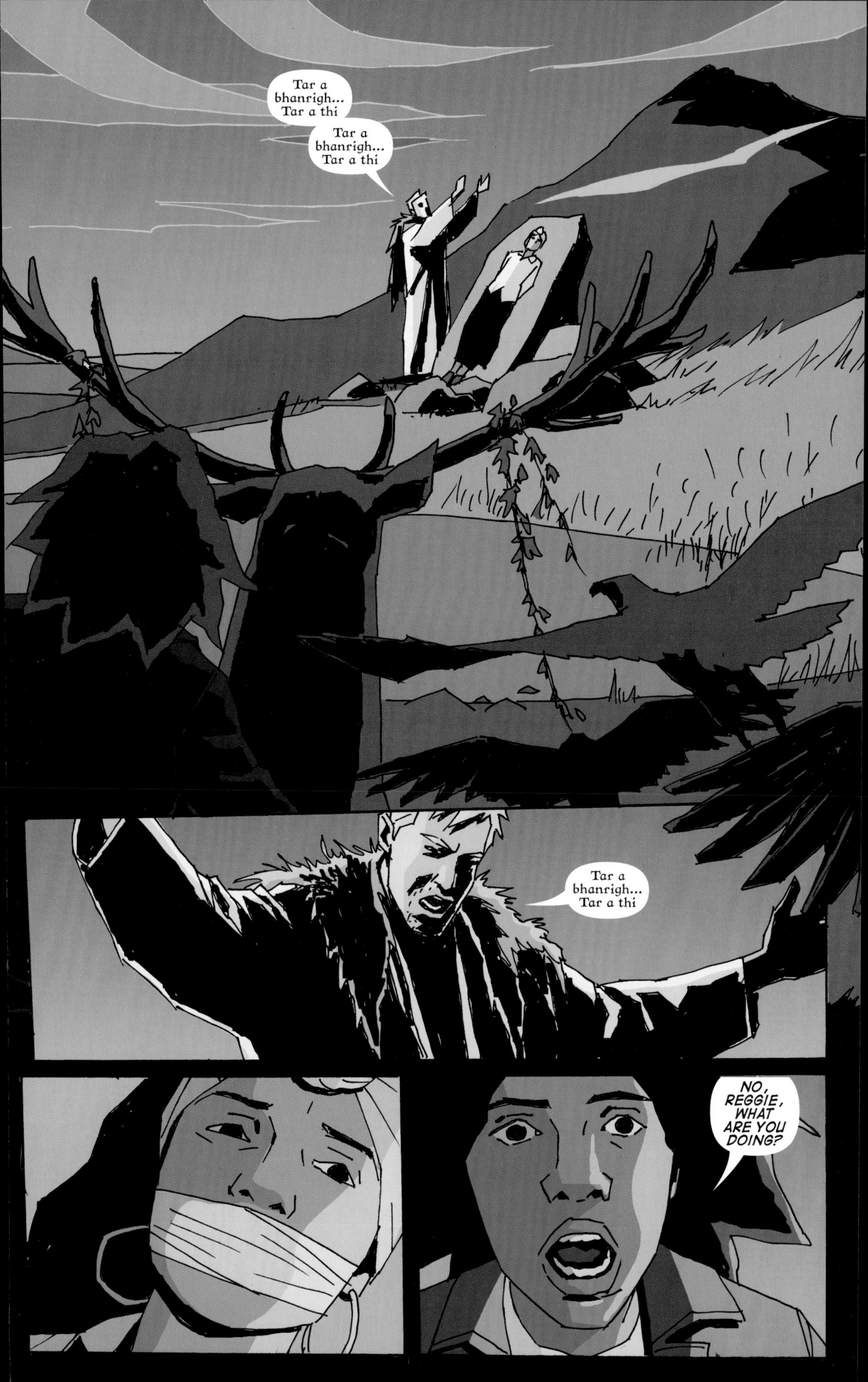
Tar a bhanrigh... Tar a thi
Tar a bhanrigh... Tar a thi
Tar a bhanrigh... Tar a thi
NO, REGGIE, WHAT ARE YOU DOING?

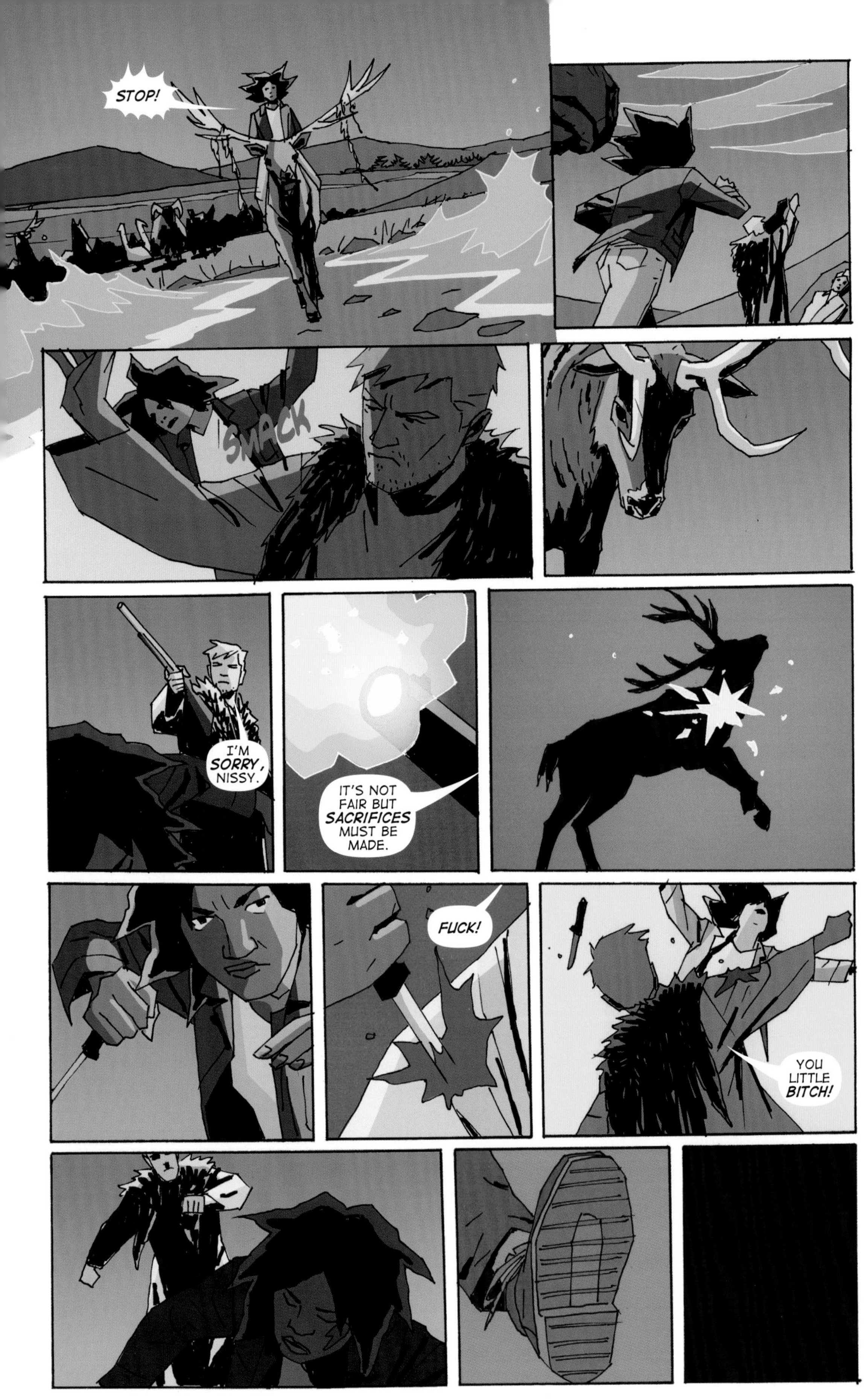
STOP!
SMACK
I'M SORRY, NISSY.
IT'S NOT FAIR BUT SACRIFICES MUST BE MADE.
FUCK!
YOU LITTLE BITCH!

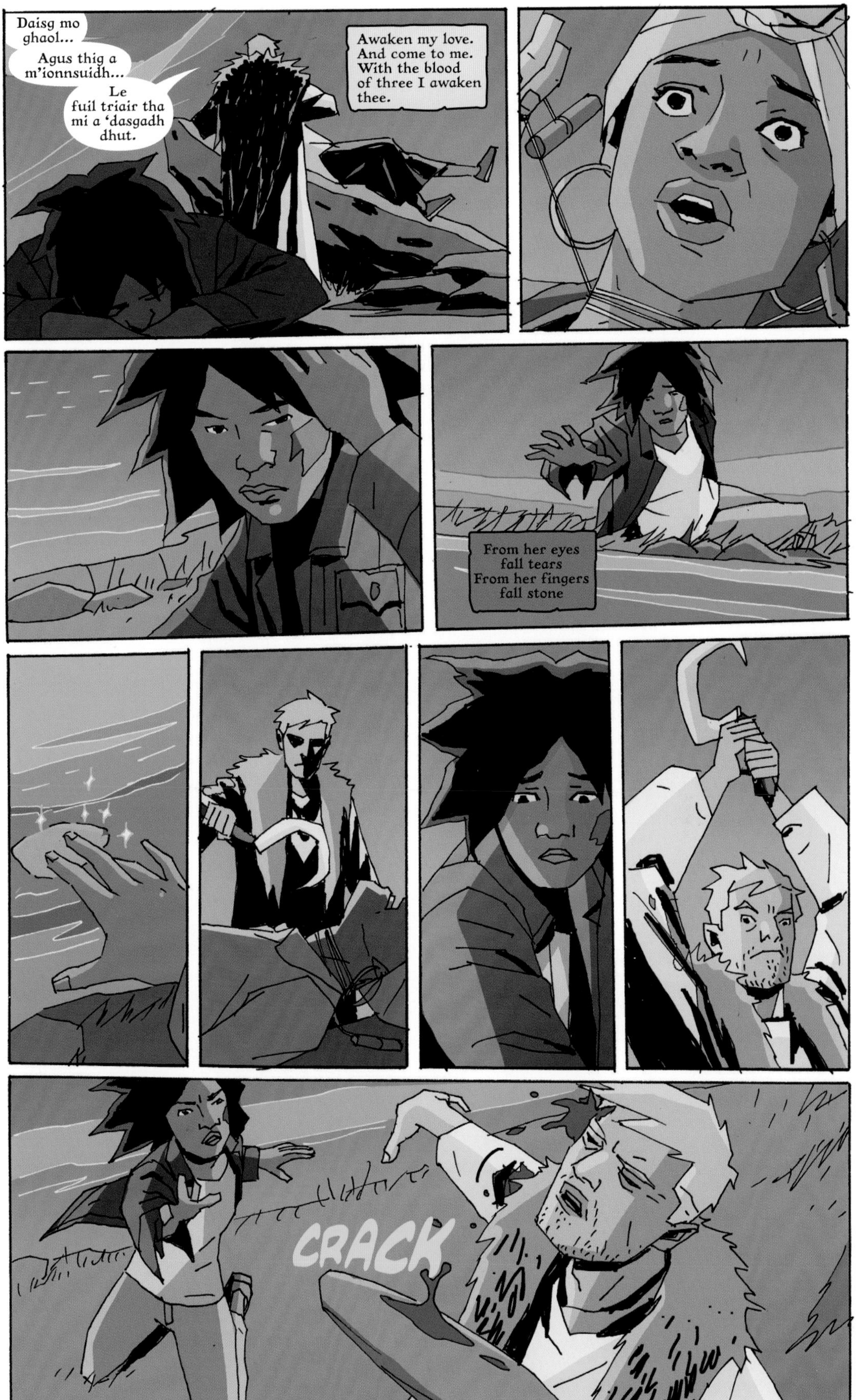
Daisg mo ghaol...
Agus thig a m'ionnsuidh...
Le fuil triair tha mi a 'dasgadh dhut.
Awaken my love. And come to me. With the blood of three I awaken thee.
From her eyes fall tears From her fingers fall stone
CRACK

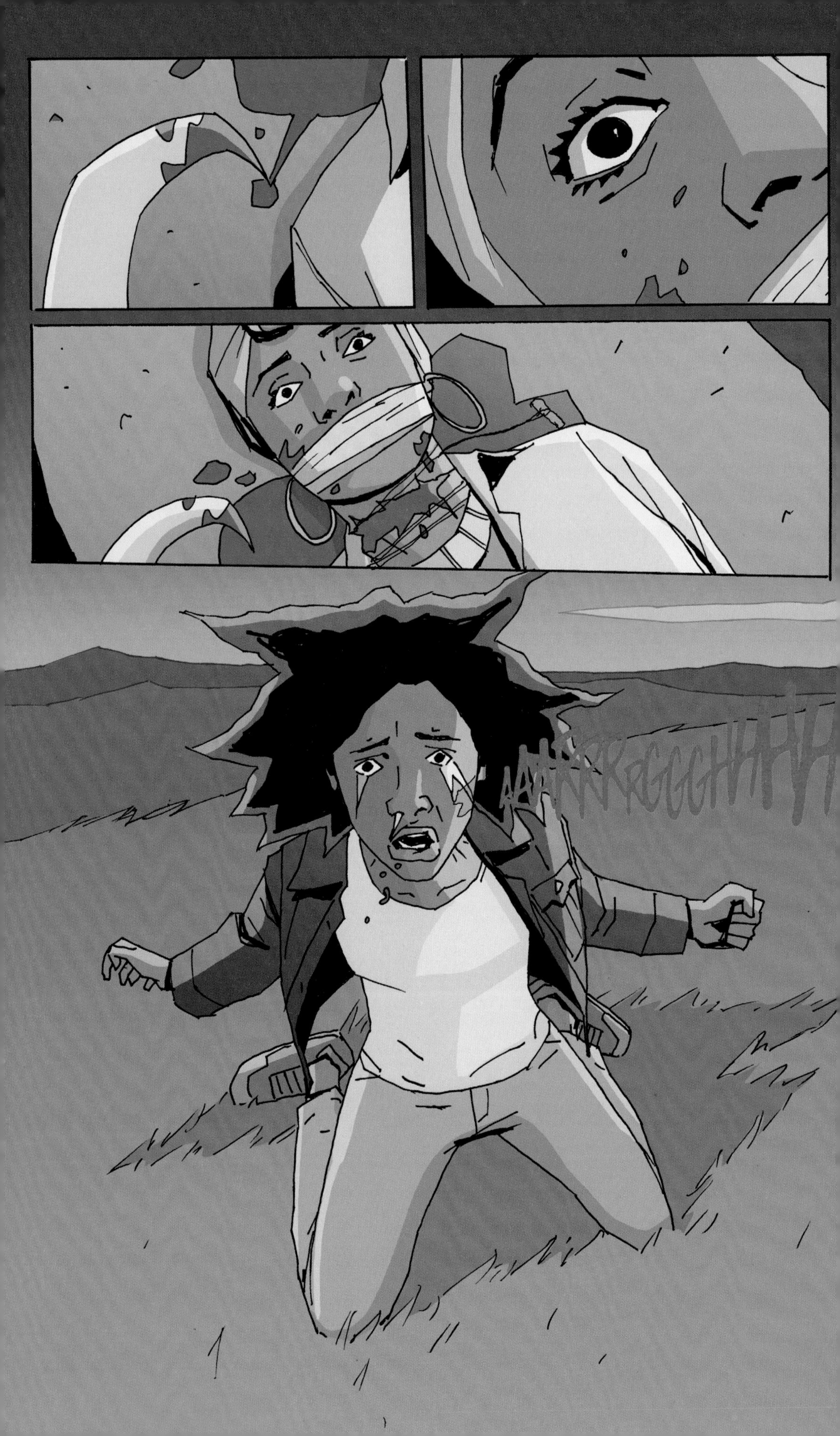
AAARRRGGHHHH

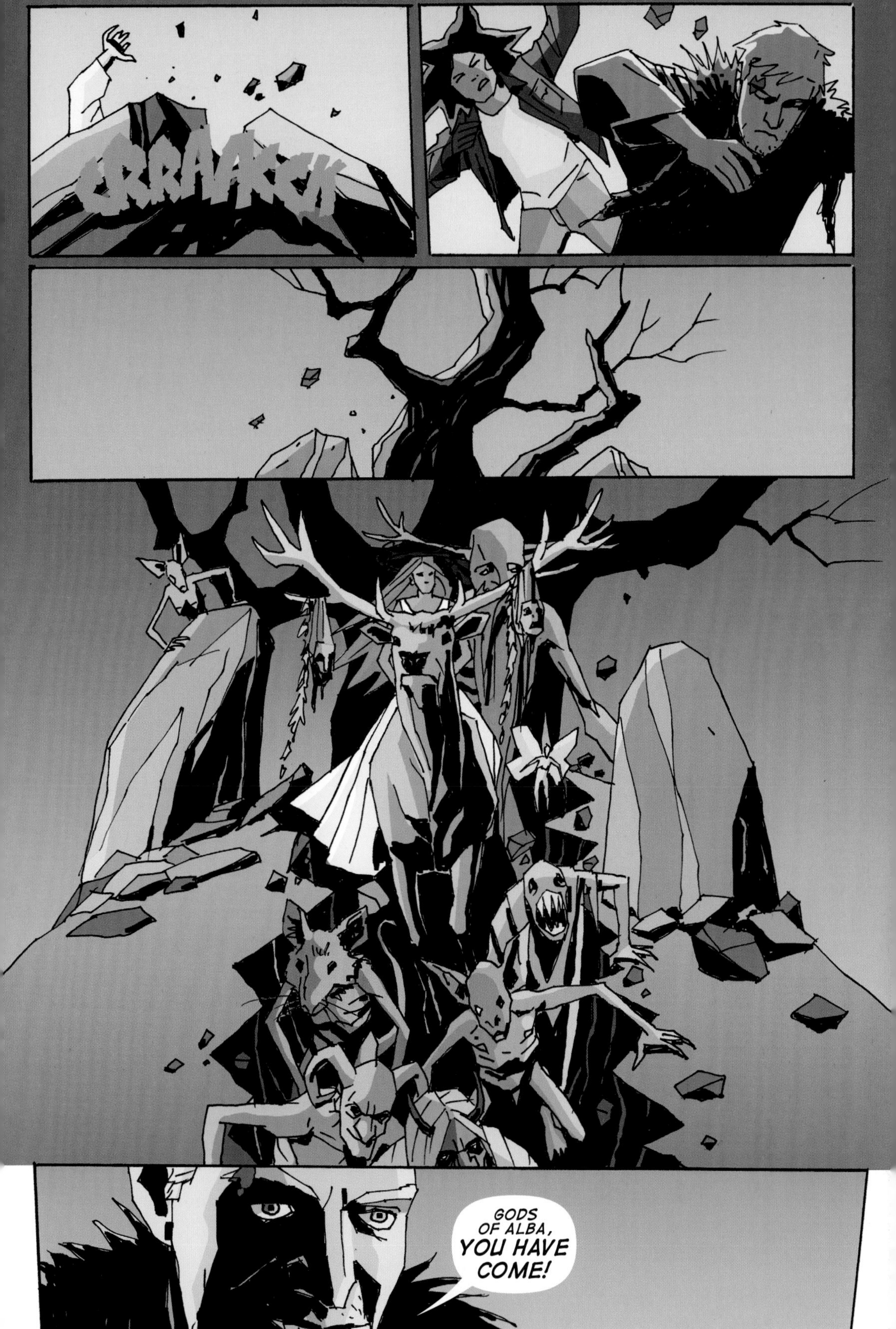
CRRAACK
GODS OF ALBA, YOU HAVE COME!

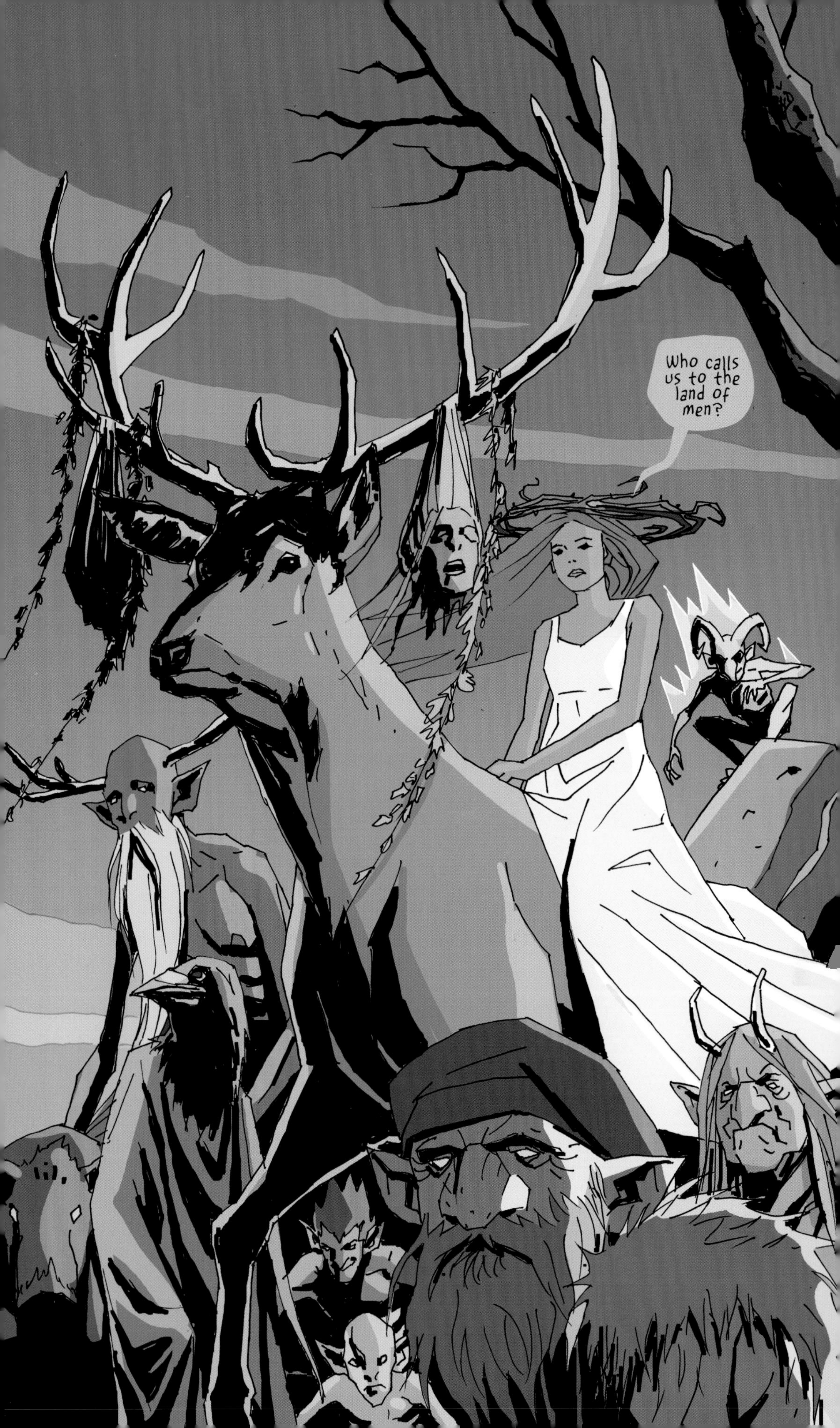
Who calls us to the land of men?

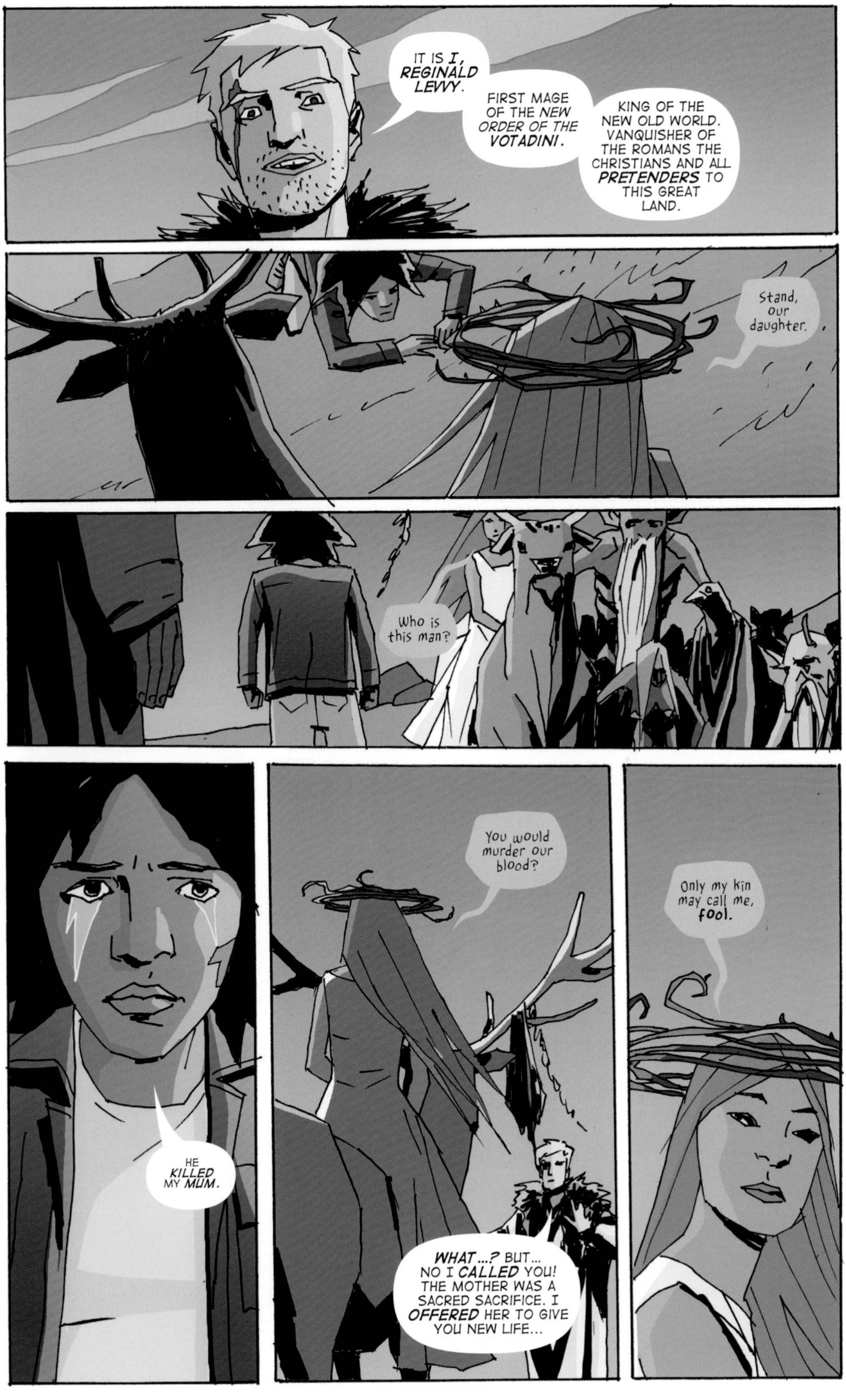
IT IS I, REGINALD LEVVY.
FIRST MAGE OF THE NEW ORDER OF THE VOTADINI.
KING OF THE NEW OLD WORLD. VANQUISHER OF THE ROMANS THE CHRISTIANS AND ALL PRETENDERS TO THIS GREAT LAND.
Stand, our daughter.
Who is this man?
HE KILLED MY MUM.
You would murder our blood?
WHAT...? BUT... NO I CALLED YOU! THE MOTHER WAS A SACRED SACRIFICE. I OFFERED HER TO GIVE YOU NEW LIFE...
Only my kin may call me, fool.

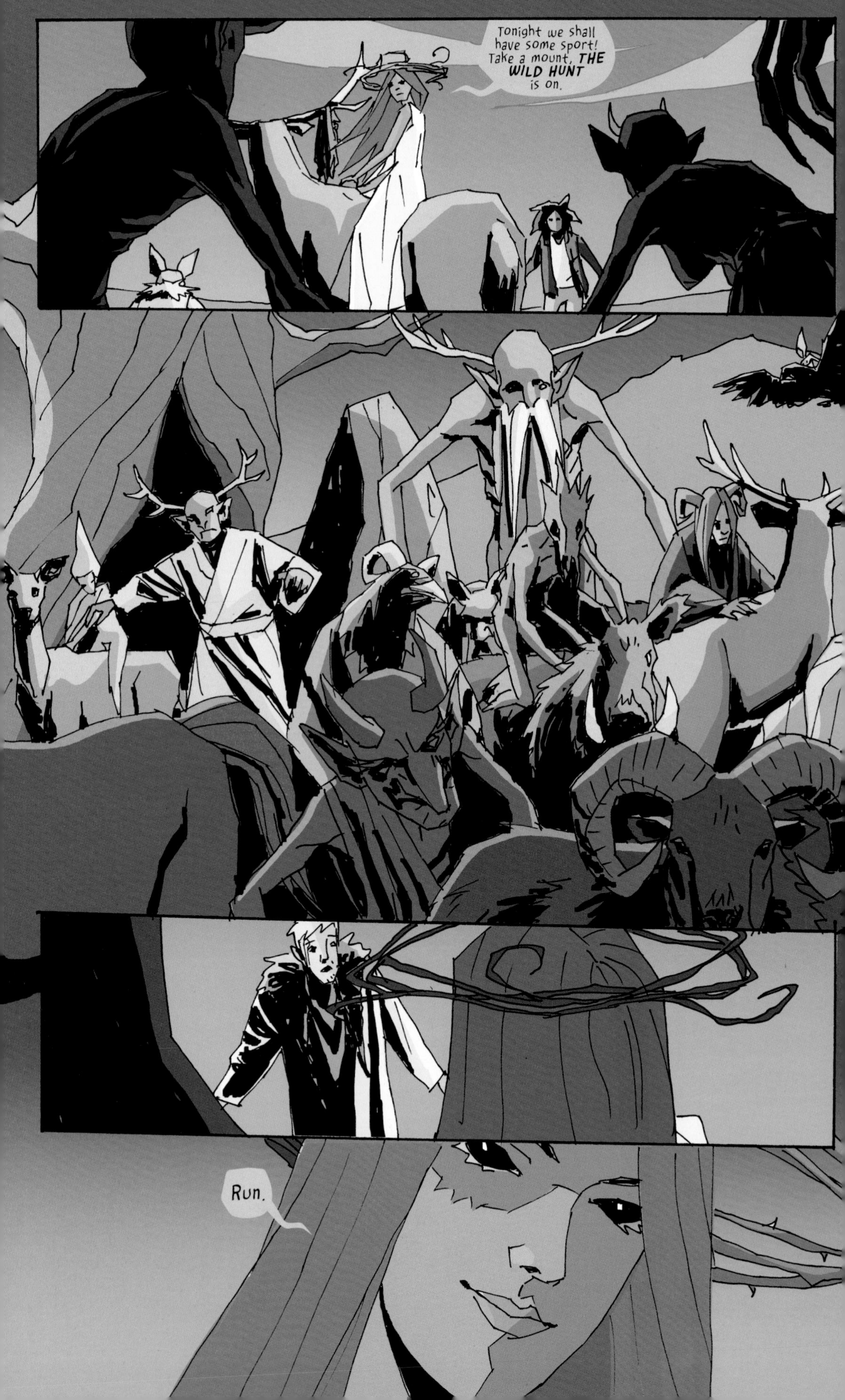
Tonight we shall have some sport! Take a mount, THE WILD HUNT is on.
Run.

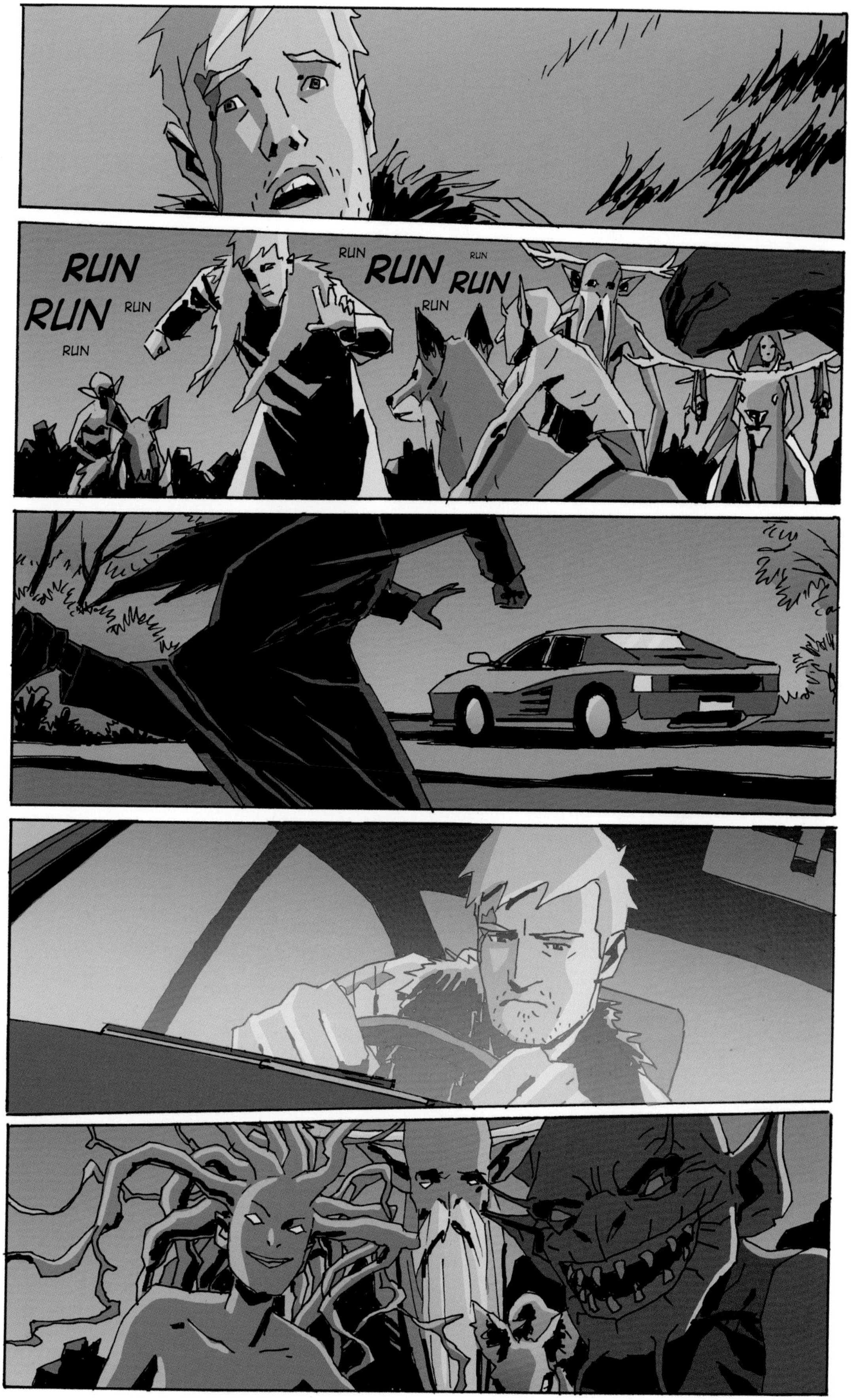
RUN
RUN
RUN
RUN
RUN
RUN
RUN
RUN
RUN
RUN

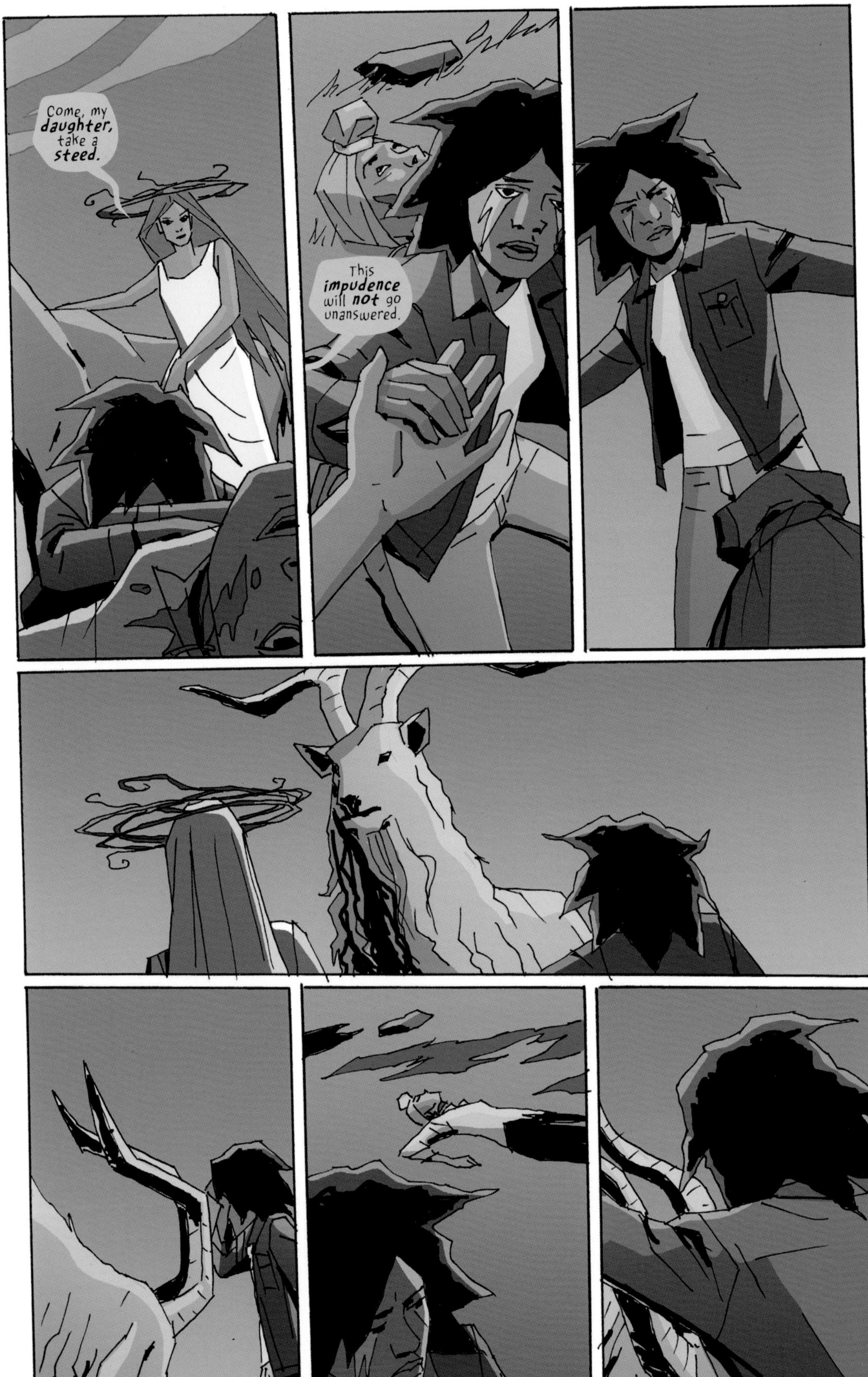
Come, my **daughter,** take a **steed.**
This **impudence** will **not** go unanswered.

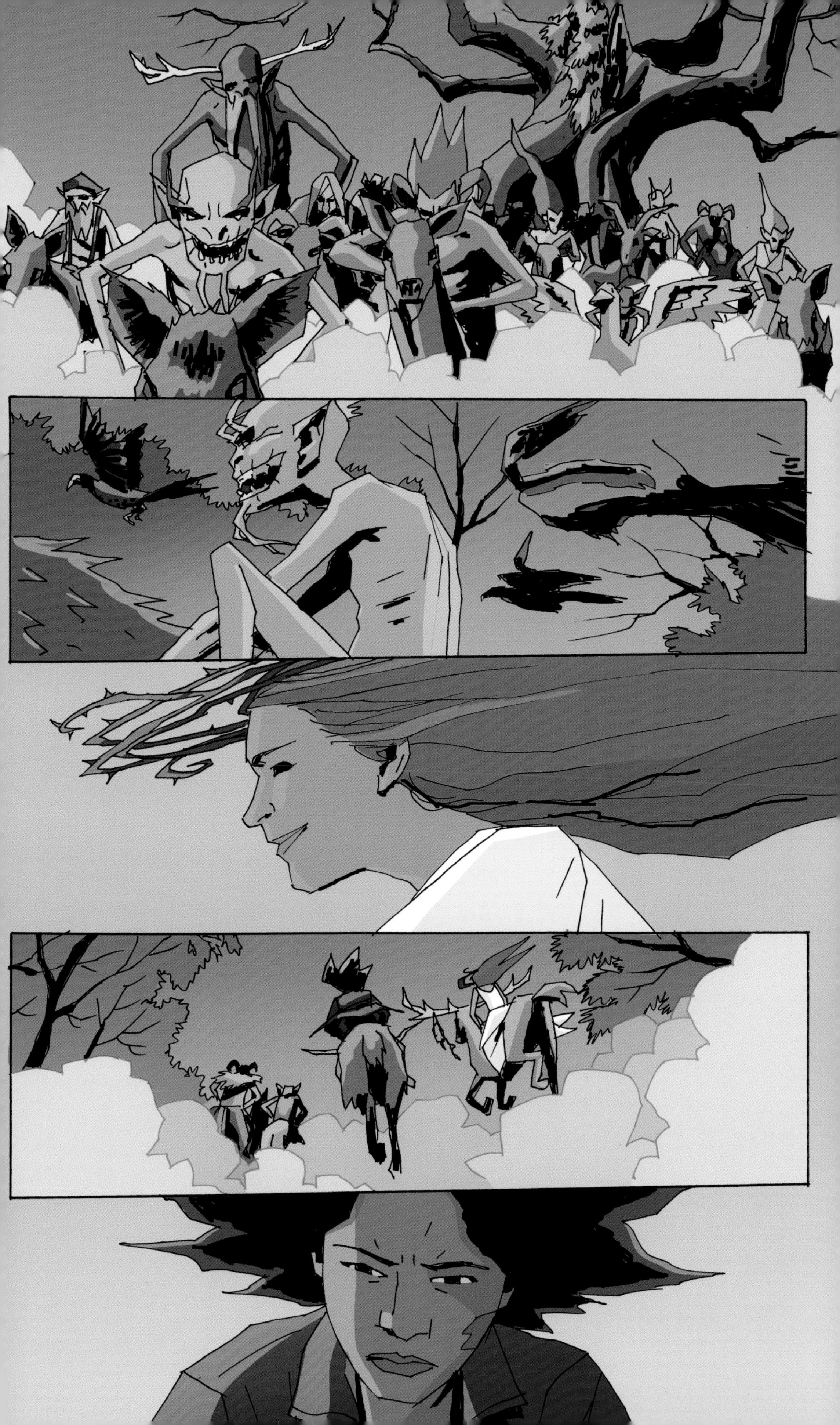

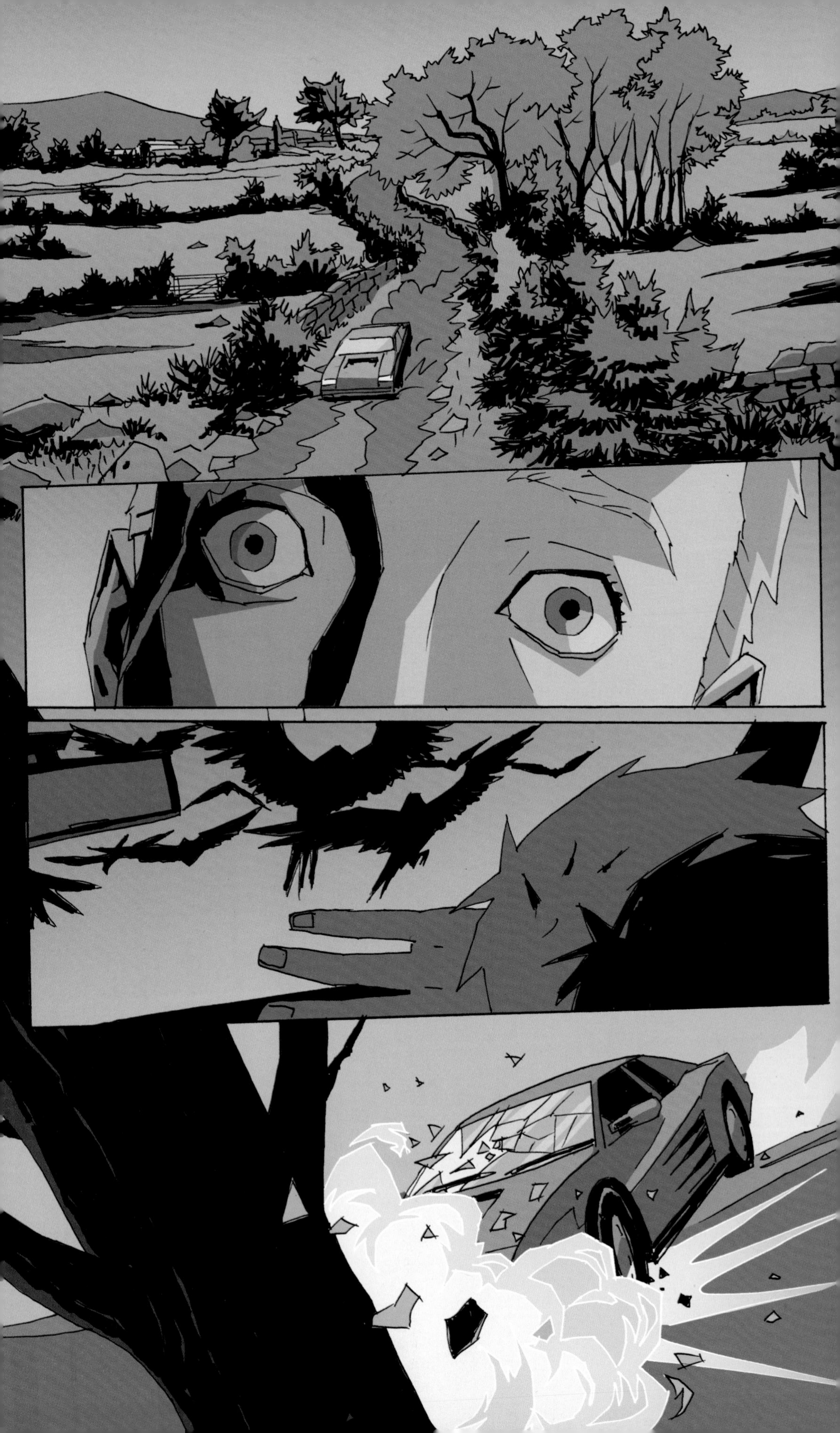

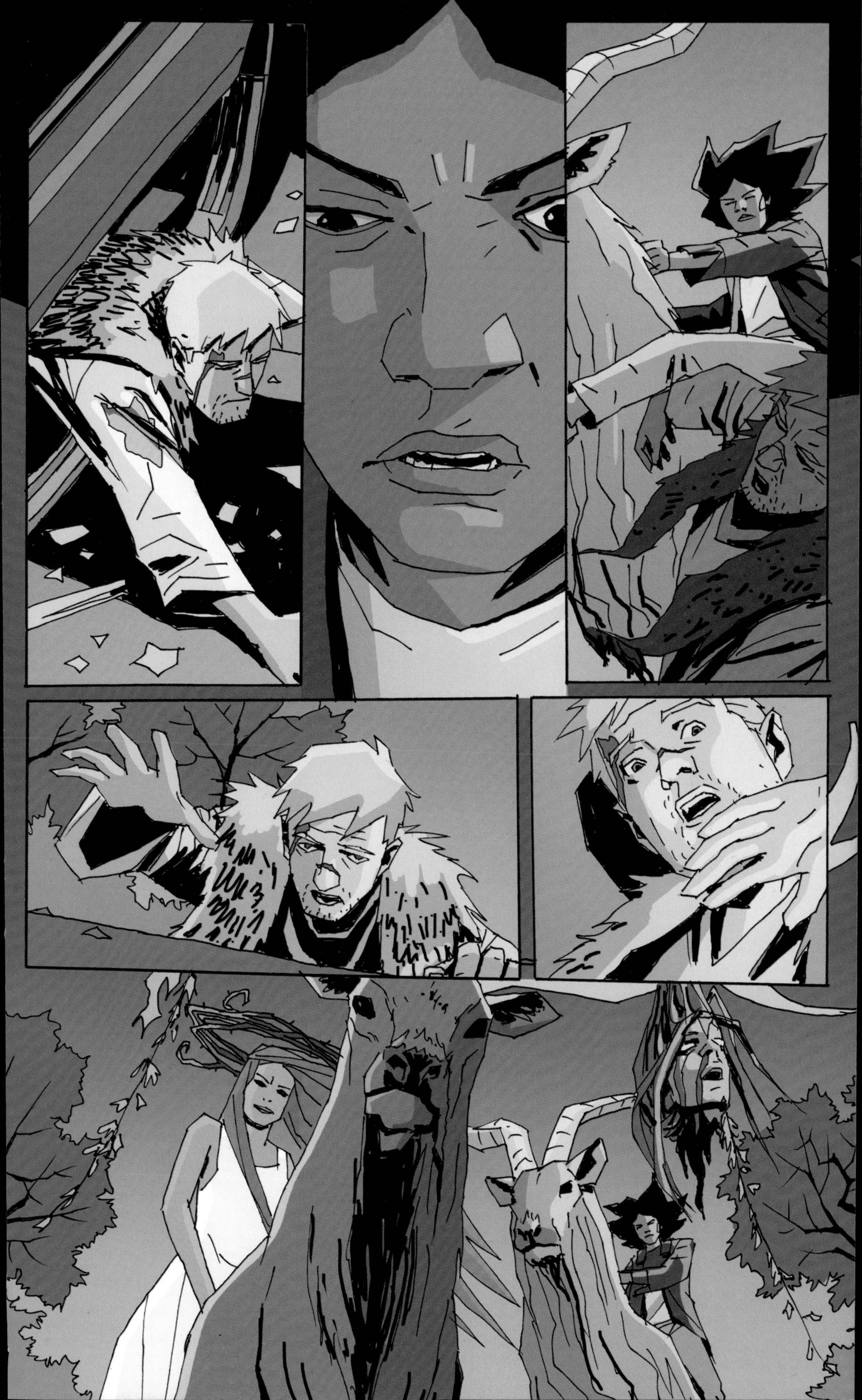

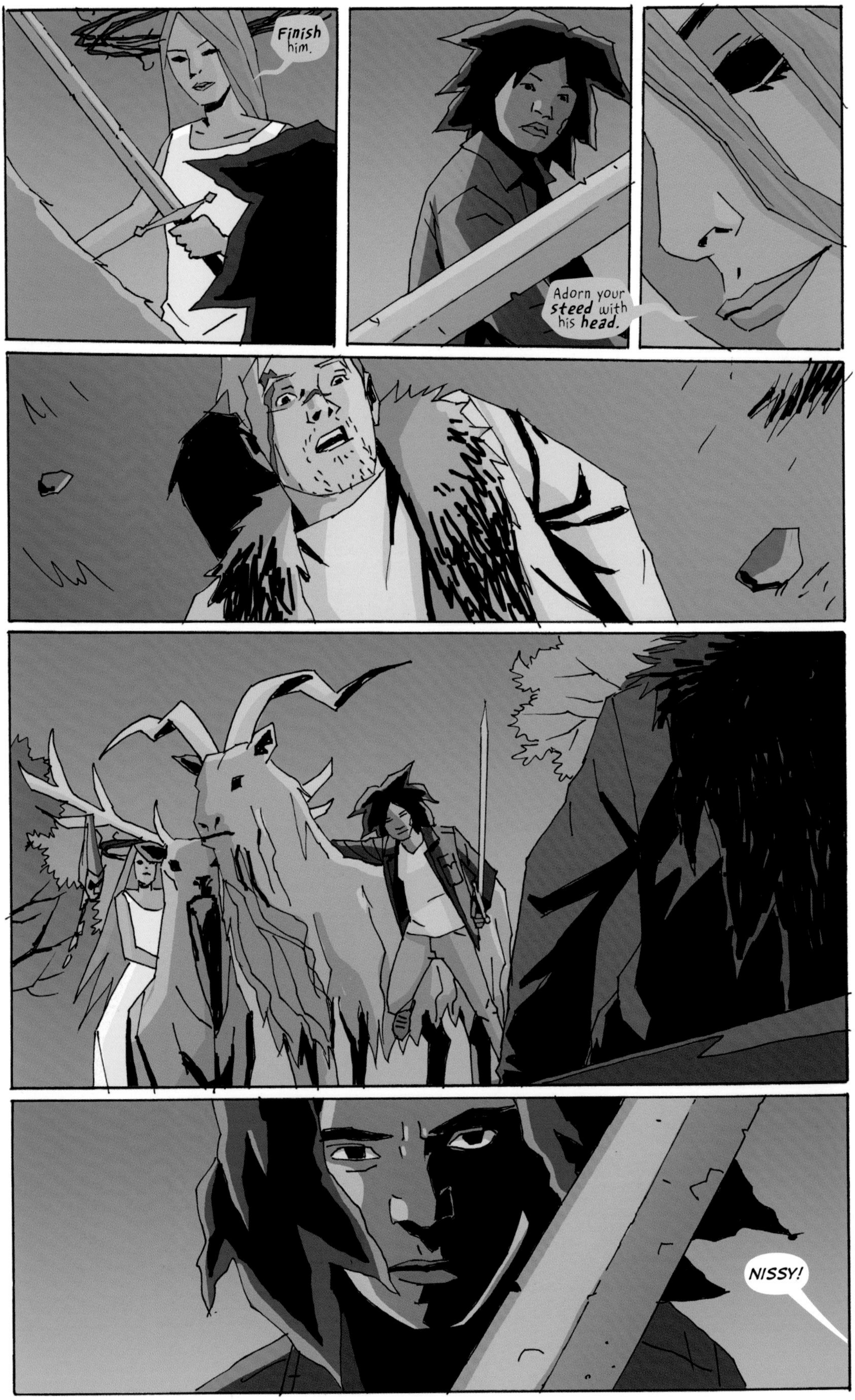
Finish him.
Adorn your steed with his head.
NISSY!

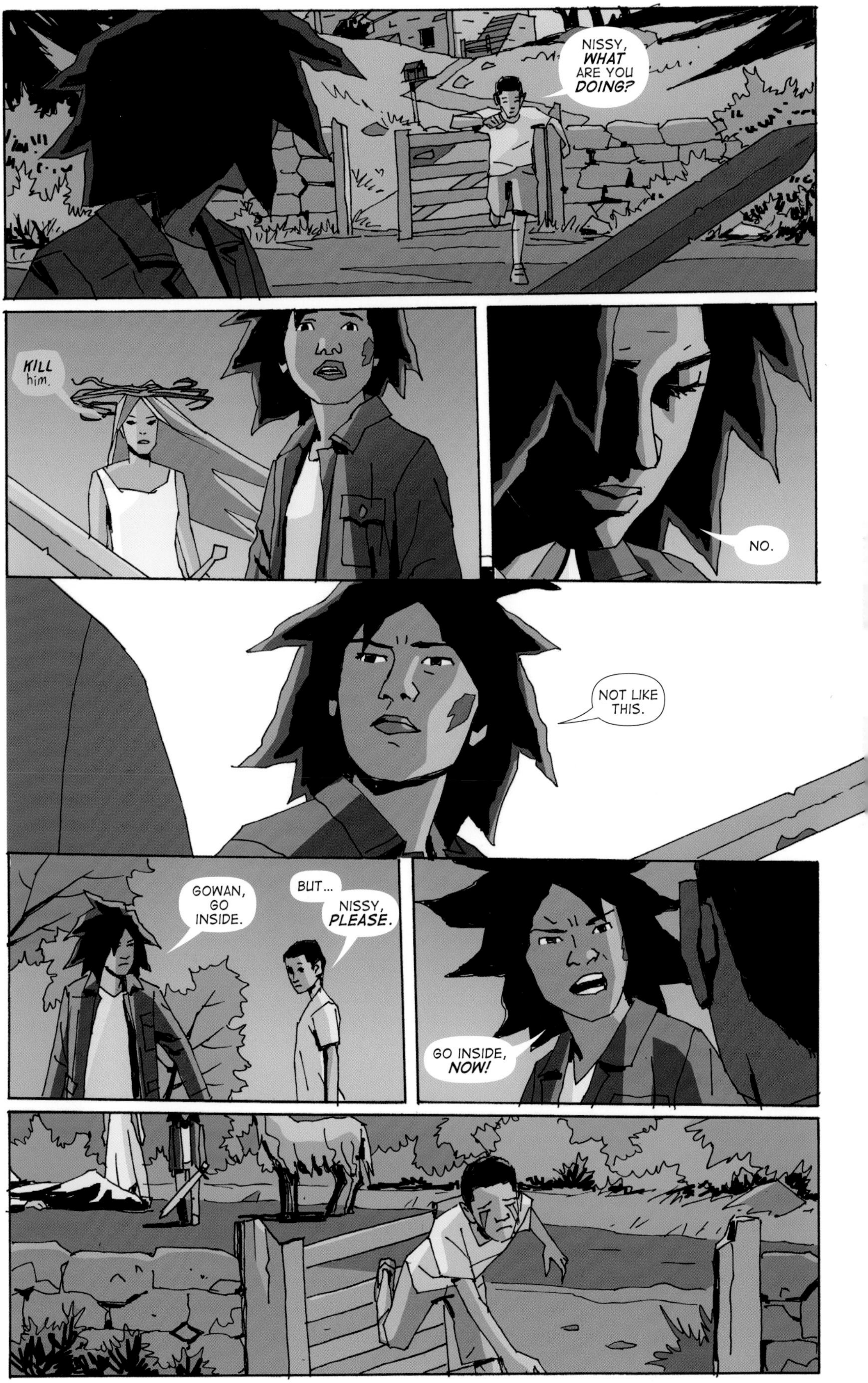
NISSY, WHAT ARE YOU DOING?
KILL him.
NO.
NOT LIKE THIS.
GOWAN, GO INSIDE.
BUT...
NISSY, PLEASE.
GO INSIDE, NOW!

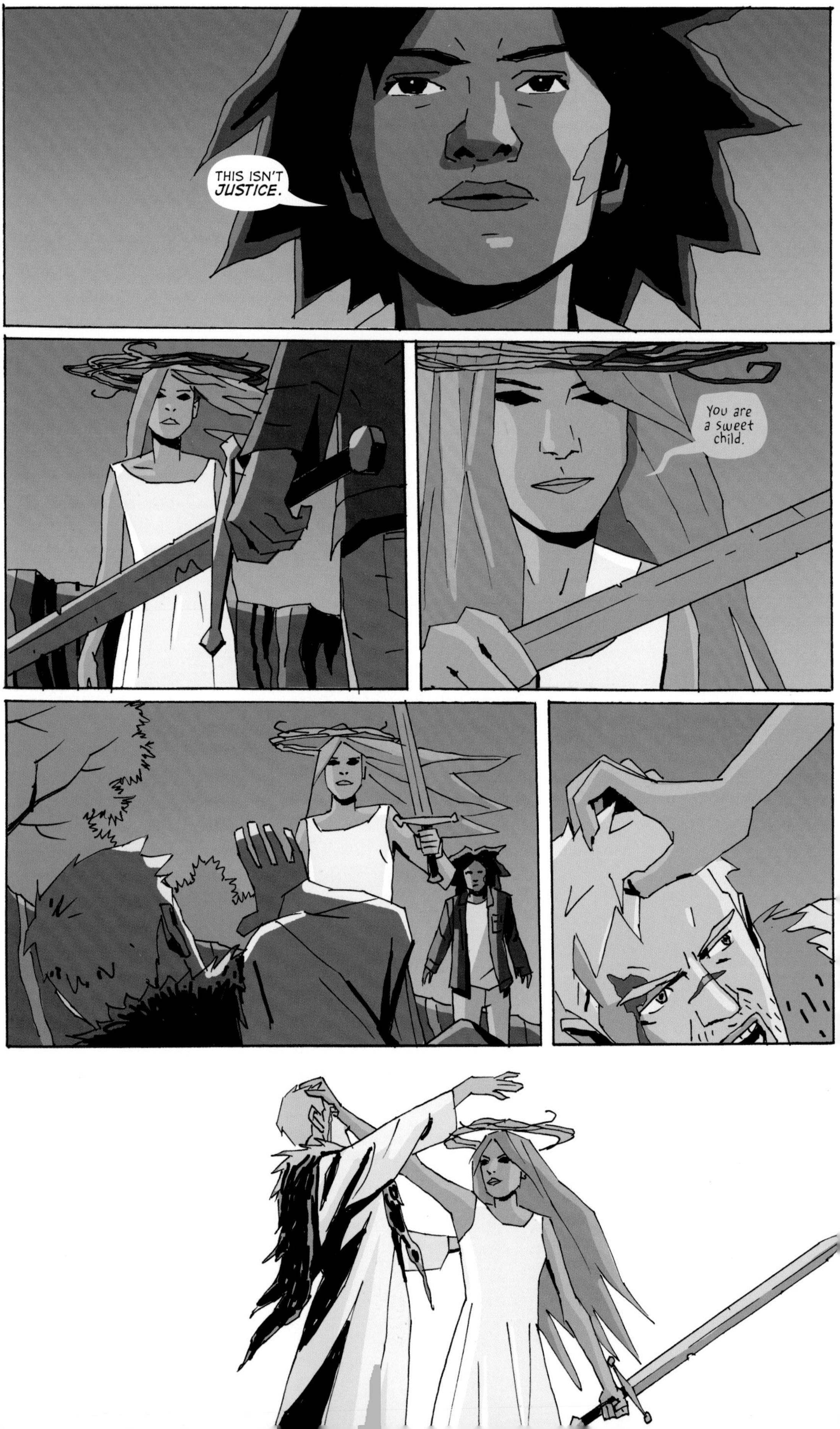
THIS ISN'T JUSTICE.
You are a sweet child.

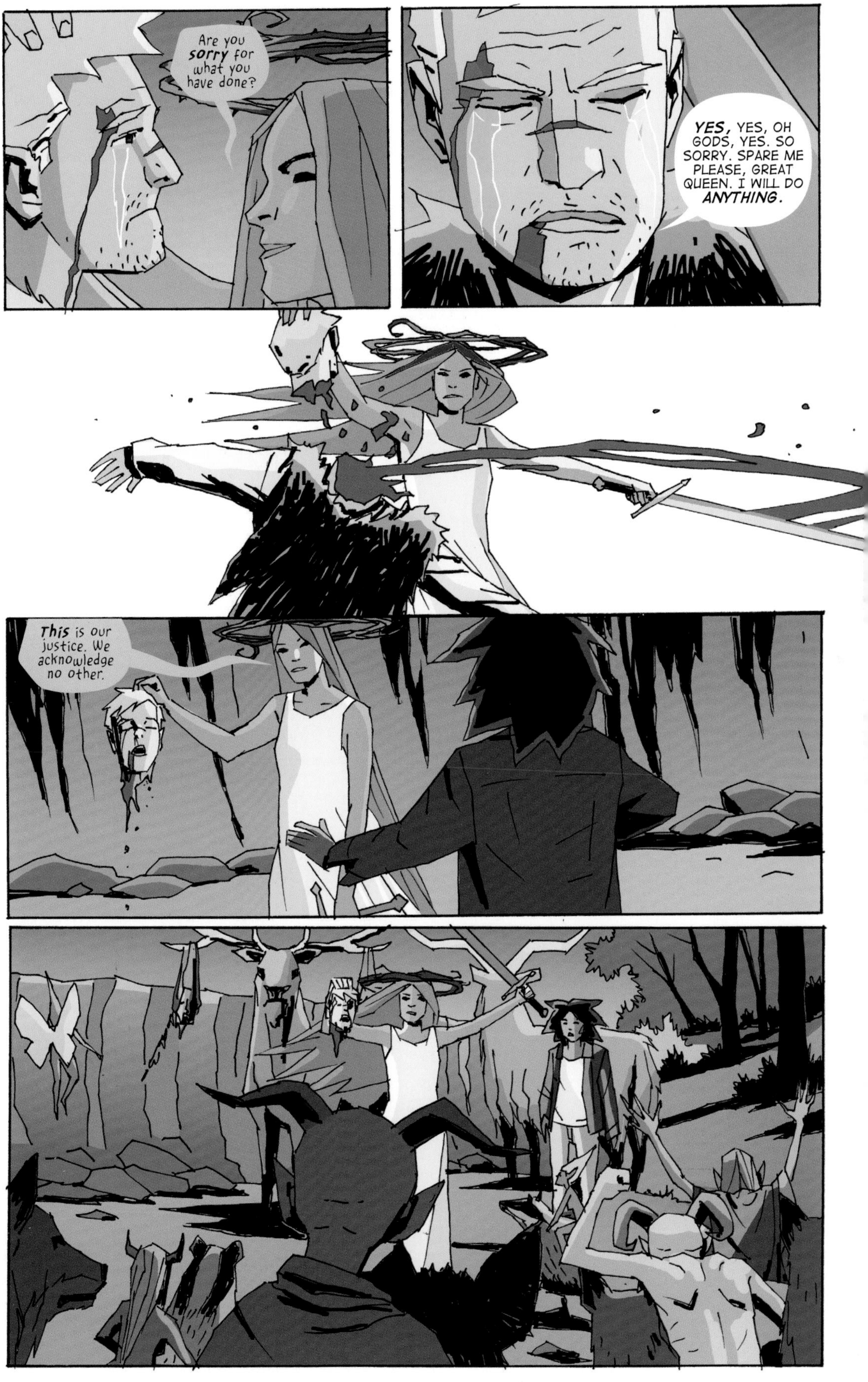
Are you sorry for what you have done?
YES, YES, OH GODS, YES. SO SORRY. SPARE ME PLEASE, GREAT QUEEN. I WILL DO ANYTHING.
This is our justice. We acknowledge no other.

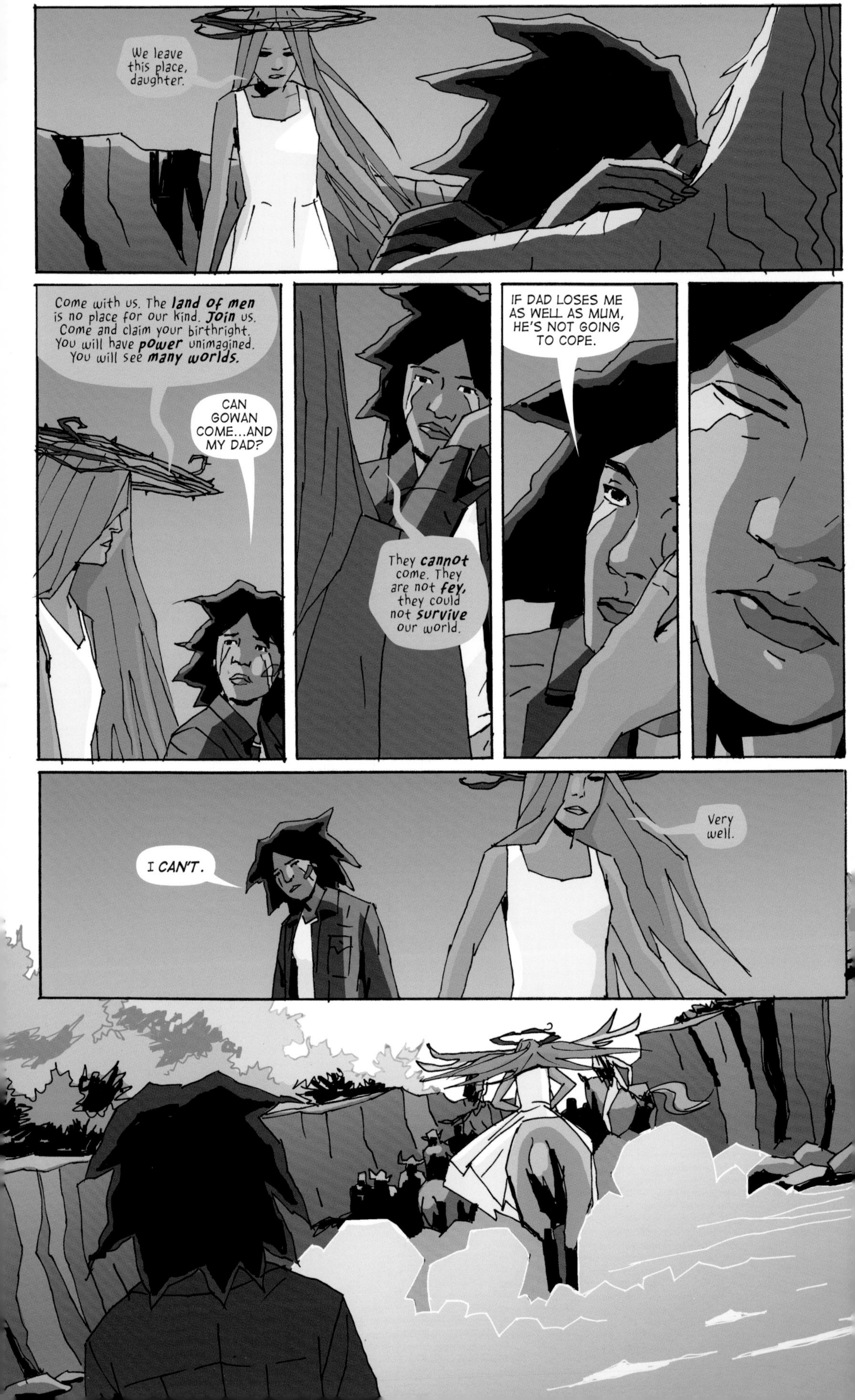
We leave this place, daughter.
Come with us. The land of men is no place for our kind. Join us. Come and claim your birthright. You will have power unimagined. You will see many worlds.
CAN GOWAN COME...AND MY DAD?
They cannot come. They are not fey, they could not survive our world.
IF DAD LOSES ME AS WELL AS MUM, HE'S NOT GOING TO COPE.
I CAN'T.
Very well.

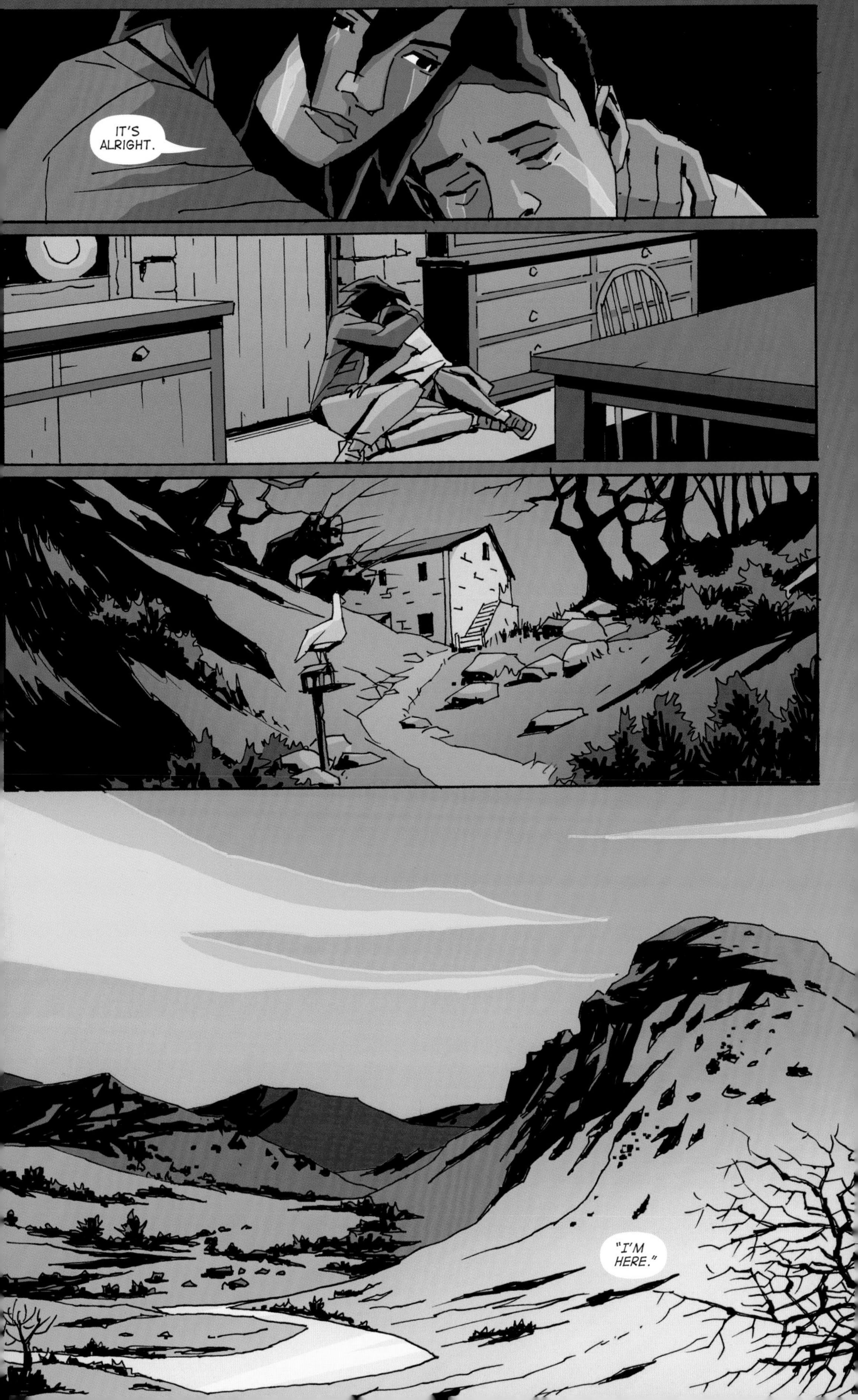
IT'S ALRIGHT.
"I'M HERE."

COVER SKETCH GALLERY BY JOCK

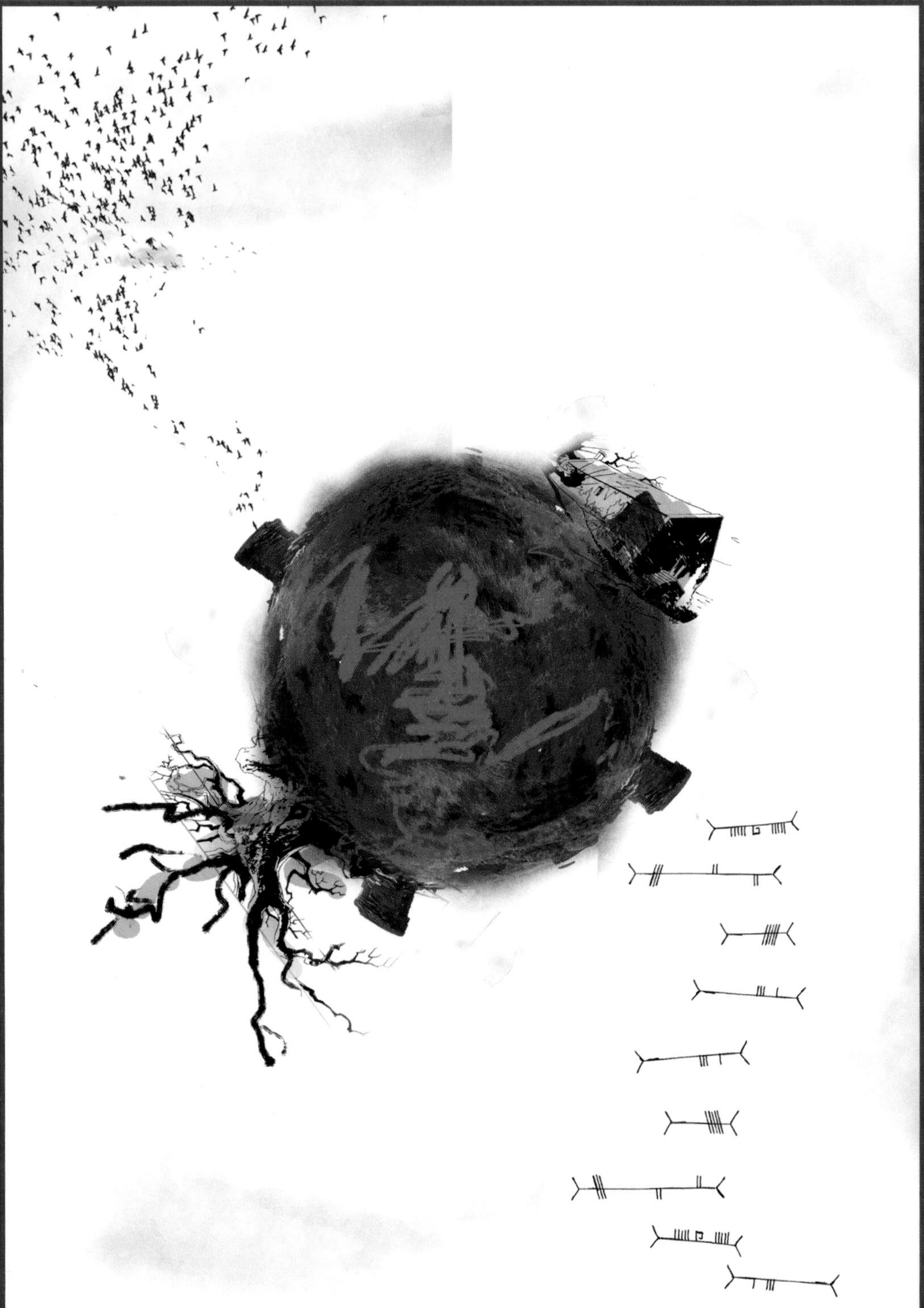

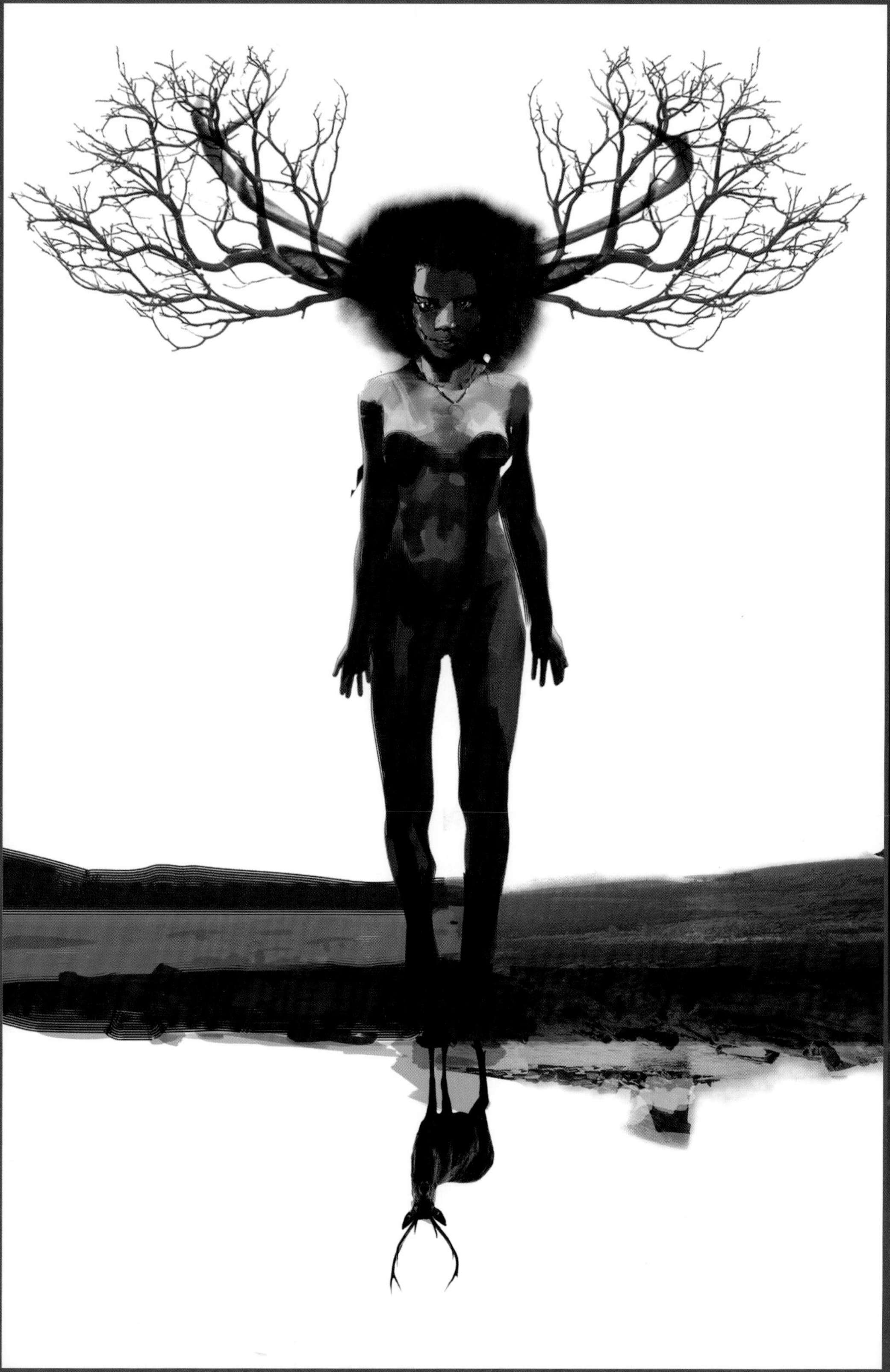

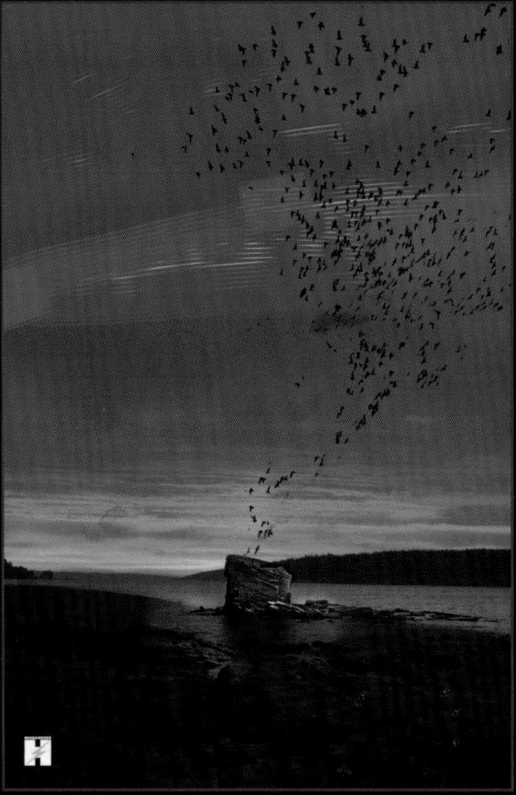
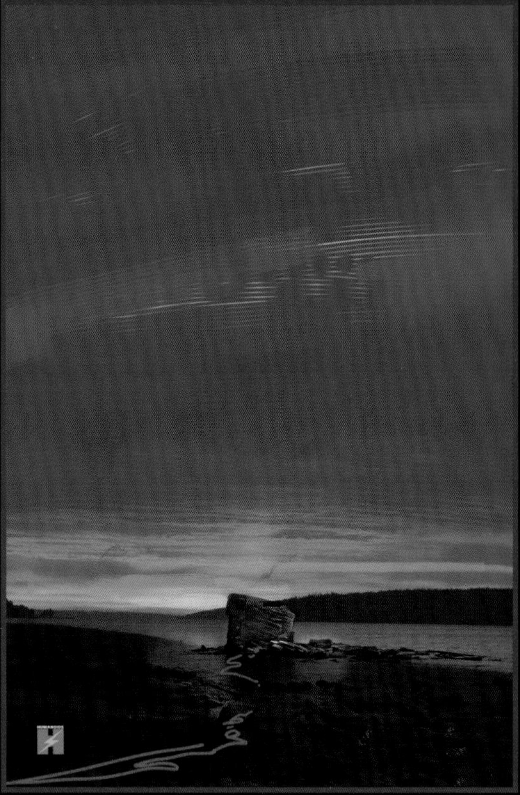
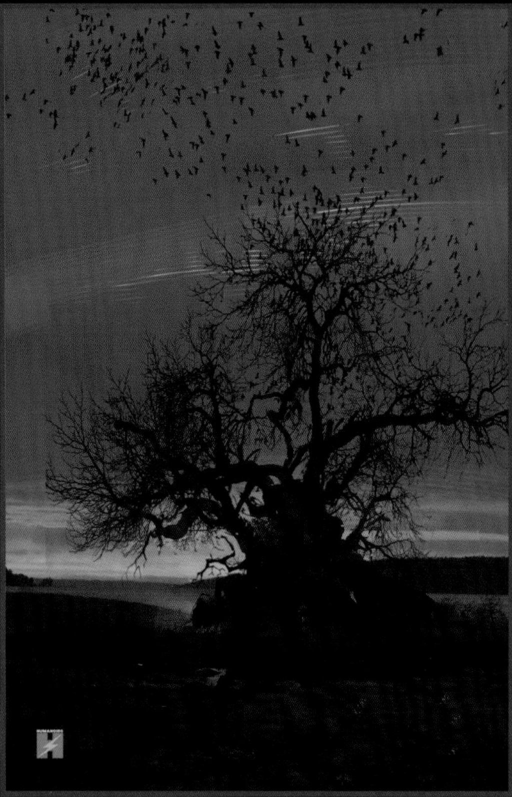
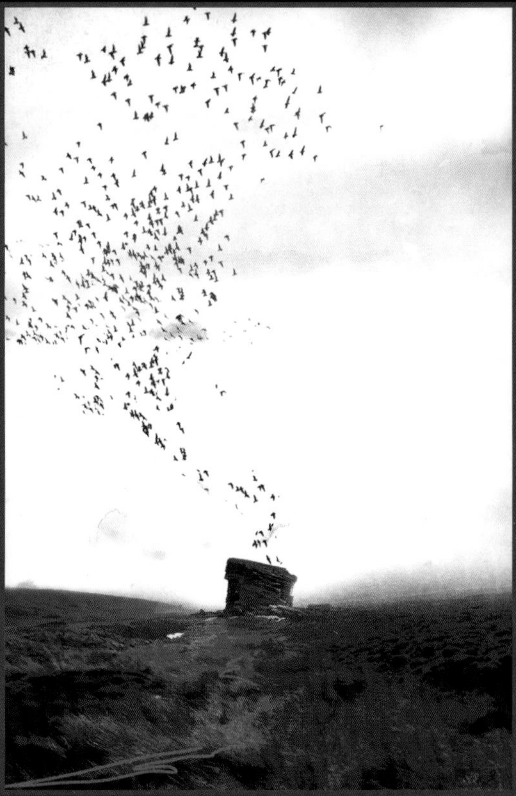

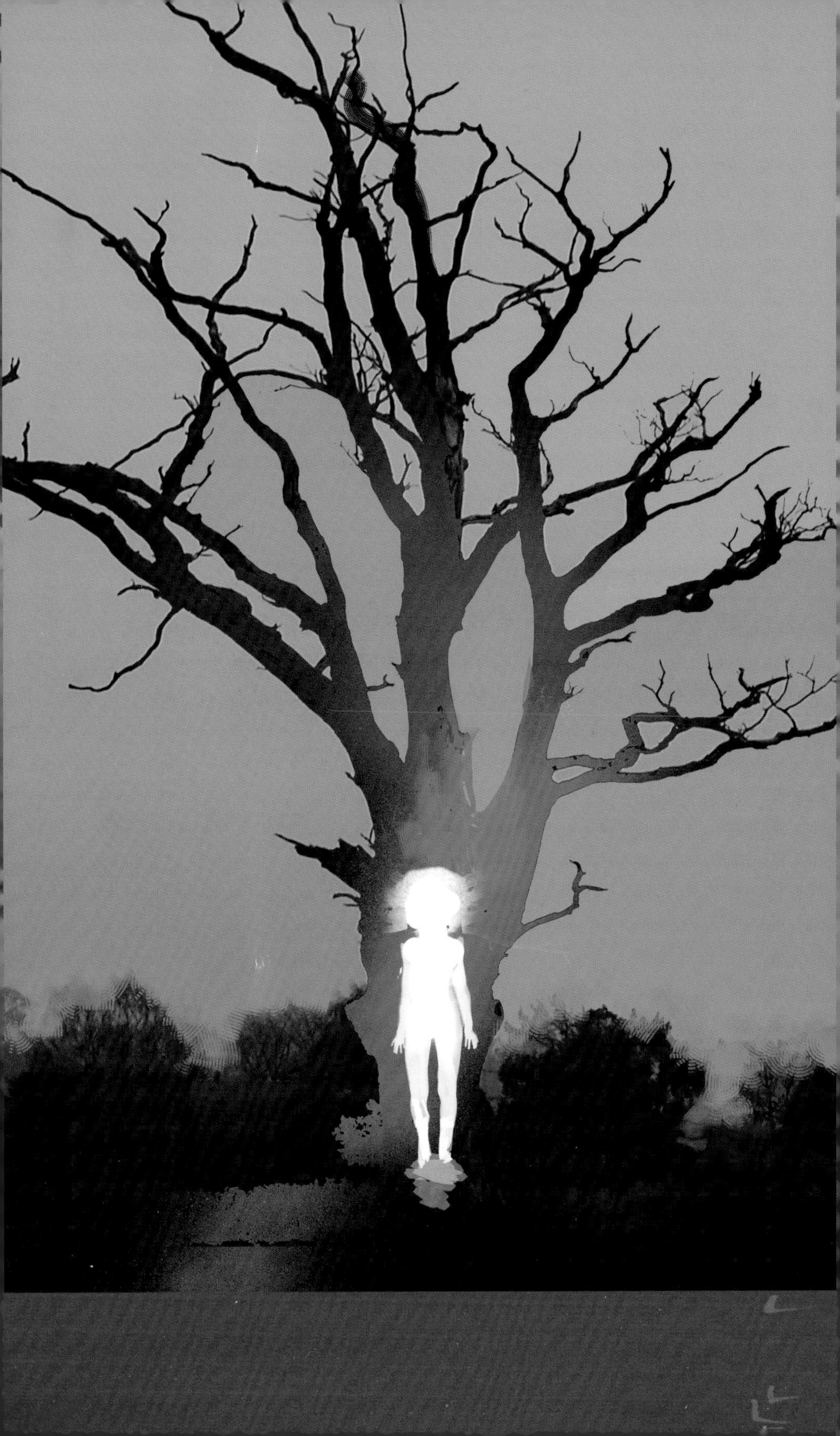

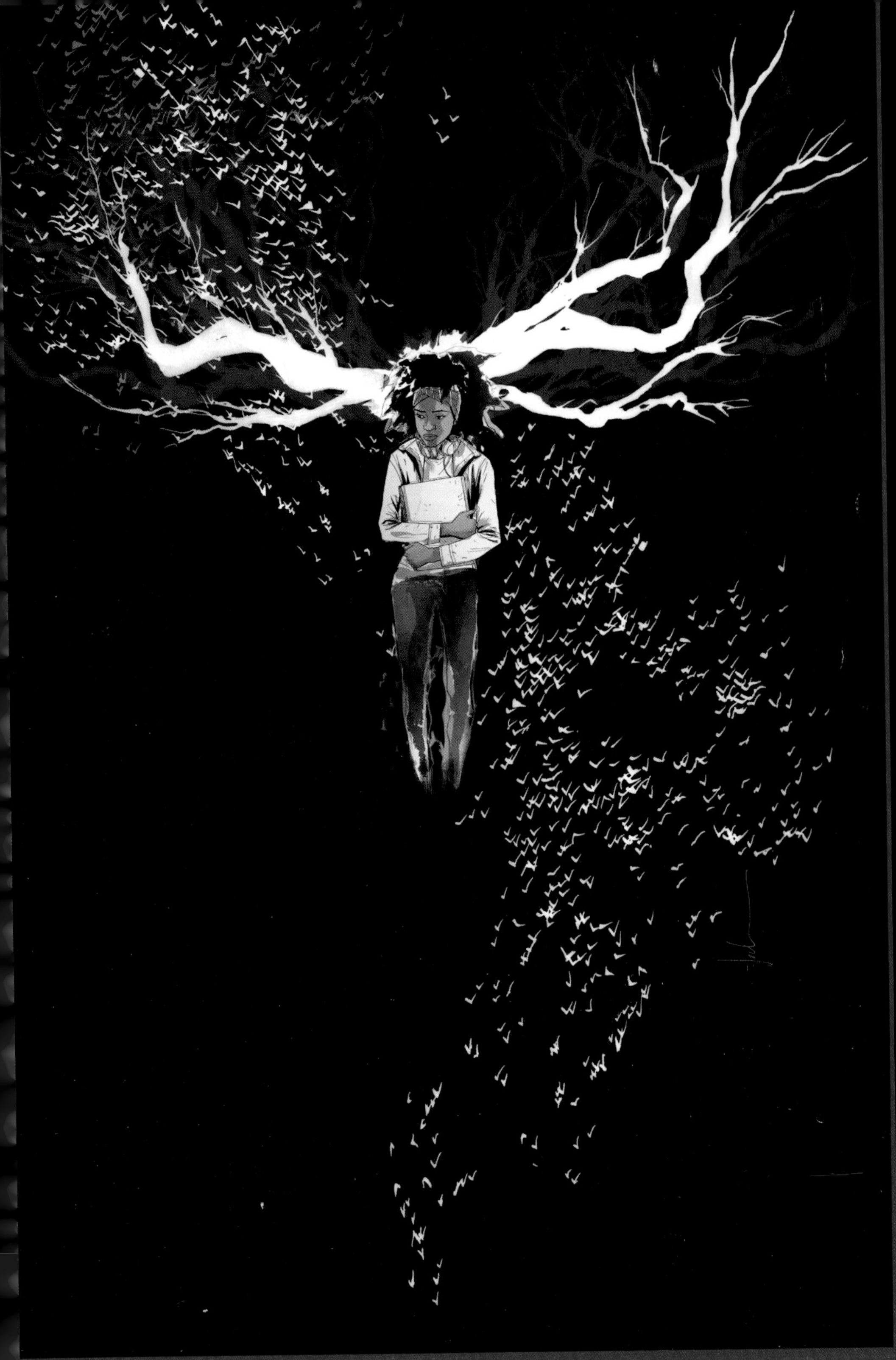

In loving memory of David Hall, forever in our hearts.